TELL ME LIKE
YOU DONE BEFORE

Published in 2018 by Lethe Press, Inc.
6 University Drive, Suite 206 / PMB #223 • Amherst, MA 01002 usa
www.lethepressbooks.com • lethepress@aol.com

ISBN: 978-1-59021-544-9

Set in Adobe Caslon and Core Magic
Cover Design by Inkspiral Design
Art by Matthew Soffee
Book Design by Frankie Dineen

TELL ME LIKE YOU DONE BEFORE

AND OTHER STORIES WRITTEN
ON THE SHOULDERS OF GIANTS

SCOTT EDELMAN

TABLE OF CONTENTS

INTRODUCTION

A few weeks after Scott Edelman sent me the manuscript for this collection—which, like Scott's previous collections, is smart and funny and terrifying and moving and downright protean in the versatility on display—the two of us went to a baseball game at PNC Park on *Star Wars* night.

(It was the major-league debut of Austin Meadows, who hit two singles and stole a base, though his Pirates still lost to the Padres, 3-2. The fireworks were awesome.)

While Scott dispensed Pez to the kids around us from Boba Fett in his left hand and Yoda in his right (a very *Night of the Hunter* touch), he said to me, "Y'know, I've been thinking. Instead of writing in the introduction about how my book is smart and funny and terrifying and moving and downright protean in the versatility on display, maybe you should explain to the readers what the theme is."

Okay, I'm kidding; he didn't actually dictate the compliment, which I came up with all by myself, thank you very much. He *did*, however, cautiously suggest that the theme of *Tell Me Like You Done Before* might need explaining, and that my introduction might be the only opportunity in the book to do it.

This I am happy to do, because *Tell Me Like You Done Before* is an exercise in something that obsesses me, as a writer and a reader: writers rewriting other writers, or writers re-imagining other writers, or writers repossessing other writers, or perhaps *being possessed by* other writers.

I learned in graduate school that Julia Kristeva called this *intertextuality*, by which she meant less a back-and-forth literary conversation than a literary bulletin board with infinite layers accruing over time—what Kristeva called "a mosaic of quotations"—or, if you prefer, a collaborative cat's cradle that gains infinite complexity as the players pass it on. According to Kristeva, no writer can avoid doing this: "Any text is the absorption and transformation of another."

Many fiction writers, I know, scoff at critical theory, but to me, Kristeva was simply doing something honorable that needs doing from time to time: stating the obvious. I knew immediately that she was talking about the relationship of *Star Trek: The Next Generation* to *Star Trek,* and the relationship of *Star Wars* to Leigh Brackett and *Flash Gordon,* and the extent to which Shirley Jackson's puckish reading of all those solemn Society for Psychical Research tomes helped her write *The Haunting of Hill House.*

Intertextuality is what writers *do*; it's what a genre *is.* It's writers all the way down.

Take zombie stories, for example. Scott has written some first-rate, original ones, as this book demonstrates, but like Robert Kirkman, Max Brooks and Mira Grant, he knows the debts *his* zombie apocalypses owe to George A. Romero's, just as Romero knew the debt *his* zombie apocalypse owed to Richard Matheson's *I Am Legend.* In fact, to write about zombies these days without relying on Romero is very hard to do, akin to writing about vampires without relying on Bram Stoker and Anne Rice.

Or consider Scott's extensive superhero-comics work for Marvel and DC, companies where generations of writers have labored to add wings and upper floors to sprawling story-edifices begun in the 1930s that seem likely to keep expanding ad infinitum, like virtual Winchester Houses. In 1977, Scott and artist Al Milgrom created imperial Kree geneticist Minn-Erva, a.k.a. Doctor Minerva. Lots of Marvel writers have deployed Doctor Minerva since, including the script squadron responsible for the upcoming *Captain Marvel* movie, in which the character will be played by Gemma Chan. To what extent are they all rewriting, or paying homage to, Scott Edelman? And to what extent was Scott Edelman, back in '77, rewriting, or paying homage to, Stan Lee and Jack Kirby, who created "the star-spawned Kree" in the first place? And what about *their* inspirations?

(On my home campus of Frostburg State University, I recently had the opportunity to introduce Scott to two undergraduates, both stone fanboys, as a *co-creator of the Marvel Universe*. They nearly melted through the floor in delight. We all should make such introductions, when we can.)

All writers, across all modes and genres and styles, write "on the shoulders of giants," as Scott's subtitle puts it. Sometimes we're conscious of it, sometimes not. Scott is more conscious of it than most, and so his homages never read like random pastiche. He selects his models with wit and finesse, so the juxtapositions that result seem both surprising and inevitable, and his deft prose ensures a smooth transition into another writer's world-view. Both techniques are on display in the Shakespearean "A Plague on Both Your Houses," Scott's first Stoker Award finalist (of eight)—a highlight of this volume, as it has been of every volume it's appeared in, these past (gasp!) twenty years. This is the type of story I most admire: ones I would not even think of, much less attempt.

I won't go through the table of contents pointing out which writers are being conjured in each story. Making those connections oneself should be part of the reader's fun. Some will be obvious from the titles: "The Final Charge of Mr. Electrico," for example, and "The Man Who Wouldn't Work Miracles" (a title I wish I had thought of). I will say, however, that I was co-editor, with F. Brett Cox, of the anthology *Crossroads: Tales of the Southern Literary Fantastic*, where one of these stories first appeared, which makes me a proud godfather to the world's only science-fiction story about Randy Newman.

The more I think about this book's theme, the more I realize that honoring his fellow writers, past and present, has always occupied a big chunk of Scott's career. He helped scores of writers into print while editing the landmark 1990s magazine *Science Fiction Age*. Many of the posts on his chatty, fascinating, and awesomely comprehensive blog are devoted to his heroes, my favorite being the backstage interview at The Bitter End that a teenage Scott conducted with George Carlin—in 1972. (The audio survives! It's online! Google it!)

Scott's *Eating the Fantastic* podcast (67 episodes and counting) showcases a different writer each episode and attempts to replicate, in Scott's words, "one of my favorite parts of any convention—good conversation with good friends over good food." (Full disclosure: I was Episode 6. What took him so long?) Stand near Scott long enough at any event, and you're likely to be swept up in some sort of dining adventure, either Ubering to the best Peruvian vegetarian place or Ethiopian buffet or rib joint in twelve states, or gaping in the hotel lobby as Scott lays out box after box of goodies from Psycho Donuts or Prantl's Bakery. "Have you tried the burnt almond torte? Oh, you *must* try the burnt almond torte!" Jamie Todd Rubin once called Scott "science fiction's Anthony Bourdain." (We won't talk, however, about the durian, which Scott sliced open not in the hotel lobby but in the parking lot—the *secondary* parking lot. Still too close.)

As you may have guessed by now, Scott also is a superb and tireless greeter. Few veterans in our field work as hard as he does, online and at event after event, to make newcomers feel welcome, and to encourage the diversification of our field. I have plenty of reasons to admire him, but that one's enough, right there.

Enough appetizers. On to the feast! I present to you sixteen stories, influenced by everybody, but written by none other than my friend, the field's toastmaster, the inimitable Scott Edelman.

Andy Duncan
Frostburg, Maryland
May 2018

Andy Duncan teaches writing at Frostburg State University in Appalachian Maryland. His third collection, An Agent of Utopia: New and Selected Stories, will be published by Small Beer Press in November 2018.

TELL ME LIKE YOU DONE BEFORE

*A*s the star-speckled black of the sky gave way to an unbroken dark blue canvas that promised a dawn, a thin man, his shoulders slumped as if he had been carrying the world upon them, rose from where he had been hiding amidst the brush.

He slapped at the dry earth which clung to the folds of his well-worn clothing. The grim expression on his sharp features softened slightly as he was swallowed by the resulting cloud of dust.

He stared down into the valley to where he knew a ranch was nestled several miles away, miles he'd had no remaining juice to cover the night before. Even though a new day was on the verge of being born, he still could make it out by but a few pinpoints of campfire.

He smiled then, a change in expression so slight that it would have been perceptible only to someone who had known him for many years.

But there was only one friend like that who still walked God's green Earth. And he was many miles away, the miles growing greater each day. Or so this weary man hoped.

Besides, that friend was supposed to be dead.

The man had made it to the start of another day, something which he'd been wise enough not to count on. He wished he could have made it to the ranch the night before, where surrounded by others he might have been lulled into a false sense of security which would have let him get some rest, instead of a broken sleep which left him as exhausted now as before he lay down, but fatigue had overtaken him there among the sycamores, and that was that.

He heard a scraping at his feet, and looked down to see a small rabbit, its bones bent, its eyes glowing, dragging itself toward him through the brown grass. Before he could react, it leapt at him, though because its frame was crippled, it could only propel itself to the top of his left boot, and no further. The wretched thing drove its incisors into the thick leather at the man's calf.

He shrieked, and struggled to kick at it with the heel of his other boot, but his angle was all wrong, and so he struck it with only glancing blows. He fell, even as he was doing so telling himself how stupid he'd been to let his throat get within the creature's reach. The rabbit dropped its jaw, a noxious liquid spilling forth, and as it readied itself for another leap, one which would end this terrifying dance, the man's scrabbling fingers chanced on a medium-sized rock. He scooped it up and slammed it hard against the thing's skull.

The coney dropped to the man's side, still wriggling, preparing for another attack, and so he quickly rolled to his knees, bashing at it again with the rock. But it kept coming, not giving up until he caught its skull directly. He brought the rock down once, twice, again, so many times he lost count.

Only then did it lie still.

The man fell back, gasping for breath, shuddering not only from the close call, but also from the memories which had haunted him ever since the night he'd pulled the trigger, embers which the violent encounter had stirred into a raging fire. He'd been haunted even before that dreadful dusk, but he'd thought that with his ultimate action, once the bullet flew, it would surely be over.

Turned out all he'd done was trade one kind of haunting for another.

He lay on his back until the sky had turned a bright cloudless blue, a color that told him he was free of any further such encounters, at least until night began to fall once more. He stood then, looked down at the ranch the morning had revealed. He'd hoped that might be the place to rest for a spell, but he now saw that he still needed to put a few more miles on his boots.

He sighed. That had been much too close. He couldn't afford to linger.

There would be other ranches.

There would have to be.

He listened for a moment to the rumble in his belly, and then moved on.

. . .

During the day, as he picked his way through the willows that lined the banks of the Salinas, hoping that it would cover his tracks and knowing at the same time that hope was pointless, he hunted for food. During the days, he could. That was when the things, and most importantly, the thing (though it hurt to call him that) which hunted him could not.

He was hungry, but even so, he hesitated when he saw his first rabbit that morning. Daylight or no, the flood of the reanimated had taught him to be wary. And there'd been so many of them killed over the years. His friend had been clumsy that way. Who knew how long they would keep coming, the parade of the damned? So his first live one of the day got away. But then, spurred on by the increasing volume of the rumbling in his gut, he shook off his close call at dawn and was able to bring himself to bring one down.

And he needed to. He had to keep up his strength, and the cans of beans he'd borrowed—he preferred to call it that rather than use the word "stolen"—had only lasted so far. He'd thought events had taken a bad turn in Weed, but on the night when he'd had to make that horrible choice, to do that terrible thing to the friend who'd trusted him more than anybody else in the world, they'd gotten worse. As worse as he thought it was possible for a life to get.

He'd been wrong. He'd been wrong about a lot.

He worried that, warm meat settling in his belly or no, he could only go on so far.

But he would have to try.

. . .

13
·

He reached the next ranch in the late afternoon, when almost all of the men were still out in the fields. He'd done that sort of thing before, shown up too late for work and gotten a meal without having to toil for it, but in the old days, that action had been a choice, and he hadn't been alone.

Of course, however it seemed, he really wasn't alone now. That was why he had to keep moving. But he'd grown wearier than usual these past few days, and had to take the risk. At least briefly.

He entered the bunkhouse and found one lone ranch hand begrudgingly sweeping the stained floor. The hand paused, leaning against his broom, and eyed the intruder warily.

"Well, aren't you the special cuss," he said. "Waltzing in here like this with the day's work just about done."

"No, I ain't nobody special. Name's George. George Milton."

George held out a hand, but the man refused to take it, keeping his fingers wrapped around the broom handle.

"Sorry," he continued. "Hitched a ride, and meant to be here early, but I got dropped off one ranch over. Had to hoof it from there. Mighty impressive spreads in these parts. Took a mess of hiking to get me here."

"You're damned lucky we're down a few hands, otherwise the boss would send you on your way like *that*." He snapped his fingers, and that action somehow broke his resolve. His grimace blossomed into a smile, and he held out a hand. "Name's Willie."

"Pleased to meet ya, Willie," said George, as the two men shook.

"So how come you're short?" asked George, after the pleasantries were done. "Times like these, no one just walks away from a job without a good reason."

"You'd think so," said Willie, his brow wrinkling. "Only, that's what done happened. Three guys just took off in the middle of the night during the last week alone, one at a time, without even the decency to say why or goodbye. Lucky for you, they didn't take any of their stuff, so since it don't look like you're carrying much in the way of supplies, you're welcome to their leftovers."

Normally, George would be grateful for that spot of good luck. There was only so much he could carry, so he'd had to leave a lot behind. But he didn't like the sound of this. Turning your back on three squares and a cot was crazy, with what the You Ess of Ay was going through in the '30s, with both food and work so scarce. Just wasn't done. Not by anyone. And certainly not by three from the same ranch, so close together.

But he didn't have time to think much further on the puzzle, because that was when the men returned from their long day in the fields.

They were glad to see him, or made a show of being so anyway, because being down a few men, their routine had become even more brutal than usual. And he was glad to see them, too, because in those few minutes of exchanging names and slapping backs, in the midst of a dozen or so men laughing, cursing, spitting, he felt almost normal. By the time the introductions were over, he had trouble remembering most of the names, but it didn't matter that he couldn't keep them straight, because he knew their types well.

Maybe they'd been bucking barley. Maybe they were just back from haying. It didn't really matter. Guys like that were the same all over.

Here was the joe who blamed the world for all of his problems, there the silent one who might be stupid or might not, but since he rarely opened his mouth, few could tell for sure (George quickly moved on from that one for fear of remembering too fully once more), here the one with the tripwire temper who was quick to anger, there the lazy bastard who hoped no one would notice but knew everyone did...

There the calm and steady one, the one George could tell people listened to. That last one's name he'd make sure to remember. Jackson. He was the rarest type of all, the peacemaker, a sort not always found in the muddle of men on ranches and farms. And he might come in handy.

Then the dinner bell rang and George met the boss around a long table as plates of tough meat and tougher rolls were passed around, and the men gobbled them down like candy. The meat tasted like horse—it was a sign of the times that he could identify the flavor, for once he'd never have been able to do that—but he was glad of any meal he didn't have to kill for himself.

The boss, a barrel-shaped man named Dix, didn't question him much, so George didn't have to explain what had happened in Weed, or what happened not so very much later a few miles south of Soledad. George wasn't a very good liar, so he wasn't sure how well he would have been able to hide the truth, but the boss seemed too needy to go hunting after possible distressing facts anyway.

After the meal, the guys pitched a few horseshoes, and smoked a few cigarettes, but they were all too worn out for much more fun than that, the men from their work, George from his long hike and close escape. Only after he'd crawled into bed did he remember that he'd intended to ask about the men who'd vanished, find out what kind of people they were, if there was a simple reason why so many workers would have gotten skittish enough to bolt so close together.

But then sleep overcame him, and he was off in dream, telling the same old story again, the story his friend had always treated as new, the one about a little house on a couple of acres, and a vegetable garden, and the rabbits.

Always the rabbits.

• • •

George jerked awake at dawn, when the sun's first rays crept into the room. He had learned what that first light meant. He'd survived another night, and nothing could get at him until another one fell. The work to come that he would normally have cursed as backbreaking would instead be a relief, because it would tell him that he was alive. Even a poorly cooked breakfast, with bits of shell mixed into the scrambled eggs, didn't dampen his mood, and when he leapt with the other men into the wagon and headed out for the barley, he was filled with as much happiness as his present life could muster.

As he worked that day, watching the sun track across the sky, he found himself wishing it would move more slowly. Ever since he'd done what he'd done, there was no end of things out there looking for him.

The big lummox had snuffed out so many of them. Only they hadn't stayed snuffed out. He couldn't even get that right.

But George must have made a mess of it big time as well. He'd shot Lennie, seen him fall. He'd shot him in the sweet spot, right where he was supposed to, supposed to so that his friend's long troubled journey would all be over.

Only it wasn't.

When he got back to the bunk house at the end of the day, he discovered that a rope had been stretched between two trees out front, a sheet tossed over it to hang limply.

"What do you suppose that's about?" asked George.

"I don't rightly know," said Jackson. George had attached himself to the man, hoping to borrow some of his calm. "Been here a piece but never seen it done before."

They shrugged and passed the setup by, heading in for another overcooked meal. When they pushed back from their plates, Dix stood up, and leaned forward with his palms flat on the table.

"I have a treat for you fellers tonight," he said. "As soon as it's fully dark, we're going to have ourselves a picture show."

The men chattered excitedly as they rushed outside.

"What do you think it's gonna be?" said one.

"I hope it's a dancing picture," said the quiet one, who surprised them by speaking up at such length. "I like them dancing pictures."

"Don't matter to me much," said George. "As long as it takes me away from here."

"Oh, it ain't so bad here," said Jackson. "We got food, a place to lay our heads. And sure, Dix can be tough at times, but believe me, I've seen worse. Who could want anything more than that?"

George could, and he wasn't the only one. He could think of a few others who would want more as well, and he knew exactly what it was they'd want. How he was the one who'd made them want it. And how he had gone ahead and ruined it for them all.

17

You couldn't blame the big lummox. He didn't know what he was doing. But George...he was supposed to know better. All that came after. That was his own damn fault.

Dix directed the men to set up rows of crates in the wide space between the bunkhouse and the stables, and then they sat there, working at their toothpicks, spitting in the dust, waiting for the purple sky to turn black. George didn't like being exposed out in the open like that, but he couldn't figure any way around it. He pressed himself into the center of the men. The boss carried out a projector and fussed with it, not letting any of the others help him with the delicate machine. That didn't stop him from cursing at Willie as the hand played out a length of cable that ran from the small generator which usually kept the boss's house lit.

"Settle down, men," shouted Dix. "I don't exactly know what we got ourselves here, but from what they tell me, it's supposed to be a doozy."

George shifted uncomfortably on his crate, and was relieved when the utter darkness was broken by a beam of light. One of the guys nearest the screen laughed and jumped up, throwing his silhouette on the sheet, but a shout from Dix returned him to his crate. Soon the night was pierced by a beating of drums, and the words *WHITE ZOMBIE* stretched before them.

"Hey, look," someone shouted, as Bela Lugosi's name appeared, "it's got that vampire guy in it."

George didn't know what the hell he was talking about. He wasn't much for picture shows, at least not lately, not when he'd had more important plans for his money. But not just with *his* money...

Best not to think of it. Best not to think of any of it, the missed picture shows, the skipped visits to fine parlors, all sacrificed in pursuit of—

Forget it. Forget it all.

Maybe this movie, whatever it was, would take his mind elsewhere. But based on how it began, it served only to refocus him more fully on his problem. Off in a country not really so distant and yet as far away to him as the moon, dead men walked, dead men who were at the same time somehow undead.

"Haiti is full of nonsense and superstition," said one character to another, but to be either of those, a thing had to be untrue, didn't it? George understood all too well the truth of his situation, that there could be life after death, though not much of one, and as the movie went on, his skin prickled with recognition. And when, about fifteen minutes in, the camera closed in tight on a huge bull of a man, his eyes wide, his soul gone, looking as if he could crush you with one hand, it all became too much. He leapt up from the center of the men, almost knocking a few of them over, ignoring the boss when he shouted at him to stay.

He fled, circling to the opposite side of the bunkhouse, cursing. He crouched down there, leaned his back against the wall, and with shaking hands rolled himself a cigarette. He could barely steady his hands to bring match to tip, and it wasn't until he'd smoked it halfway down that his trembling stopped.

Jackson was suddenly there with him.

"Mind if I join you?" he asked.

George shook his head, and waved with his free hand at the patch of ground beside him.

They sat there quietly for a while. George wanted to say something, anything, to cover the sound of the movie which whispered at them around the corners of the bunkhouse, but he couldn't think of a damn thing.

"So what was that all about?" Jackson finally asked.

George had half a mind to tell him everything. He remembered another man like him, one who took George under his wing after the deed was done. He got George stinking drunk, and made him think that life could go on after what he'd had to do.

Life went on all right, but not the way either of them had thought. Now Slim was dead, George was on the run, and there was something after him, which though no longer capable of running, seemed pretty much unstoppable. But how to begin to tell something like that?

Before George could speak, a shuffling sound came from out of the desert, one which could barely be heard over the movie's buzz on the other side of the bunkhouse. George noticed it first, his senses having been made more alert to such things due to his recent situation.

Jackson noticed him squinting, and followed his gaze.

"What are you looking at?" he asked. "I don't see anythi—why, would you look at that!"

A small dog crawled toward them in the darkness, one of its front legs broken. Even so, it managed to close the gap between them quickly. George pressed his back more forcefully against the wall of the bunkhouse, unable to move any further, even as Jackson stood up and took a step toward it.

"Jackson, no!" George shouted.

But before Jackson could heed George's warning, he was on his knees beside the thing, reaching out to stroke it. It responded by biting hard into the meaty part of the man's thumb. Jackson yanked back his hand, but the animal wouldn't let go, and so was pulled into the air as he jumped up. He leapt around in pain, flinging his hand about, snapping the animal this way and that to no avail. It clung to him with the hunger of another world.

Jackson's yelps finally propelled George to action. He slid his work gloves from where they were tucked into his belt, and grabbed the thing by its hind legs, angry memories flooding back. He knew who had broken that one leg. He knew who had killed it. And yet not even those injuries, sudden, foolish, and fatal, had been enough to stop its vicious hunt. It had still kept coming, tracking him, sensing him out, and if George didn't act quickly, it would turn the man who'd come between them into another victim of his unwise choices.

He pinched at the hinge of its jaw, forcing it to release its grip, and hurled it to the ground. He brought down his heel, catching it in the midsection as it made to escape, flattening it as surely as if it had been run over by a wagon wheel, but though it burst, intestines spilling out, that wasn't enough to stop it. It still struggled for them. He slammed down his heel again and caught it near one ear, while Jackson continued to yowl in pain, cradling his arm, unable to help.

George could hear a crunch of bone, but because of his angle he didn't think that had been enough to take care of it.

Though its lower jaw now hung at an ugly angle, he could see that he hadn't yet finished it. It moved away from the two men, more quickly than George thought would have been possible, and he had a choice. He'd always had choices. Wasn't that what had brought him here? Too many had died because of him, and so he knelt beside Jackson, held him as the creature vanished into the night.

"What the Hell was that thing?" said Jackson, puking. He slumped against George. "Oh, I don't feel so good."

George helped Jackson to his feet, and saw that they were still alone. Good. The fact that they were still by themselves meant that thanks to the sounds from the movie and the whoops of the men, no one had heard anything. There was still time, time to save Jackson and time to keep his secret.

But not much. Jackson's eyes were dilated. His tongue lolled in his mouth.

"Do you want to live?" asked George. Jackson jerked his head, but George couldn't tell whether the man was nodding or shaking it. "Jackson, listen to me. You want to live, don't you?"

Jackson was beyond answering, so George answered for him. He dragged him into the bunkhouse through the back door, and laid him down on his cot. He got a knife, a candle, and a bottle of whiskey, and then took a brief furtive look out the front door.

The men were still mesmerized, not giving a damn that two of their comrades were gone. George pulled back from the door, avoiding even the slightest glance at the screen. That would be too much, even now. *White Zombie* be damned.

George lit the candle, and held the blade of the knife over the flame. He poured the whiskey, first on the heated knife, then down Jackson's throat. The man hardly had the power to swallow, and barely even had the power to choke. George crushed one corner of the bed sheet and jammed it in Jackson's mouth.

George held the knife against the base of Jackson's thumb, which by then was almost black, and oozing a foul pus. He held the knife an inch below the bite marks, pressed it against the part of flesh where the skin was already turning from pink to gray.

"There's no other way," said George. "I wish there was, but there ain't."

He took a deep breath and sliced as cleanly as he knew how, while Jackson howled through the cloth, which thankfully dampened the sound of it, and then fainted. George poured another slug of whiskey onto the wound, then wrapped the hand tightly with scraps from a shirt that had been abandoned by one of the men who had vanished.

Having just encountered the undead cur, he now was pretty certain where they had gone.

He'd answer Jackson's question when he woke, tell him *exactly* what that was all about. He swore he would. Because though he may have decided he'd just have to get used to being one of the loneliest guys in the world, something which he never thought he'd have to be, there was no way out of this life alone.

Tonight proved that.

· · ·

The men never saw how the movie played out, whether or not the fancy pants hero managed to save the day against "that vampire guy." George ended it all when he came running out of the bunkhouse, screaming, his eyes wild. He sprinted up to the boss, shouting hysterically, grabbing his collar, calling out Jackson's name. They all followed him back inside and found Jackson stretched out there, his hand a ball of bloody cloth.

George tried to explain what had happened, what he wanted them to think had happened, but couldn't be heard over the chaotic questions from the men. Dix had to fire a shot into the ceiling to shut them up. With the room silent, George was barely coherent, or at least tried his best to be, and Willie insisted he down some whiskey, which helped in his pretense, especially considering he'd already taken a few shots on his own before sprinting outside.

He explained how a coyote had attacked them as they'd been talking there quietly in the dark, and how they'd fought it off, but not before Jackson had lost a thumb. One of the men, who'd almost finished high school, and had done some book reading, peeled back the sodden makeshift bandages. George could see that the blood ran red, thank god, and so what he'd done had been worth the funny look the man then gave him. George looked away as the man did his best to sew up Jackson's hand, though he heard him explain it would be several weeks at the least before he'd be able to return to work. George then saw the guy whispering to Dix, who walked over to him angrily.

"Are you sure you're telling us what really happened?" he barked.

George protested that he had, and Dix seemed to take his word for it. At least at first, for he did glare back at him suspiciously after he returned to stand over Jackson.

George hoped that once he woke, the man would be able to keep his story straight. George's life, George's plan, depended on it.

George's life? Hah!

One way or another, it would have to end.

• • •

George spent the next day toiling in the field while wondering how Jackson was doing, what he was saying, and how everything could have gone so wrong. Nobody was in the mood to talk much, and the men kept their distance from him, so he had plenty of time in which to wonder.

He'd sworn, though his intentions then were not what they were now, that his aim had been true. He'd pressed the barrel of that gun right where the spine and the skull joined, but he must have closed his eyes, or looked away at the last moment, or done something to stop the shot from firing straight. How else to explain it? It was love that had caused him to do what had to be done, but he guessed that it was also love which had left space for the mistake which had allowed his friend to come back.

The day passed quickly, because even though he pressed himself to work like a dog, harder than he ever had before, in an attempt to forget, he wasn't really there, since that attempt was a failure. He was instead off in that clearing in the brush where it had all gone down—Had it truly been only a few weeks before? That seemed impossible—but also lost in the night before, when in the instant Jackson was attacked he had made a decision. So he was in those two places, not out under the hot sun. He had no way to undo either of those events, but he could damn well make sure that there would be no other such events in the future. If only Jackson could remember what George had whispered to him through his delirium.

By the look Dix gave him when the crew returned at the end of the day, it seemed as if he had. George nodded at his boss, and the man nodded back without judgment. As the rest of the men ran to the dining table, George slipped away to sit himself down next to Jackson's cot. Jackson, propped up by a pile of sweat-soaked pillows, was clear-eyed, and appeared fully himself again.

"I'm sorry," said George, his voice cracking.

Jackson studied George, taking his measure of him, and then nodded.

Then George told him everything.

He told him all about Lennie, big as an ox and just as dumb, and how Aunt Clara had asked him to watch out for the poor bastard, and all the promises he had made, and livin' off the fat of the land, and what happened to drive him and Lennie out of Weed, and about Curley, and Curley's wife, and it all tumbled out breathlessly, right up until that horrible night in the clearing near the brush by the river.

And through it all, Jackson kept nodding, his expression revealing nothing. So the tale he never thought he'd tell anyone kept pouring out of him, those impossible things that came after, how Lennie, and the things he had killed, had started to come back. Back for *him*.

Finally, there was nothing more left to tell. Nothing. Except—

"I need your help," said George.

Jackson held up his crippled hand.

"Help?" he said, snorting. "What can I do? What good would I be?"

"More good than what all of the others could possibly be put together," said George. "After what you seen, you'll believe."

Then George told him of his plan.

"Will you do it?" said George. "As far as I can figure, that's the only way to make it stop."

Jackson whistled.

"You're a crazy bastard, you know that?" he said. "Crazy as a wedge."

"Maybe. But that don't mean it won't work. Will you help me?"

This time, Jackson didn't hesitate.

"From the sound of it, you saved my life," he said. "Wouldn't seem right not to."

George reached out to shake Jackson's hand, then frowned, letting his own undamaged hand fall back into his lap.

• • •

By the time George finished laying out what the two of them would do next and got to the dinner table, most all of the food was gone, but it didn't really bother him. His hunger had been dampened by his plans. He mopped up some gravy with a heel of bread and mulled them over. That would have to be enough for now.

Once the meal was done, and the men poured outside to unwind with jawing and horseshoes, with one an excuse for the other, and it was never clear which the excuse and which the thing that had brought them there, he snuck back in and made his way to the deserted kitchen. He packed a bindle with half a loaf of bread, a rind of cheese, and a couple of cans of beans. Such a theft had become far too familiar to him, and he hated that, but depending on how things went, one way or another, this would be the last time he did this.

He returned to his bunk, hid the supplies under his covers, and pretended to sleep. When the snores of the other hands began to echo through the room, he slipped to his feet, tucked his boots under one arm, and made his way over to Jackson. He nudged the man, who snapped awake.

"It's time," he whispered.

George grabbed Jackson's things so that he wouldn't have to use his bum hand to fumble with them, and led him out the door, feeling crazy for doing so as the darkness swallowed them.

•   •   •

They hadn't been on the road for more than a couple of hours before they came upon Curley's wife shambling toward them in the moonlight.

Seeing her make her way unerringly in his direction through the bramble, each step clumsy yet determined, George realized that if they hadn't left when they did, this encounter might have occurred at the ranch, and then he would have been responsible for even more wreckage than he'd spread so far. Three men whom he did not know were already dead. He wouldn't have been able to bear the burden of more.

Her right leg was twisted in a way a leg shouldn't be able to go and still function, while her left shoulder seemed dislocated, the arm that hung straight down from it dangling limply.

"Damn you," screamed George. "You done this! If not for you, we still coulda been back there, still hoping, still dreaming, still pulling together our stake. But you had to go and mess things up, didn't you, you had to—"

Jackson dropped his good hand on George's shoulder.

"She can't hear you, George," he said. "There ain't nothing left inside of her to hear."

"Maybe you're right," said George. "Considering what we gotta do to that woman, I sure hope so."

George pulled out the pistol he had taken, a theft for which he hoped Dix would forgive him, but Jackson tapped his wrist with cold metal of his own and shook his head. George could see that he was grasping his baling hook.

"Save your bullets," said Jackson. "From what you been telling me, we're going to need them."

The two men separated, moving in wide circles to take up positions on opposite sides of the woman, their hands filled with curved steel. That she moved toward George without hesitation, whether from conscious thought or just some primal animal instinct that remained, ignoring Jackson as if he was nothing more than part of the landscape, told him, as if he needed any more convincing, that all his running had been pointless. He could never run far enough that she, or something like her, would not have been able to follow him.

As George looked at her then, her once shining sausage curls now dull as they hung from a grizzled flap of scalp, the splotch of red smeared across her mouth no longer lipstick but rather fresh blood, the hatred he'd been carrying around for her suddenly vanished. Whether that was going to make what was about to occur easier or more difficult he could not reckon.

He didn't have much time to figure that out, either, because he could see Jackson coming up behind her, beginning to make his move, and so he dashed in and dropped to his knees, swinging wildly to slash at the tendons in her calves. Unable to die or not, that would at least slow her down. As she bent toward him, he rolled to one side, and as he hacked at her again, Jackson joining him, she toppled like a downed oak.

With her face in the earth, Jackson leapt upon her, pressing both knees into the small of her back. He plunged his hook into the base of her neck, tearing through the gray flesh. George was right there with him, alternating his blows so that they only slashed her, and not each other, their hooks occasionally getting stuck in her skull and needing to be pulled free. The ichor flew like ribbons in the wind each time they raised their fists to the sky, and they did not halt their attack until what had once been Curley's wife stopped wriggling beneath them on the ground. Then they fell back, gasping for breath, dropping their weapons into the dry earth.

George poked at her with the toe of his boot. He felt the bile rise in his throat, felt as if he was about to retch, but he somehow managed to hold himself back.

He'd only known the woman for a little while, and still it had been difficult. But Lennie...Lennie was like a brother. He couldn't imagine how much more painful that would be.

He looked across her broken body at Jackson.

"The next one won't be so easy," said George.

Jackson looked at the blood seeping through his bandages, and nodded. He glanced down at Curley's wife, and suddenly grew solemn.

"She deserves a decent burial after all she's been through, don't you think," he said.

"She's already had one," said George. "And one is more than most of us ever get. Besides, we just don't have the time."

So they piled stones on her until she could no longer be seen, though George doubted that any animal would be drawn in by what was left of her and be tempted to feast. He said a short prayer to keep Jackson happy, even though he believed in God less now than ever.

They stood silently for a moment, until George could bear no more, and then they continued on.

· · ·

As George led Jackson back, back to where this final chapter had begun, the journey made him feel as if they were traveling not just in space but in time. If only that were possible, if only he could have undone it all with different choices, instead of what was coming. But that was wishful thinking, and he had no more wishes left.

He did not follow a path which would lead them there directly, because he did not want them to meet head on the one who followed, but rather force this to be ended where it seemed right that it should be ended. So they circled back around the far side of the valley, made their way as far up the foothills of the Gabilan Mountains as they had the energy to spare.

George wanted no possibility that they would meet at some random midpoint. Rather, he wanted to draw his friend back, back to that place in the brush by the sandy banks of the Salinas River.

Lennie would remember that place, even with all that had occurred, even with what he had become. George had made sure to drum that hiding place into his feeble brain until it stuck like tar. If all else was burned away, that would remain. George was sure of that.

It took them several days to reach the spot, and several further encounters with pets which Lennie, when living, had not been able to help but kill, and by the time they arrived, night had already fallen. George could barely see the outlines of the place, but in his bones, he knew. This was where his friend had been reborn.

"What do we do now?" asked Jackson.

"We wait," said George. "It shouldn't be long now until he returns, until it's over."

He knelt, ran his fingers through the soil on the patch of ground where his friend had fallen.

"I don't know that I'll be able to sleep," he continued. "But I have to at least try. Why don't you take the first watch?"

George threw himself down under a sycamore tree, and closed his eyes, but even though he was exhausted, his eyelids atwitch with fatigue, sleep would not come. Somehow beyond conscious thought he must have sensed that he should be aware of that stretch of final moments before he did what he had to do, and not pass through them unconscious. He looked at the branches above him, and then closed his eyes to think about his next step, and when he opened them, he found that he must have fallen asleep anyway, for Lennie was there, crouched beside him.

George quickly glanced over to where Jackson was supposed to be keeping watch. The fool was slumped over, having fallen asleep, instead of preparing to do to Lennie what they had done to Curley's wife. He cursed, not at Jackson, but at himself. It was too much to have asked of him, after he'd already undergone so much.

George looked back at Lennie, who sat there as if frozen. He could have been a statue in the moonlight, rather than a man, a dead man, but still a man. George could make out a wound at the base of his throat, the bullet hole not where he would have imagined it to be. He hadn't been able to look before, but now he knew for certain he must have pointed the gun down at the last instant, missing the brain completely. It had been enough to kill him. It just wasn't enough to keep him killed.

They sat there, unmoving, and in George's mind it was almost like the old days, a night like any other in a long string of nights, and he was being asked to tell him like he done before, asked this time not with words, but with silence. And he knew that he would answer that request, as he always had.

"Guys like us are the loneliest guys in the world," said George in a whisper, not because that was what he intended, but because that was all that would come out at first. "They got no family, nothing to look ahead to. But not us. No, not us. Because I got you to look after me, and you got me to look after you!"

George looked over at Jackson, his sleep unbroken by the bizarre conversation occurring so close beside him. George raised his voice, hoping to rouse the man.

"We're gonna get the jack together and get a little place," he continued. "We're gonna live off the fat of the land."

That was when Lennie would normally have punctuated the speech by clapping his hands together. George hesitated, leaving a space for the old familiar answer. He waited, looked for any movement, however imperceptible, from his old friend, but none came.

"We'll have chickens, and a vegetable patch—and rabbits. Rabbits, Lennie. *Rabbits!*"

George was shouting now, but no matter how loud the words came, Jackson would not move. He could see then in the moonlight that the man wasn't sleeping after all.

Arrayed around him were dozens of undead mice in various stages of decomposition, and all the other animals Lennie had in his clumsiness put down. Every watchful eye was aglow. The puppy they'd encountered earlier sat curled in Jackson's lap, its intestines draped over the man's legs like ribbons.

His neck was bent and broken, and what George had earlier taken to be a shadow from the brim of the hat pulled low over his eyes had actually once been a waterfall of blood, a waterfall now stilled. George looked back at Lennie to see a matching patch of color smeared across his face.

George stood slowly.

"I guess I'm not going to get to tell you about the rabbits no more, am I?" he said.

Lennie answered by also getting to his feet, and once he started rising, he kept on rising. George tilted his head back to look him in the face, the way he'd had to for years. He was surprised that even though it hadn't been that long, he'd already forgotten how amazingly tall Lennie had been. His friend stepped closer, but George did not retreat. There would have been no point.

And besides, all was as it should be.

He'd made a promise to Lennie's Aunt Clara, a promise to watch over him, to make sure no harm came to her addled nephew.

He'd failed. Failed them all.

Failed Lennie, and Clara, and Candy, and Crooks. And now Jackson. And himself. Most of all, himself.

He'd made endless promises, and he failed to deliver on any of them, and whatever happened next in the remaining moments of his short, hardscrabble life, he deserved it.

Everybody in the whole damn world was scared of each other.

But George wasn't scared no more.

Not even when Lennie's teeth ripped through his stomach to what lay beneath.

George had always told Lennie that someday his friend would be living off the fat of the land.

As his life seeped from him, as he began to lose consciousness, he managed in his last moments to be strangely comforted by the sudden awareness that even though the alfalfa and chickens and rabbits would now be forever out of reach, even though he had fulfilled no other promise on this Earth, he had at least fulfilled that one.

WHAT WE STILL TALK ABOUT

Selene, blue pill cupped in one palm, wondered where she would find the strength to raise the small lozenge to her lips. The longer she stared out at the harsh landscape, the heavier the morning dosage seemed in her hand.

The dome had hoped that she and her husband would find the vista in which it had chosen to place them that morning pleasing, but for Selene, the generated location was a failure, as had been its other recent choices. Karl would perhaps feel differently, but for Selene, as the rocks stretched on, rough and dry and red, the scene brought to mind nothing so much as the interior of her own heart.

She closed her fingers tightly around the pill, and could feel its smooth metallic surface grow sticky from her sweat.

"Does anyone," she said, in a soft, uncertain voice, "remember how to get to Earth?"

The words spurted out of her so suddenly that she was startled. Her question had exploded on its own without even the thought of an audience that might receive it.

"Did you hear what I just said, Karl?" said Selene. "Or did I only think it?"

"I heard you, darling," said Karl, lifting wiry arms above his head as he stretched out on rainbow sheets which shimmered with his movements. "It just took me a moment to digest it. I haven't thought about Earth in years."

"Oh, please, Selene," said Karl, entering through one of the bedroom's irises while bearing a tray of drinks intended to cool them from their lovemaking. "Earth is so boring. Promise me that you're not thinking of going back there again. You're not really—are you?"

"It's not very far," shouted Karl from the opposite dome from which Karl had just entered. Selene, peering through the connecting biolock, could see him busy at work, his fingers encrusted with a yellow dust from pollinating the wall for the coming season's sculptures. "No, it's not very far at all. But then, these days, what is?"

"Good," said Selene. "Then let's go."

She tossed the pill in her mouth and swallowed too quickly; the pill stuck in her throat. She took the drink which Karl held out to her, swirled the sheer cup until the thick liquid began to spark, and forced the pill quickly down.

That was that, then. Her choice had been made. There'd be no more thinking, no more worrying. Not for today, at least.

"This will be fun," she said quietly, almost to herself. She licked away the last of the sticky blue residue that remained in the folds of her palm. "I love you, Karl."

"And I love you," said her husband.

"And I love you," said her husband.

"And I love you," said her husband.

The joyful harmony of his voices caused her heart to skip a beat, its pulsing overwhelmed at being the focus of her husband's love.

"Let's get started then," she said, jumping to her feet.

"Right now?" asked Karl. He flung the bedsheet toward the ceiling and then, as it billowed, stepped beneath it. As he lifted his arms, the flowing fabric descended to wrap itself tightly around him. Mere molecules thick, his garb was less clothing than a second layer of skin, as if his nude form had been dipped into a vat of multicolored paint. He snatched the second mug from Karl's tray.

"Why not?" said Selene. "I see no reason to wait. There's something to be said for spontaneity."

"Yes, something," said Karl, dropping his empty tray to the floor, where it was quickly reabsorbed into their dome. "I've never been sure exactly what that something *is*, though."

"Which flitter should we take?" asked Selene, strong enough now, as she might not have been before, to ignore her husband's joke. She looked into the sky and tried to see past the moons above.

"Why a flitter?" asked Karl. He left a yellow trail of powdery footprints that suffused with red behind him as his steps germinated. "All we need to do is simply think our destination, and we're there."

"No," said Selene firmly, still intent on the distant Earth that hid somewhere in the sky. "This is something that must be done real, or at least as real as anything *can* be done these days."

"As if projecting our way to Earth wouldn't be real," said Karl, shaking his hands by the wrists until the bedsheet extruded opalescent gloves that grew to his fingertips. "As if the new choices are any less real than the old ones. It's all real, Selene. You have too much love of old-fashioned things."

"Which explains why I keep you around, I guess," she said.

Her husband reached out simultaneously to swat her on the rump. Karl's hands collided one-two-three before they continued on the final few inches to make contact with her, the sort of overlap that she knew only occurred in those rare instances when she touched a nerve. She smiled, and they hugged, his arms weaving together to embrace her at the center of a warm cocoon. She murmured peacefully. For a brief moment, she forgot about blue pills, about the endless red rock, about the pleasant, tickling memories of ancient Earth.

Then Karl had to speak, bringing them all back again.

"We should really ask Ursula and Tomas along," said Karl, his words echoing wetly in the confines of their flesh.

"Oh," said Selene, stepping outside of the curtain of Karl's body. "I was hoping that we could all go alone."

"All?" said Karl, looking from himself to himself.

"Why, yes," said Selene. "All. All alone. It's been so long since we've all been away alone together. Too long."

"Too late," said Karl, coming up behind her. "I've already invited them. It never occurred to me that you'd object."

"You should have thought about it a little more carefully before you thought them an invitation, Karl," she said, slowly turning away from her husband.

"You're right, Selene," said Karl, from beside her. "But it's too late for that now, unfortunately. You know how Tomas and Ursula are. I wouldn't want to hurt their feelings. I'm sorry, Selene."

But what about my feelings?, she thought, and then, almost before that emotion could claw its way to full consciousness, the feeling effervesced, as all such feelings did, if only she made the right choice each morning. She turned back to Karl, and touched her husband's cheek, while by the dome's outer window, Karl watched as a flitter blossomed from the rocks around them. A jagged skeleton slowly rose up that was but a whispered promise of the vehicle that would carry them light years away. Molten ore feathered through the air like spun sugar and wrapped about the flitter's core.

"Look," Karl said, as the process completed and Selene's name etched itself into the finished skin of the ship.

"Hello," tickled Tomas in her ear.

Selene smiled, perhaps at the flourish her husband had provided, perhaps at the arrival of her friend. Perhaps both. She felt the familiar good mood wash over her as the nanobots massaged the chemistry of her bloodstream.

"Thank you, Karl," she said. "Hello, Tomas."

"Ursula will be along shortly."

"But never shortly enough for you, Tomas, right?" said Karl.

"I can be a patient...man," he vibrated, everywhere and nowhere. If he had chosen to sneak up on them, they wouldn't even have known he was there. "Someday, she'll grow tired of a material existence, and then, there won't be anything left for me to have to be patient *about*."

"Other than enjoying your practice of such restraint, Tomas," asked Selene, "how have you been?"

"Bored," he vibrated. "The universe continues to hold far too few surprises. So I'm glad that you asked us along."

"How could you possibly be bored with all this?" asked Karl, as he stepped through the iris back to his wall work. "I can't remember when I've last been bored."

"Oh, it's more than just that, Karl," said Tomas. "It's that you can't remember, period. I never have been able to figure out how you manage to keep yourselves straight."

Before Karl or Karl or Karl could answer, the ground rumbled, and Selene jumped in quickly. She needed the day to go smoothly.

"That would be Ursula," she said, as the dome compensated for the clamor outside, and the room regained its silence. "You know, Tomas, for someone so willing to take the greatest of leaps, your emotions can be awfully old-fashioned."

Ursula plodded towards them from the short horizon, her robotic feet crushing rocks into crimson sprays of dust. It wasn't until she arrived at the flitter, overshadowing it in a tower of chrome, that Selene was able to judge the size that Ursula had chosen to carry that day. Ursula had felt like being a giantess, and so she was.

"We're all here, then," said Selene. She had made her own choice about what she was to be that day, and she intended to stick to it. "Let's go."

Selene walked in the direction of the flitter, and when she arrived at the dome wall, kept walking, and flowed effortlessly through it, passing as if through the fragile skin of a bubble. A thin membrane clung to her as she continued walking, and stretched the wall outward, and as she drew closer to the flitter, the connection snapped, and the skin sealed shut behind her. The flitter extended a tongue in her direction, and as she mounted the walkway, she waved up at Ursula from within a self-contained atmosphere.

"Are you feeling any better today?" said Ursula, her faraway speakers booming deeply.

"How I'm feeling doesn't really matter," said Selene. "It's how I'm *doing*. And right now, I seem to be doing something at last."

Selene paused near the top of the walkway. She turned and gestured back at the dome, making the assumption that her movements were being watched.

Karl seemed to be the first to follow her and vanish inside the flitter, though with Tomas around, she could never be completely sure. Once her husband was inside, Karl then followed. He brushed past Selene on the walkway and stopped at the hatch. While she looked up at him, Karl came along, stepping up behind her and wrapping his arms about her waist. Karl smiled down at the two of them from above, then turned and vanished inside the ship.

"Do you really need all of me?" Karl whispered. The pliant membrane allowed her to feel his breath hot in her ear.

"Yes," said Selene. "This time, I do. Please, Karl."

Arms locked, they strolled up the rest of the walkway together and entered the ship. Karl and Karl were already seated within a teardrop-shaped room otherwise bare of furniture, a compartment larger than the ship in which it was contained. At the narrowest point of the teardrop, Karl and Selene dropped back off their feet, trusting that a couch would ooze up from the floor to catch them.

"Ursula?" called out Selene.

The opaque wall which curved about them grew steadily transparent until Selene could see her friend framed by the landscape outside. She swelled even larger, and was soon crouching down above them, her head alone as big as one of their dome rooms.

"I have a feeling that this is going to be fun," said Tomas. "Yes, darling, it's time. You know what to do."

Ursula scooped up the flitter, growing even taller as she hugged the vehicle to her chest, carrying them to where the atmosphere was even thinner. Staring into her friend's ever-more-enormous face, Selene felt as if she was instead shrinking away. At times like this one, she always found it hard at first to tell which one of them was actually doing the changing. Ursula lifted the flitter behind her head for a moment, and then pitched it high into the air. As it neared the top of its arc, great flames spouted from the soles of Ursula's feet, and she rocketed after her friends. She overtook them and slammed into the rear of the ship, adding the thrust they needed to escape the gravity of the small planet.

Once Ursula and the ship she'd propelled were both fully free of the atmosphere, the gleaming plates that made up her body receded into each other. As they overlapped, she shrank until she was down to a size capable of entering the airlock. As she fell back into the circle of her friends, a seat sturdier than the others grew up to greet her.

"How long do you think this will take?" she said with a dull buzz, as she brushed meteor dust from one shiny shoulder.

"That all depends," said Karl, looking out at the stars.

"It will take however long Selene wants it to take," said Karl, looking intently at his wife. "That isn't something that can be timed."

"Then I think I'll have a drink," said Selene.

Karl pressed his hands against the front wall of the small ship, which extruded mugs that he handed to Karl and Selene and Karl. Ursula pressed a few buttons on her wrist, and a small door slid open in her chest. She took the offered drink and poured its contents down into a permaglass funnel. Karl offered Ursula a second mug, which she balanced on the flat of her knee joint as liquid gurgled pneumatically within her. As the level in that beverage dropped, Selene could hear a gentle slurping.

"Thank you," said Tomas. "So tell us, Selene—why Earth?"

"And why now?" buzzed Ursula. "I don't remember Earth being so thrilling the last time that it was worth this kind of effort."

Selene stared off ahead of them through the clear hull of the flitter, and then looked at the empty mug in her hand, unable to remember having drained it.

"I'm not entirely sure," said Selene. "It just seems like the thing to do."

"It's those movies, you know," said Karl, refilling her drink with a pass of his hand. "She's become hooked on them. I have no idea why she wants to go there *now*, but she loves those movies."

"We could have watched them at home," said Karl.

"We could have watched anything at home," said Tomas.

"I don't quite understand the attraction of those dead art forms," said Karl. "They're so simple. Simple and simplistic. Like children's stories."

"As if you remember children's stories," said Tomas.

"As if *you* remember children," said Ursula.

"There's more than one kind of simple," said Selene, struggling to put into words the static that warred in her head. "It doesn't always have to be derogatory. What I like is that those people had their limits."

"Maybe they only seemed to," said Tomas, playfully. "Maybe you only thought they did. You only know them from their movies. Maybe they were just like us."

"They weren't like us," said Selene. "They couldn't do everything. They couldn't rewire their bodies or dissipate their souls or wear whatever flesh suited their moods or...or just take a pill. They had to deal with whatever they were dealt."

"And you think that make us any different?" asked Ursula. "You're getting lost in the details. They were just like us."

"But look at us," said Selene, her eyes suddenly filled with tears. "*Look* at us."

Karl leaned forward to peer at himself in Ursula's chrome shoulder, then looked at Karl, then looked at Karl, then laughed. Tomas laughed with him.

"For some of us," said Tomas, "that's easier done than for others."

"Life is a metaphor," said Ursula. "Just because we get to choose a few more of them each year doesn't make us any freer in the grand scheme of things. We all believe what we're programmed to believe."

"Or what we choose to believe," said Selene.

"I choose to believe that there wasn't really a need for this," said Karl. "As I said, there was no need to travel back to Earth, dear. Whatever you wanted to see of it back home, you could just have asked for it, asked for any dream you wished, and we would all have been able to see it."

"Is taking a trip with me really that much trouble?" said Selene. She dropped her cup and was pleased to see it shatter before it was reabsorbed into the floor. "What else were you doing that was so terribly important?"

"Nothing," said Karl.

"Nothing," said Karl.

"Nothing," said Karl, "is so important that I wouldn't stop doing it in an instant for you. I'm only thinking of you, Selene. I only mean that you can have the prize without all this effort. Such a dead art form can't be worth all this."

"Sometimes the effort *is* the prize," Selene said sternly.

"Now *that* isn't boring, Ursula," said Tomas, here, there and everywhere. "Can you remember when she last spoke to him in that way?"

"I can remember everything," said Ursula, tapping at the databanks buried deep in her waist.

"Brava, Selene!" said Tomas. "Keep going."

"No," said Selene, her feelings fluctuating wildly. "No more talking just to fill the time if this is what we still talk about. Let's get to Earth *now*."

And so they did.

41

But when they rose and spread out against the walls of the ship, peering in search of a planet, all they saw was the same vaporous space that had been their companion for the first part of their voyage. The flitter, which should have popped across the universe and come to rest in orbit around the birthplace of humanity, instead floated in a void. The sun shone blisteringly hot at them with no intervening atmosphere.

"Where are we?" said Selene. "This can't possibly be right."

"And yet it is," said Karl.

"We're exactly where we're supposed to be," said Karl.

"We're exactly where you wanted us to be," said Karl.

"But we can't be," said Selene. "Where is the Earth?"

This time, Selene felt for sure that she would lose herself to a wrenching bout of tears. It had been a long time since she had felt pushed to that extreme. And then, as she heard her husband speak again, the notion was flushed away.

"There's no reason that it shouldn't be right here," said Karl. "These spatial coordinates should have placed us in exactly the same relation to the Earth as when we'd arrived the last time."

"That's impossible," said Selene. "The Earth couldn't just disappear."

"Nothing is impossible," intoned Ursula.

"How long has it been again?" asked Karl.

"How long *has* it been?" said Selene.

"No," said Tomas. "Definitely not boring."

When Tomas shivered with delight, Selene could feel the goosebumps.

"I didn't come this far just to talk about it," said Ursula. "I'm going out."

She pushed herself from the hatch to hang in space. Selene watched as her friend slowly somersaulted beneath the ship. There should be blue below her, blue oceans and white clouds and cities and the ruins of men.

"Selene, dear," said Karl. "We may just have to accept the fact that the Earth is gone."

"Can we be sure we're in the right place?" asked Karl.

"Oh, we're in the right place," said Karl. "There's no doubt about it."

"But what could have happened?" said Selene.

"At this point, does it really matter?" said Tomas. "Planets are born, and planets die. Just because this planet happens to be Earth doesn't mean that it gets to go on forever. It could have been attacked. Or perhaps someone blew it up for spite. Or maybe the last person simply turned out the lights, and then it just ceased to exist, expiring from lack of interest."

"It doesn't matter why," said Selene. Even as she said it, she realized she'd spoken a little too quickly, even for her. "I don't really care why. We've got to put it back the way it was."

"All the way back?" asked Karl. "Is that what you want, dear?"

"Should I gather the pieces?" asked Tomas. "Should I bring them all back and make them bustle once more? It might even be a challenge. I've never puzzled out a working world before."

"No," said Selene. "Not all the way back. That would be meaningless. Just restore the Earth to as it stood when I was here last. When I was here with Karl last."

"Isn't that the same thing?" said Karl.

"You didn't let me and Ursula tag along with you here that last time," said Tomas. "I'll need a reference. Do you mind?"

Selene shook her head. In a moment, she felt an itching in her brain, and then, as quickly as he had entered, Tomas was gone.

"Ah, I see it now," said Tomas. "I see how it was."

That's all that it took, for suddenly, Earth was there below her. Spinning there, it was just as Selene had remembered it, the swirling clouds hiding a purer past beneath. And having experienced Tomas's work a thousand times before, she was sure that it truly *was* exactly as she had remembered it.

"Let's go down," whispered Selene. "I can't wait any longer."

"Ursula, dear," Tomas called out. "We're going down now."

"I'll meet you all Earthside," said Ursula.

She tucked her chin into her chest and kicked her feet away from the planet. Rockets ignited in her heels to push her down toward the surface below. Selene watched hungrily, jealously, as her friend became a dot in the distance and then vanished from sight.

"Should we just—" said Karl.

"No," interrupted Selene. "We shouldn't. The old-fashioned way. We're doing this the old-fashioned way."

The flitter dropped into a low orbit as Selene surveyed the terrain.

"What are you looking for, dear?" said Karl.

"What are any of us looking for?" said Tomas.

"You've grown much too metaphysical of late," said Karl. "Go join your wife."

"I'm already with my wife," said Tomas. "And besides—I put a planet together today. Don't you think I've earned the right to wax a little metaphysical?"

"What do you see, dear?" asked Karl.

"I see us there," said Selene, jabbing a finger at the horizon. "We're going there."

The sky turned blue as they descended to an even lower orbit. Ursula pulled up beside them and waved, spiraled about the flitter while laughing, and then sped ahead. Moments later, they dropped to the surface, setting the ship lightly down in the center of a deserted city. The frozen moment resurrected by Tomas reflected a time when no one was left to greet them. Some of the buildings still towered over them, but others no longer did, and lay in rubble. Tall grasses swayed. Stepping from the flitter and pausing to listen, Selene could hear the sound of birds and the occasional thunder and crash of a collapsing building. The abandoned planet was once more a dying planet, and now that Tomas had set its clock ticking again, Earth hurried along again to its inevitable end.

"It's exactly as I remember it," she said. "Perfect."

"Why didn't you want me to return Earth to its glory, rather than its decline?" asked Tomas. "I would have welcomed that. It would have been more of a challenge."

Selene didn't answer. Selene couldn't answer. Selene merely stood transfixed, studying each inch of territory between her toes and the horizon until Ursula landed with a thud beside them.

"Well, we're here," said Ursula, setting right a car that had flipped on its side ages before. "What are we supposed to do now?"

"That's entirely up to Selene," said Tomas. "This is her party. We're just here as her guests. Or witnesses."

"Witnesses?" said Ursula. "It isn't as if this is a wedding."

"Dear?" asked Karl. "It's up to you."

"Come," said Selene, holding out her hands to her husband. "Let's take a walk together."

Karl came up on her left side, and Karl came up on her right, and Karl stepped ahead to walk before them with both hands dangling back to join theirs. Ursula cleared a path ahead of them, concrete and brick being crushed into a smooth powder beneath her. She came across a tumbled lamppost, and laughing, tossed it toward the sky. Selene never saw or heard it fall.

"Remember the first time we came here?" asked Selene, giving her husband's hands a squeeze.

"How could I possibly forget," said Karl in her right ear.

"It was our honeymoon," said Karl in her left.

"It seems like a lifetime ago," called Karl back over one shoulder. "But I'm sure that it was much longer than that."

"When Ursula and I decided to bind ourselves to each other," said Tomas, "we went *everywhere*."

"Earth was quite enough for us," said Selene.

"I'm sure it was very nice," said Ursula.

"Who needs the entire universe, when this is where it all began?" said Selene. "Not just us. *Everything*."

"Poor Selene," said Tomas, wickedly. "Feeling overly nostalgic? They have a pill for that, too, you know."

"Tomas!" blared Ursula, turning to the sky. "If you had a neck, I'd wring it."

"What did I say?" said Tomas. "I never meant that in a bad way. We're all friends here, aren't we?"

"Pretend that you have a tongue," said Ursula. "And hold it."

"I want to see it all again," said Selene, unshaken by Tomas's words. Playful or punishing, they could not affect her. In that place, at that moment, for one of the very few times in her life, she felt like a rock. "I want to visit the museums, see the movies, and...and everything. I want to see the way that people lived before. I want to watch what choices they had to make."

"Assuming, of course," said Tomas, "that in their art, truth was being told about the way that people lived before."

"Tomas!" said Ursula.

"I'm only saying—"

"Enough," said Ursula. "Selene, do you think all those things you need could possibly still be here?"

"Except for a little more decay here and there, it's just as we left it," said Selene.

"Thank you," whispered Tomas.

"I recognize this city," said Selene. "I recognize this street. Karl, do you recognize this street?"

There was no answer, not from Karl nor Karl nor Karl, which made Selene squeeze his hands all the harder.

"We've just a few blocks to go," she said, pausing for a moment in the middle of an intersection. "And then you'll all see what I mean. That way."

"Let's do it then," said Ursula.

Ursula swelled from her default size into her gigantic self. With hands the size of couches, she scooped her four companions high up into the air, and ran in the direction Selene had pointed.

"No!" shouted Selene, bouncing several stories above the cement. "Ursula, please, it can't be like this. Put us down."

Ursula froze so suddenly that her metal muscles squealed. She shrank in on herself until Selene and the others touched lightly down.

"Thank you, Ursula, and please forgive me," said Selene. "But what happens here today, you have to understand, I don't want it to be done our way. I need it to be done the old-fashioned way."

"If it's important to you," said Ursula, "then I understand."

"Well, I don't," said Tomas.

"Tomas..."

"But whatever you need, Selene," he quickly added.

"This is where the art museum was," said Selene, gesturing to the decrepit building in front of which they stood.

The front wall of the marble and granite structure had collapsed, so they were forced to pick their way across a field of rubble. They climbed atop a pile of huge shards that blocked the entrance, and then slid down inside through where a wall had split open. Most of the paintings were no longer on the walls, having fallen in some past catastrophe. Tomas wrapped himself around one that had dropped face-down in the dust, and the large canvas rose and floated in the air, presenting its face to each of them in turn.

A man and woman gazed out at them, their hands lightly touching as they stood in a flowering garden. A young girl sat between them in the grass, hugging a ball in her lap. They stared at the painter who had captured them, stared, without being entirely aware of it, into the future Selene occupied. Selene stared back, trying to peer into that past.

"Is that all we once were?" said Ursula, as the canvas spun again to her. "They look trapped in their flesh. Except for size, they look almost exactly the same."

"For them," said Selene, "that was difference enough."

"At least, that's what they had to keep telling themselves," said Tomas.

"Come along, Tomas," said Ursula. "Let's give Selene and Karl some time alone."

Ursula climbed back out the way they had come. As the painting dropped against a wall, Selene hoped, but could never be quite sure, that Tomas had followed his wife. After a moment, Selene could hear the slamming together of great objects. She smiled.

"I hope Ursula is having fun," said Karl.

"Some people just know better than others how, I guess," said Selene.

Selene and Karl and Karl and Karl made their way through what remained of the museum, where she tried to feel as a long-ago tourist might have, visiting on a summer day for a break from her busy life. She imagined how it must once have looked with its walls arranged neatly, its paintings organized according to a lost scheme Selene could not comprehend, its halls populated by contemporary visitors in search of a mirror. Selene lifted up each painting as lovingly as would a mother a child, and found each a place amidst the ruins where it could be seen and perhaps understood. She had no desire for blotches or geometric patterns today, though, and when Karl would overturn anything reeking of the abstract, she quickly abandoned it. She needed only the representational today. She needed...life.

A great fish, trapped at the end of a line, frozen in midair, yanked toward a small rowboat. A bowl of fruit that was only a bowl of fruit, and nothing more. A dog, its fur sparkling, proudly posing with a limp duck hanging from its maw. And the faces of the people, the endless faces of the people.

She mostly studied their eyes. They did not look unhappy to her. They did not look discontent. She was not fooled into thinking that their lives as they lived them were perfect, no, she was too smart for that, but she knew that what problems they had were not just symptoms of their times. They did not seem enslaved by the paucity of their choices. In fact, they were probably just as bewildered by the multiplicity of them as she was by her own.

"Selene," said Karl. Her name startled her. She lost hold of the last painting she had been studying, and Karl and Karl had to stumble forward to catch it. "Sorry. But Selene—what are you looking for?"

"I don't know."

She studied her husband's faces over the frame that was between them. Their eyes were equally sincere.

"What's wrong?" asked Karl.

"I don't know that either."

Karl tugged at the frame that separated them, but Selene held it in place. Karl stepped back and left them like that, coming around to place a hand on the small of Selene's back.

"Selene," he said. "Let's go."

"I can't," she said.

"We can't stay here forever," he said.

"Can't we?"

A deafening crash thudded outside. Selene could feel the vibrations through the soles of her feet.

"Obviously not if we want this world to remain in one piece," said Karl, smiling.

When they climbed back outside, the front of the museum was entirely clear of debris. Ursula stood in the midst of several perfectly balanced columns of wreckage.

"Much better that way, don't you think?" said Ursula. "And I could use the exercise."

"You don't need any exercise," said Selene.

"You must stop being so literal," said Tomas.

"Where have you been, dear?" asked Ursula.

"Everywhere," said Tomas. "I've seen it all now."

"All?" asked Selene.

"Yes," said Tomas. "The museum. The city. The world. Is it time for us to go?"

"There's much more the rest of us still have to see," said Selene. "Go back and take a second look. It isn't our fault that you can see everything so much faster than we do."

"Actually," said Tomas. "It is."

"Tomas!" shouted Selene. She wished she had the ability to tell whether her sudden anger was a good thing or a bad thing.

"Don't bother," said Ursula. "He's gone again."

"How can you tell?"

Ursula shrugged, her shoulders clinking. Selene sighed.

They walked single file through the rubble, first Selene, then Karl, then Karl, then Karl, then Ursula, this time, none of them touching. At a building where Selene recalled a movie theater once had been, she stopped. There'd been tuxedos there on the screen, she remembered. Tuxedos and dancing. But now the marquee was fallen, blending with the broken concrete of the sidewalk to block their way. Ursula pushed through to the center of the mound and effortlessly lifted a girder over her head.

"No!" Karl shouted.

"That's right," said Karl. "Put that down."

"Yes," said Karl. "The old-fashioned way. Selene wants this done the old-fashioned way."

"If you insist," said Ursula, lowering the girder slowly and moving back beside her friend.

Karl dove into the pile, squeezing through the narrow path that Ursula had started. Karl tossed a small chunk of brick and concrete to Karl, who flung it on to Karl, who grunted as he caught it and then stepped outside the field of rubble to lay the clump at Selene's feet.

"A gift," said Karl. "A gift of the old-fashioned way."

Selene laughed.

"Good," called out Karl, from where he continued to work. "You keep doing that."

"There hasn't been enough of it lately," shouted Karl, struggling next to him.

Karl bounded away to rejoin himself within the forest of brick and metal and glass, and continued widening the path. Pulling away the wreckage that barred the door, the three of him passed the rubble among himself like the hands of a juggler, and Selene laughed yet again, at her husband's playful love, and at the sight of the entrance that she'd been remembering with such hope.

Karl bowed on the left, and Karl bowed on the right, and Karl waved her forward, and Selene responded with a curtsey, as she had seen the native Earthlings do in those movies made so long ago.

Then, before she could step forward to entwine her husband's arms with her own and go inside, she heard a deep rumbling as loud as the death of stars.

The pavement cracked open in front of Selene, and her husband dropped away and vanished into the crevasse. Before Selene could move, the front wall of the theater spilled forward, sliding into the hole after Karl and Karl and Karl. From the ragged split, smoke and ash plumed upward, blinding her. She screamed, but no sound came out, her throat clogged by a harsh dust.

Ursula dove forward into the chasm, pushing debris aside and hurling rubble out of sight into the distance. Tomas returned, bringing a wind that blew the clouds of dust away. As soon as Selene could see her way clear, she stumbled down the lip of the pit to stand beside Ursula.

"Selene, you shouldn't be here. It's much too dangerous."

"Where is he? Where's my husband?"

"Selene, you don't want to see this," said Tomas. She could feel Tomas surrounding her, beginning to lift her, and as she started to be wafted away, she shrugged him off.

"Leave me be!" she said, as she saw limbs, ghostly with dust, protruding from beneath the rubble. "Karl!"

As Ursula removed the last bits of debris that were keeping Karl's broken body hidden, Selene threw herself alongside him and started to howl.

"This can't be," she muttered, when speech finally returned. "This is impossible. He's dead. All of him is dead."

"I don't think I can remember anyone ever dying," said Tomas.

As Selene rocked and moaned, Ursula grew once more into a larger self, and cupped her friends in her hands. This time, Selene did not object as Ursula cradled them all and returned them to the flitter. Kneeling, Ursula carefully placed them inside the flitter as if arranging the figures in a doll's house. A chair rose up to greet Selene, but no pallet responded to support any of Karl's bodies until Ursula waved her shrinking hand across the floor.

"It can't be over so easily," said Selene. "Not now. Not today. This isn't how it was supposed to be."

She moved from body to body, touching a bruised cheek here, flattening out a curl of hair there. As she traced a deep gouge in one of Karl's legs, terror welled within her, terror that was then tamped down. She didn't know what would happen if she was allowed to feel such pain.

"There's nothing we can do," said Ursula, moving to her friend's side. Ursula's fingers felt colder on her arm than they ever had before. "We should leave here, Selene. Don't you think?"

"Selene?" said Tomas.

Selene could not speak. Was there anyone left who needed to hear her voice? She did not think so.

"Let's just go, Selene," said Ursula, as softly as she could. "There's nothing more for us here."

Selene could feel her friend's fingers in her hair, and did not want to feel them.

"Go?" said Selene, struggling to keep her voice from cracking with rage. "Why should I go? Why should I go back home now? There no reason to do anything any longer, no reason to come here and no reason to go back. If only I hadn't made us come here! If only I hadn't insisted *all* of him come here. Leave me. You go back. Just leave me."

"Why *did* you want to come here, Selene?" asked Ursula. "What was the reason? What was it all about?"

Selene looked at her husband and her husband and her husband. She stroked his smooth face and his bruised face and then had to turn away from where there was hardly any face left at all. They'd begun their day in love and ended it in death, and love would not come again.

"What was the reason?" Selene whispered. "What *was* the reason?"

It had seemed so important, back when she woke on the other side of the galaxy. Earth, and all it represented, was more than just a goal, it was the journey as well, and had seemed dreadfully important. And now...now nothing was important.

"You're right," said Selene. "Let's go back. Let's go back now and let's go back fast. And let's not talk any more of the old-fashioned way."

"That's what I've been saying all along," said Tomas.

And as swift as the thought, Earth was gone, with no sense of a trip having been made. Selene, when she could bear to look out again through the transparent flitter walls, could see that they had arrived back outside her dome. It appeared exactly as they had left it that morning, in a prior dawn that was light years away. She looked from the dome to her husband and back, with no idea how she could ever live in one without the other again. She would have to have the dome destroyed.

Later, after Tomas and Ursula left her alone, perhaps she would have herself destroyed as well.

But before Selene could think the dome away, a figure pressed toward her through the membrane of its walls, and as a shell tightened around the approaching form, she could see that it was Karl. She struggled to cry out, but her mind was too numb to speak before he did.

"What happened?" he said, as he ran inside the flitter and embraced his wife while surrounded by his own dead bodies. "One moment I was clearing a path for you, and the next...nothing. I was cut off."

"How can you be alive?" she whispered, cradling his head in her hands. "The building fell and crushed you, all of you..."

"I was going to tell you," said Karl, "but I figured that if there could be three of me, darling, why not four? There was so much work to be done around here, and I knew that once I explained, you wouldn't really mind."

"You bastard!" she shouted, and pushed him away. "How long has this been going on?"

"Only since the moment you left. As Ursula launched you all into space, I launched a new me down here."

"But I wanted to see Earth with you at my side. I *needed* to see Earth with you at my side! How could you choose to stay behind and miss that? How could you live without me? I thought you loved me!"

"But I *saw* Earth with you, Selene. I was never without you. I was there the entire time."

"I could kill you," said Selene, slapping at Karl through the tears.

"If you're going to do that," said Karl, letting her succeed in slapping him a few times before catching her hands, "I'd better make sure that there are a few more of me first."

He drew her close with a single pair of arms and kissed her. Her knees buckled, and she crumpled at his feet, sobbing, laughing, howling, giggling, her emotions in full revolt against her senses.

"We should leave the two of you alone," said Ursula.

"Or however many of them there are," said Tomas. "Let's go, dear."

"You'll let us know how it goes, Karl, won't you?" said Ursula.

Selene eventually stopped trembling, and was able to realize that she and her husband were by themselves. As she let Karl help her to her feet, the flitter dissolved around them and was reabsorbed into the planet's surface. As she stared into the shadows spilling off the dry, red rocks, she realized exactly how much time had passed them by while they'd traveled through the void and explored Earth the old-fashioned way.

An entire cycle had passed. It was that time again, if she still wanted it to be that time.

They entered their dome, and she studied the view out of the bedroom's picture window. She almost thought she could see Ursula, curving through the sky like a shooting star off in the distance. Selene replayed her friend's last words in her mind, until...

"None of today was real, was it?" Selene whispered. "Not a moment of it."

She waited for him to reach for her, hoping that he would, hoping that he wouldn't.

"Tomas and Ursula, they were both in on it, weren't they?"

"We just wanted you to have an old-fashioned experience," said Karl. "We just wanted you to be happy, that's all. I thought you would like it."

"And I appreciate the gesture, Karl," she said. "I really do. But could you leave me alone for just a moment?"

"Are you sure?" he asked. "Is everything all right?"

"Everything is fine," she said.

Once Karl exited through a biolock, Selene sat on her side of the bed. On a small table nearby, perfectly centered, was exactly what she knew would be there: a small, blue pill just like the one that had been waiting for her the morning before, and the morning before that, and all the mornings she could still remember.

She snatched at, and choked it down quickly. Then, while thinking with terror of the old-fashioned ways, she held out a palm in wonder and supplication until a second pill appeared, and then swallowed that one even more quickly than the first.

THE WORLD BREAKS

The world breaks everyone, and afterwards,
many are strong at the broken places.
-Ernest Hemingway

Dear Annie,

I hope to God that you never have to read this letter. If we're both lucky, instead of it being delivered to you back in Travis by some stuck-up officer, I'll have it handed back to me at the end of my rotation so that I can destroy it.

I've put off writing this for months. But the guys tell me that this is something I'd better do, especially now, and so even though thinking about never seeing you again is the last thing I want to do, I've snuck away tonight to spend some time with you, the same way I used to climb out the bedroom window of my parents' old home and shinny down the gutter to meet you in the cornfield. Maybe writing this will be less painful for me if I can pretend that's all I'm doing right now, getting together for a late-night heart-to-heart with you.

The meat of it is, Annie, things don't look so good. I don't know whether you or anyone else ever gets to hear back home what's really going on over here. I doubt it. They don't want the truth to get out, so they candy-coat for you what we see on the ground each day, and feed it to you with a smile. They need you to swallow it, because if you ever knew that truth, none of us would be over here for even one more day. This war, even though no one likes calling it that, chews up men and spits out body bags, and—

Forgive me, Annie. I really shouldn't talk like that. It feels good to rant, but this really isn't the place for it. The things I've seen...

It's hard not to think about the worst.

I've never seen things this tense, and it could go either way. If this breaks big, we'll all of us be lost. Unlike those bar fights I kept getting in back home (how you were able to keep smiling each time you showed up to bail me out I'll never know, but I've always cherished that forgiving face, you know that, don't you?), this fight will do more than just break a few mirrors and chairs when it blows. This fight could take out the whole world.

I've thought about that a lot during the time I've been stuck out here in the sand. I've always been a little angry—and a little jealous, too—about those Air Force guys. They get to fly way overhead and never see the blood first hand. But what really steams me are the ones back home who sit in windowless rooms, their fingers on buttons. Or on charts and reports, which is worse, because with them they manage to turn us into numbers. They have air conditioning, and warm meals, and hot showers, and...and they can see their families, too, which means that they're not forced to write stupid letters like this, meant to be read in the event of...well, you know. You'd think those perks would cause them to appreciate life more, make them think twice before acting stupid, but it doesn't seem to help.

Anyway, I seem to have gotten away from myself again. I didn't mean to write this letter just to complain about the brass. I wanted to say a little something about us while I still had the chance, just a few words about you and me and what we had.

I love you, Annie. I guess I never said it enough when I was back home. I guess no one ever does. But I sure think about it every day. It's what keeps me going. In fact, if I close my eyes, I can see myself back there with you now, watching a football game, going for an ice cream, steaming up the car windows at the drive-in.

Oh, damn, Annie. Especially that drive-in.

We should have gotten married before I shipped out. We should have had a kid, and bought a house, and...

We should have done a lot of things. But if you're reading this, that means it's too late. We're not going to get a chance to do them.

Don't let yourself get too sad over that. Don't waste your time mourning too long over me. Have a life, Annie, a good life with someone else. After all, that's why I'm here anyway, right? To make sure that you and others like you can have a good life.

I've gone on long enough. I really should get some sleep before tomorrow's mission. It's going to need all I've got. Hopefully, while I sleep, I'll dream of you.

I usually do.

After all the hurt I've shown you, it doesn't seem right that God would let us get back together. I'll make sure to pray tonight, ask Him to show us some mercy. Maybe He'll decide to show the human race some mercy while He's at it.

I once heard Father Dixon preach that if we each got what we deserved, the world would be in pretty bad shape. Who knows? Maybe that's what's going on right now. We're all just getting what we deserve.

But I can still hope that in the end, there'll be mercy.

I guess this means Slipper is yours now. He's been a good dog to me. Treat him right and I'm sure he'll be good to you, too. Remember to give him a scratch from me in that special place behind his left ear every now and then.

And remember me, too.

Love,

Danny

•   •   •

Hey, little man,

If you're reading this, then I guess you're the big man now. Remember what I told you the last time we spoke, back on the day I headed out to look for your brother? How you had to take care of Mommy while I was gone? Well, this letter, the fact that you're reading it, means that I won't be coming back the way I hoped I would, and it's going to be up to you to watch after Mommy from now on. It's a big responsibility, but I know that you'll be up to it. I know in my heart that you're going to make me proud.

I'm writing this just before I leave so you'll understand why I'm not with you right now, even though remaining in Travis is one of the things I want most in the world. When I explain it all to you, I hope you'll understand why I couldn't stay. I'd like to believe that others would tell you what happened to me and to the world, and tell you why I'm gone, but I can't be sure. Sometimes people try to hide things from kids, and this is just too big to be hidden. So in the few hours I have left before I've got to go, I want to try to explain it to you.

I don't know when and if you'll read this, but right now, it's only been a few days since the lights went out. I don't know whether, by the time this gets to you, that you'll even remember the night. You're so young, and early memories often fade. Perhaps it's better that you don't remember.

We were waiting for your brother to get home so we could sit down to dinner. Mommy had made a big pan of lasagna, his favorite meal, because it was his birthday. John was off fooling around with his friends for the afternoon, and we expected him back any minute. But then he called home to say that he was going to be late. So we started eating without him. I'd just filled my mouth with a huge fork of lasagna when the lights went out, so my curse only came out as a mumble.

I was already angry about your brother, and sitting in the dark didn't make me any less so. Luckily, our generator kicked in, so we weren't that way for long. With the power back, I turned on the television to see whether there was any news, but all I could get was static. Same thing with the radio. And I couldn't raise a dial tone on any of our phones. All of which made me nervous, because it meant that whatever had happened, it was more than just a local problem.

A normal person might have stayed home and eaten his dinner. In a warm house, with a belly full of lasagna and maybe a glass or wine or two, I could have pretended that nothing was wrong. But you see, Bobby, Daddy's a policeman, which means that it's my job to take care of people. The way I've always done my best to take care of you and your brother. And so I had to go out that night to make sure our town was safe.

I hit the road, and as I drove, the car's headlights were comforting. It helped me continue to pretend that there was just a glitch somewhere, that a fuse had blown that would soon be replaced. I found a lot of our neighbors wandering aimlessly, perhaps for that very reason. But there were no answers to be found anywhere. Not even down at the station. Even though their emergency generator had also kicked in, they couldn't get in touch with the world outside Travis either.

Two of my fellow officers decided to drive the seventy miles over to the next town to see if anyone in Buxton had figured anything out. I wasn't sure we could even spare that. It took everything the rest of us had to keep order. You see, people have less sense than animals sometimes. When it's dark, most animals lie down and sleep, but not people. They take the darkness as a sign to head out and cause trouble. So we ended up with more crime that night than any other night since I first took the job.

It was all petty stuff. Drag racing down Main Street. Shoplifting jars of pickled eggs from the all-night grocery store. A couple of fist fights down at the bar. I had to keep cruising until the sun came up and people had the sense to lie down. But it was my job to make sure that no one got hurt. Or hurt anyone else. By the time the sun had come up, we were all of us exhausted, and I was finally able to come home to see you.

You were asleep, so you don't know that I looked in on you before collapsing. But I did. Because I needed to know that you were safe, too.

Your Mom shook me awake around noon to tell me that your brother still hadn't come home. She shoved a mug of coffee in my hand and told me the truth about how he had planned to spend his birthday. Turns out that he hadn't just been hanging around locally with his friends. Instead, they'd gone on a road trip to the city. He'd never really intended to be back for dinner. He'd told your Mom the truth when he'd called about missing dinner, and she didn't tell me then because she didn't want me to worry. But he should have been home by midnight. And now, with the phones out, there was no way for him to tell us if anything had happened to him, whether he needed us to go get him.

I went back down to the station to see whether our guys had returned from Buxton, but they hadn't. So we were still clueless. No one had any further information than the night before. My gut told me to get in the squad car immediately and take off for your brother, but I couldn't. There was too much chaos right here, and I had sworn an oath. I had heard of other cops who had abandoned their posts during natural disasters, and I didn't want to end up like one of them. I couldn't have lived with myself. So I spent another day on the job, this time stopping looting and cleaning up after car crashes, all the time wondering what was going on in the rest of the world. We had no way of communicating with anyone outside Travis, and no one was bothering to check up on us. It was if the world had broken, and we had slipped into a crack somewhere.

But after another day, with still no word, I couldn't bear to wait any longer. I had to get your brother, the same way I'd come get you if you were in trouble. So no matter what you hear people say, that I ran, don't believe them. It's just that family had to come first.

So I'm going after him, knowing that whatever's happening, I don't have to worry about you and your Mom. Because you'll be safe here in Travis. That's what a hometown is, the place that protects you. That's what a hometown does. Never forget that. I can go after your brother knowing that you'll be here when I come back. And I do want to come back.

But still, I thought it best to write this note first. This is what we used to do in the service. You'd go out each day and you'd never know for sure whether that was the day you might not return. And though I plan on doing everything in my power to get back to you, just in case I don't, I wanted you to hear why from me.

I'm going to do my best, but if you're reading this, then I guess my best wasn't good enough.

I'm going to give this letter to someone I trust, and when enough time has passed, when it looks like I didn't make it, he's going to bring it to you. He's someone you can trust, too. You're going to need someone like that in your life.

I'm sorry I won't be there each day to do the things a father is supposed to do with his son. It hurts me now just thinking about it. But let him try to be there for you, the way I know you're going to be there for your Mother.

Be strong for me, son. Make me proud.

Always and forever,

Your Father

• • •

Dear Jason—

Know this—Americans don't let themselves get pushed around. Not by anyone. Not even by other Americans. *Especially* not by other Americans.

I tried my best to teach that to you that while I was alive. I sure hope it stuck, because if you're reading this letter, it means that I won't be around to try to teach you that or anything else any more.

Actually, it wasn't so bad at first. At least, not here in Travis. I could have lived without the power—after a while that didn't feel like so much of a burden. No TV, no phone, no Internet. Hell, that's how my grandparents lived, and they seemed pretty happy. That's how most people lived back to the beginning of time. And we could have gotten by here. That's the kind of people we are. We're pretty self-sufficient.

Most of us who lived in this town worked in town as well. We weren't dependent on the outside world. We can grow most of our own food anyway, taking care of at least our needs, if not always our wants. I ate too many Oreos anyway. And as for those other things we couldn't make ourselves, well, we quickly discovered we didn't really need those as much as we thought we did either. Without the gossip mags, radio talk shows, new movies and so on, we remembered that there were more important things in life, things we hadn't always had time for before. Like each other. So life wasn't as tough here as it might have gotten in other places. We could have easily gotten by.

That's another thing you have to remember about Americans—when things get tough, they take care of each other.

But then the army arrived and told us that we had to leave, which changed everything. That was when we learned what had really happened to the rest of the world, why the men who had been sent out to explore every few days never came back. That's because the world out there that they were trying to communicate with was gone for the most part, Jason. The soldiers who brought us the bad news wouldn't tell us the whole truth of it—I'm not even sure that they themselves knew the whole truth of it—but the gist of it is that one bunch of madmen did the unthinkable, and then another bunch of madmen did the unthinkable in return. Which side started it didn't really matter. Just that it got started at all. There was enough blame to go around.

Which led to the army at our door telling us that we had twenty-four hours to gather our things and abandon our town, to go with them to an evacuation center. They said that the fallout would soon make it unhealthy for us here. All I can say is that once it's unsafe in Travis, it's not going to be safe anywhere else on Earth.

Your great-grandparents came to this country with nothing, Jason. They helped build this town. I know what it meant to them, what it means to everyone here. And I wasn't going to let anyone destroy it. This is where I was born. This is where I fell in love. This is where I met your father. And this is where I buried him.

This is where I hoped that after I'd died in my sleep surrounded by my grandchildren, you'd be burying me.

The colonel who stood on the steps of City Hall yesterday and laid out our timetable—a timetable he said he could not alter for any reason—looked honest and trustworthy enough, I guess. Under other circumstances, I suppose I would have done anything he asked. He had that kind of look to him, the look of a leader. I could understand why his men would follow him. But that day, his words did nothing but make us all boiling mad. Almost as bad as us having to leave at all was the fact that he told us that we could each only bring as much as we could carry.

I could pack up the first lock of your hair, but your first crib? What about your grandfather's grandfather clock? Or the barn your uncles helped raise? How could I carry away those? Our home holds history, generations worth of history. And that wasn't something I could fit in a backpack. I didn't plan on even trying, no matter what threats the soldiers made.

I'm not going anywhere I didn't choose to go myself. I love this town too much to abandon it. I love this town too much not to try to save it.

I only have a few hours until the army returns to City Hall to scoop us up and take us away. I need to get my backpack ready. It will take everything I've got if I'm going to change their minds. I don't know if I'll succeed—only you will know that—but I've got to at least try. For your grandparents. For everyone who ever lived in and loved Travis. And especially for you, Jason. This town deserves that much. It can't defend itself. Only we can do that.

When you hear what I have done, I hope that you'll understand, and be able to find a way to forgive me. You will probably ask yourself, why did my mother have to be the one to do this? Why couldn't it have been one of the men?

I guess because I'm the one who thought of it first. But also, any of the others would have seemed too threatening, I think. They might not have been able to get close enough to pull off what needs to be done.

The house is yours now, Jason. The town is yours now. Take care of them both.

I'm sorry for all the mistakes I made. I know that I wasn't the best mother in the world. Didn't even come close. And the fact that you're reading this means I'm not going to get any further opportunities to prove how much I love you. But I hope that once you hear what I have done, you'll understand that it was done for you. I hope that I've managed to make it right between us. Sometimes the only way to fight the madness of the world is with a little madness of your own.

Stay strong, Jason.

Don't forget to feed the fish. They shouldn't have to suffer on my account.

Your mother

. . .

My dearest Maggie,

The sun is rising, so you know what that means—I'm thinking of you. I always hear people saying that the way for a marriage to last is to make sure that you never go to bed angry, but you and I know the real answer, don't we? It's to instead make sure that you always wake up happy. How you start out the day determines how you end it. Those who wait until their heads hit the pillow before paying attention to their marriage are too late. They've already lost. But we always knew that, Maggie, didn't we?

I always think back to those mornings with you whenever the darkness begins to fade. Waking up in your arms, your breath hot against my neck, one of your ankles crossed over mine. And that look that came into your eyes when you were fully awake and you realized we were still together. I'm pretty sure you were able to see in my eyes what I saw in yours back then. At least I hope so.

That's what hurts the most, actually—not what I have seen and done in service to my country—but the string of mornings I have spent without you. I look forward to the day when those mornings come back to us again. That's the only way I find myself able to function.

But there are no guarantees in this world. That's what I tell my men to persuade them to write letters like these to those they love. I've never heard of a soldier who did this willingly. All the time I've been gone I've been avoiding writing one myself. I didn't want to admit even the remotest possibility that another of our mornings wasn't going to come, that a day could arrive when one of us would wake without the other. But after having too many of my men taken from me, I can't fool myself any longer. This has to be done. And so I take my own advice, and write this letter to you.

We're camped several miles outside a small town in the Midwest right now. I can't tell you its name, or even what state we're in, because the censors would just delete that information anyway, even though these letters are supposed to be delivered unread. We went in yesterday to tell the people who lived there what had happened to the world and what was going to happen to them, and their faces were heartbreaking. Unlike you, who knew everything right from the start of this mess (one of the benefits of being an army wife), these people knew nothing. And strangely, once I started bringing them up to date, it didn't seem as if they *wanted* to know anything.

I came to help them, Maggie, that's my job, that's what I swore to do, but these people didn't see it that way. As I stood on the front steps of their City Hall and told them what we were going to do when we returned today, I saw anger in their eyes. But it wasn't the same anger I'd seen elsewhere. This was a quiet anger.

I'm used to people shouting and screaming. I can deal with that. That can be defused. Those sorts of people can eventually be persuaded to do what's right. But these people were seething in a way which leads me to suspect we will see some trouble there today. And so I'm finally writing this letter I didn't want to ever write and that I don't want you to ever read.

I hope that I'm wrong. As we drove out of town after my announcement, this certainly didn't seem like a town worth dying for. It was the sort of place I had escaped as a kid, the kind of town any sane person flees at the first opportunity, rather than takes refuge in. It's what I joined the army to get away from. But I could tell by the look in their eyes that they saw something I did not, and that could make them dangerous.

Well, Maggie, the sun has come all the way over the horizon now, which means that our special time is gone. I have to go make sure that my men are prepared, because when the sun is directly overhead, we'll begin shepherding the civilians to the camps. We've already been doing this for quite a while without too much trouble, so it should all go smoothly.

But you never know.

If you're reading this, something went wrong. Either I screwed up, or one of my men did. Or maybe it was just my time.

Please don't let that make you an angry person. One of the things I've always loved about you is the lack of anger in you, which is a miracle considering that you've had to put up with me, who carried so much. I don't want anything that happens to change that about you. You knew this might happen when you married the kind of man you married. So don't hate the army, or the civilians either. None of us asked to be in this situation, and none of us knows how to get out of it either.

I always regretted a little that we never had children, though I never said it out loud. I didn't want to make you sadder than I knew you already were about it. But now I think that we were lucky. I don't know what kind of world we're going to have once we come out the other side of this, or even that there will be another side, and I'd hate to think myself responsible for condemning anyone else to it. This may not be a world that wants people in it any longer.

I'm sorry each day that I can't be with you to help protect you, but it helps to know that you're safe on the base. And I have a job I must do for my country. For our country. I have to go do it again now, so I must cut this short. I hope that the job will go well, so I can return to you.

But if I don't, Maggie, think of me each time you see the sun rise.

With more love than you'll ever know,

Kenneth

• • •

Dear Momma,

You remember Peggy, don't you? She owned the movie theater, such as it was. By the time a film got there it had usually already shown on cable TV, but that didn't make it any less fun. It's been a while since you were well enough to leave the home and be taken there, but I hope that you can still remember it and her. Do you remember who I mean, Momma?

Well, Peggy did something horrible today. And the way things are going, that means that I'm probably going to have to do something horrible, too.

You haven't heard about any of this yet, of course. None of your friends get out much from that nursing home, and though you might have been able to hear some of the loud noises from in there, the doctors probably didn't want to have to explain to you what had happened. Once people get to a certain age, they forget how to handle change, and the nurses didn't want to rile you up. They have enough trouble getting you to cooperate. Ordinarily, I might not have told you any of this either. But if things continue on the way they've been going, I won't be able to come around to visit anymore, and you should know why.

This is an odd feeling for me, Momma. I never had to say goodbye forever before, except to Dan, and with that bastard, it was a pleasure. I know you've already forgotten about Dan, Momma. I wish I could do the same. But it doesn't look as if I'll live long enough to start forgetting the way you do.

But this all begins with Peggy. I never knew she was that brave. I'll tell it to you as simply as I can, Momma. See, some bad things had happened out in the world. I'd hoped you'd never have to know about them. But because of those bad things, we were all brought together in the Town Square so that Travis could be evacuated. The government had promised to take us away to someplace better. But do you know of any better place this side of Heaven? Of course not. Me neither.

And we all lined up, apparently just getting ready to go along with it, just like sheep. Your doctors were going to go along with it a little later, too, just pack you up in the backs of trucks and ship you off. Travis would have become a ghost town. And it angered me that we were all just calmly collaborating in its death.

But not Peggy. You would never have suspected it to look at her. She wove through the crowd quite casually, as if she was just angling for a better view. She didn't make eye contact with anyone until she stood immediately before the City Hall steps and looked up at the colonel who was rattling off the agenda of what we could expect for the rest of the day. A line of trucks trailed off from the square to the outskirts of town, and we were supposed to peaceably climb on with our belongings. But Peggy proved that she wasn't feeling so peaceable.

As the first truck pulled up, Peggy, instead of hopping in the back, ran up the steps to the colonel, and embraced him. I could see then what I hadn't noticed before—the wire coming out of her backpack near her neck, running down the back of her shirt, down a sleeve, and then out into her hand. When what was about to happen registered, I threw myself to the ground, so I didn't see what came next. But the result. I saw the result.

The City Hall steps were shattered, suddenly no more than a crater filled with rubble. I backed away from the action through the smoke and screams into the lobby of Elton's Drug Store. It was only later that I realized I'd gotten inside without having had to open the door. All the glass had been blown out, and I'd just stepped right through.

I hid under the counter. Though I covered my ears, nothing could blot out the sound of gunfire and roaring engines. I waited inside until the streets were silent again. And what I saw out there, Momma. There were a lot of dead, both soldiers and civilians. The soldiers I couldn't recognize, but the others...they were our friends.

With the army gone, the town was strangely quiet. But the soldiers would be back, I was sure of that. And I knew in that instant that Peggy had the right of it. We couldn't let them succeed. Travis was ours. And nobody was going to take it from us. But if we didn't do something...

I wasn't going to let them take you away from here, Momma. This is where you were born. This is where you spent your life. And this is where you should be buried.

So I'm ready, Momma. Ready to fight back in the only way I know how. Tomorrow I'll be ready for when those soldiers return. And when they do, when their trucks come for us again, I'll be thinking of Peggy.

And of you, Momma.

And I'll be thinking of fresh corn. And the field of daffodils you planted as a girl, the one that's still out there. And the sound of owls in the night, calling one to the other. I always used to lie in bed in the dark with the windows open and hope that they'd find each other. I'd like to think that they always did. I hope that you and I get to find each other again someday, too.

If all these things I'm telling you should become too painful to you, then put this letter away. Give it to one of the nurses. Tell her to hide it from you, and you will soon forget. I never thought I'd be relieved at the ability to forget that's come over you, but I am now.

You kept me safe for so many years, and now it's my turn to keep you safe.

Your loving daughter,

Linda

• • •

Dad,

You tried to teach me to always tell the truth, that that's what a man did. It never took, not when I was back home. I just never could seem to do it. But suddenly it seems pointless to lie. I guess I only let myself get away with lying because I always knew that there'd be time later to straighten things out. But now I don't think I'm going to get any more later.

Things are really fucked up now. I thought they were fucked up before, but believe me, Dad, they've gotten even worse.

I'm on my own here. We're all of us on our own. Our leaders are gone. No chiefs any more, Dad, just us Indians. I always used to think that there were too many of them, but it turns out that too many were better than none at all.

I don't know how much time I have left in which to write this, but I figure I needed to say something. You deserve that much. There are so many things I should have said, but didn't really feel a need to say until now. Funny what brings you to that place in which you can do those things you weren't able to do for years, but couldn't.

We're camped outside a small town right now, a town that looked to us like any other at first. But it wasn't, Dad. We were under orders to move the inhabitants to the closest camp, and long story short, they resisted. Oh, other civilians have talked big, and occasionally shown us their weapons. But this is the first time that anyone's ever actually fought back.

They've been blowing themselves up, Dad. What the Hell is up with that? American suicide bombers? What were they thinking? How could anyone bring themselves to do that? I didn't join the army to die for my country. That's not what a soldier does. I joined to make the other guy die for his. So how could they go ahead and *choose* to die? It doesn't make sense.

After it began, I did some things I'm ashamed of. You have to, to defend your buddies. But no more.

I don't even know whether you're ever going to read this letter. Not because I don't know whether anyone will deliver it for me should anything, you know, happen—my buddies wouldn't let anyone stop them from bringing it to you should that become necessary—but because I don't really know for sure whether you're even still alive. I hear that the big cities took the first hits and are mostly gone. Only small towns like this may have a chance to survive.

I guess these people all knew that. I guess they were right, and were willing to die because they knew they were right. Well, I'm not so sure that I'm in the right any more. So while some of the men are preparing for a final assault on the town, me and a bunch of the guys, we've decided we've had enough. We're getting out of here, and we're going to head home instead.

Which might mean that we're only heading for where home used to be.

As I wrote at the top, there's no one in charge anymore to stop us. I'm not sure whether we'll make it. I'm not even sure we'll get out of here before the town begins another attack of their own. And so I write this letter, just in case.

If you do get to read this, Dad, I hope you can forgive me for all the crazy things I did. There. I said it. If only I could have said it to you then rather than joining the army to avoid saying it at all.

I hope this letter reaches you. I hope I reach you, to say those things myself. At this point, I don't know which is more likely.

Whatever happens, know that I love you.

Jimmy

P.S.—If you ever see Shelly, let her know that I'm sorry for all the things I did to her, too. I hope to tell her myself, but, well, you know.

P.P.S—I hope the people who got us into this mess man up and say they're sorry, too.

· · ·

Dear Jessica,

I'm calling you that even though I don't yet know whether you'll turn out to be a boy or a girl. Not for sure anyway. I never made it to the hospital to find out, and the way the world is now, I don't know that I'll get the chance. But a mother dreams. And a mother knows.

I used to worry a lot about whether it was right to bring a child into this world, what with global warming, pollution, the threat of war and all those other dark futures waiting for us down the road. But the perspective is different from here. Maybe I only worried so much because I never had the chance to do anything about it before. Now that I do have that chance to help make things right, I no longer feel so bleak.

By the time you're able to read this letter, if you do ever read this, you'll probably want to know about your father. And I won't be here to tell you about it. That's why I'm writing this, to answer those types of questions for you.

But honestly, Jessica—and this is hard to have to say, especially to you—I'm not really sure who the father is. Please don't hate me for that. That's just the kind of person I was. That's the kind of life I lived. I wasn't a saint. I did drugs. I slept around. And pretty much everyone in Travis knew that. As a result, most people here didn't like me much, and I didn't like myself so much either.

But that was then. Now that you're on the horizon, I don't live like that anymore. Now I feel I have something to live for. Someone to live for.

And that someone is you.

I can see your face in my mind, a face I haven't yet seen, but that I already know so well. You're looking up at me, trusting. Expecting the best. Thinking that only good things are down the road for you, that life could be all rainbows and ponies. I was that way once. I wasn't that way for long. I used to regret that, but now I think perhaps that's the only reason I survived for as long as I did.

Maybe, if we're both very lucky, and if Mommy makes the right choices, you won't have to toughen up the same way I did. Life isn't much fun with a callus between you and the world. But that may be why I was able to return alive from what I just did.

See, honey, bad men had come to Travis and were going to take us from it. I couldn't let that happen. It's almost hard to explain why, what with all the crappy things done to me here. But still, I wasn't going to let it happen. Taking me away from Travis angered me as much as if someone was going to take you away from me. Travis was my mother as much as I am yours. Our stories are entwined forever. Whatever is to happen to me, however I'm supposed to end up, it's meant to happen here. You and me and Travis. Together.

I didn't realize we had a choice at first, though. When the bad men came the first day to take us away, I never dreamed of saying no. I hadn't ever learned how, which was one of my problems in the first place. So I packed up my things as I was told and got ready to go.

But then a very brave woman decided to fight back, showing others the way, inspiring us all. And our kidnappers retreated.

But not entirely.

We knew they were still there on the outskirts of town, readying for one final attempt. I'm not sure that they still had either the men or the will to do by then what they'd set out to do when they first rolled into town. I think their minds were just full of revenge about the terrible things they'd forced us to do. Which meant that for Travis' sake, for your sake, I knew what *I* had to do.

I went to visit them just this morning. I walked up to their camp in the bright daylight. I didn't want them to think I was sneaking up on them. After the events of the previous week, they didn't let me get too close. But close enough for what I needed.

They could see the vest I was wearing. They could see what I was ready to do. And when I held that vest open, Jessica...

They could see you.

That was when the soldiers who remained started shouting at me the loudest. Some of them even began to cry. One fell to the ground and vomited. They insulted me, questioned me, shrieked while pointing at you. But I did not answer them. I just held my hands out toward them and let them see the wires wrapped around my palms.

I closed my eyes and remembered the saints I had been taught about in Sunday school, what they had been willing to endure because of what they believed. I listened to the world beyond those men, listened to the birds, the sound of the nearby stream by which they had camped, the rustling leaves. I felt an almost unbearable peace. I knew that whatever happened next, we would be together, one way or another.

I didn't open my eyes again until I heard their engines. I stood there unmoving as they pulled out. Then, when they were gone, I was the one who fell to the ground and wept.

Then I came back to town and told the others what I had done, what I had seen. I think we're safe now, Jessica. I don't think that they're coming back. But it wasn't my doing. It was yours. You're the one who convinced them that we were never going to abandon this place. If not for you, Travis would be no more. Remember that.

We'll have a good life here, Jessica. I look forward to watching you grow. I look forward to being able to look into your eyes and tell you these things. I'd rather you didn't have to read them here. But there are no guarantees in this world, which is why I'm writing it anyway.

When we came home just a little while ago, I did not disassemble the vest I had worn. I just hung it in the closet. The time may come when I will have to wear it again. Only when that time does come, having put it on, I might not have the option of taking it off.

So I will leave this letter where you can find it someday, and know what your mother was willing to do for you. I learned today that I was stronger than I ever thought I would be. I hope that someday, you will be stronger still.

Love,

Mother

P.S.—If we're both lucky, you won't ever have to read this letter. Maybe, if the world is lucky, this will be the last such letter anyone will ever have to write.

AND THE TREES WERE HAPPY

The old man slowly and carefully lowered himself onto the stump—
for, after all, everything he did these days had to be done slowly and
carefully—and as the ancient wood pressed against his bony flesh, he
was surprised by the surge of emotions that brought on a sudden welling of tears. He looked up through wet eyes at the empty air where a
tree had at one time towered above him, and recalled how he had once
swung effortlessly through branches which, if he had not cut them
down so long ago, would now have shielded him from an oppressive sun.

The twinge of pain traveling through his hips as he connected with
the stump was something he would never have imagined, back when
he was a young boy, waited in his future. And yet somehow, as he settled in, he found comfort there, as if it had been carved for him alone.
The walk through the orchard had been longer than he'd remembered
it being, and his need to sit was overwhelming. But then, most things
these days were longer than he remembered. Longer, more difficult,
and often filled with an almost unendurable sadness.

Still, he had managed to endure. And unexpectedly, after years—
decades actually—return.

He felt a bit foolish to have done so, though, even as he knew the
return had recently become inevitable. He'd been haunted lately by
ancient memories he found he could not elude, and drawn by them
to this orchard close to his childhood home. Drawn, more specifically,
to this tree, or the remnant of same, at the site of which he had passed
so many of his life's most important moments.

Many of his memories of this place were cloudy now, and as he
sought them out, he suspected, too, that they were surely muddled

by an old man's brain. As a boy, he had spoken to the tree, treated it as a friend, of that he was certain, and he saw nothing wrong with that, for that is what boys, what children, do. But—and here is where he did not believe what he remembered—had the tree really spoken back? Surely that was not possible. He assumed this was only the hot sun inserting those memories into his mind. Because... what else could it be?

He should have remembered to wear a hat. Or should, at least, have brought along some water. For he was thirsty, a thirst which resurrected on his tongue the taste of the apples which had once grown above him, and which had quenched his thirst like nothing since.

But those apples were gone now, first to be sold for money so he could buy toys, then because he needed the branches which bore them to build a house, and finally due to his hewing of wood for a boat. And now all those things were gone as well...money, house, boat...plus the wife and child those first possessions had gotten him.

The wife who would have reminded him about the hat. The child who would have trailed after him to gently place a bottle of water in his hand.

No, now he had nothing, nothing save the clothes on his back and the elusive memories which had brought him here.

The memory of the stump on which he sat. The memory of what it had once been. The memory of what *he* had once been.

If only he could taste an apple again! If only he could go back. He would do anything for that. But he could think of nothing which could be done. Because there was nothing which *could* be done. The orchard's other trees, the other apples, they were not like this tree, those apples.

Which made his return...pointless.

As he wondered why he had bothered, why his childhood had intruded on his life once more in a way he could no longer reject, he noticed that the sun had dropped behind the orchard's closest row of trees, the nearby branches casting a shadow across his face.

How odd. How could so much time could have passed, high noon transforming into those elusive moments before dusk, without him being aware of it?

But as he looked into the shade-filled gathering of the trees, he quickly forgot that, for he could make out an abundant display of heavy apples tugging at their branches. The weight of them was a living thing, and he wondered...if he rose, if he reached out his hand to pluck one, if he held it to his lips, touched it to his tongue...would it be as sweet as memory? Could anything ever be?

He knew he had to try. He stood, and took a step forward toward them, but then stumbled—for his rear foot had caught under one of the stump's exposed roots.

He fell to the ground, a pain shooting sharply up his leg. Had he broken an ankle? Based on the ache that remained, it felt as if he had, but he'd endured so many pains in recent years, he couldn't be entirely sure. He wiggled his foot, which seemed trapped where it had become wedged between the root and the stump, and no matter how hard he tried, could not pull it free.

"How could you do this to me?" he almost said aloud to the stump, feeling betrayed by a thing which he knew could not possibly have the sentience to betray him, but caught himself, silenced himself, before he acted even more foolishly than he already had by coming there. This was no one's fault but his own. And for whatever reason—a momentary distraction, the clumsiness of his gait, which over the years had turned into more of a shuffle—his foot was stuck.

Out of breath, and unable to pull loose his twisted foot, he lay on his back and looked up at the darkening sky. He wondered how many hours, how many days, it would be before anyone wandered by this remote place who could help, and what they would think of the silly old man when they found him.

Slowly, a branch from the nearest tree grew nearer above him, lengthening into his field of vision, a lone apple at its tip pushing forward to hang tantalizingly close. The fruit pulsed with possibility, and he held out a hand, but could not reach it. The more he stretched, the more tightly the root squeezed around his foot, preventing him from closing the infuriating gap.

"Please," said the old man. "Please let me have just one more apple."

As if in response, the branch above him trembled. As if in response, the root beneath him squeezed. And then the tree which had grown toward him impossibly fast to tease him with its tempting fruit spoke, its words all around him, its words *in* him.

"Do not worry," said the tree, though as its words filled his mind, the man knew it was speaking, not just for itself, but on behalf of the entire orchard. "The fruit will be yours. If you truly want it, that is."

"I do," said the man, embarrassed by his greed and glad no one else was there to hear the naked desire quivering in his voice. "But I can't quite reach it. My foot, you see. It's become stuck."

"We know," said the tree. "But it hasn't *just* become stuck. It's become trapped. *You've* become trapped. There has always been a part of us that loved you too much. It loved you too much then. It loves you too much now. It wants to stop you from eating the apple that would let you see things clearly. Even now, even after all you have done, it wants to keep giving. But now it's time for a giving of an entirely different kind."

The branch shook, its leaves rustling like the wind from another time, and the dangling apple danced seductively at the end of its stem. For a few agonizing moments, it looked as if the stem would hold, and the man dared not breathe, but then the fruit broke free and landed with a plop in his hungry palm.

He held it to his nose, the aroma dizzying. As he did so, he could feel the root pulse against his ankle, and he knew it was urging him to drop the apple. At the same time, he could almost hear it whisper. But whatever it was trying to say was unimportant. He was beyond convincing.

He bit roughly, and as his teeth broke the skin of the fruit and the moist flesh touched his tongue, his foot was released.

And he was young again.

And so was the tree on whose stump he'd been sitting.

Its trunk thrust high above him, leaping for the sky. Its branches bent to offer shade and extend an invitation.

He accepted that invitation. Laughing, he shinnied up the trunk until he could touch the lowest branch. Then he leapt, and swung, and crouched atop it. He jeered the ground so far below, dared gravity to have its way with him, but he knew it could not, for wasn't he a boy?

He gathered leaves as he had in days past and once more wove himself a crown so he could declare himself king of the forest. Ruler of all he surveyed, he swung from branch to branch until he tired, and then had his fill of the sweetest apples in the world before settling in the shade for a nap.

When he woke, he was...older. A teenager, perhaps? He had grown so old in the world outside this vision that he could no longer gauge the age of the young, not even when he was the one who was young. And as he filled a basket with apples so he could carry them away and sell them to buy things he believed would bring him fun, it was as if he was both doing and observing, and he saw more than he'd experienced when he'd lived through it the first time. Now he could see that the tree was not as happy as it had claimed to be at his taking. No, it was sad, for it had meant the apples to be his alone. He saw that now, and it made him sad to have made it sad. But it was too late to change that. It was too late to change anything.

And then more time passed in the living of a life he'd moved through blindly the first time around, and the tree offered him first its branches, and later its trunk as well, so he could build things and be happy. And he had been happy (or so he'd thought), and the tree had been happy (or so he'd thought as well), only...it was not. It had never been. It wept silently as he'd removed its limbs, not wanting him to see its pain, and he hadn't, so desperate was he for the things he thought he would die if he did not have.

This time, he winced with each cut. This time, every swing of the axe, every slice of the saw, cut into his own heart as well. But again, he could not change what this vision let him see. The doing of it was done.

And then, a final vision—that day he'd returned after a long absence to sit on the stump for the first and only time up until now, that moment of rest being the only gift the tree had left to give.

But he did not stay for long. He could not. Perhaps, somewhere deep inside and unacknowledged, he knew what he had done, what he did not want to face, so he left to abandon and forget.

And with that forgetting caused the thing that loved him most the greatest pain of all. Until dreams and memories and the call of an angry orchard drew him back.

"I didn't know," he whimpered as he returned to the reality of what was left of his life. "I didn't realize. I thought—"

"What was it that you thought?" said the tree, on behalf of all trees.

"I thought," he said, pressing his back against the stump which he had made. "I thought that's what love was."

"And yet, you are alone," said the trees.

"And yet, I am here," said the man.

"And you expect your presence, a presence which would not have occurred without our call, to be enough? You expect your return to make up for what you have done? How would you like it if we were to make of you what you have made of part of us?"

The man's mind filled with an image of grasping branches tearing his limbs from his body one by one, until what remained was as helpless as the stump on which he'd sat. He gasped, but did not object. Because he was weary, and now knew far too well the revealed truth which he had long fought to keep hidden.

"It would be no more and no less than what I deserve," he said.

"Then," said the orchard. "So shall it be."

Other branches stretched out to fill the sky, joining the one which had offered him the apple. They reached for his arms and legs, and as he raised his head to them, as he held his arms wide, he was ready.

But then the earth around the stump behind him rumbled, and what remained of the tree rose out of the ground, thrust upward by its roots. It walked clumsily on those wooden legs until it covered the man's body with its bulk, shielding him from harm. And in his mind, the man could make out the whisper he'd thought he'd heard before, but had been unable to decipher.

"Come, boy," it said as he curled beneath it.

The branches sought him out, but the stump scrambled this way and that, repeatedly blocking them.

"You would do this?" said the trees in conversation with themselves, pausing the attack. "After all that has been done to us?"

"I would," said the stump.

"But you have loved too much," said the trees. "You know that. And you have loved wrongly."

"If I have loved wrongly," said the stump. "At least I have loved. At least *we* have loved."

The branches trembled slightly, their leaves like sighs, and then, after a pause during which the man did not know what decision he truly wanted the trees to make, they retreated.

The stump crawled away and exposed him to a sun that was low in the sky, but no longer hidden, then settled into the earth once more.

And the man rose shakily to his feet, his joints cracking, his chest pained.

He moved closer to the stump, hoping to sit there one more time, but could not reach it, and fell to his knees a few footsteps short. He reached out to rest his hands where he had once so callously rested his ax.

"I am very tired," he said, gasping for breath. "And very sorry."

"Well," said the tree, once again as tall and proud as when the man, then a boy, had first run through the orchard and spotted it in the distance. "Lay yourself down and rest."

"I will," said the boy. He stretched out beneath the magical tangle of branches, placing his head softly on a moss-covered root.

As he closed his eyes, he dreamed he was king of the forest.

And then he dreamed no more.

And the trees were happy.

MY LIFE IS GOOD

I. POLITICAL SCIENCE

Last night I saw Randy Newman on the time machine, with some smart, rich New York Jews. I still had hours to go in my shift, and was already at that familiar point in my day where I was so sick of his smug face as to worry that I wouldn't be able to find the stomach to see it through.

Since the Visitors had come, this mind-numbing study of each vapid moment of Newman's life was a daily irritant for me, and up until then it had been another typically boring evening. The time machine had been bringing me only scenes that I had already witnessed before, recapping a life dedicated to mocking the privilege that had molded it, but the tableau that this time confronted me on the screen was new to me.

I waved a hand to dim the subbasement lights so I could make out his features more clearly on the tiny window to the past. Newman was smiling, but dressed as he was, I don't see how it was possible for him to maintain that grin. He wore a plaid suit that could only have been bought at a store that catered to unsuccessful used car salesmen and the most insecure of television evangelists. The tie that strangled his fleshy jowls was a chaotic patchwork quilt of overlapping Confederate flags. This garish ensemble was out of character for the man I'd unfortunately come to know, and on top of that seemed completely wrong for its intended audience.

Perhaps he thought he was being funny. I'd learned right at the beginning of this that being funny had always been one of Newman's greatest problems. Or rather, *thinking* himself funny had been, when in fact he'd been far from it. The man on whom the Visitors had me waste so much of my time spying was literally addicted to satire, a flavor I despised, and I had no further patience for his uncontrollable habit.

But this outfit, this setting, seemed more than the usual idiocy; things were too off-kilter, even for him. For one thing, during all the hours I'd put in studying the man, I'd never before caught him willingly in a suit and tie, garish or otherwise. One of the other things I'd learned quickly was that when he'd lived, Newman had not been a formal sort of man, and was unlikely to have kept that unflickering smile when trapped in such a getup.

The picture made little sense to me. At first I thought that the time machine had captured Newman at a costume party of some sort, but since the rest of the crowd that milled about him in the oak-paneled ballroom had forgotten their costumes, I cast that theory aside.

The women dressed as rich women did in that not-so-long-ago time by the calendar but which the arrival of the Visitors had now made inconceivably distant. They were statuesque in their jewels and furs, and the plastic surgery which gave them the appearance of youth and firmness had obviously been obtained from the best, for their scars were barely visible. The men did not bother to trouble themselves over their physical appearance. Their doughy forms were stuffed into dark wool suits, and they'd already had too many drinks. They laughed too loud. A few of them had checkbooks in their hands, and one was already pressing a folded donation into Newman's breast pocket with fat knuckles.

I'd long been looking back to keep my eye on Newman, but I'd never before seen anything like this. It worried me, but not so much that I was yet willing to alert the Visitors upstairs and have to look into those saucer eyes again. My worries were still more about the future than the past. My hopes were that it was the machinery, rather than the timestream, that was askew. I called Pall, the technician, and had him examine the equipment. He was happy for the chance to be in the room while the time machine was operating, because the Visitors did not give him much opportunity to do so. They trusted me, and me alone, to be a witness to Randy Newman's life.

Unfortunately, Pall found no hardware problems. The troubling picture was real. Something had happened that had never happened before. I let Pall continue to huddle with me before the small screen, Visitors be damned.

"What do you make of it?" I said. "I've never seen anything like this before. Look at his face. Look at those eyes. It's as if those aren't the same eyes. He's changed somehow."

We watched the normally-awkward Newman move through the crowd as if he had been born to it, shaking hands, clapping the men on their backs like brothers, kissing the women on their cheeks until they flushed, and collecting more checks in the process.

"Is there any way we can hear what they're saying?" I asked. "As soon as this scene started, the sound crashed."

"There's too much static," said Pall. "I don't know why. But why don't we try this? Let's detach the focus from Newman himself. Unlock the gaze and let the machine's point of view wander. Maybe that will show us something."

I manipulated the controls to stop targeting Newman, the maker of my weary days. The image slid from him sluggishly, and shifted to let us see glimpses of the rest of the room. At first there seemed no answer to the mystery there. A bustling wet bar. A coat rack. A buffet table overflowing with bowls of jumbo shrimp, decorated with an ice sculpture of Huey Long, a man whose profile I would not have recognized without having been forced to study him thanks to Newman.

But then we both saw a tall poster, ten feet high, filled by Newman's face. Pall didn't know enough of my mission to react, but the sight made me dizzy. I was stunned to see that above the smiling photo were the words:

EVERY MAN A KING

Below the photo, in large red, white and blue type, was written:

A NEWMAN FOR A NEW DAY
RANDY NEWMAN FOR PRESIDENT

"Something has gone terribly, terribly wrong," I said. My gut inflamed at what this meant my next step would have to be. Those eyes. I would have to suffer them again. "I'm going to have to tell them."

"You lucky bastard," Pall whispered.

His words pushed me back from the screen. I'd had enough of Newman for this day or any other day.

"You can have my luck," I said coldly, immediately regretting the tone I took with Pall. It wasn't his fault. The blame rested entirely with the Visitors. "You can't possibly know how sick and insignificant I feel when I have to face them."

"But you realize what this means, don't you? This must be what they were waiting for all along. This must be what this project is all about. You *are* a lucky bastard."

And then Pall, in a voice washed with awe, uttered the words I never thought I'd live to hear.

"They're going to have to send you back."

2. THE WORLD ISN'T FAIR

I once thought I had a life of my own, but now I only have his. Randy Newman's. A minor American singer-songwriter with a voice like a tortured cat and a heart like a pumice stone whose tunes were more smirk than sincerity.

Maybe I was only fooling myself about that life business, though. Before it all changed, I'd been lost in the world of theoretical physics, stepping beyond that arena only to do what I had to do to stay there, and as little as possible beyond that. So perhaps maybe I never really had any life at all. Maybe living Newman's life vicariously for twelve hours a day is better than having none at all.

But upon reflection, I don't really think so.

Until the Visitors came in their shower of blood and thunder and set me to the task, I'd spared no time for popular music. Other people may have needed it to give their lives meaning, but I had the more basic poetry of the quark. I was deaf to song, and not entirely by choice, either, but rather by constitution. As I studied particles dancing just beyond the edge of perception, the songs the singers sang were unintelligible to me.

Randy Newman, with whom I've been ordered to spend my days, created the most unintelligible of them all. With his uncle Alfred scoring Hollywood movies and winning Oscars in the process, Randy Newman was born to make music. Instead, he only made noise.

The fact that he'd been able to garner any fame at all is as senseless as the songs themselves. He had the superior attitude of the frat boy, without the substance to back it up. He sang that "Short People" had no reason to live, but he meant us to understand that he really didn't mean it. "I Love L.A.," he wrote, but from the words, who could really tell? He called southerners "Rednecks," but didn't seem to mean it in a pejorative way, and wanted license to call African-Americans "niggers" in the name of his supposed art. Why did he think people would want to struggle to unravel meaning and intent from a song, when all they were seeking was a distraction? Give me a song that is what it presents itself to be, with no ambiguity. There is enough mystery in the world without adding more.

No wonder that when the Visitors summoned me to set me to my task, the difficulty of my research was almost overwhelming, because in this century, Newman's musical corpus seemed as dead as his physical one.

Regardless of my difficulties or distaste, I could not protest, only submit. After the day that they announced themselves and gave that first terrifying proof of their power, no one dared question the Visitors.

Whatever they wanted, they got. With their inarguable supremacy, they could have plucked the treasures of Earth.

Luckily for the world, they didn't want much.

Unfortunately for me, one of the few things they did want...was me.

I didn't know why. I still don't. I was as far from suitable for the assignment as it is possible for one human to get. When I was taken from the university and told by my government that henceforth I would be using a time machine given us by their alien technology to peer into the past, I was ecstatic. I thought that everything my life had been headed towards was about to be fulfilled. I'd finally arrived at the fruition of my impossible dreams. But it turned out that none of my physics training was to mean anything. They could have grabbed any semi-comatose couch potato, thumbs thickened from wrestling with the remote control, for all the manipulation I ever had to do of the device they gave us. I was to watch the pictures of Randy Newman as they paraded by, and report on any anomalies.

The promise I'd thought the universe had kept had instead been broken. I lived my days in pain, as if in the grip of a disease.

I could never tell them that. I'd decided I'd rather live. They wanted me, and so they had to have me. But though I'd suffered in silence, that suffering still raced through my mind as I waited to tell them the news of the aberration. I tried to avoid meeting with them, did my best to share the information with them over a holo, but they forced me to stop before I could tell them what I had found.

They wanted to see me in person.

I did not like the way I could look into those large, liquid eyes and see myself looking back. Their gaze made me feel as if they were able to read my mind. I am not a paranoid man, and yet, they were able to make me feel like one, and I did not want to have to stand there and let them see again how stupid I felt wasting my life this way for them. I could barely hide my discomfort from Pall and the others I was assigned to work with, so how could I hope to hide it from them?

But I had no other choice.

As I sped inside the high-speed elevator from the subbasement that housed the project to where the Visitors dwelled on the skyscraper's top floor, I wondered if Pall could possibly have been right. Was this what we all had been waiting for? Would it really cause me to be sent back in time?

As the doors began to open and reveal a place I dreaded, all these thoughts emptied from my mind. What was left was fear. That fear grew when I saw their tall, attenuated forms and realized that though I'd never before seen more than one of them at a time in person, there stood two. So something out of the ordinary had indeed occurred, and they already knew it. They stood at opposite ends of the large, windowless room. The elevator that left me dead center of the room recessed into the floor, placing me pinned between them in the dimness.

I could not tell the two Visitors apart. They had no distinguishing features to individualize them. No difference in eye color, nor scars, nor variation in tone of voice. Seeing them this way made me wonder about my past visits to the top floor, whether either of these had been the one I had seen my few luckless times before, and in fact, whether their sameness now meant I had never seen any Visitor more than once, but had only thought so.

I stayed silent until they spoke, not due to any conscious decision to show respect, but rather because, this time as always, their presence left me speechless.

"You have news to report," said one, sliding closer.

"I do not understand why, but the subject is not who he once was." So great was my anger at Randy Newman for wasting my life this way that I did not like to say his name aloud, particularly in front of the Visitors, who would surely hear my contempt. I spoke to them formally because that was the only way I was able to bring myself to speak at all. "Something has changed about the past. I have looked at this moment before, and each time all was always as it always was, but now he is no longer a man who writes music. The timestream has altered. He appears to have entered politics."

"That is…not good," said the other, taking its own fluid steps closer to me.

"He must be…protected," said the first.

"But he's in the past," I said. "How could he be in need of protection? What's happened has happened."

Said one, its voice becoming louder as it approached, "What's happened has not happened yet."

Said the other, "What's happened never really happened."

"You're speaking in riddles. What does that mean? Is the past truly fluid? Has the past put the present in danger? Will this alteration catch up with us here? Tell me, please. Is something terrible going to happen to our timeline if he is allowed to become president? Am I going to the past to protect our future?"

I was rambling on, verging on hysteria as the distance between us shrank. I was going to say more, but then they were suddenly upon me, and words were no longer a part of my palette.

"You must fix this," said one.

"Go now," said the other. "Put it back as it was."

One of the Visitors reached out a hand towards me. I shrieked as the elongated fingers grew near. I started babbling, speaking as I'd never dared to speak before, questioning them out of a greater terror than I'd ever known.

"Why?" I shouted. "Why do you care? Why have I been doing this? Why does it matter to you?"

My questions would have horrified Pall. In challenging the Visitors, I was risking everything, including my own life. But with a Visitor about to lay hands upon me, all propriety had fled.

"Just go," said the other, answering my frustrated questions by beginning to reach for me as well.

When their flesh touched mine, an explosive energy coursed through me, blinding me, and they, the skyscraper, and all of the world I knew, were gone. For I had come unstuck in time.

3. MAMA TOLD ME NOT TO COME

I popped back into existence on the twenty-seventh-floor observation deck of the Louisiana State Capitol, a setting which on its own merits told me that this was an earlier century than my own. I felt a sense of freedom to be back in a time before the Visitors had razed such buildings to the ground to get our attention, but it was only a momentary emotion. I knew I was not truly out of their reach, and could not pause to enjoy this place. I had to get on with it.

I blinked into the morning sun and admired the Mississippi as it rolled toward the Gulf of Mexico. Louisiana's state capitol building, when it still stood, had been the tallest of such buildings, which was a good thing, for it meant that the structure contained enough square footage for the Visitors to have found a spot in which to have me appear that would not attract attention.

I'd had no time to prepare for this trip. Luckily, the Visitors had prepared for me. My tunic was gone, replaced by a finely woven suit that could easily allow me to pass as a member of this century's elite. As I stood there, the wind had a different feel to it that morning, and when I touched a hand to my head to figure out why, I discovered that my shaggy hair had also been altered. It was now closely cropped in a style I loathed. I could only hope that when at the end of all this nonsense I was allowed to return to my own time, my hair would return as well.

My physical shell wasn't the only thing that had been made right for this time. How else would I know without a doubt the spot on which I stood? How else would I know instinctively that I was hundreds of feet above Baton Rouge, and that if I walked mere yards to the south, I could look down on the grave of Huey P. Long, the former governor of Louisiana, felled by an assassin's bullet to then be musically commemorated by Randy Newman? As I walked along the deck so I could study where the martyr was buried, I felt as if I belonged here, and I realized that the Visitors had filled me with enough of the essence of the time and place to pass as one of them.

And then I realized something else. I was not alone.

I did not at first recognize the man who was leaning against the rails. My approach took me up to him as he stood with his back turned, and that was a side of him that the time machine, focused on telling me his story as it was, had never let me witness. As I drew to the right side of him, could see him there with his eyes closed, I was momentarily stunned. Randy Newman, whom I had known up until then only as an historical figure on the flat screen of a time machine, was before me as a living, breathing man. And I once more cursed the Visitors and mourned the loss of those I would have chosen to see on my first excursion back in time—Galileo, swearing that the Earth still moved; a young Einstein, still working at the Swiss patent office; my parents, before they'd met, before the thought of me had even entered their lives; my own self, paradoxes be damned.

Newman's head was bowed, and beneath the halo of his graying curls, he seemed lost in prayer. His forehead rested against the fleshy fingertips of his clasped hands. What was he praying for? To be the next president?

Even though almost everything I had seen of him during my long hours with the timescreen had offended me, this offended me more. And not just because I was the first human to travel through time, and I was trapped having to pay attention to *this*. But because I knew who he was supposed to be, and this was not it. I preferred to think of who we are as immutable. He was supposed to be mocking governors, not being one, and certainly not one on the road to the White House. From all I'd learned of him, from the clowning deviousness of his songs, I knew he was a buffoon, not a statesman. Maybe that would be good enough for Louisiana, but not for the rest of the country. That must be why the Visitors wanted him stopped, why this fracture in the timeline had to be extinguished. If Newman could not be turned from this path, something bad would come of this, or why else would the Visitors have expended so much effort? Maybe, if allowed to proceed unchanged, this timeline could ripple forward to catch up with our own, and end the present as we know it.

Randy Newman had to be stopped.

The Visitors had given me information, but not a plan on how to use it. Standing there, staring at him, I was frozen. How do I begin to change the universe? Better that they'd sent someone else. Someone who was a strategist, or a private detective. Someone who did not hate Randy Newman so much. Someone who could see what had to be done.

Yet I had to get through this somehow. Without that, I knew that there was no getting back to my own time.

Newman opened his eyes, but kept his head bowed against the early morning sun, and took a moment to survey his city. He lived. He breathed. I was still startled to behold him. I could not take my gaze off of him until he started to turn his head in my direction, and I lowered my own before he spotted my hungry attention. I shifted my look to Huey Long's grave, and quietly said a little prayer, but it was not the one Newman thought.

"I'm usually the only one who feels a need to take in the view this early in the morning," he said. His voice seemed friendly, in tones that were now familiar echoes to me, but there was a wariness to it as well.

"You're not the only one who feels the need to commune with the governor, Governor," I said.

I was startled to discover that the Visitors had not only altered my brain and my body, but also my voice. When I spoke, it was with a lazy Southern drawl. I bade him a good morning, just to hear myself speak, and then laughed softly at the sound of it. He didn't seem to take it amiss.

He nodded towards the sacred spot hundreds of feet below.

"They would like to laugh at him, you know," he said. "Laugh at us. Let them, I say. So he was a cracker. Well, I'm a cracker, too. From the sounds of it, so are you. But he bound the people together like no one else before or since."

He laughed.

"Look at me. I'm getting goddamned maudlin on you. But that isn't just a metaphor. Why, do you know that you can't get from one end of the state to the other without passing over at least a half a dozen of the hundred and eleven bridges he built us. And the roads! The son-of-a-bitch added over twenty-three hundred miles of them. In

1931 alone, the state of Louisiana employed ten percent of the workers involved in building roads nationwide. Man, what I would give for the power to do that. He was a unifier, in more ways than one."

"You'll get no argument here, Governor."

"I like the man. Without him, Louisiana wouldn't be what it is today."

"With your love of Louisiana, I don't see why you'd want to leave it. I don't see how a man of your temperament could stand the air of Washington."

"I couldn't leave Louisiana behind, no matter where I end up. It's in me. But, you see, there's so much more that I can do, not just for the people of my state, but for my country as a whole. The world isn't fair. I'm just doing my best to make it so. And that's a job I just I can't do from Louisiana."

I was suddenly startled to realize that I liked him better this way. It was as if that part of him that was inside-out had been burned away, leaving what was pure and true and honest. And at least this way he wasn't singing and writing any more of those sarcastic songs.

I was tempted to leave him this way. He could surely do no more harm to the world than his other self had with his endless cynicism. But I knew that the aliens wouldn't see it my way.

"But why? Why do it? Why care enough to make that sacrifice?"

He leaned in close to me, and whispered.

"Now, you wouldn't happen to be a reporter, would you?"

"I'm just a fellow southerner, like yourself."

"Then come with me."

I followed him inside, where two bodyguards were surprised to see me with the governor. The four of us took the elevator down to the first-floor executive corridor between the House and Senate chambers.

"This is where they got him," he said. His voice quivered as he pointed at the spot. "If they hadn't gunned him down, he'd have been president for sure. So since he can't make it, I will have to be president in his place."

Newman was silent for a moment as he stared at the site of Huey Long's assassination, and then his face hardened.

"When I was a small boy, my mother often took me to get ice cream. Ice cream can be a very powerful motivator for a small boy. If only it wasn't."

He scratched his full stomach and laughed ruefully.

"One day, we went to one of those one-man ice cream wagons," he said. He spoke as if he was not there, as if he was not chatting up a potential contributor. He was far away, traveling in the only time machine most of us ever know. "There were signs on the side. One side of the cart was meant for Whites, and the other side was for Colored. You don't look quite old enough to have ever seen such signs yourself. Two black children were already being helped there when I arrived. The man turned from them the instant I appeared, and ignored them both. I didn't think it fair, but I did let it happen. Because I wanted the ice cream, you see. We all want the ice cream. Only—we can't always be allowed to have it. Or else, life isn't fair."

"But why did it have to be politics? Why not choose music? After all, both of your uncles..."

"When has a song ever changed the world?" He hesitated then, and looked at me oddly. He took a step back, and glanced at his beefy guards. "You seem to know an awful lot about me and my family."

"No, I assure you, I don't." I'd sent the wrong message, but I had no idea how or why. "No more than any other proud Louisianan, governor."

Newman stared down with wide eyes at the spot on which he stood, where an earlier governor had fallen, and blanched.

"Oh, no," I said, realizing where his thoughts were heading. "I would never do such a thing. Please don't think that."

But he did. And as he started to shout for help, I turned and ran.

I heard shouts, followed by a gunshot. Then another. I have no idea whether it was the bodyguards who fired, or some other good Samaritan. This was Louisiana; undoubtedly half of the building was armed.

I felt no pain, but I must have been hit, for the world faded away and I thought, *how meaningless, to die, here, for this.*

4. GOOD OLD BOYS

I returned to myself not yet dead on a blazing summer day, the only relief from the heat being the cool ice cream melting down a stick onto my fingers. I winced under the assault of the sun directly overhead, my eyes and mind still back in the damp cavern of the Louisiana State Capitol. I had no memory of purchasing an ice cream bar, and no hunger that would have caused me to do so. I had only an anxiety that caused my temples to pulse with the tension of it. I tilted my hand so the drips would hit the dusty pavement instead of running down my shirt cuff.

I was in yet another past, one even more distant from my own time. Randy Newman's past.

I looked around for the ice cream cart that I knew had to still be near. That was why the Visitors had not yet brought me back. My first excursion had been for information only. There was still work to be done. The wagon was half a block away, surrounded by children. From this distance, I could pretend that it did not bear the signs marked "White" and "Colored." Not only had he told me about it in his time, mere minutes ago that were impossibly still decades in the future, but I had been forced to listen to him sing about it in my time. Over many months, the Visitors had insisted that I listen to that part of his oeuvre and all else. I moved closer to see what was to come.

An elderly woman walked by, dragging behind her a small cross-eyed boy. She sneered in disdain at my sticky hand. The boy looked at me with one eye and away with the other, and from his split stare I realized it was Newman. The painful operations to fix those eyes would not come until later.

As the woman tugged him along, it became clear to me that he hadn't been looking at me at all, but rather at the melting confection in my hand. He wanted it very badly. A chill went through me at that desire, for I knew then with a certainty that not only was this boy a young Randy Newman, but that this was the pivotal day as well.

Still holding her hand, he skipped slightly ahead of the woman so that he was pulling her along instead of the reverse. He pointed at the ice cream wagon, and the pleading began. Even with the weight of this event heavy on my heart, I could not help but smile. The young were always able, whatever their time. It didn't take too much pouting to get her to acquiesce, and she reached into her purse to find a coin. She planted herself where she stood and watched as he skipped down the street to the cart. I dropped my ice cream bar to the pavement, and muttered to make the action seem accidental. I needed a reason to pull near, and so I grimaced and looked at the cart as if deciding whether to buy a replacement. The Visitors had made an actor out of me.

I moved closer to young Newman, his nose as yet unbroken by all the things that would come later, and watched as he stepped up behind two small black girls, only to be shooed by the jeering vendor around to the other side of the cart. I stepped up behind him and watched as one of his eyes read the sign that said "Whites" and the other seemed to study the two girls who had just been abandoned by the server.

"They were here first," said Newman in a high-pitched voice.

The server coughed.

"Don't tell me how to run my business, son," he said. "What'll it be?"

Newman turned and looked at me. Well, *half*-looked at me. I was an adult, and he hoped that I would solve this for him. But I could do nothing. Yet.

"Mister, you saw it," he squeaked, his voice a whistle. "They were here first."

I grunted. What was I to tell him there, with others still listening? That life wasn't fair? It wasn't time for that. He would learn that soon enough himself.

"Well?" asked the ice cream man, seeming to take joy in Newman's discomfort.

The boy shifted his stance, turning his back on the girls, as if that was the only way he could find within himself the ability to place an order. He looked at the coin that had been dropped in his hand.

"Do you want an ice cream or not?" said the man.

"I do, I do, only—"

"Only what?"

Newman bit his lip and, unable to speak his order aloud, pointed to a picture printed on the side of the cart. The man thrust it in his hand through mist from the dry ice and then looked at me, the two girls still ignored. I quickly got a bar to replace the one I had dropped.

Newman had not yet gotten too far, his relative still a short distance away. I quickened my steps to catch up with him, trying at the same time to look casual about it for anyone who might be watching, as if I'd just happened to approach him on the way to somewhere else.

"E pluribus unum," I said to him.

"What was that, mister?" he said, blinking, unsure I was talking to him.

"E pluribus unum. It's a phrase the founding fathers decided to put on our money. It was stamped on the coin you just gave the man. It means, 'Out of many, one.' One people, all the same and equal. Because that's what the founders envisioned this country to be."

Newman stuck out his lower lip, his ice cream momentarily forgotten.

"Someone should make it be that way, then. Someone should change things so that they're the way they're suppose to be. If I were president—"

"Oh, no," I said. "Not president. If I were the sort of lad who wanted to make a difference in the world, a president would be the last thing I'd be. Presidents don't really change things."

"Well, who does then?"

"No, definitely not," I said. "Not politics. Politics is definitely not the way to go."

"Well, what then?" he demanded petulantly, snapping at his ice cream bar in frustration. "What am I supposed to do?"

He looked back at the wagon where the seller, without a smile, was still attending to the first of the little black girls.

"You know who really changes the world?" I said. "Writers. Particularly writers of—"

"Randy! Come over here this instant!"

A stern voice cut me off, and I looked up to see the woman striding towards me, holding her purse as if ready to use it like a weapon.

"Get away from my boy this instant! You, sir, are being far too familiar!"

I stumbled away, having run out of time.

"Remember, Randy," I cried out. "Remember what I told you. You must remember that."

I walked swiftly away, the woman continuing to stride past the boy so she could further hector me. I raced around a corner to escape her and found the hot street suddenly gone, for I discovered myself cloaked in the cool dark of a New York City hotel ballroom.

5. MAYBE I'M DOING IT WRONG

I realized that I was back in the same room that with its fractured glimpse of Randy Newman had begun my trip through time. And not only was it the same room—I sensed that it was also the same crystal of time that had held that catalytic fundraiser. The South was behind me now, if the South could ever truly be said to be behind me as long as I was forced to focus on Randy Newman. Perhaps Pall was up ahead in the future, watching me now, studying the moment to see how things were going as I had once watched, peering into the past to see if the timeline had changed. There was no way for me to tell; I could not return his gaze. But at the same time I felt reassured by seeing around me in person the same dark wood paneling that I had once watched—or rather, would watch in the future—on the compact screen of the time machine.

As my eyes adjusted to the dim room, I was relieved to see that the walls had no posters blaring of a presidential run. People were squeezed into ragged rows of chairs that faced an empty podium. I saw neither furs nor pinstripes around me, nothing that smacked of the elite fundraising crowd that had been there earlier. (Or was that later?) The crowd contained T-shirts and long hair, scraggly beards and a general sense of poor hygiene. The rich had been replaced, and now I was surrounded by an army of songwriters.

Newman came into the room then, and he, thank God, looked the way I remembered him. A blinding Hawaiian shirt draped his gut, and he had the sardonic twinkle in his eyes that I had come to expect. I did not realize that I'd been holding my breath until I sighed. I'd done it. This is how that earlier scene had obviously meant to be. A crowd of songwriters gathered to hear from the songwriters' songwriter. (He obviously wasn't, and never would be, a lay audience's songwriter.) My words had nudged him in the right direction. It was over.

He stepped behind the podium to applause. He smiled as a few attendees started to whistle and hoot, waved and smiled at someone he spotted in the front row, and began before the sound that had greeted him had stopped.

"I love you sons of bitches," he said, and the room filled with laughter. It felt good. Things were right again. *I sure don't love you, you son of a bitch*, I thought.

I leaned back against the wall behind me, and waited to be returned to my own time. My own life. I'd soon be back to it. It was a miserable life, but it was my own. Maybe now that the puzzle of Newman's life had been put back the way it should be, now that my mission was over and I had accomplished what the Visitors had intended, they would leave me alone now. I would be freed from the bondage of studying a man I did not like on the screen of a time machine I envied. I don't often pray, but I prayed then to be taken from this place, as I was taken from the Louisiana State Capitol, as I was plucked from the hot summer streets of an even more distant past.

Instead, when I opened my eyes I was still trapped listening to the buffoon talk. What more did the Visitors want of me? Why did they want me to undergo more of this suffering?

"You're the only ones to pay attention to what really matters in this world," continued Newman. "Others may waste their days delineating the mundane, wasted lives of college professors, but only you know that there are galaxies being born right next door, and that somewhere there are civilizations being snuffed out as galaxies die. I am home here, with the only people who understand me. The hell with the talented myopics who can only write stories of things that are thrust under their noses, when the issues that matter can best be described with metaphors that don't yet exist, that we can only imagine—aliens and planet-hopping rocket ships and time machines. You know who the real audience is for my novels? You are. I'm so proud to be one of you."

He paused, choked with emotion. It appeared that there was more he wanted to say, but could not. He returned his index cards to his pocket, and could only repeat:

"I love you sons of bitches."

I was dazed by his confusing words. What did his ramblings mean? Why was a tunesmith talking to his peers about novels and time machines? Randy Newman had never written a novel in his life. As far as I was concerned, he had barely written songs.

I was the only one who seemed bothered by any of this; the audience ate up every word. Looking at them more closely, I could see that some of their T-shirts bore pictures of scientific formulae, others had spacecraft, and the faces of aliens looked out at me with visages much like the Visitors themselves. I raced to the closest audience member and grabbed a booklet from his hand. Newman's face was on the cover of the pamphlet, but by the words that accompanied the caricature, I could tell that this wasn't the gathering of songwriters I'd originally thought it to be. Instead, this was a science fiction convention! That was the reason I was still trapped here, pinned to the past by my pain.

I'd only been half right. My message had gotten through to him as a child, but I had been interrupted before I'd been able to deliver the whole of it. I screamed my frustration to the world, but by the time the audience turned from Newman to me to see what had caused the commotion, I was no longer there to be seen.

6. LAST NIGHT I HAD A DREAM

A square of moonlight hit the boy's face as he drooled against the pillow, dreaming of...of what? That was what this was all about, wasn't it? I sat uncomfortably on the other side of young Randy Newman's dim bedroom, contorted in a chair meant for a child. As I looked at him, with his smooth face and his mussed hair, the boy did not look like someone destined to cause me pain, seemed indistinguishable from any other sleeping child, but there was potential in him I had to derail. A potential for what, I did not know. But he had become fractured from what the universe had originally planned for him, and it was up to me to set his life back within the groove before disaster struck.

Gazing at him, I could not tell, now that I was back once more in the deeper past, whether this moment was a time before or after the incident at the ice cream wagon, or even, perhaps, some other timeline entirely.

It struck me that this was one of the few times I'd ever seen him without his glasses. He appeared peaceful and serene.

I don't think I've ever felt such hate.

If he were to die right then, I thought, I would be far better off, and so would the world. He would never then grow into the man who would make music that was more curse than song, and would never attract the attention of the Visitors. I would never be sitting there where the Visitors had put me, a place where I had no right to be, hoping to be freed from this. Perhaps that was the way to solve this, by ending the matter entirely rather than trying to reinvent him. It seemed the far easier way to stop whatever disaster they meant to prevent.

Those thoughts fled when I heard the murmur of a voice, and I tensed, fearful that the approaching sound was his mother creeping up the stairs. But then I realized that what I was actually hearing was a low humming, as of someone preparing to sing. It scared me, until I realized that the vibrations were coming from my own throat. Then it no longer scared me.

It petrified me.

I have never been a person with an inclination to song, another reason why the whole assignment has been so painful for me. During my commutes, I always chose talk radio of any kind over music of any flavor. Yes, I understood music scientifically, the relationship of one note to the next, the effect they are supposed to have on the listener, how music can make emotions rise and fall, but I find no pleasure there, nor a true empathy for the pleasure it causes in others. If you were to tell me that music was a hoax, I would think, "Ah, yes, finally they tell me the truth," and believe you.

Yet here I was, readying myself in a dark room to sing a small boy some sort of reverse lullaby. Instead of putting him to sleep, I was to wake him to a new potential.

Without even knowing what was to come next, I found myself singing the opening verses of "This Land is Your Land." Surprisingly, I didn't sound half bad. In addition to everything else the Visitors had given me for this journey, a decent voice seemed to have gone with the package.

Little Randy Newman awoke halfway through, and I continued on to the final verse that is rarely sung, the one that rails against the private ownership of land. He rubbed his eyes as he looked at me, but did not say a word. So I told him about Woody Guthrie, and the various causes he championed, and how he'd had inscribed along the edges of his banjo the phrase, "This Machine Kills Fascists."

I sang songs to him from times that had come before him, but also times that had not yet occurred, though it was doubtful he'd see the difference. I sang him Joe Hill's "Casey Jones—The Union Scab," followed with "I Dreamed I Saw Joe Hill," and sketched in the effect they both had on the beginnings of the American labor movement. His eyes grew wide as I told him the story of student protesters shot by the National Guard, and sang Neil Young's "Ohio." I told him of

103

the civil rights movement and how "We Shall Overcome" helped power it. I told him about the antiwar efforts of John Lennon and sang "Give Peace a Chance." I sang "The Times They Are a-Changin'," but I don't know that he got the full effect, because the voice the Visitors had given me was better than Bob Dylan's. I did my best to let him see how people paid more attention to songwriters than they did to politicians or novelists. That much I could give him. The cynicism that would put him back the way he'd been still had to come from within.

When he finally spoke, it was to say, "I'm still asleep now, you know, mister." His voice was insistent as he pushed out his bottom lip. "I think it's time I had a different dream."

He closed his eyes. Searching for another song, I found nothing. I had run through them all. I waited there until he opened his eyes again and glared at me.

"Go away," he said.

I would have liked nothing better. But the choice was not my own. I would not know I was ready to leave until I was gone.

"Just remember what I told you tonight, Randy," I said. "Remember what the martyred Joe Hill said. He wrote that a songwriter is the only kind of writer that has meaning in this world. He wrote, 'A pamphlet, no matter how good, is never read more than once. But a song is learned by heart and repeated over and—'"

The door opened suddenly, cutting me off with a shaft of blinding light. His mother stepped into the room and moved towards her son, his arms flung over his face.

"What is it, dear?" she said. "I thought I heard you cry out."

I tried to slip out behind her into the hallway, but the floor creaked beneath my heels, and she turned to see me.

"You!" she shouted. "You're that man who was bothering us yesterday!"

It was only then that I realized I was in the same time stream I had visited earlier.

"I can explain," I said weakly as I backed away, then said nothing more. The Visitors had filled me with knowledge, but had not given me the words to deal with this.

She raced from the room, but did not look afraid.

"Now you'd really better go," said Newman. That smug look on his face reminded me once again why I hated him so.

"Just remember," I said. "Please."

There was no way to explain to him that that was the only way I'd ever get home.

I slipped out a window and dropped to the yard below. As I limped along the quiet street, a shotgun exploded behind me. After a life without violence, gunshots were chasing me for the second time that day. Between the blasts I heard a high-pitched voice shout, "Mother, no!" and then all went black.

One way or another, I prayed for it to end. I no longer cared how.

7. THE WORLD ISN'T FAIR

So silent was my pop back into existence in my own time beside Pall that at first he did not even realize I had returned. I was at his elbow as he stared at the time machine, and on the screen I caught a glimpse of myself vanishing from the dark street just as bullets breezed through the spot I had just been inhabiting. The picture then vanished to be replaced by static. Pall cursed at the blizzard and backed from the screen, and only noticed I was there as he bumped into me. When he turned, his cursing increased. He lifted me up in a bear hug as I complained.

"You did it!" he said. "You traveled through time."

"Yes," I said, reaching out to touch my world of now, the chairs, the walls, the blank time machine before us, almost as if I thought they would all be quickly taken away from me again. "I traveled through time."

"I witnessed it," he said quietly. "All of it. They let me see you. What was it like?"

"I don't know," I said quietly.

Pall shook his head.

"I can't accept that. You were the first human to go backwards in time. I know you. I know what that must mean to you. You must feel *something*."

I looked inside myself, and all I saw were things I needed to forget. What I felt could not be expressed in words without driving me insane. Even thinking them as abstract emotions was difficult enough, but to make them concrete...

All my life I had wondered if such a thing as what I had just accomplished was possible. If it were possible, I would surely be the man to figure that out. There were so many things I wanted to see and do on such a voyage into history, so many precious moments I wanted to collect.

To have it handed to me in this way, like spare change tossed to a beggar, that made it worthless. And to be led around the past on a leash for as insignificant a reason as Randy Newman, that made the whole thing even more insulting still. Some pain was not meant to be endured.

So all I could say was, "I feel...nothing."

And then hope to forget.

The interference on the screen faded, and there was Newman again, as he had been all those months before, as he had come to haunt my dreams. There he was as a young boy watching his uncle Alfred conducting an orchestra on a sound stage as snippets of film flickered above them. There he was meeting his first wife, and then later writing a song about their marriage dying, and yet later again writing another about how stupid he felt to be still loving her after all. There he was, losing an Academy Award, which pleased me. All the pieces came together into the cynical mosaic of his life as it always had.

I had succeeded. I had saved the world from whatever great unknown it was the Visitors had foreseen. Maybe they would now let it end.

"So what was that all about, anyway?" asked Pall. "Did you save the world? What was he going to do as president? Did you avert a nuclear war?"

I sat in the chair that had owned me for too long.

"I don't think they'll ever tell us."

I hoped that it was over. Now that all was well within the time stream, perhaps I would not ever have to watch Randy Newman again. I reached behind the machine, unplugged it from the wall, and sighed.

It was a good sigh.

That was when the voice in my head said, "Turn it back on."

8. THAT'S WHY I LOVE MANKIND

My life is good.

At least I, unlike many others since the Visitors have come, have a life. I must be thankful for that.

I have grown used to spending my days as I do. The pain of it is duller than when I started my vigil. It has become bearable. I accept that though I have watched him be born, watched him live, and watched him die, I will be forever deaf to all he does. Even as I wince at it, I accept that I must be his eternal witness.

I have grown to know the rhythms of Randy Newman's life as well as I know the pulse of my own blood, the music of my own lungs. I watch constantly, and when an aspect of his life goes awry, when he jumps the track of his enforced destiny and creates something other than those infantile songs of his, I can sense the disturbance immediately. And almost before I can alert the Visitors to what needs to be done, I am gone, sent back by them again to set things right.

I have seen him become a short order cook, a comic book artist, a television weatherman, a vagrant, a school teacher, a radio deejay and more, and each time I have put him gently—and sometimes not so gently—back in his place.

I have been doing it for years now, and I still do not know why. I have asked the Visitors and have been given only silence. So I no longer ask. I try to find comfort in Pall's belief that I have saved the world many times over, but I gain no solace from that. I cannot be sure of that. I can be sure of only one thing.

I once had a dream, but now only have dreams of him.

I was going to be the one who would figure out how to unravel time, only I have instead found myself knotted in it. I was a man who liked his music straight and honest, if forced to have a choice in music at all. I was a man with little use for irony, and yet Randy Newman serves me a portion every day, mocking slavery, making fun of the homeless, and meaning neither. Or so he says.

How ironic that the last person on Earth who should be doing this job is the very one forced to do it.

How...ironic.

As that thought began to gel, another thought intruded on my own: "Come to us," it said.

I slumped in my soul and went to join the Visitors. It never got any easier. I was terrified to see, when the doors opened around me and the elevator slipped back into the floor, that this time there were a dozen of them. Never before had I seen more than two at a time, such as when I was launched on my first mission, and the ones that followed. As far as I knew, no human had ever seen more than two at once. I tried again, petrified, to distinguish them one from the other, looking for scratches, discolorations, differences in appearance of any body part. I hoped that their increased number could help me find distinctions. But they could have been stamped out by a machine, so identical was their flesh. It was hopeless.

"Do you know why we have called you?" one said.

I could not speak, could not even shake my head.

"We thought perhaps you already understood," said a second.

"It is time," said a third. Or maybe it was the voice of the first speaker again. I could not be sure. Their intonations were so similar that they could have been speaking with one voice.

"It is time," one of them said again.

"Time?" I asked, my voice a dull croak. But even before I finished spitting out that single short syllable, I already knew what they meant. They intended, at last, to explain it all.

"Then tell me," I whispered. "Why, then?"

After years of sparse and cryptic sentences, the words came this time in a torrent, first from one, then another. So many words after so long a time. I try to avoid attributing emotions to aliens, but now it was as if they were as excited that this time had come as I was. I looked quickly from one to the next, trying to keep track of who was speaking, but soon their voices melded together so that I did not know which of them had spoken. The unleashed sentences came barreling out of them so rapidly that what I heard carried the qualities of an uninterrupted soliloquy.

"We thought you were smarter than this, little one," they said. "Don't you perceive it? Don't you yet see the truth? You know, you were on the verge of figuring it all out when we called for you. You were so close to the answer, so close that you almost thought it yourself. You should not have to ask us why. You will undoubtedly figure it all out on your own soon."

I feared for a moment that they were dismissing me. If they had brought me this close to the brink only to leave me dangling, if they intended to send me back to the time machine with no answer, I did not think I could survive it. If this moment was just meant to be a malicious tease, I doubted that I could live much beyond the day. I needed to know.

"Do not worry. We will be the ones to tell you so that we can see your face as it happens. Think back. What was it that you were thinking when we summoned you? Do you not recall it? You were thinking that you were the last person on Earth who should be doing this job. Well, you are right. You meant it as a metaphor, but it is true...literally."

I grew dizzy, and flung out an arm, but there was nowhere to support myself in the bare room.

"And we would know. You see, we have come to love irony. Irony, we have discovered, is the most delicious of all emotions, a thing we have learned well in our travels throughout the universe. It is our hunt for the highest degree of irony that put you in charge of this project these many years, and it is irony that has left you there."

"You're saying I am here precisely because I shouldn't be?" The anger in my voice for the first time overcame my fear. "That I am the most unfit candidate for the job, and you know it? So you're torturing me deliberately? You mean you crossed a galaxy for that? What kind of creatures are you? You came up with a stupid project designed to be the opposite of who I am just to watch me wriggle?"

"You must not call Randy Newman stupid!"

The sound in my head was deafening, and I fell to my knees. Their words continued to bombard me, each one opening a new wound.

"Do not pride yourself on thinking that it was you who came first. This wasn't designed around you, it was Newman, first, last, and always, and it is you who were chosen around him. It is this project that takes precedence. Why is it that you think we came here? Do you think that Earth's sunsets are more beautiful than the ones on other planets, or that your air smells sweeter, or that your goods are worth our export? Actually, we can see that you *do* think that. But that is not so. We come here for one reason, and that reason is Randy Newman. Without him, do you think that we would bother to keep Earth alive? No, without him, Earth would be a ball of ash. We have seen the universe entire, and we know that Earth produces the most flavorful taste of all, for he is the king of irony. You are engaged in the only thing worth doing on this planet, which is keeping his life on track, so that he can continue to produce that delicacy."

"But I thought you were trying to prevent him from going astray because of something horrible he might do, not to protect the things that he did do."

"You hoped that you were saving your planet from a nuclear holocaust? We would not care if your entire race save one went up in flames. No, we needed you to keep the shifting timeline on track, to make sure that nothing occurred that would keep Randy Newman from blossoming in all the fullness of his spirit. He sees life as it truly is. He is the only one of your entire species. As for you, there is only one reason why you and your exacerbated frustrations are involved, a reason you were close to realizing on your own. You were chosen because of your potential, because now the story of your life is as full of irony as any of Randy Newman's songs. It's all very simple, you see."

I could not speak for the horror washing over me. I covered my ears so I would not hear the judgment that they were about to deliver, so I could avoid the summation of my life, but their words seeped through my fingers anyway, and drove straight to the core of my brain.

"We want you to hurt like we do."

PITY THIS BUSY MONSTER NOT

*J*ulian found himself sitting at a narrow counter which ran along the coffee shop's front window, a coffee shop which he knew should have been familiar to him, even though it was not. His head was down as he frowned while working with too great an effort on what should have been an easy crossword puzzle. He was frowning twice over, in fact, for he wasn't just frowning because he found the clues which ran down the page to be tough ones. He was also frowning about even frowning over that crossword puzzle. For as far as he knew, he didn't *like* crossword puzzles, at least, not that he remembered, which explained, he guessed, why he also couldn't recall ever attempting to do one.

Actually, he wasn't quite sure what he liked or didn't like, was only sure that he shouldn't examine too closely the nature of his uncertainty just then. So he returned to his struggling, a mental exercise accompanied by gently tapping the cap of his pen against his lip, a habit he found comfortable, and recognized as his own, even though he had no idea why, when, or where the gesture had become his in the first place.

He searched his memory, which he knew in his heart (he had a heart, didn't he?; yes, he felt it there, beating) to be wide and deep (though he clearly had no true proof of that in this instant) to remember the name of a certain actress from a certain movie made during a certain year. This attempted dive into the past made his head hurt, because somehow he knew, somehow he was aware, that he should have remembered information like that easily. He always had before, hadn't he? Though he wasn't sure how it should be possible to remember that remembering, while at the same time having no clue as to the information itself.

Sighing, he lifted his gaze for a moment from the newspaper. It had been the only moment he'd raised his head since sitting down with his puzzle and his coffee and his banana nut muffin, and in that moment, he chose to glance out the large front window and onto the street.

He could have looked elsewhere in that instant. He could have turned his head, perhaps, looked to his right, and studied a wall decorated by a trompe l'oeil mural of coffee beans growing on a hillside. Or he might have tilted his head back, looked up, and admired the fanciful lighting fixture formed there by a spiral of glowing coffee cups. But no, instead, he chose that moment to stare straight ahead, to feel the sun on his face for what seemed like the first time, and so he, not just for what seemed like the first time, but for what actually was the first time, saw *her*.

Had he changed this element of his posture a moment earlier, she wouldn't have yet reached that narrow stretch of side street, and so he'd have lowered his gaze before she passed, missing her. If he'd stirred himself a moment later, she'd have already been gone, having turned a corner, escaped the moment of their maybe, never to be seen by him. But, luckily for him, luckily for her, the puzzle which had been confounding him disturbed him just enough that he'd looked up at exactly the right moment.

As he saw her, this woman he would have sworn he knew and swear he didn't know, it seemed to him as if she contained not just all that mattered in the universe, but all the matter *in* the universe. His body grew suddenly too tight to contain his soul, and he feared that if he stared at her any longer, if she did not pass quickly from his field of vision, her presence would burst him from his skin and split his shell to tatters. But his heart was pounding now in a way he'd never felt a heart pound before, making him aware of its presence with an urgency he'd never known, so he had to dare it anyway.

He would not look away. He could not look away. And then he didn't have to look away.

She was gone.

He dropped his pen and dashed out to the street, leaving his muffin barely nibbled, his coffee hardly sipped.

But once there, he was unable to spot her in any direction. As he scanned the city, a city in which he'd spent his entire life, it did not seem familiar to him the way he knew it should, and now, because of her, he assumed, it was only an impediment, a maze, its marvels meaningless, and not worth his time.

Because of her.

If the woman he sought had already entered a building, he knew he'd have lost his only chance, and would never find her again, but perhaps, oh, perhaps, if she'd only turned the corner...

He hesitated for the merest fraction of a second, trying to make in that infinitesimal fraction of time—one so small, it didn't seem possible for a human to measure it—what he knew would be his life's most important decision: Which way to run. Then he simply ran, knowing he had time for but one choice, knowing that if he'd chosen wrong, this would be the end of it, though an end he would never forget, and so no end at all.

He reached the street which instinct—or something grander—had headed him toward, looked in one direction, and saw nothing but a string of food trucks mobbed by a crowd he could immediately tell did not contain her. But when he looked the other way—ah, when he looked the other way—there she was.

He'd made the right choice. Or perhaps the universe had made the right choice for him. He'd have looked skyward and said thank you had he believed there was anything to which to say thank you.

After he called out to her, the expression revealed to him on her face when she turned told him, however...she didn't at all think he'd made the right choice.

• • •

Barbara'd had enough of strange men calling out to her on the street as if they had a right to, shouted at by so many she couldn't remember them all even if she'd wanted to. Which she did not. So she had made it a habit now to ignore them, and to make it seem at the same time as if she wasn't ignoring them, merely as if she'd never heard. Life was easier that way. Safer, too. She knew that even though she wasn't sure how she knew that, couldn't conjure up more than just a few of their faces even though she'd have thought they'd be burned into her memories, but if her mind wanted her to forget things, if her memory had become porous, she figured there had to be a good reason, whether she could extract that reason or not. So she let go of the attempt to remember which the cry from behind her had raised.

This time, as opposed to all of the other times except for the first, which she was aware of instantly without really remembering...she decided to turn. To confront.

Though the words said by the man behind her weren't by themselves offensive, his call had come when she'd had just about enough—he hadn't been the first that day; at least she thought he hadn't been the first that day—so who it was and what was said this time didn't really matter. She'd had enough, and though she wasn't sure what she was going to say, she was going to say *something*.

But when she spun, ready to speak, and trusting the words would be there when she needed them, she couldn't tell at first which of the others on the street had even been the one to accost her, as no one was looking directly at her. The dozen or so people were mostly in motion, hurrying for their destinations, with none headed toward her, while the ones who vibrated in place were all occupied by tasks which had nothing to do with her—hailing a cab, studying a store-front, lighting a cigarette. But the way his voice had reverberated so recently and so close behind, she knew he must still be there, and realized that it had to be *him*, the man looking down in confusion at a newspaper in his hand, as if he'd forgotten it was there, as if its presence had distracted him and caused him to forget *she* was even there. But then he looked up, and saw her, and she could see him remembering where he was, and why he was, see a smile blossom across his face from that remembering. A smile. Not the leer she'd come to expect from a string of faces she couldn't conjure up. (And why not? But better not to ask, she knew.)

He lifted the newspaper, shook it slightly so her eyes were drawn to a partially completed crossword puzzle, and asked whether she knew the name of a certain actress from a certain movie made during a certain year. A question which took her aback. Both because it was so unlike anything any stranger had ever said to her, but also because she *did* know the name of that certain actress who'd starred in that certain movie made in that certain year. Why, she'd been discussing it just the night before with one of her girlfriends. How remarkable was that?

So she told him.

His smile grew wider, a smile of happiness that she was right, not only in her answer, but...*right*.

He then looked at his other hand, the one not holding a puzzle, and smiled a different smile, a crooked smile, and asked whether she had a pen he could borrow. He stepped closer and ran a finger down the column where the name of the actress she'd given him should go. She shook her head, apologized, telling him it had been a long time since she'd had to write anything down that couldn't be done electronically. Writing with ink on paper seemed like something an ancient people would have done.

It seemed longer ago to her than it actually was. She knew that. But she didn't really care.

Oh, he wasn't quite as old as that, he told her, then pointed at an empty corner of the puzzle, and tapped the clues that went with it. He wondered whether she'd care to help him further. He knew of a coffee shop around the corner where they brewed excellent coffee, and the muffins weren't that bad either. And if they were lucky, no one would have yet thrown away the pen he'd left behind.

She looked at him, and for the first and last and only time (she was surprisingly uncertain of many things this morning, but not of that) thought...oh, why not?

. . .

That didn't seem right.

Did you really expect it would? It was a long time ago.

What are you saying? That just because that was then and this is now, nothing needs to make sense? How did he know which way to go to catch up with her? How did she know to stay after he'd found her? How did he know she was the one? How did she know he was the one? How did either of them know anything?

They just knew.

It doesn't seem possible. They didn't have enough information to be able to know. Not the way they were constructed in the old days. They didn't have the tools. And even if they'd had them, they wouldn't have known how to use them.

Maybe it's not that. Maybe we're reading them wrong. The information that survived from those times is incomplete, you know, so when we reanimate them, when we inhabit them, there are gaps. We might not be getting a complete and accurate picture.

Well...they did seem awfully uncertain at times...

And whether our knowledge of them is fragmented or not, how can their knowing what they knew of each other be the thing that disturbs you? And not that he was struggling to complete that puzzle when the answers should have been immediately accessible from the air around him? Not that he was having to eat and drink—what were those things they put in their mouths anyway?—in order to continue living? Not all those cars they needed to move from place to place? Or their inability to fight the force which kept them pinned to their planet? I had almost forgotten all those things.

And I couldn't remember any of them. But those mysteries made far more sense than this knowing what could not possibly be known.

But the question is, did any of that, or the others we reconstructed and ran simultaneously, help you decide? You have been delaying this for eons.

Time is infinite. We won't run out of it. Infinity, it's the only thing we won't run out of. I think we need to see more. To be more. No need to be hasty.

If you say so.

Do you disagree? Once we proceed, once a decision is made, there'd no going back.

I neither agree nor disagree. I am merely...patient.

Then let's keep going.

• • •

Sylvia couldn't open her eyes, even though she wanted, oh, how she wanted, to open them. But she was unable to summon the strength, barely had enough even for a coherent thought. And yet, she was still aware, though she was uncertain how she was aware, as she hadn't raised her lids once since entering the room, that the darkness without matched her darkness within. Only a few blinking lights kept that darkness from being total, she knew that as well, even though she'd never seen them blink, not even when her lids were intermittently lifted so her condition could be checked, for her eyes, well, they were beyond seeing. Those lights twinkled like stars, stars that felt like home, stars that comforted her, as if she had always lived among them, stars she knew very well, as well as she knew her own soul, without knowing how she knew them very well.

Their glow cast barely perceptible shadows upon her face, a face smoother than she'd thought it would remain for her to have ended up in such a place as this, not that she'd ever thought she'd end up in a place like this. They'd made themselves a promise, the two of them, she and her lover, that neither ever would. They'd made a pact, in fact, one they'd hoped they'd never need, but swore to each other would be fulfilled if necessary. But then life intervened, speeding up and sneaking upon them before they saw it coming, and they had no choice. And now that Sylvia was beyond doing any of the choosing, Jane, poor Jane, had to do the choosing for her.

Unable to see, unable to move, there was little for Sylvia to do save listen to the hums, the whirrs, the beeps of the sustaining machines which surrounded her, and the answering call and response of the meat symphony within—the air passing through her lungs, the blood coursing through her veins, the crackle of electricity allowing her to think those thoughts, none moving with the force they once had, but with enough, just enough. She was amazed that body continued to function at all, even as a part of her, a part she'd never noticed before, was also amazed that it had ever functioned in the first place. Bodies were messy things, and that hers had survived this long as the vehicle for the part that mattered was miraculous.

She became aware that beneath those sounds, barely audible, hid the sound of crying. As that sound came closer, grew louder, she recognized its maker. She wanted to sit up, to reach out, to place a hand against a cheek, to make the tears stop. But she could do none of those things. She could only lie there as she knew one of them eventually would, and listen, and be grateful. She'd known this was coming. It was foretold by the promise they'd made. But that didn't make it any less of a surprise when it finally arrived.

She could hear the weeping grow louder, though no closer, for they were already close enough that she could feel dampness on her face, tears which were not her own, and she knew that if she opened her own eyes, if she could somehow regain that power, she would see *her* eyes, the eyes of the one she knew so well, the eyes she'd chosen to gaze into forever (a forever which had been sadly shortened), above her, damp and overflowing. But though she strained, though she exerted all that remained within her, she could not even do that.

She hoped her lover knew she'd do that if she could.

She knew her lover knew she'd do that if she could, and knew it with a certainty which made all her earlier certainties only faith.

Then, interrupting their reunion, there rose the voice of another, a stern voice, and when it spoke with words Sylvia could not make out, that crying stopped for a moment, so there came a deafening silence which was almost unbearable, but then a cacophony followed to fill it which was more painful than the silence—yelling both from the one she loved, and from an angry voice, no, two angry voices, neither of which she recognized.

The voices grew louder, but no matter how much she concentrated, she could not understand what they were saying, for she was beyond concentration, behind understanding. She was adrift in a sea of her brain's own making, and as she struggled to make sense of the world around her, a world she could not see—but felt as if another would let her, she could, she could—those voices grew more guttural, grunting rather than speaking, and then her bed shook, as if others were bumping against it, others she could not stop, wrestling with another she could not protect, and she tried in the center of this chaos with all her soul, all her remaining will, to rise, to help, to protect...but could not. For whatever remained of her was simply not enough.

And then the room was silent again, silent save for the sounds from the gleaming machinery without which tried to keep her from dying and messy machinery within which was doing its best to disobey.

A room in which, though together they'd chosen another path, she knew she would die alone.

. . .

Jane had never done anything illegal in her life—well, except for the way she *lived* her life, but why should that be illegal, they had no right—and now, this was the time to take that step, because something illegal was being done to her. Well...not *illegal* illegal, not literally illegal, but definitely immoral and definitely something that should have been made illegal long ago, and someday would be. She knew that with a certainty, wishful thinking aside, knew that humanity would one day be beyond this, beyond barriers of laws, of concrete, of flesh—of flesh?—though she was unsure why that certainty beyond faith should be instilled within her now, considering how bleak things looked. Considering what she was considering doing.

More than merely considering. *Actually* doing. That was what they had pushed her to.

She'd bought an outfit that looked like something she thought a nurse would wear, wriggled into it in her car in the hospital parking lot, waited at night until she saw a legitimate nurse step outside for a cigarette break, and then slipped past her and inside before the door could shut, into the hospital where she was forbidden to be. The hospital where a photo of her was pinned to the wall by the front security desk. Where Sylvia lay in a bed, her wishes ignored, being kept alive in a way she would never have chosen.

Nothing was going to keep the two of them separate. Nothing was going to keep Jane from doing what her love alone could not. Nothing.

The corridor revealed off the rear lot was unfamiliar to her, looking nothing like the maze beyond the front entrance out of which she had been escorted so many times. She felt lost, but it was necessary that she feel lost. For here there were no guards to stop her from wandering, and that was all that mattered. She trusted she'd find her way. She'd been lost before she found Sylvia, and yet she found her, hadn't she? Being lost was but a temporary stage before what mattered. The world would not be so unkind as to prevent her from fulfilling her mission.

She entered a stairwell—she didn't feel she could dare risk one of the elevators, worried she'd be too visible there—and walked up with what she hoped would seem to anyone who saw her to be a nurse's determination rather than a madwoman's urgency. No one spotted her, though, and so she made it safely to what she remembered as Sylvia's floor. Then a wave of horror passed through her as she thought—what if they'd moved her in the week since her last visit?

But—surely they wouldn't have, for where else would they have moved her *to*? The hospital was already doing all it could, and Sylvia wasn't going to get better, so there was only one other place for Sylvia to move on to from here, and Jane didn't want to have to think about it. Not yet. Not until she had to. Because it would have meant Jane had failed her, and she wasn't sure she could bear knowing that. But at least…she wouldn't have to bear it for long.

She exited on a corridor without a view of the nursing station, for which she was grateful—as she could probably be taken as a nurse by those who'd never seen her face before, but not them, not them—and made it to the remembered room with no false turns, which surprised her, because luck was never usually on her side. Well, except for having found Sylvia.

Sylvia.

She lay in the bed in the dark, her breathing more a series of arhythmic gasps than the gentle flow of air, the sound of which had helped Jane fall asleep all the years since they'd gotten together. Wires and tubes led from the body she knew so well to the machines which surrounded her. Her eyes were closed, her face expressionless. Somewhere inside was Sylvia, but her body, it could have passed for dead.

This was the end they'd promised they'd keep each other from. They'd had a pact, promised they'd never let it progress like this, never let these people get their hands on either one of them. Though if she were honest with herself, Jane, being the older of the two, had always thought, if they'd erred and let things get this far, *she'd* be the one in the hospital bed, with Sylvia doing for her what she couldn't do for herself...but one doesn't get to choose.

She stood by Sylvia's side, ready for what she was meant to do, but found herself unable to reach into her pocket for the hypodermic. It had to be done, she knew it had to be done, but her hand would not obey. All she could do was cry. Her tears struck Sylvia's cheek, making it appear as if *she* were the one crying. She wondered whether Sylvia could sense the dampness on her face. She wondered whether Sylvia even knew Jane was there. Whether either of them was there.

Neither of them believed there was anything after this life, they'd discussed the matter many times, but as there would soon be nothing left of this one, Jane knew...she'd better start pretending.

She was about to place a hand against her lover's cheek to draw strength for the next step when the door behind her slammed open. She knew they'd come, so that was no surprise—she just didn't know they'd come so soon. Before they could reach her, she grabbed the railing on Sylvia's bed with one hand, while simultaneously reaching into a pocket for the handcuffs, which she slammed down against her other wrist. But she wasn't fast enough, and before she could attach herself to the bed, they pulled at her arm and twisted it behind her back. They knew who she was, shouting her name, shouting other things which she couldn't believe they'd dare to shout, words she'd been called many times before, but not here, not now.

Jane went limp, dropping to the ground, uncertain even as she fell whether she'd done it deliberately to prevent herself from being dragged off, or if her knees had buckled from the rush of emotions.

Down on the linoleum, curled into a ball, she screamed at them, cursed them, demanded they think about what they were doing, but none of that stopped them doing it, no matter how loudly she insisted she loved Sylvia, how they couldn't possibly be so inhumane, how they should let the two of them be, regardless of what Jane's estranged family had insisted. Couldn't they see? Didn't they understand? They would someday, they all would someday. She knew it. *She knew it.* But that helped little now.

They ignored her words as they yanked her to the door. And as she was pulled from the room, she kept fighting, kept foolishly hoping they'd find it in their hearts to let her fulfill her promise, but most of all kept her eyes on Sylvia, only on Sylvia, until the door slammed shut and she saw her no more.

· · ·

That was terrible. It can't possibly be true. Can it? Were they really once like that? Were we really once like that?

Once like what? Bound in bodies? Or blind to what that imprisonment did to them? Both, I fear. But it doesn't matter whether it's true or not. We're beyond that. We don't need to have anything to do with them.

That's not really something we can choose. They either were us...or were not. Facts are facts. History is history. It's not a matter of choice.

Of course we can choose. We're no more required to believe in them than we are to accept the truth of a myth, or the laws laid down by a religion. Besides...the information we have...who knows whether it's accurate? There are holes. There are mysteries. Didn't you sense them?

Our presence...it seems to be filling those holes. We're doing more than watching untampered recreations. We became a part of them. We're not the only ones sensing things. Didn't you sense them sensing us? They're aware of what we're doing. They're aware of what we're trying to decide. So we're not getting a perfect picture of how they really were. The evidence that was left behind by those we once were...we've tampered with it. Infected it. Our trail from there to here is no longer true.

Oh, there's been some transference perhaps. They surely did not have that certainty we're picking up about times to come. Our times. We're bleeding through. But enough of it remains true. Enough for you to decide.

I know.

You still have to decide.

Yes. I know. So...we can be what we want to be? We can be what we are?

We already are what we are.

But that's not what this has been about. That's not what we're trying to decide. We've been embodying them to determine whether to become what we are not yet.

I don't know that we're ready.

Then it's a good thing we have all the time in the universe. Time enough to replay every one of them if necessary.

I'm not sure I could bear many more of them. They feel so...constricting. How were they ever able to stand it? We, at least, have a choice, but they, they had none.

It doesn't seem as if they could stand it. Maybe that's what drove them mad. Maybe that's why we two are all that's left. But that doesn't matter now. What matters is, since you've yet to decide...do we dive in for more?

We must. We'll dive. We'll learn.

We'll choose.

• • •

Gwendolyn is a genius, something the world long ago acknowledged, as any scan of the Internet would reveal, but she'd never consider calling herself one. The scientists on whose shoulders she stands, those are the geniuses. She sees herself as someone merely making real what those others had already proven possible, for everything she's achieved over the years seems obvious to her even as the world calls it miraculous. She wonders, as she rehearses one final time in her head the presentation she's about to give, the momentous step she is about to take, why she's thinking of herself in those terms now. She'd never used the world genius to describe herself, would never think that way, so for a moment she's confused, feeling not quite herself at the exact moment she needs to feel most herself.

Perhaps it's her old fear, one she'd thought she'd long gotten past, suddenly asserting itself again as she prepares to stand before a crowd and speak, something she's never much liked doing because of the way the looks on their faces would sometimes signal they had too many questions about the way she presented herself to be.

Perhaps something else.

On another day, without the pressure of what was about to occur urging her to get on with it, she might have paused to examine this feeling more closely, figured out why she was having thoughts which seemed not her own. But she had no time for that now. And so, as best as she could, she shook off whatever it was, and raised her head to look out once more at the reporters who surrounded her now that the culmination of her work was at hand.

Studying their faces, she wished she could have found a different way. She wished the others in the scientific community would have listened, allowed her that. But those whom she'd thought her peers but had proved not to be felt her latest findings ridiculous, didn't want to help her let the world know of this project through the usual sources, so she'd had to pursue other means. She'd always scoffed at those who'd choose to reach out through the popular press rather than scientific journals, but she was beyond that now. The whole world had to get beyond that.

It was time to move on.

She activated the equipment behind her, and the hum as the lights flickered and intensified quieted the murmuring of the reporters. It was as if a galaxy was unfolding before them, and she found surprising comfort there. She wondered why. Reluctantly, she turned from it, turned to them who would let the rest of the world know.

We are far more than our bodies, she explained to them. This is nothing new, she said. We have always been more than the meat which imprisons us. But until now, there has been no way to unlock the prison gate. Until now, the body ruled the spirit. Until now, there was no way to become immortal.

She could tell they were confused. This sounded to them like New Age nonsense. This was not what they'd come for. She was, after all, a scientist. A genius. (Where had that come from again? Enough.) But Gwendolyn knew they wouldn't have come if they'd known what they were coming for.

Our only hope for survival when the world burns up isn't rockets, she told them. Not generation starships to carry us to another Earth far away. We have no need of other Earths. We can have the universe. Because only meat needs metal. The mind does not.

The mind need no longer be at war with the body in which it is trapped. The mind can be free. The mind can span galaxies.

The words she spoke did not seem like the kind of words she'd speak—they were far more philosophical than she was comfortable with—but they were the only words she seemed to have left. Good thing she had more than words.

She raised a hand to the equipment behind her and explained what was going to happen even though she knew they could not understand. But she had written it all out, provided documentation, blueprints, everything necessary for others to replicate what was about to occur. She attached the wires to her temples, her ankles, her wrists, her heart. And she told them goodbye, that after this meeting, she would be able to tell them no more, that it was up to them to spread the word of what they were about to see, so others could join her, so no one ever need feel imprisoned again, so no goodbye would ever be permanent.

And then she pressed the button.

She crumpled to the ground, her head striking a corner of the podium on her way down, but no matter. Some of the journalists leapt forward to check on her, see what had gone wrong, not understanding that all had gone right. Others remembered their roles, which they'd later come to regret, then later come to not, and kept snapping photos.

Let them.

Gwendolyn looked down upon the body she'd abandoned, the body she had wrestled with for too long, and was glad to be rid of it.

Would they tell her story? She smiled, surprised she could still feel the sensation of smiling when she had nothing left with which to smile. Ah, yes. They would tell her story. Her bifurcated life and apparent death would make sure of that. And eventually, someone would understand the documentation she had left behind, figure out what she had done, and join her. Others would follow.

And who knows what might happen then?

· · ·

We have much to be thankful for.

That we do. Those bodies were uncomfortable. Unwieldy. Unnatural.

Well...that last is something they can't be accused of. They were natural, all right.

And they had all the flaws that came with being natural. How did they ever survive without going mad?

They didn't. Survive, that is. Not more than a fraction of them anyway. But luckily, by the time the world went away, enough of them had decided to become us. Or what was to mix and merge and coalesce and eventually become us.

Coalesce...yes. We are all who remain made two. Without bodies to keep us apart, without the membrane of flesh between us, why not? Once those walls began to fall, why let any other walls keep us apart? It wasn't until the barriers of the spirit were shown to be unnecessary that we could see they were even more claustrophobic.

And yet...

And yet? Am I not convincing you?

I feel the tug, I really do, sense the gravity of consciousness calling, pulling us together. But still...I hesitate.

Inhabiting the psyches of the billions past, or what remains of them for us to know, was of no help to you?

Nothing we saw answered the question, will we be lonely when we are no longer two? There has never before been a universe inhabited by only one.

Well...except...you know.

Yes...well. It's not the same thing, though.

No. No, it's not. However...procrastination ill becomes you. It's time for you to decide. Can you really deny it? That this, that that, is what was and is meant to be? Isn't that what we learned from inhabiting those who came before? Isn't that what this sorting through our particles has been all about?

Yes, you're right...but...I'm afraid.

So were they, you know. But they were afraid because they were apart. And if we weren't afraid, we wouldn't be human.

But we're not human. Not anymore.

Oh, but we are. We are human still. Nothing has changed. What matters is the wine, not the bottle.

That makes no sense. We have no need to drink any more. We are the stuff of stardust now.

Hush. Listen to them. Then let go.

· · ·

Julian and Barbara and Sylvia and Jane and Gwendolyn and a million million others felt a sudden disturbance as they lived their lives— or perhaps it wasn't their lives which were interrupted at all, perhaps it was merely an unexpected pause in a shadow play, a breach of their recreations as they'd been worn like a mask during the search for truth in making this ultimate decision. But whether alive or illusion, real or only memory, at this point, after more time had passed by far than the entire race had ever lived, was there really a difference?

Julian and Barbara, too old to be living independently, having moved in now with their oldest daughter, looked at each other with smiles, then up at the wall to the completed crossword puzzle they'd had framed so long ago, then back to each other, their skin tingling—

Jane, standing over Sylvia's grave, her trembling hand pressed to the stone engraved with a date of death from decades earlier, felt an electric charge pass through her, turned around because she felt someone was there, saw no one, but knew, without a doubt, that someone *was* there—

Gwendolyn, drifting away from Earth to circle the sun, paused in formless wonder, suddenly connected to a future she had dreamed into being, and quivered with ecstatic urging—

And Dana and Masud and Luc and Robert and Mary Jo and Li Xia and Jeremy and Hani and Amelia and Felipe and a billion others stopped what they were doing, suddenly unconstrained by the scripts of what they thought were their lives, and cried out:

"What are you waiting for? Get on with it!"

• • •

And the final two became the only one, transforming into a fine specimen of hypermagical ultraomnipotence, and delighted itself, no longer alone, by going off to explore a hell of a good universe.

OPOSSUMS AND ANGELS

*A*nn woke before dawn, snug in her sleeping bag beside the big rock by the swamp, and looked up at the stars which would soon fade, trying to remember how many months it had been since she'd last seen what the men had taken to calling angels. She frowned, unable to count the time, as her struggle to survive had left one day looking very much like the next. But of one thing she was certain—it had to have been longer ago than when she'd last tried—and failed—to rise to the challenge of killing herself.

As the sun rose, she turned her head to the epitaph she'd scratched months before along the rock face, though the fact she was still around to read it meant it was still merely words, and had yet to actually become an epitaph.

Her marks were difficult to make out at first, but then the rising sun cast shadows within the gashes she'd made, and soon the letters were legible again—

HERE LIES THE SECOND MEANEST PRIMATE ON EARTH

Reading that, she felt chastised by her former self, felt as if she ought to apologize to her for not having gone through with it, but she just hadn't been able to do it, she couldn't, even though at least once each day she promised herself she would. If only she could have been sure she wasn't the last woman on Earth, it might have been easier. If she knew, perhaps, that another was safely tucked away in some Easter Island cave, waiting for the right moment to rise up among the moai, then ...

But...she had no way of knowing. So maybe she *was* the last. And if, in fact, she was, it didn't seem right for her to go out that way. Not by her own hand. Not when it meant that men—and the glowing visitors they mistook for angels—would win.

So it was just as well she was cut off from the rest of the world, more cut off than even she—as the horror of what was really happening dawned on her—had expected she would need in order to live. She'd thought she'd been remote enough in the mountain cabin toward which Barney had pointed her (Barney, oh, poor Barney), but it was only this—sleeping where nothing but animals slept, eating raw fish so no cook fire would reveal her existence, rubbing herself with animal fat so the smell of anything but a woman would spill off her—that had kept her alive, due to both isolation and ignorance. If she'd known there were others out there like her, other hidden women who'd managed to survive the brutal days when men went mad but didn't know it, she might have been able to let it all go, fulfilled the promise of those words above her. Words no one would probably ever read, not human, nor supposed angel either.

"I saw them, Amy," she whispered, during that bridge moment prior to being fully awake, realizing as soon as she spoke what she'd forgotten and been forced to remember hundreds of times before, that her daughter was not there. But a mother's mind plays what tricks it can, and self-delusion was much easier than living with the constant knowledge your husband had filled with bloodlust as inescapably as any other man, and had killed her. Amy, her beautiful, precious Amy, dead at Alan's hands. Alan, the most gentle of men, who'd fought so hard to protect them. Until the angels, who once she finally saw one herself she realized were nothing but aliens, turned his loving instincts into murder, and gave him a reason to kill, as all men had been given a reason to kill all women. And all women *were* killed.

All, perhaps, but her.

She rose from her sleeping bag and headed back down to the cabin after weeks—at least she guessed it was weeks—away. She'd had to abandon it when men started sniffing around (oh, she'd dealt with them quite handily, at least the first few, until there were too many, much too many), but now...did she really have to keep hiding? If they were going to get her, if they were going to fulfill their task of clearing the Earth for what was to come, they'd surely have done so by now.

The front door of the cabin hung loose, and its contents were trashed, as she expected they'd be. She had carried away what she could when she fled to the swamp, but much had to be left behind.

Plates had been smashed, the Turner print on the wall had been punched right through, the sheets on which she'd slept had been shredded, even the sturdy cot was now shattered into pieces, the bent branches from which Barney had shaped it splintered and scattered to the corners of the room. She could imagine them, the men who'd lost their minds, puffed up with rage, growling like apes, driven mad by the pheromones she couldn't help but leave behind, destroying everything they could because they were unable to destroy her.

Though the mounds outside the cabin, beneath which were buried the ones who'd come for her first, and singly, showed they weren't the only ones capable of destruction.

She built a fire, and as she gathered what paper she could find to get it started, it wasn't clear to her whether she no longer cared whether attackers might be drawn by the smoke, or if she hoped they'd all been destroyed anyway, having turned, at last, on themselves. Beneath one of the piles, apparently dropped and forgotten during the ransacking, she found a well-read copy of Reverend McIllhenny's ludicrous pamphlet *Man Listens to God*, which attempted to justify the slaughter. She crumpled its pages one at a time and happily tossed them into the flames. She watched the pages blacken, wishing she could gather and burn every copy. God had always justified a lot, could even make aliens over into angels.

Well, it looked like the aliens had gotten their way, and Earth was devoid of people. Almost anyway.

So why had it been so long since she'd seen one? They'd gotten rid of the native population with no mess—no craters, no radioactivity—so why hadn't they returned yet to claim it for their own?

As she hunched over the flames, the hinges of the hanging door behind her creaked, and she spun to see a man, a shaggy, filthy man, standing there in the open doorway, holding his right wrist tight with the fingers of his left hand, waging an internal war against what the aliens had planted inside him.

"Stay back," he croaked, his jaw twitching. "Keep away from me."

Stay back? He was the one who'd come for her! And what had he to fear? It was his kind who'd slaughtered all of hers, and it seemed to her as if he was about to continue the bloodbath. No man had yet been able to win against the new self he'd been given. So, no, she would not stay back, not even though she could see his struggle to remain rational.

No time to drop to her boot for the knife she kept there, so she slipped a hand into a pocket for the fishing hooks which had fed her, and launched herself at him.

She wedged the barbs between her knuckles and swung for his face, shrieking out her hate for him and all like him. She knew, no matter how overwhelmed he was by the bloodlust the aliens had instilled in all men, that he couldn't help but flinch. She'd seen it before, when taking down men larger than him. Those reactions were planted even deeper than what the conquerors had left behind.

"Wait, you don't understand," he said, backpedaling away. "Stay away from me. Please!"

He retreated as she neared him, tripping over the lip of the door and falling. When she was almost upon him, his pleas faded, and his demeanor changed. At first, he'd been blank and exhausted (though no less a threat; there was no longer such a thing as a trustworthy man in this world), but suddenly he was angry and filled with energy. As she leapt atop him, he flailed, growling.

"Bitch!" he called her gutturally as his blows went wide. She was too close for him to swing cleanly—his forearms collided dully with her shoulders—but just close enough for her to do what she needed to do. She'd been a doctor in the old world, so knew just where to press, and for how long...and that was that.

Once he was still, she stood, panting, and wondered what to do with him. She should kill him, she knew, she'd done it before, after all, and had even gotten better at it, though she still had to force herself to think of Amy and the aliens each time. But she'd never done it like this. She had killed no one yet who wasn't in the process of trying to kill her. Looking at the man, she knew she might have to get over her reluctance and do it anyway, but decided...it didn't have to be right then. Besides, it had been so long since the last time she'd had to kill a man she felt she might learn something by talking.

She dragged his body to a tree by the well out front, propped him in a sitting position with his back against the trunk, and wrapped fishing line around him again and again, enough so it would hold him until she was ready to do whatever it was she had to do next. Then she went back inside Barney's cabin for one last look. That he had found her meant she'd been too optimistic. She'd have to abandon the place for good this time. The war the aliens had started was not done yet.

By the time she returned outside, he was awake. It surprised her to see he wasn't struggling against the line. That was what she'd have been doing, if she'd found herself in that situation. He lifted his head, considering her cooly, as if he was used to always being in control, and was the kind of person who would never admit either to himself or to her that his current predicament had changed that.

"Smart girl," he said, jutting his chin down toward where his chest was bound.

"I'm no girl," she said. She thought of her own girl again, and what had been done to her, and almost went for her knife right then, but resisted the impulse. For now.

"No, you're right," he continued. "You wouldn't be a girl, couldn't be, not to still be alive. A girl would never have made it this far."

She started walking toward him, and he began to shout.

"Don't come any closer!" he cried, the muscles of his shoulders jerking. "Back up, back up! Stay over there, and we might have a chance to talk."

"So you're infected," she said, taking a few steps back while keeping her eyes on the line she'd wrapped around him, hoping she'd bound him tight enough. She wasn't sure, as she'd never had to do anything like that before. All she'd ever done to the other men was kill them.

"Weren't we all?" he said.

"No, we weren't all," she said, bitterly. "Just men."

"Just men," he repeated.

"Why are you here?" she asked.

"Isn't it obvious? I had to find you. And you had to be found. You're the last woman on Earth, and I'm the last man."

He shrugged, or rather moved his shoulders in what would have been a shrug had he not been tied up, as if to say, *do I really have to tell you what needs to be done next?*

"How can you be sure we're the last?" she asked, ignoring what he'd left unspoken.

"I just know," he said. "Know without knowing. Turning men into killers wasn't the only change they made in us. We can sense you. Your existence is an itch we need to...scratch. So eventually, we find you."

"Doesn't sound as if that change worked out very well. Yes, you found me. And so did a few others."

She nodded toward the mounds nearby.

"But not all men," she continued. "If what you say is true, there should have been an army hunting for me up here."

"After we turned on you, we turned on each other. Isn't that always the way? Not that many survived. And out of those who did, not many had the skills to survive this far north."

"And you had them?"

Her question hung there, ending with a tone that signaled she was seeking more than one answer, so he gave her what she wanted.

"Don," he said. "Don Fenton. And as to how I'm still alive, let's just say Uncle Sam taught me well, and leave it at that. And you?"

"Ann Alstein," she said. "*Doctor* Ann Alstein."

He smiled. She did not like it.

"Doctor," he said. "That's good. You'll be able to understand better than most what needs to be done, and why, for now at least, you should stay exactly where you are."

"Don't you dare tell me what I should do," she said, taking a step forward. His breathing quickened in response.

"Look, I mean it," he said.

She took another step, and his lips curled, his hands balling into fists.

"Stop it!" he said. "This isn't a game. I'm trying to fight this thing, but I won't be able to if you keep coming closer. We need to talk, and talk calmly, and I can't do that unless you back off. Please."

"Talk about what? Seems to me the only thing we need to figure out is whether you'll kill me or I'll kill you. What else is there to talk about?"

"That it doesn't have to be that way," he said, his legs trembling, as if he were a dog, running in its sleep. "That things are different now. That they're gone."

"Who's gone?"

He closed his eyes, beginning to breathe so quickly she thought he'd hyperventilate.

She took a step back. Then another. Then a few more until she was almost standing in the doorway over whose lip he had tripped.

"The aliens," he said, beginning to be more relaxed.

"You don't think of them as angels then?" she said.

"No. No, I don't."

"Most men do. Most men use it as an excuse to..."

She didn't feel she needed to say it. And no matter what he might later claim, she knew he'd probably done those things she didn't say.

"I know better. I've known that from the beginning."

"How could you? I didn't know that until it was almost—almost the end."

"Because these aliens...they were not the first. There were others."

"What did you see?" she said slowly, and with a hard tinge to her voice. She took half a step forward, fighting down her desire to get into up his face. She pulled her foot back, breathed deep, tried to calm herself. "Tell me."

"It happened when I was down in Cozumel a few years back. I was hoping to make it to Belize to get some fishing done. But I never go there. My plane crashed, and before we were rescued, we saw those...things."

"We?"

"Me. My pilot. And a couple of women. I went off for water with one of them so we could stay alive until we were found, and instead we found them. Actually...they found us."

"Angels? That long ago?"

"They looked nothing like angels. They weren't glowing, couldn't have fooled anyone they were on a mission from God. They were tall, and white, and with limbs that could stretch out even longer than their bodies. They claimed they were students—or at least I think that's what they were saying—and once they helped us, they were gone. But the fact they'd been here at all showed me—we're not alone in this universe. So when the next ones appeared, I knew. They were no angels. I knew who they were. And I know who *we* are."

Ann stared at him, silently, until he looked away. She could tell it was a thing he did not do often, or lightly.

"There's something you're not telling me," she said.

He did not respond, keeping his head turned to the nearby mounds.

"What happened to the women?" she asked.

He laughed, and it was an ugly laugh.

"She wasn't even the same species as me, she said. Claimed she was as different from me as I was from an opossum. That's what's she thought of herself as, you know. Merely an opossum. They're all around us, she said, but we don't even see them."

"What the Hell are you talking about? Tell me what happened to the women, Don."

"You're just like them," he said. "I should have realized it before. Just another opossum."

"Tell me now, Don! *What happened to the women?*"

She found herself coming closer before she was even aware of thinking of coming closer, and he writhed uncontrollably until the cord cut through the cloth of his shirt, cut through more than just cloth, and blood was running down his arms. He gritted his teeth, and rocked forward, surging to meet her approach, but could not reach her.

"I'll kill you!" he shouted, his veneer of control defeated. "I'll gut you and kill you!"

"Did you kill *them?*" she asked, standing over him as still as he was wild. "Is that what you did to the women, Don? Kill them?"

He shook his head, gritted his teeth, grunted, and smacked his head back against the trunk until tears ran down his cheeks. She could hear, as he grimaced, the cracking of a tooth.

"No!" he shouted. "I didn't kill them. They're gone! The aliens took those two crazy bitches. And they wanted to go! Said they didn't belong here. That they were a different species. Can you believe that? They wanted to go! They...wanted...to...go!"

He repeated that last sentence over and over until it seemed as if he would never stop, in the grip of a fugue state which would have killed them both if she let it. She backed away, circling around to the opposite side of the cabin, and sank to the ground against it, relieved to have it between them. Eventually, his whimpering stopped.

"We're it, you know," he said, his voice calmer now that she was out of sight and further away. "You and me, that's all that's left. That's why I came here. That's why I've been trying to control myself. If we don't do something, if we don't take action, the human race dies here."

"Are you serious?" she called out, suddenly parsing his meaning. "You really believe you're going to get a chance to fuck me?"

She laughed, and even though it was a hateful laugh, one she hoped hurt him, the laughter over his dreams of action—action, what kind of a euphemism was that?—felt good, because it had been a long time since she'd had a laugh of any kind.

"This world is not ours any longer," she said, once her laughter had stopped. "It belongs to them now. I don't know what they have planned, but those plans don't include us. That's what this was all about. This planet...we've lost it. How have you not figured that out?"

"We won't have lost it until they come back," he said. "And don't you see? Who knows how long that will be? Who knows how the aliens

139

even measure time? It could be years before they return. Decades. And if we're lucky—centuries. We've got to try, Ann. We can't let it end here. We've got to keep living. Surely you can see that."

She thought of herself, night after night by the rock beside the swamp, and how many times it almost did end there. She looked at her wrists lined with scars, too many to count, but none quite deep enough. He was crazy if he thought the species could go on, crazier if he thought they could do it together.

"And you think, you really think, you'll be able to get near me?" She didn't hide the disgust in her voice. She didn't even try. "To mount me and shoot the future into me? You think they'll let you? You think *I'll* let you?"

She thought of Alan then, Alan's voice, Alan's touch, the promise of what they'd foolishly counted as infinite tomorrows. Damn him! Why couldn't he have stayed in Colombia? Why did he have to rush back to her? If only he'd waited...

 But if what Don said about his being the last of men was true, waiting wouldn't have saved him.

"We'll think of a way," he said. "We can't allow ourselves to be the last. We *have* to think of a way."

Did they? She had no answer to that, no *way*, not even a desire for a way, and so she sat quietly, not replying to his calling of her name. She regretted even telling it to him. He didn't deserve to be the one to use it.

Eventually, night began to fall, and the stars started to come out, looking oh so very different than they had that morning. She shivered at the increasing cold. She rose and went to the front of the cabin, and kept her eyes on him as his gaze tracked her to the door. He didn't speak, which told her he had at least some sense. Inside, she took the remains of a tattered blanket and draped some of the shreds about her shoulders. She carried the rest to the man, only approaching as close as she needed—which wasn't very close at all—to toss the rest around his shoulders. Then she backed away to sit against the cabin and watch him in the moonlight, wondering which of them would break the silence first. They stared at each other like that, the last man and the last women, one wanting everything, one wanting nothing.

"I didn't come here to kill you," he said eventually. "You have to know that."

"And my husband didn't come home to kill my daughter," she said. "And the Sons of Adam and the Pauline Purification Cult, they didn't want to kill either, they only wanted to become closer to God. What you want doesn't matter, and if you think you didn't come here to kill me, you haven't been listening to the blood pulsing through your veins. Blood which is right now outside you, running down your arms. Don't lie to me, Don. Don't lie to yourself. You came here to kill me, all right."

"Perhaps you're right. Perhaps I'm lying to myself. But as long as we keep our distance, nothing bad will happen to either one of us. I'm in control. I'm okay."

"No," she said. "No, you're not. You're a bear trap waiting to be sprung. And I can't have you around, worrying every moment that you'll snap shut. When my time comes, it's not going to be at your hands. You don't get to win. They don't get to win."

"I'm telling you, it doesn't have to be that way. If you'd known me before, you'd know I'm about as much of a cynic as you can get. I was never one to get sentimental. But I believe life can go on. We can do this. We can be another Adam and Eve."

She snorted.

"That's just the alien in you talking, Don, hoping to convince me to lower my guard so you can end the job they started. Besides, there's no way you can knock me up if we have to always keep thirty feet between us."

"There's always a way, darling."

She grimaced at that word.

"Darling?" she said, then laughed. "Jesus. You're mad. Well, I guess after all this time, I'm mad, too."

"Neither of us is mad. It's more like we're...inevitable. Just like—"

Now he laughed.

141

"Like who?"

He shook his head, astonished by something he'd yet to share.

"Like Captain Esteban and that Althea girl."

She frowned at the word, but he jumped in before she could speak.

"No, really, that one *was* a girl," he said. "And you see, the thing is, when her mother and I went for water, what I didn't realize until later was, she'd left them alone deliberately. She wanted her daughter to get herself pregnant and carry a kid away to the stars. The same way we got left here alone deliberately by the universe so that *we* could bring a kid into the world right here. It all makes sense now."

"Wait, she—what? Someone's pregnant? Up there?

He nodded.

"Up there, Lord knows where. She knew. Oh, that Ruth Parsons, she knew exactly what she was doing when she volunteered to head off with me. She knew both of them would be leaving, and she knew wherever she was going, she'd need something more for the race to live on. On a planet circling one of those stars, somewhere out there, there's a baby. A baby unlike any human baby that's ever been. Or maybe...not a baby anymore. Time could work differently out there, remember. Who knows where he's been? Who knows what he's seen? The last of us now. Well, except for those two opossums. But he doesn't have to be the last of us."

"The last of us," she repeated, saying coldly what he had said so hopefully. She stared at the blood which by now was seeping through the strips of blanket. "I'm sorry, Don."

"Sorry for what?" he said. "There's no need of sorries now."

She stood and began walking toward him, knowing now what she'd have to do next.

"Wait—what are you doing?" he said, his voice beginning in fear, but ending in anger. "You shouldn't come any closer. I warned you not to do that. Ann, Ann, Ann, stop it! Think of what you're doing. Bitch, get back! Get back, you stupid bitch!"

But she would not get back. She continued approaching slowly, watching intently as the bloodlust overtook him. She needed to see the change occur, needed to see his humanity slip away, to do what she had to do. What she must do. She knew she couldn't bring herself to do it otherwise. She wasn't like that. Or perhaps...she didn't want to *admit* she was like that. She stood over him, fishhooks again in one hand and knife now in the other, watching him curse and convulse, and she was grateful in that moment, grateful she'd been unable to get to her knife earlier, for that would have meant she'd never have learned about the other aliens, and the women who'd escaped with them, and the star child somewhere way overhead. She'd never have learned what she was now free to do.

"Get this off me, you filthy whore!" he screamed as he continued to struggle. "I'll kill you, I swear! I'll kill—"

And then, his brain beyond thought, his body beyond pain, the line snapped, and so did she.

As he rose, she slashed the knife across his throat, and though blood spilled down his chest, the force of his forward motion carried him to her, brought her down.

His body pinned her there, but she no longer had anything to fear from him, as he only twitched once...twice...and then no more. She didn't try to move at first, but simply lay there, feeling his weight atop her, his final warmth oozing into her, and gasped, catching her breath as the stars twinkled down on them both.

She looked at them, thousands there must have been visible in the crisp night, and wondered once more which one they had come from, the invaders who had seeded the Earth with madness. She'd wondered that often before. But this time as she studied the stars, her eyes sought out a different star, the one toward which the women had fled, taking a child, a future, with them. Was it that bright one over there? Or the one over there, that blinked more quickly than any other? Ann had no way of knowing. She knew that she would never know. But that not knowing didn't seem to matter.

"Thank you," she whispered into Don's ear, even though he could no longer hear her. "Thank you."

And then she slid from beneath him, and went off to do the last and final thing she was now free to do.

• • •

Barney, dear Barney,

I don't really know why I'm bothering to write this, or why when I'm done, I'll shove my note into a plastic baggie and stuff it into the crack in that rock we agreed we'd always use for messages. Even when I was doing this before, I always suspected I was fooling myself, that no one would ever read my words...but now that's more than just a suspicion. You're gone, all men are gone, and I'm no longer just the last woman on Earth, but the last *person* on Earth. Still, I feel compelled to write one final note for you, and leave it for you as I promised I would, acting as if this were the old days, acting as if you and I still had hope.

So one last note for dearest, dearest Barney, who snuck me out from under the noses of those who would have gutted me, and made sure that here on planet Earth, I'd be the one to turn off the lights.

Remember the creatures I told you about that I'd finally seen, told you in a note I now must admit you never got a chance to see? (Oh, Barney, I hope your end was not *too* painful.) How I saw them, those who'd come and erased the world, those aliens we called angels? Well, they're gone, based on what my eyes and a very foolish man have told me, just as the human race itself is almost gone.

But as important as that is, it's not the most important thing right now. What matters is that not only are we not alone in the universe, we are even less alone than I'd originally thought. For there are *other* aliens out there, a species not dedicated to our destruction, a species who are our true angels. For they took some small part of us with them, before the plague contaminated and killed the human race, which means we will survive.

Which means I no longer have to.

I learned today why I'd hesitated earlier to do what I'd so longed to do. When I believed I was the last, I now realize I felt I couldn't make that decision on behalf of all humanity. It wasn't my decision to make. But now that I know there's something more...something more up there...

Goodbye, Barney.

There'll be no need for me to scratch out an epitaph. I did that many months ago, and my stone has been waiting. It has been patient while I decided whether I had permission to put down this burden.

Oh, Barney, I wish you could feel the quiet of the world, now that I am the last. It's beautiful. And it is, I fear, the way the world was meant to be.

But soon it will be quieter still.

Out there, however...out there...humanity will continue. I can feel it. As for here, though...as for Earth...

It's funny this should be the last thought of the planet's last person, but, you know...

It's a nice place, if it wasn't for people.

FIFTH DIMENSION

Dear Mr. Klein:

It's been wonderful reliving the golden age of television these past months in your magazine via Marc Zicree's guide to *The Twilight Zone*'s classic episodes. I've been a lifelong Rod Serling fan, so it's heartening to see that the market will support a magazine dedicated to carrying on Serling's dream of quality fantasy.

But now that the series is nearing its end, I'm worried that Zicree is going to leave out some of my favorite episodes. As far as I can tell, he's already skipped at least two—the one that had John Agar as the small-town bully whose life is changed when he switches places for a few hours with the meek schoolteacher he's been taunting, and the unforgettable tender comedy in which Irene Ryan plays a struggling writer's muse. How could he possibly have forgotten them?

Sincerely,

Scott Edelman

· · ·

Dear Mr. Edelman:

I'm afraid I'm unfamiliar with the two episodes you mention. Are you sure you have your facts straight?

Puzzled,

T. E. D. Klein

· · ·

Dear Mr. Klein:

You've got to be kidding, right?

I've been watching *TZ* reruns on my battered old Zenith for as long as I can remember, and I know all of the *Twilight Zone* trivia—cast listings, writing credits, plot convolutions, twist endings, etc. I would have sworn that you'd have all of it down pat, too. I guess I figured it came with the job.

Next thing you'll be telling me you never saw the episode with Sebastian Cabot as a third-grade math teacher who has an insolent pint-sized Jackie Coogan in his class, playing the boy who may very well be Cabot himself as a child. I just saw it on my set for what must have been the twentieth time last week.

Sincerely,

Scott Edelman

• • •

To: Marc Zicree

From: Ted Klein

Do you know what the hell this guy is talking about?

• • •

To: Ted

From: Marc

This Edelman guy is either senile, deluded, or lying. I'm sure these episodes were never filmed; none of the people I've interviewed for my *Twilight Zone* book remember writing or acting in any of them.

Tell him that April Fool's Day is long past and to stop bothering busy New York editors with his fruitcake fantasies.

• • •

Dear Mr. Edelman:

None of us at *TZ*—including Marc Scott Zicree, out in Los Angeles—has heard of the episodes you claim to have seen. Would it be possible for you to tell me a little more about them?

Sincerely,

Ted Klein

• • •

Dear Mr. Klein:

I'll do better than that. Take a look at these 8" x 10" glossies I shot off my Zenith last night.

Sincerely,

Scott Edelman

• • •

To: Marc

From: Ted

Check out these photos. If this is a hoax, this man has hired the best damned photo retoucher alive. There's one I find particularly intriguing; it shows Rod Serling delivering his monologue beside an obviously henpecked Wally Cox while a fierce-looking Billie Burke smashes Cox's record collection.

This can't be the real thing...can it?

• • •

To: Ted

From: Marc

I've studied the enclosed photos. This has *got* to be a dream...so you'd better rush over to Brooklyn for a peek at that television set before we both wake up and regret it!

• • •

To: Carol Serling

From: Ted Klein

Please sit down when you read this letter. What I'm about to tell you may seem strange at first, but I'm sure you'll agree after you watch the enclosed videotapes that all is as it should be.

You will see a *Twilight Zone* episode about a pacifist G.I. (William Bendix) forced to fight with Death (Raymond Massey) to win life for his platoon. You are going to watch Larry Blyden become the first comedian to make a Martian laugh, and shiver at the reward he gets from the citizens of the red planet. You will be amazed to see Rod introduce us to Ed Wynn as an oddball inventor who solves all of mankind's problems and then is visited by a very unhappy President of the United States (Bob Crane) who finds that without miseries to try to cure, the government is slowly losing its power.

I'm confident that Rod, somewhere, is still creating the magic that makes people happy and makes people think, and that if you stay up late enough in Scott Edelman's apartment with just the right dosage of fatigue and the correct degree of insomnia, you will be able to see him at work with a crew of otherworldly compadres. But the eerie fruits of his labors can only be seen on one battered television set in Brooklyn.

And to answer the question I've already asked myself, which is where the signals this set picks up are being broadcast from, I can only let Rod's words speak for him.

"There is a fifth dimension, beyond that which is known to man..."

I WISH I KNEW WHERE I WAS GOING

I'd left work early that day, the knuckles of my right hand still sore from where they'd finally—or as my wife, Lori, would surely say, inevitably—met the chin of the man who signed my paycheck. Not the smartest thing in the world to do, and yet, instead of being shocked by what I'd done, I was only surprised that I'd managed to hold off as long as I did. Jerry had it coming. With yet another less than amicable resignation behind me, I drove aimlessly through the nearby streets, my hands wrapped tightly around the steering wheel.

I knew that if I hadn't left the office, my hands would have ended up wrapped tightly around Jerry's neck instead.

I wanted to go directly home to Lori; really, I did. But I just couldn't. I'd had to explain too many of these incidents to my wife over the years, and our marriage wasn't in such a state as to support another one easily. I was not looking forward to the conversation awaiting me whenever I got home. I turned on the radio, then turned it up, and tried to ignore the future.

With my only possible destination something I was trying to keep at a distance, I was in no hurry at all, and quickly grew bored with the clogged city streets. Each woman I'd pass would look up at me with a frown. *Get back to work*, their expressions seemed to say.

Instead, I headed for the highway.

That's where I always got my best thinking done. No stop lights to demand my attention, no sudden turns to pull me out of my reverie. I didn't need an autopilot button on my dashboard, I had one in my brain. On highways, I would drift into a peaceful meditative state, floating along the road beyond conscious thought, until whatever problem it was that had been eating at me washed away, and I was ready to return to the real world.

It's always worked for me. And I haven't had an accident yet. At least, not one that I couldn't walk away from.

I eased onto the ramp, peering over my scraped knuckles, unsure whose blood was dried on my ripped skin, mine or Jerry's. At that point, I didn't much care.

About a hundred yards along onto the highway, a slight old man stood with his back toward the flow of traffic. His worn coat snapped in the breeze stirred up by the car's passage, almost yanking him off his feet. He didn't seem much to care, though, as he walked slowly along and continued to stare at the waist-high weeds.

He looked as if he could use a meal. Since I hadn't lasted long enough at the office that morning to eat lunch, my untouched sandwich was beside me. I reached for it, then grimaced, looking away as I passed the man by. I should have chucked the brown bag out the window, but I wasn't feeling too charitable that day, especially not in a world that didn't seem to have any charity left over for me. I pushed him from my mind quickly. The only thoughts I had room for now were about Lori.

How could I explain to her that yet again, I had done what I had sworn I would never do? Those late-night promises I'd make while licking tears from her cheeks were never easy to remember in the light of day. I only—and always—remember them *after* whatever it is I do. I knew I could not improvise on my return home and succeed. I needed to plan the speech I would give her. I needed to decide what to do.

As I crested a hill much too quickly, I saw a hitchhiker by the side of the road in the depression below. His thumb was already thrust out, as if he'd known that I was coming. He must have heard the motor of my car, or so I figured. After all, when you keep losing jobs the way I do, you can't afford the best.

With all the aimless driving I did after getting worked up like this, you'd think I'd see more hitchhikers. But not these days. I guess people considered it too dangerous now. If you can't even trust your friends anymore, how can you trust a stranger?

I couldn't make out his cardboard sign, not even when squinting. As I slowed while nearing him, I could see that the ink had been turned into an unreadable spider by too much rain, too many long, unsuccessful nights. The sign might as well have been blank.

I stopped, and waved him over. His hair was long and his beard was full.

"Where are you headed?" I called out to him.

"Not sure," he said, shrugging. "That's not always an easy question to answer."

"Then get in," I said.

He dropped his backpack between his feet on the passenger side and meticulously connected his seat belt. That did nothing toward making me want to put on mine. I began to drive on.

"You really should wear these," he said, as we accelerated, "if you don't want to go through the window."

"And you really should learn not to bitch to the driver," I said, in no mood to listen to the complaints of a self-righteous freeloader, "if you don't want to go through the door."

We drove on in silence. I mostly looked at the scenery, trying to figure out why I'd bothered to pick him up. I guess I felt I owed some debts for the times people stopped for me. I wasn't sure why my normally lax sense of responsibility had chosen today to assert itself, because with him present, it was harder to think about the things that really mattered. A confrontation with Lori was waiting for me, and doing a good turn wasn't going to make it any easier when the encounter finally arrived.

Winter was coming, and the branches we passed were growing as bare as my heart. The trees, stripping down for the darkness to come, yet knowing in their own way that they were headed for another spring, were a slap in the face of my life, a refutation of all that I had done with what I had been given. Even a tree knew where it was headed, but I, with darkness at my own shoulders, just ignored the ticking clock and drove aimlessly.

In that instant, I saw myself clearly, and it hurt. I found myself speaking, me, a man who disliked pouring out my inner guts even to Lori, the words coming out almost before I was conscious of them.

Before I could figure out a way to stop them.

And almost as if we were singing in a harmony of despair, my passenger said the same words along with me:

"I wish I knew where I was going."

I turned to look into his eyes the moment I heard his voice. And I *knew*.

It was like looking back at myself. They were my own eyes, only younger. I'd been too fixated on my despair to notice it before. A wild honking pulled my attention back to the road, and I swerved to miss a truck that was shifting back into my lane in front of me after passing. As the truck rumbled on, I pulled clumsily to the side of the road, my spinning tires tearing up grass. My heart was pounding, though not from the near-miss.

It was from the eyes.

I shut the engine, and shifted toward to him. Toward me. He didn't seem to care that we'd almost had a collision. He poked at my lunch bag.

"Still ham and cheese, right?"

"You're me," I said. I was amazed that he could be so calm as to talk about sandwiches.

Beneath his beard was the chin I now wore, though smoother, and without the hard knocks I had taken there from the years he had yet to see that would pass between us. His flesh was not yet as chunky as mine had become; he was still a walker, who worked through his problems by moving his feet, instead of randomly spinning a steering wheel.

He nodded serenely.

"Always was. Always will be."

"How?" I asked. "Why?"

He shrugged as he had earlier, and this time I recognized it as the casual way I once used to.

"You don't seem very shocked."

He shrugged yet again. I was beginning to see why everyone I'd known had always found those shrugs of mine irritating, and why I'd eventually stopped. He unwrapped my sandwich, and took a quick bite.

"I guess I figured," he said, talking through the food, "that if I kept sticking my thumb out long enough, something like this would happen."

"But I don't remember anything like this."

"You've forgotten a lot of things."

I felt shocked and insulted by my own presence. I was unsure of what to say, yet also unsure whether even if I'd miraculously known what to say, that I'd have been able to say it.

My emotions were at war. I wanted him—me—out of my car; I wanted him with me, at least until I knew why he had come. I hated the way he so easily seemed to accept this; I needed that calmness to anchor me, to keep my own final faint traces of calmness from floating away.

I would have stared into those eyes forever, frozen like a deer pinned by headlight.

But then:

"Drive on," he said.

He finished the sandwich, neatly folded the bag, and dropped it into his pack. I started the engine, and took a deep breath. Once there was a break in the traffic, I pulled out. The noon rush hour was building, and all those others who, unlike me, had managed to last until their appointed times were starting to join us.

"But we don't know where we're going," I said.

"We'll get there anyway," he said.

He placed a hand gently on the steering wheel. A crumb of cheese was stuck beneath his thumb. We steered together clumsily, each responsible for the way we went and each at the same time not, with the same diffuse liability one feels when guiding the marker of a Ouija board. But somehow we stayed on the road. We did not crash. It did not take long for the highway to fall away, to be replaced by streets again, streets like the ones I had earlier tried to escape. Streets with homes, and presumably, with families inside. I had always believed, as I drove, that those sheltered families invariably knew how they had gotten into those boxes, and also exactly where they were going. I had always believed that I alone was aimless. Now, still aimless, I wasn't alone any more. I had a partner in my drifting.

He did not release the wheel until we were parked in a driveway. I did not peer out of the car to check our destination. Instead, I watched his thin fingers as he pulled his hand away. He was the one who first peered out of the car, toward the house in front of us. I guess I was not as interesting to him as he was to me.

"This is where I live, isn't it?" he said.

I looked up, surprised at where our journey had taken us.

"No," I said. "This is where *I* live."

He leaned forward to grab his pack, but I stopped him with a light touch.

"Let me go in first," I said, quietly. I trusted that he would listen. I think because that's what I would have done once. "There's a lot to explain."

He shrugged again, my mirror memory self, and I left him there.

Even though I'd only found him a short while before, I felt suddenly alone walking toward the house. Leaving him behind that way made me aware of a hole within myself that I'd never even considered. He'd temporarily plugged a cavity which I had not known had previously existed until we parted. I didn't feel grateful for that lesson, the fruits of which I suspected would remain long after he left.

When I entered the house, Lori was in the kitchen. She turned toward me, and a warm smile slipped out, but she quickly pushed it away, tightening her lips. She'd gotten good at hiding herself like that.

"You're home early," she said.

I shrugged now. Damn! Her eyebrows went up. I could see she was trying to figure out where that shrug had returned from, and why. I would have told her if I truly knew.

"I tried phoning you an hour ago," she said, her voice shaking. She was working hard to hold back her judgment. "Liz told me that you took a swipe at Jerry."

"He deserved it," I said.

"They *always* deserve it." With that, her body joined her voice in its quivering. She hugged herself to try to make it stop, and I knew I should have hugged her as well so that we could make it stop together, but I did nothing. "Mike deserved it and Carlos deserved it and Jerry deserved it and anyone who ever tried to tell you what to do, god damn it, they all deserved it. Is that it? Sure, that must be it. None of it could ever be your fault. Not even goddamned once."

As tears began to rake her cheeks, she turned away. She never liked me to see her cry.

"Come on, Lori, it's not that bad." I had gotten good at lying on this subject, or so I thought. "You're acting like I do it deliberately. It's no big deal. I can always get another job."

"And how long will you keep that one?" She leaned against the sink. One hand gripped the counter far too close to the knife block. "Things will start out fine, they always do, you're great at first impressions, you really are. But each morning when you leave, I'll have to worry about whether *this* is the day you'll screw it up again. No. I don't want to have to wait that way again. I'm getting too old for this. I can't do it anymore. We're going to end that kind of waiting. You will go back to Jerry today, apologize, and get your job back. If you can get through that, if you can be grown-up enough to pull it off...then I'll know you'll stay."

"Lori, you're not thinking straight. I can't go back. I *hit* him, for Christ's sake."

She did not answer me, not at first. She turned on the faucet, and bent low over the sink to scoop water against her cheeks. Then she paused and watched the water run. When she spoke, it was without turning toward me.

"If you don't go back and at least try," she said, "then I'll go there and beg. I swear I will."

Her cheeks were red when she turned back to me. Her face was damp, but what was water and what was tears, I could not tell. I did not like doing the things that made Lori look that way, but somehow I could never stop. And somehow was a terrible word, because "somehow" meant I could never figure out the *why* to it. Before I could think of a way to empty those eyes of tears...

I entered the room.

Lori turned, and the hot flush paled from her cheeks.

"I thought you were going to wait," I said.

"So I waited," he said.

She looked from me to...me. Her expression did not change. I held my breath. She finally nodded.

"Yes?" she said. She seemed to accept so easily, as I had. There is no room for doubt, I guess, in the face of a true miracle.

"Look, I was going to explain," I said to her. "I was getting around to it. We just got sidetracked, that's all."

"What's there to explain?" she said.

"I'll explain," he said, sitting at the kitchen table.

He reached into his pack and pulled out a cigarette. With his thumb, he flicked open a matchbook cover from a bar that had been torn down ten years ago. He coughed as he took his first drag.

"I don't do that anymore," I said.

"You see," he started, ignoring me. He looked around for an ashtray. Finding none, he shrugged, and pulled an empty Coke can from the pack. "Let me tell you something about your husband. It's something that I hope you have already figured out, but no one's ever bothered to tell him. He's not used to being thwarted. In fact, up until he graduated college and entered the real world, he never was. So when the way he chose to order his life began to be threatened, he didn't take too well to it. He didn't know how to deal with it. He may try to hide it under a million logical excuses, but what it comes down to is that if he can't get things done his way, he won't hang around to do it any way at all."

"His way isn't working any more," said Lori. It hurt to see them together.

"His way never works. Not in the long run."

"Don't psychoanalyze me," I said.

"Sorry," he said. "But who knows better? It all fits, though, don't you see? Face it. You just never learned how to make it in the real world."

He tapped the cigarette ash against the can. The smoke hurt my eyes, as if I needed anything else to make me regret the fact that I'd brought him into my home. I saw the way Lori was looking at him. He was the one she'd fallen in love with, not me.

Me, I was just what she'd ended up with.

"How long will you be staying with us?" she asked. "I'm sure we'll all have a lot to talk about."

"Not very long at all," I said, jumping in before he could answer. "I picked him up hitchhiking. He has other places he has to be."

She didn't buy it. She looked at him for the answer instead.

"I don't really know," he said. "I don't know how I got here, and I don't know how I'll be going. So I guess I'll be here as long as I have to. And then I'll go. I don't think it's up to me."

"It's up to me," I said, moving toward him. "You'll go now."

"Wait," said Lori, moving between us. "For God's sake, after what's happened today, can't you see that's not the way? We...I don't know, it sounds ridiculous, but we need him now. I think that without him, we may fall apart. He's only been here for minutes, but still, he's what's holding us together right now. Damn, don't look at me that way, you know what I mean, not him, but the part of him that's still in you."

"I don't goddamn need him," I said, "or any goddamned part of him."

I stormed out of the house. They followed me to the car, but I locked the doors before they could get in. I pulled out fast, and left them standing there on the front lawn I had so often been nagged into mowing. Lori's head was hung low. He just stood there, staring at me hard. I could tell he wanted to hurt me. The last I saw before turning a corner, he touched a hand to her shoulder.

I can be such an idiot.

I sped back to the highway. My heart was pounding. I tried to think. I tried to slow down my thoughts enough so that I could hear what I was thinking.

I hated to do this to Lori, run away in fear and anger, spitting gravel on her love, but I just couldn't stop myself. He was right. And god damn it, how it hurt to admit that stupid, idealistic kid could be right about anything.

I *don't* know how to deal with the things that refuse to fall into step with my plans. I wouldn't bend for anything. Not for the companies where I worked, not for her. Not for *anyone*. But would I have admitted that? No. That morning, had I been asked, I would have said that except for an occasional unavoidable flare-up, much like those that anyone might have had, the world and I got along fairly well. Afternoon came, and I realized that was an illusion. I'd been kidding myself for years. The easy confidence of my college days had given way to the realism of an adult world that threatened to crush my soul. I'd been so sure of myself before I'd begun playing the game of life, when I was just on the sidelines, but now that I was *in* the game, the rules did not come so easily to mind. I hadn't realized until today that one man had turned into another. I wasn't able to fix the problem because I wouldn't admit there was a problem.

I could not go on this way any longer. Lori was right. My way wasn't working. I had to change. Maybe that was what my younger self had been sent to tell me, the message of his mission. He came to force me to see where I had gone wrong, how far I had fallen from where I once was. Yes! It was at last within my power to change. I had promised Lori many times that I would change, that next time and then yet again another next time things would be different. And each sincere promise always turned out to be a lie.

This time it would not be a lie. I was sure of it. This time my life would depend on it. My love depended on it.

I started to cry out of happiness. It had been years since anything like that emotion had been a cause of tears. Exultant, I spun the car through a cloverleaf, and headed back to my wife and myself. Toward where they were both waiting to show me the way. I laughed, and tasted my tears.

As I raced toward home, I saw the same little old man whom I had spotted earlier. He walked slowly, his shoulders drooping, no more than a mile along the road since I had seen him before. He seemed to be carrying all the weight I had just cast off. This time as I neared him, I felt generous. From now on, the world was going to be a different place, and I wanted to share my happiness.

I laughed once more as I pulled beside him. When I popped open the door, I could smell the sweat and dirt of him, but I figured that if he had to live with it for the entirety of each day, I could endure it for a few minutes.

"Come on in," I said, tossing a newspaper under him as he sat. "I can only take you as far as the next exit. It should be easy for you to catch a ride on from there if you want one."

I pulled out on the road again, and thought of Lori, whom I was fast approaching. I thought of the life we would have from then on, a hard but joyous one that I considered guaranteed. I saw it there before me. I'd find another job. I'd find once more the heart of my marriage.

The old man coughed then, a long rattle that broke my concentration, and almost my right eardrum as well. He hunched forward as he coughed, and when he fell back against the seat, he wheezed, and then spoke in a small, bewildered voice.

"Oh, God," he said. "I wish I knew where I was going."

The scabs on my knuckles popped as my hands tightened on the steering wheel. I turned, ignoring the urgent bleating of a car horn behind me.

I found myself looking into the solemn and bloodshot eyes of the poor, old man sitting next to me, and realized that though I had thought that at last I knew where I was going...I had been wrong.

THE TREMBLING LIVING WIRE

Iz slowly tightened his grip around Mozart's pulsing neck, savoring the last moments of life that remained. He paused, offering to the dog the gift of several final panting breaths. The beagle had earned that. After all, Mozart had been the key to unlocking Juliet's heart.

Yet what difference did one breath more or one breath less really make, Iz thought. All lives, however short their sputter, however long their flame, still seemed ridiculously brief. And except for the lives of a very special few, poignantly pointless as well. Rare those were, extremely rare, but rarer still the ones who could be shepherded to ripeness under his tutelage. One of those was young Juliet, and as soon as he accomplished this final step, all he'd need do was to pluck her.

As the eyes of the dog whom he had trained to trust him widened in response to the narrowing circle of his fingers, Iz became aware of a second, more human, gaze upon him. He dropped his hands from the animal and moved back, suddenly both alert and confused. It had been decades since he had last felt off balance like that—or had it been centuries?—and the unfamiliar emotion prickled.

He had trained himself to leave no witnesses behind to the sort of action that he was about to take, yet...how could there even be any? He considered the unfolding of his previous hours, perfect and tantalizing.

The evening's plans had proceeded smoothly. Juliet was now innocently asleep down the hall, slightly drugged, resting that beautiful, budding instrument of hers, and she would not rise until the timing was right, a timing Iz alone would control. Her parents, at the foot of whose bed he had been ready to act, were more deeply drugged, and would be unconscious at least until morning, if not beyond.

If there was any gaze upon him, it should only be that of the pet itself, and nothing more. But as Mozart lay there, one ear twitching eagerly as it anticipated what it mistakenly thought would be a comforting caress, it looked off toward a dark window on the far wall, eyes narrowing as if making a connection with the eyes of another.

Iz stood, and moved carefully, quietly, to the window outside of which something had apparently captured Mozart's attention. With long, delicate fingers, he slowly widened a gap in the curtains by a few inches so he could peer out from the darkness of the room to the darkness of the street. As he searched the night for a hypothetical unknown observer, his heart was the darkest of all.

The streets were empty, as they should have been in the town he had chosen, at least for this decade, to call home. It must have just been nerves, nothing more. Ever since the local paper had sewn together seemingly random incidents over the years into a string and called it a pattern, tensions had emerged in the town. No one had yet deciphered what it all meant (how could they?), but there was just enough unease floating freely there that Iz had begun to have his own fleeting moments of worry.

Perhaps it was now time for him to move on, to choose a new feeding ground, as he had been forced to do countless times before. But those intermittent feelings were quickly suppressed, for who would suspect *him*, kindly Mr. I, apparently old, outwardly frail, wanting nothing more each day than to pluck the heartstrings of his students until a bolder note might swell?

He closed the curtains more completely this time, leaving no gap to be used by a potential prowler. As he turned back to the bed, he momentarily considered Juliet's parents. If he could only explain to them what this sacrifice would buy, they would understand, he knew, in their hearts and souls, if not their minds. He was certain of that. But he could never share that bit of information, for his voice was not up to the telling. That task was beyond him. Though vocal gifts were his to be given, they was never his to possess.

And so best be done with it, and done with it quickly. He could already see through the blackness of the deed to Juliet's shining future. The short, sharp sound of a snapped neck would inevitably be followed in the days ahead—as so many other snappings and smotherings and shortenings had been followed—by the most beautiful sounds of all.

But Mozart was no longer atop the folded blanket at the foot of the bed. Which was itself as much an impossibility as any witness, for if the creature had moved, Iz would surely have heard the scratching of its nails on the hardwood flooring. No sounds escaped his ancient ears, which was both his blessing and his curse. He searched the rest of the house for the wandering beagle, but Mozart was nowhere to be found.

It was a puzzling absence, which Iz did not like, but what was more distressing than that oddity is what it meant—he would need to end his mission. He supposed he could suddenly and spontaneously escalate things, shift his attack from animal to man, but it was not yet time for him to move on like that. His life's work must not be rushed. For Juliet's sake, this composition was to be performed con adagietto, not con affrettando.

Never con affrettando.

He took one long, last look at Juliet asleep in her bed, tucked in by his hand. Not that she would remember. If he had calculated the dosage correctly (and he always did), that moment would be gone, now possessed by him alone, though if he had been especially precise she might still dimly remember the dinner which had preceded it. He curled over her, a question mark awaiting its answer. He caressed her throat, and leaned forward even more deeply to listen to the shallow breaths emanating from her lips, out of which such wonders were meant to spring.

That evening's music lesson would have to wait.

But not for long.

· · ·

As Iz took attendance the next morning at Helen Keller Middle School, the faces which ringed his own filled him with nothing but disappointment. That day, they failed to remind him, as they so often did, of the possibilities held out by the hours ahead. Instead, they only brought him back to the fact that his previous night had not gone as planned.

The classroom left him with no way to avoid that conclusion, for all of the faces which had been there the day before were with him still. Juliet, one foot tucked beneath her while she twirled this way and that in her seat and chatted with her neighbors, should have been missing. She should have been at home stewing in her pain and growing more flavorful for the private concert to come, but instead, there she was, her eyes offering no sign that she remembered his hands on her from the night before. Her presence—poignantly tender, intensely innocent, little knowing of the shadow which had almost passed across her face—distracted him as he tried to remain casual while taking the head count, but none of the students seemed to notice his estranged mood.

Not that they ever noticed much of anything, even on those rare occasions when he managed to prod them into more elevated and focused conditions. He moved behind his podium and tapped his baton, attempting to rouse them from their electronics-induced fugue states. Their relationship didn't have to be this way, which Iz knew better than anyone living could, because it *hadn't* always been this way. Unlike once upon a time, students and teachers seemed to exist these days in separate worlds, a hard, unyielding membrane keeping them artificially apart, and though the two groups could occasionally peer across at each other, they usually could not touch, and having any sort of impact was nearly impossible. But luckily, Iz had found a way to continue effecting change. As the text messaging and gum chewing gave way to the first tentative notes, each student seeking to find the proper key, he was grateful for his discovery, that such a way existed. For there were times that the music each produced was so excruciating that he saw not children, but merely many broken instruments in need of his expert repair, and in the absence of such an answer...well. Then there would have only been despair.

Iz started off the period with a quick run-through of the number which the chorus was to perform for the parents at the following week's Spring concert, a song taken from a Broadway musical in which the singers looked forward to those better times which would surely come tomorrow. Considering the limitations of the talent pool before him, and the failure of his most recent mission, Iz felt that his own tomorrows were running out. He did not see how the group could possibly be ready by then.

As he moved his hands through the air, trying to knit the discordant collection of children together into a voice that spoke as one, Iz glanced from one round, open mouth to the next, feeling a bit like a mother bird about to feed its chicks. But at the same time, he acknowledged that he lacked the true rearing instinct, for he did not see the need to save them all. He was always judging, constantly winnowing, looking to separate those with potential from those who could never, even with his tutelage, be more than merely adequate. And no matter how closely he examined his flock, the pick of the litter was always Juliet, poor Juliet, whose sweets and sours flavored his otherwise dull days.

His heart broke for her, as he picked out her tone from the rest, her voice a crystal. However, it was one a little bit too clear, not yet purified by the life experiences which seasoned one's soul. She was supposed to have been changed the night before, her spirit transformed by mortal inevitabilities, but instead, here she was, the same as always, good but not yet great, a sterling example of promise unfulfilled. As Juliet stretched for each note, projecting them one by one to the back of the room with a tone and control with which the average music teacher would have been satisfied, Iz was constantly aware of the potential there, and of how it could be wasted, always cognizant of the gap between what she could yet become on her own, and how far short that destination would fall of what he could make of her. He managed to hold those fates in his head simultaneously, both how much she had achieved on her own and what she might never achieve. Not without his guidance, a guidance which had given so much to so many.

As his fingers continued to dance, leading the choir along, he was able to hear not just the ones who that day performed bodily in front of him, but all the others who had come before, a long, unbroken string of everyone whose instruments he had tuned. In his mind, they were arrayed about him in a holy ring, interspersed with the contemporary chorus.

There was Ruth, whose voice had been merely pleasant, until the time she woke to find her favorite horse gutted beneath her bedroom window, and then it became magnificent. Michael's airiness grated, but after his house mysteriously burned to a husk, taking with it all the child held dear, his nature was properly grounded. Alyx, whose soul had appeared forever stunted, was one of those who required more extreme measures; an offering of her younger brother was required before she could break free of the bounds of the mediocre. And nearby was Rose, with a sweetness that could be treacly, until her father's death endowed her with a maturity well beyond her years, which encouraged her timbre to follow.

He had nudged them all, and countless others like them, to the fullness of their talents, and in his mind's eye they joined the serenade. They did not judge him for what he had done, and he believed that was not just because they did not know that the characters each accredited to chance had instead blossomed because of his more directed intent. Even if they'd known, Iz felt they would have forgiven him. Anything could be forgiven in the service to art, if one loved that art enough. After all, the world had tolerated castrati for centuries (no, more than tolerated—embraced) as a necessary sacrifice to music, as a gift offered up to the Lord, and what Iz had done, what Iz still did, was more or less the same, kinder even, as no one was left physically unmanned. Not that there might not yet be someone out there who might someday have to be.

The music, both that in the room and that only in his head, wafted him away to a place more like Heaven, but the slamming of a door clipped his wings and brought him harshly back down to Earth. His hands froze, and without his direction, the singers came to a ragged stop. He spun from the podium, prepared to snap at the intruder, but then held his tongue. It was Principal Trottle, whose status shielded him from the abusive outburst Iz had been prepared to give. A shadow of a girl stood beside the man, her head down, straight hair obscuring her face, her spirit so withdrawn that it took Iz an extra beat before he registered that she was even there.

"Good morning, class," said Trottle, and then gestured for Iz to approach.

"Excuse me, class," said Iz. He turned his back on his first-period choir and joined the visitors in a corner near the classroom door.

"This is Cecilia," said Trotter. "Cecelia, this is Mr. I."

Cecelia did not look toward Iz, but instead studied the rest of the class with an aspect that appeared like fear bordering on terror. Iz wished the girl would instead look at him directly, so he could gauge her prospects, make his first guess as to whether she would give the choir lift, or only weigh it down, but she would not meet his gaze.

"She's just moved to the area," continued Trottle, "and she'll be attending our school from now on. She's supposed to be quite a singer."

From anyone else, Iz might have accepted that evaluation, but Trottle was a moron, who wouldn't recognize good singing if entertained by the starry choir itself. Iz would have to be the judge. The girl didn't seem like much, and at first glance, didn't appear to have the self-confidence necessary to be a decent singer. Oh, perhaps Iz could whip her into passing shape for the upcoming mandatory performance before the parents, but he doubted that she'd be worth any more of his attention than that. He could likely tweak her to fool an untrained ear—he could do that to just about anyone—but he probably couldn't make her of interest to the only one who truly mattered.

"Thank you," said Iz. "I'll make sure she feels at home."

Once Principal Trottle was gone, Iz led the girl to the front of the class and placed her to stand with her back to the other students. Maybe the illusion that the two of them were alone together would assuage her fear and lend her an unconstricted voice.

"So the principal tells me you can sing," he said.

"Yes," she whispered, barely projecting far enough so that he could make out her answer.

Iz sighed, and rapped his baton sharply.

"Then let's see what you can do."

Before he could steel himself against the stillborn tone he was sure she would utter with a volume that would barely register and a pitch that would wound his ears, Cecelia tilted her head, the curtain of hair parting but slightly, revealing her mouth, but little else. She threw open that mouth and sent forth a pure and perfect note, and as it washed over him, its beauty was such that he almost sang a perfect note himself, that note which he dreamed about, and which he thought he could never utter, but only struggle to prod into existence in others.

Startled, he dropped his baton and gripped the podium tightly, offering up a prayer of thanks for its support, for without it he might have toppled backward. The silence once her note had been completed was staggering, the void that followed it too blank for him to dare to fill with his own voice. All eyes were on him, waiting for him to speak, but he could not, for language had fled. He slowly raised one hand, urging the class back to the song which Cecelia's arrival had interrupted. Cecelia did not move from where he had placed her, just stood there, the veil of her hair hiding her face once more. Iz wished that she would join in with the rest—didn't any teenager already know at least part of that song?—but she remained silent as the class continued at the same level of competence at which they had begun. This time, however, he did not care about the uneven tempo or occasional forgotten word, nor that their tone had become, by sudden contrast, hollow. Iz had grander things in mind.

He had them repeat the tune endlessly until the bell rang to dismiss them. As the other students started to shuffle out of the classroom, returning to their electronic distractions, he asked Cecelia to remain. He needed to provide her with the sheet music and other paperwork she'd need to catch up with the rest of the class, though even if there had been no reason to speak to her privately, he would have manufactured one. But before he could begin speaking to Cecelia, Juliet stepped up beside them.

Juliet. He had to think for a moment before he could remember her name. Cecelia's arrival had caused him to forget that she was even there.

"How did I do today, Mr. I?" she asked eagerly. Her words returned to him memories of her rich voice, but suddenly, today, that voice was no longer sufficient to excite him.

"Fine, fine," he said absentmindedly, waving her off.

"But Mr. I, don't you have any more tips for me, don't I need to—"

"Hurry along, Juliet," Iz snapped, interrupting her. "You mustn't be late for your next class."

Juliet glared at them both before heading out to join the throng in the hallway, not quite sure what had just happened, ignorant of how much happier her life would end up being in the future from the accidental gift of being ignored.

Once Iz was sure that they were alone together, he pulled a chair over to where Cecelia stood, and sat beside her so that their heads would be level. He handed her a quickly assembled packet while attempting to pierce the veil she had created and look into her eyes. But it was useless. She had built a shell around herself, whether intentionally or unconsciously he could not tell, but either way, he could not get inside. He would though. In time, he would.

"Your voice is remarkable," he said. "Let's talk about how you'll best fit in."

"But don't I need to get to my next class, too?" said Cecelia. "I don't want to be late either. Especially not on my first day. I want to make a good first impression."

"You're right," he said, returning to the professional persona which had served him so well for so long. It wouldn't do for his true self to yet show through. Not now, with such a prize at hand. "You run along. We'll talk later. Very nice to meet you, Cecelia."

Iz sat where she left him, quiet, thinking of nothing but her, and a first impression which had almost stripped him down to his soul, until the students for his next period exploded into the room and tried to flush her from his mind.

But they could not.

· · ·

At day's end, Iz rushed from the school to the employee parking lot in back. He pulled out ahead of the other teachers, who, though equally motivated to put the school behind them, had merely mortal reasons for their desire to escape, and thus did not have quite his speed. Driving slowly to the side of the red brick building, he parked alongside the string of school buses and watched the children as they boarded for home.

He knew them all, as the district forced each child to take a music class of some kind, even those for whom the experience was obviously pointless. He'd heard them all sing—or at least, attempt to sing—at the beginning of the school year as part of the sorting process to determine whether each would struggle with a tuba or limp along with him, though he rarely noted their names. He tended to remember them only by their flaws. There stumbled the boy whose low notes reminded him of a hyena with something stuck in its throat, here ran a girl who could only hit the proper key after first sampling all the other ones first. They were defined by their shortcomings, and once Iz knew those, he was free to forget all else.

Scattered randomly through the sea of mediocrity that pulsed before him were those few who mattered, rare children who had potential. He watched them board, too, such as Sarah, who had surely swallowed bells, Travis, whose voice had just that year begun to change from broken glass to stained glass, surprising them both, and Juliet, poor

Juliet, with tones of honey and spice, who until the start of the day he had thought his finest.

He watched them vanish into their buses with no sense of loss, because now, he cared only for one remarkable voice, hoped to spot just one special face. It had only taken a single note to tell him that. He had played this waiting game before with others, and now it had become her turn. His anticipation had never been so high, but then, neither had been the reward.

When Iz finally spotted her, Cecelia was walking slowly down the front steps of the school, her eyes on her feet as the other students swirled around her. Instead of boarding one of the buses, she ignored them each in turn, and walked past the line to exit the school grounds and take to the streets. Iz waited impatiently for her to proceed a few blocks ahead before he pulled out to follow her slowly. Did she understand how lucky she was to carry such a gift, to have been chosen like that to fly so high, to have come so close to touching the sky? He doubted anyone her age could, which was why the gifted always needed him. This one had come the furthest on her own of any he had seen before save one, but that only meant that she also had the furthest still to go.

Cecelia paused every few blocks, as if she had forgotten something, at which point she would then kneel to paw through her knapsack. She apparently would find nothing, or so it seemed to Iz, no matter how often she looked. Each time she stopped, he would tap his brakes as well, trying to blend in among the parked cars of the suburban streets. He knew what he would have looked like to anyone who could have seen and connected the two of them, but no matter. He needed to track that voice back to its source, to perhaps hear the sound of it once again so he could better envision the voice that would surely come after he had exercised his craft.

After one more stop to rummage, Cecelia turned suddenly, and started walking back in the direction of the school, which also meant that she was walking toward *him*. He turned the steering wheel, but before he could pull out, make a u-turn, and avoid any confrontation, she caught a glimpse of him and began heading his way. He surveyed the street. They were alone. He tried to calm down. Perhaps he could use this accidental encounter to his advantage.

Cecelia came up to his car and tapped on the glass. He lowered the window, and hoped that he was not blushing with love.

"Hello, Mr. I," she said, as if she saw nothing extraordinary in finding him there, parked in a car along her path home. She let her book bag drop solidly to the pavement, and grunted.

"Hello, Cecelia," he said. "What a surprise."

Cecelia shrugged, nearly imperceptibly.

"My backpack is heavy, Mr. I.," she said. "Teachers load you up with so much stuff the first day."

"Then you should probably have taken the bus, Cecelia," he said. "Why didn't you? Isn't that what your parents were expecting?"

"I don't...I don't like buses," she said. Even with their faces close together as they were, he could not make out her expression. "Do you think you could drive me home, Mr. I? It would just be this once. I'll figure something else out for tomorrow."

"Will your parents mind?" he asked, feigning concern for anyone's desires save his own. And God's.

Cecelia looked down for a moment, which he could barely make out through her curtain of hair.

"There's only my father," Cecelia said, in a whisper that belied the voice he knew was there. "My mother died, Mr. I. That's...that's why I don't like buses. Besides, why would he mind?"

Iz surveyed the street, and finding them unwatched, decided...why not? When God provides you with an opportunity, you should take it. He quickly cleared the passenger seat of the stacks of private records he was never supposed to have removed from school property in the first place, and she climbed in next to him.

"Make sure to fasten your seat belt, Cecelia," he said, out of sincere concern. If anything were to happen to her...it would be like trampling a Stradivarius. "Now, which way do we go?"

Cecelia directed him, and as they zigged and zagged, he tried to fill the small space that enclosed them with small talk, but none of his usual patter seemed to work with this girl. Could it be because whatever had caused the soulfulness of her voice had already lifted her beyond the usual childish concerns? Whatever the reason, their talk as he drove was elevated far beyond his usual chatter.

"So what is it that you don't like about buses, Cecelia?" he asked. Because she was looking out the passenger window, her head tilted away from him, and did not answer at first, he wasn't sure that she had heard him. "Cecelia?"

"My mother," she finally answered. "My mother was killed by a bus. She was crossing the street and didn't see it coming. That's why I don't like buses."

"I'm sorry, Cecelia," he said.

But he was not. He was glad that Fate had pushed Cecelia so far before he'd arrived to intervene. The special qualities in her voice were there for a reason. She now only needed just one final push, but what should it be? Iz could not take from her other parent, because if he did, she might then be taken from *him*, sent away to a relative or a foster home, and he'd never get to personally experience the fruits of his labors. But he wasn't worried. Once she led him to her house, he would surely find the special something he was meant to remove from her young life, a taking which she would someday come to realize was really a form of giving. He could almost hear her future song, and so abandoned his attempts to make conversation, lapsing into silence so that he could attend to that promise as he drove. He didn't stop listening to it until Cecelia's cry of, "Right over there, Mr. I!"

The house looked like many another in the neighborhood. There was nothing remarkable about it, and even from just a glimpse of the outsides, he could tell that Cecelia and her father had obviously not been there long enough to individualize it. There were no curtains on the windows, no decorations on the porch. In fact, if Cecelia hadn't led him to it, if he had just passed it in his wanderings, he would have taken it to be abandoned. Iz could visualize its layout easily, for he had surely been in one like it over the years, meeting with unsuspecting parents, bonding with children in preparation for his special sessions. Perhaps he had once even been in this very home, helping develop a unique talent in his unique way.

Before he could unlock his car and walk her to the door—he'd hoped that he'd be able to steal his first peek inside to begin his calculations of the next step—she had already sprung from his car and was up the path, giving him no time to follow. Cecelia turned in the doorway as if only as an afterthought, waved at him, and then slowly shut him out.

No matter. He now knew where she lived. There would be plenty of time to get acquainted later.

• • •

Iz called in sick the next day, the first time he could remember doing so, surprising both the school administrator and himself. He had just never found it necessary before. Not that he was actually feeling ill—he didn't know whether that was even possible—but suddenly, he was not content to wait for the workings of his relationship with Cecelia to play themselves out at the usual pace. His need to better understand what was to come, and understand it quickly, had become an urge, and so instead of showing up at work to pretend that he cared any longer about the other students, he instead stole the time to retrace his path of the day before.

He rolled slowly by Cecelia's house, then turned a corner onto a side street and parked as far away as he could while still being able to keep an eye on the front door. He watched intently as Cecelia left, walking in the opposite direction toward the school, keeping to her decision to avoid the bus, followed shortly thereafter by her father, leaving for whatever dead-end job of which he was still capable. Iz could not make out the man's face as he drove off. He knew what the mother's death had done to Cecelia. But what had it made of the husband? The inside of the house would tell soon enough.

Iz circled the car around to a more remote section of the subdivision, one where it was less likely to be noticed, and walked through a dense stand of woods to approach Cecelia's property from the backyard. The door and windows of the house were locked, but he entered easily anyway, one of the tricks that time had taught him. Once inside, he moved through the home slowly, for after all, he did have all day. As he pored over their possessions, he interpreted the meaning of each object, inventorying her soul, looking for that thing which when subtracted from her would add to her the most. His task that day wasn't as easy as it usually was, however, because the environment into which he stepped had not yet developed a personality. The messy canvas of life was blank. The rooms were mainly filled with moving boxes, the contents accrued by father and child still hidden. Very little had yet been unpacked.

By Cecelia's bedside was a family photograph, seemingly taken not that long ago, for Cecelia was basically unchanged from how Iz had just seen her. Both parents were hugging her, one on either side of the child, three smiling faces. The mother was beautiful, and Iz could see a sadness there, even with the smile, but it was a sadness that would be as nothing compared to that which would eventually visit Cecelia.

But how best to deliver it? He could not kill Cecelia's mother, because the woman was already gone in a bizarre traffic accident. But if Iz studied Cecelia long enough, he knew that he would find something. He always did.

Iz spent the rest of the day peering into boxes, seeking a sign. But he could sense no direction in clumsily-made summer-camp ashtrays, posters of movie stars too distant for any affecting tragedy to be possible, and paperback romance novels, or in the cache, found hidden under stained work shirts smelling of tobacco, of the father's pornography. It was a good beginning, but with the heart of the home still hidden by the move, he saw that he wouldn't be successful that day, no matter how much time he had to devote to it. He would have to wait as the house blossomed into a home, as the placement of each object told tales of their significance, to see if any further clues would be delivered.

When he felt he had lingered long enough, he moved the car back to his earlier vantage point and watched as first Cecelia, and then her father, returned home. He sat there until the skies grew dark and the lights inside Cecelia's home spilled over onto the front lawn.

Then he closed his eyes and trembled.

• • •

The following week pulsed to a steady rhythm, one to which Iz tried with great difficulty to surrender. It was difficult to remain adagio when his heart screamed that all should proceed allegro. Too much time had to be spent in pretense, keeping up the outer shell of his life, but he had lived that way for too long to abandon the face the world knew, not even with the stakes so high. So he continued to spend his days in attempting to teach the unworthy, while the afternoons which followed were filled with rehearsals with those he had cherry-picked for the Spring concert performance. Only the evenings were truly his, and he devoted them to studying Cecelia.

He would park in the secluded back street he had found and walk to her house, always approaching the structure the same way, from the woods by its backyard, and never from the street. Once he did what had to be done next, he did not want to have left behind the memory of any chance encounter with a bystander which could expose his involvement. He found a stump, well hidden, and topped to just the right height to act as his perch for the evening. He would stare at the well-lit windows that dappled the darkness, glad that the mother was gone, even though that meant he could not take her to give Cecelia the push she needed, because a woman would have put up curtains immediately upon moving in, and he would then have been unable to play voyeur. From this side of the house he could make out the kitchen and the den downstairs, and the two bedrooms upstairs. He watched for hours, rapt by the silent shadow play.

The action would begin on the first level of the house, as Cecelia prepared dinner for her father, who sat dumbly in the breakfast nook, head down, while his daughter worked. Because of his angle of observation, Iz could not see just *why* his head was down. Was he lost in a fog of mourning for his wife? Or just reading a newspaper spread out upon the table? Iz hoped it was the former. After they ate, they would sit together in the den, watching television. He could not make them out at all, just the flickering of the screen. He could not hear the sound of it, nor their conversation, but as he imagined it, there wasn't any; they had been cut off from each other by the great tragedy which had staggered them both. Occasionally, Cecelia would get up and move to the kitchen, returning with a beer for her father, then once more vanishing from view. After several hours of this, and more than several beers, the downstairs lights would be extinguished, and the two moved upstairs to their separate rooms. The father paced for a few minutes, then quickly became invisible. Iz imagined him falling asleep stop the unseen bed with the lights on, unable to bear the darkness.

Cecelia, however, would sit at the desk Iz had seen there the previous day, her face perfectly framed by the window. Alone in her room, with nothing there to hide from, she would run her fingers through her hair, pushing it away from her face. She was beautiful, too, like her mother, but unlike her mother, she was one of those girls, would become one of those women, who obviously did not know she was beautiful. Sometimes she looked down, perhaps reading a book, or doing her homework, or even writing in a diary, for that last was what he had learned all young girls did, even though he had not found one yet. Sometimes she just stared off into the darkness, not knowing that this time the darkness was staring back. Iz would stay that way, soaking in her unconstructed essence, until her light would go off, and then he'd sneak quietly away, sleeping but little until the cycle resumed again.

• • •

Iz took Cecelia aside after class one day and offered to tutor her privately. She would need it, he told her, to catch up with those he had been teaching far longer and be ready for the concert, even though she was in truth far more advanced than any of the others. But she seemed to accept what he had to say. He could not tell whether she actually agreed with him, or was just too stunned by life to care one way or another any longer about how that life proceeded.

During one of their sessions, while running Cecelia through her scales, scales which Iz had never heard performed so perfectly before, he thought that he could make out the incursion of a certain...coarseness. And so he stopped her.

"What is it, Cecelia?" he asked. "You seem distracted."

"It's nothing," she said, from beneath her curtain of hair. Now that he was seeing that face each night, even though it was from a distance, he found that her veil did not disturb him quite as much.

"I don't believe you, Cecelia," he said. "It's something. Something is bothering you. A music teacher can always tell. You should know that. Your music teacher is the only one in the school who can truly see into your soul. No guidance counselor, no school psychologist can do that. You can't hide from me, Cecelia. Now, what's wrong?"

"It's my father," she said, so quietly that he would not have been able to hear her had his ears not been so well trained by the ages.

"Yes?" he said.

Her mouth opened, but no sounds came out. Her silence extended for many beats.

"What is it?" he asked.

But she would not reply further, no matter how many times he prodded her.

"Is your father hurting you?" he asked. "Is that what's going on? You can tell me."

Even as he told her that, Iz could see—no, she couldn't tell him. There was just no way. So they sat there in silence until a tear dropped from her chin. He hadn't even been able to tell that she'd been crying.

"Let's just sing, Mr. I," she finally said.

"Yes, let's," Iz said. "You don't have to worry any more. I know just what to do."

And he did, realizing suddenly, as they returned to the scales, that the answer to how next to temper Cecelia's talent was now his. He now knew the final step. Whatever it would mean for his ability to see Cecelia in the future, the father had to go. Her voice demanded it.

• • •

Iz decided that he would take action the night of the Spring concert, an event which would provide just the distraction he needed. It had become a Helen Keller Middle School tradition that once any concert was over, the teachers would take the children out to Skiddoo's for ice cream, with a few parents tagging along as chaperones. Iz knew that Cecelia's father wasn't going to be one of them, but then, based on what Iz had seen, he had never expected him to be. Iz wasn't even sure that the man was going to be able to stir himself for the concert itself. He had been lost to a fugue state ever since the death of his wife, and apparently hadn't been really fully present since. Iz had no idea how the man had been able to summon the energy to move his truncated family to a new town. He barely had enough energy to make it to work each day. Iz didn't see that Cecelia's father would be that much worse off after what he had planned for him than he currently was.

Iz was too distracted to be fully present himself for the concert, because as far as he was concerned, the true performance would not be until later that night. If any of the children noticed, they didn't show it, and as for the audience, most of them were too busy tinkering with the controls of their cameras and camcorders to be present themselves. After it was all over, the principal thanked him as usual, hollow compliments indeed. Iz then excused himself from the pack of squealing children, and hurried off to Skiddoo's. He needed to arrive there first, so he could make sure that all was ready for his unseen departure.

Once the children and their chaperones were present, and having been served their rewards for having survived the experience, Iz tapped his spoon to one side of his ice cream sundae and stood.

"I'm proud of you all," he said, surveying the children as he spoke, while struggling against dwelling overlong on Cecelia. "I know that for many of you, it wasn't easy. But nothing worth doing ever is. Enjoy yourself. You've earned this night."

As the restaurant filled with applause, Iz slipped away to the men's room, sneaking from there through a window he had previously made sure was unlocked. He sped out of the parking lot and rushed to Cecelia's neighborhood, and then returned to the house via his usual route, picking his way through the underbrush in the darkness. He would be quick about this, and be back with his group before it was time to settle the bill. As he approached the home, the lone light inside came from the glow of the television. The father was obviously hypnotized by it, as he usually was of an evening. Iz slipped into his gloves, and opened the back door slowly and quietly, not that he'd have been heard over the din from the television even if he'd slammed the door open and rushed in.

He moved silently down the hall, wafted along by his memories of Cecelia's voice earlier that day, pulled forward by the even greater song which would spring from tomorrow's sorrow. Before entering the den where he planned to extinguish the father, Iz pulled a bowling trophy down from a nook where it had been placed during the previous week.

What was to occur had to look like the work of a random intruder. Iz would be there to comfort Cecelia, to show her what solace was to be found in music. He flexed his fingers around the base of the trophy, raised it over his head, and stepped quickly into the den.

Only—Cecelia's father was not there. Just Cecelia herself, seated calmly on the couch, hands folded in her lap.

Then...darkness.

• • •

When Iz woke, his head aching, the first thing that filled his field of vision was Cecelia's face, fully revealed, her hair swept back and tucked behind her ears. They were no longer in a dark room lit only by a flickering television. He could see that they were now in the basement, where she knelt beside him as he lay on his back. When he tried to touch the pulsing area behind his right ear, he found that he could not move his hands. Tucking his chin into his chest, he looked down the length of his body to see that he had been bound by piano wire. Iz heard a thud of footsteps behind him, but he could not turn to see the source. Then Cecelia's father shambled into view, a baseball bat in one hand, the bowling trophy which Iz had last been holding in the other.

"What's going on, Cecelia?" said Iz, speaking as steadily as the situation would allow.

Perhaps it would have made more sense to have talked to the adult in the room, but from the leaden look on the man's face, one far more dull than any Iz had yet seen on him, no one was home to hear any appeal.

"You know, you're not the only one who's figured out how to sneak out of a party, Mr. I."

"Untie me, Cecelia."

Iz struggled against the wires which wrapped tightly around him, but no matter how much strength he put behind his movements, they would not snap. His years spent in exile might have given him the accrued knowledge he needed to plan his tasks, and a certain canniness necessary to carry them out, but he had never been made as a repository for might. He remained as vulnerable as any mortal. As he wriggled against his restraints, he knew that there was only one way out, and that was through Cecelia.

"Let me go," he said to her.

"I don't think so, Mr. I.," she said. "For once, I think you're exactly where you need to be."

And then she closed her eyes and began singing a song so sad, he wept. Not for himself, even though that should have been the most proximate cause for weeping, with the wire cutting into his wrists and his future uncertain, and with a hulk of a man looking down at him blankly, a bloodied bowling trophy now hanging in his hands. Not for Cecelia either, who had in his presence *become* the song, transformed into a channel for sorrow. But rather for the whole human race, that it could produce such a voice. He cried for its beauty, and for those who would never get to hear its beauty, and for the miracle that he was lucky enough to be there in its presence, however bound. And as Cecelia held the final note, stretching it out so long that Iz thought it might go on forever, almost as if it promised that there might be no other moment on the other side of it, he remembered once teaching that same song to another. Another young girl whose raw talents demanded instruction in another city, at another time.

"You recognize my song," Cecelia said. "I see it in your eyes. That's good. You're starting to remember. But do you remember it all? Do you remember teaching it to my mother?"

He should have known, but he'd been too swept up by the remarkable voice, too distracted to have picked up on the resemblance between the faces, so similar at similar ages even with her attempts to hide it. He should have known.

"Cecelia, I—"

"Do you remember the other things you did to her? I do. She told me all about them before she left us."

"I'm sorry that she died, Cecelia, but—"

Cecelia suddenly leaned in so close she could have bit him if she chose. Or kissed him.

"My mother didn't just die, Mr. I. She killed herself. She tried, after all of the torment you put her through, to have a normal life. She married. She had *me*. But it was too much for her. You had worn her down. That was no accident that killed her. She left us a note, telling us everything. She stepped in front of that bus willingly. She just couldn't go on."

"But don't you see, Cecelia?" Iz said, tears of joy streaming down his face. "I may not have planned for your mother to have been snuffed out that way, but the grief was all for a greater good. Listen to your-self! If not for me molding first her and then through her you, you wouldn't have been blessed with this magnificent instrument. I was meant to find you someday. This is part of an eternal plan."

"No, Mr. I.," said Cecelia. "I was the one meant to find *you*. You think our move to this town was a coincidence? You think anything that happened here was accidental? While you were watching us all week, I was watching, too. This all went according to plan. *My* plan."

She stood, and backed away from him until she was at her father's side.

"You're close, Cecelia," he cried out. "So very close. Let me keep teaching you. I promise you, God Himself will weep. I'll give you a voice to silence the stars."

"Oh, there'll be silence, all right," she said.

Cecelia nodded to her father, and as the man approached, lifted the trophy high over his head, and brought it crashing down, Iz himself finally uttered the perfect note which had eluded him for centuries.

A PLAGUE ON BOTH YOUR HOUSES

Dramatis Personae
JONATHAN, a gravedigger
SAM, a zombie, freshly risen
VINCENT, Mayor of New York City
CARLO, the Mayor's son
EDDIE, his friend
LEOPOLD, King of the Zombies
DOLORES, his daughter
MARY, her maid
WOMAN REVELER
MASKED PARTYGOERS

Scene. Manhattan Island. Sooner than you think.

PROLOGUE.

A graveyard in lower Manhattan.

(Enter JONATHAN, a gravedigger.)

JON. Diseased New York, the setting for our play
　　　Has lost its glitter, trading it for grue.
　　　Cold dead come back, in graves they will not stay.
　　　The living bear no young, and dwindle few.
　　　I am an old man. I've seen many things:
　　　A walked-on moon, democracy again,

The death of tyrants, privilege, nations, kings.
Now hope is weak. I fear the end of men.
I plant them deep, yet somehow they thrust up,
As if Spring's breath has touched their wint'ry souls,
Enticing them to once more grasp life's cup,
and mount the stage, demanding their lost roles.
Is this a fate mankind deserved to earn?
Watch, and listen, and perhaps you'll learn.

(SAM, *a zombie, speaks from the grave, his voice muffled.*)

SAM. Hello, up there! Hello, world I once knew!
    Evicting dirt and worms from my parched throat,
    I cry out loud. I call for you, yes, you!
    Announcing, to the surface I must float!

JON. Dear friend, dead friend, are you so sure it's wise
    To spurn God's gift of your eternal rest?

SAM. This second life has come as a surprise.
    But who are you to judge for me what's best?

(SAM's *fist rises. His fingers uncurl like the petals of a flower.*)

JON. How dare I? I am he who oft' has dug
    The beds for those who should have stayed below.
    Thousands have I made forever snug,
    Yet now, like you, they do refuse to go.
    I'm one whom time has given weary arms.
    My bones seem less mine each passing day,
    Till I myself desire death's own charms.
    I'd take your grave if I knew I could stay.

SAM. Again, I say, you cannot speak for me.

Impertinence, is that thy Christian name?
Help me now. The sunlight I would see.

JON. My stomach will not let me play this game.
If you would live again, it's not my style
To interfere with what God means to be.
So though I think I'll rest with you awhile,
I'll watch, not interfere with fate's decree.

*(JONATHAN sits atop the mound of the grave,
setting his spade across his knees.)*

SAM. I wish, sir, if you're disinclined to help,
You'll stand, and hold me down not with your weight.
Assist or not the birthing of this whelp,
But please, sir, do not seek to bar the gate.

(JONATHAN sighs, and slowly rises to his feet.)

JON. Quite right, dead friend, forgive my actions rude.
Old age has brought a torpor to my soul.
I'll strive to demonstrate a friendly mood
And do my best to aid you to your goal.

(JONATHAN begins digging in the loose earth.)

SAM. I thank you, sir. You prove a kindly man.

JON. Kindness? No. No kindness in this flesh.
It's simply one man doing what he can
To help the live and zombie peoples mesh.
No longer are things as they once had been
When your kind ravaged mine, blind hate was strong,
And coming back from death was called a sin.

I'm just providing help to right a wrong.
My reticence was but resentment's trace
That my life's work has proven worthless now:
Unburied stay the children of your race.

SAM. I think not, friend, for to your skills I bow.
Long decades have you made your job the dead
As you have set them in the frigid earth.
But if those dead become a living mob,
Can you not act as midwife to their birth?

(JONATHAN pauses in thought, spade in hand.
By now a growing pile of earth rests beside the grave.)

JON. I never thought to find a new employer.

(SAM sits up, his head and shoulders becoming visible out of the grave.)

SAM. You've served the living, now you'll serve the dead.
Do not think of this plague as job destroyer.
Good men need never fear to earn their bread.

JON. Dear friend, dead friend, you are a man of wit.
I feel much younger now, with you to thank.
Ennui has fled. I'm like a new-born kit.
Here, let me help you from your prison dank.

(JONATHAN takes SAM's hand, and pulls the zombie up onto the stage. SAM
brushes clumps of earth from his tattered clothing.)

SAM. I'm glad, sir, that the captains of our race
Have made us into partners who can deal
With one another in this strange new place.
Time was you would have made my breakfast meal.

JON. If you in your new life are so relieved
　　Imagine how I feel. Your words have joyed
　　This one who surely would have felt aggrieved
　　To see myself as luncheon meat employed.
　　Times have changed. The world has made its peace
　　With how society transformed in decades past.
　　I'm pleased that you whom we do predecease
　　Now see us more as friends than as repast.
　　Let's celebrate the way the world has changed
　　From times of bloodshed filled with undead hate
　　To where our people's moods have rearranged,
　　So that we two can stand here and relate
　　How such a friendship could have come about
　　Amidst a world that did not value love.

SAM. Of love's transcendence there can be no doubt
　　Our God's transplanted heaven from above.

(JONATHAN and SAM face the audience and speak the next lines jointly.)

BOTH. Attend now as our players speak their parts
　　To see how hate must fade before true hearts.

ACT I.

City Hall. Afternoon.

(Enter VINCENT, Mayor of living New York City, with EDDIE, his son's closest friend.)

VIN. Dear Eddie, you are like my second sun

Which warms the dark spots of this troubled life,
And Carlo long has known that you are one
Who'll be there if he needs you with your knife.

ED. Of late that fact it seems he does forget.
He acts not as the Carlo whom I knew.
Instead, his features tremble with regret,
And though I try, there's little I can do.
As weeks have passed, I've marshaled every skill
To draw my friend your son from out his shell,
Used travel, women, sports, food, drink and pill.
But nothing's worked to wrench him from his hell.

VIN. That's why we meet today. I need your aid
To lift his mind from what has brought him down.
And so I will announce a masquerade
Where we two joined will rob him of his frown.

ED. I fear his stupor's far worse than you think.
It won't be awed by song, nor gaudy masks,
Nor laughter, magic, dancing or strong drink.
Lord Mayor, you could have chosen simpler tasks.

VIN. And yet, it's ours, I'm certain that we must
Soon free my boy from what has captured him,
For someday age will my keen judgement rust.
Then Carlo must rule, or else life will turn grim.

ED. I'll try, sir, for my love of him and you
To breach the walls he's built to keep us out
And though there may be nothing I can do,
I'll swear to fight till his dark side I rout.

VIN. Wait! Here Carlo comes, his head hung low.

No word to him of this, our secret plan.

ED. Let me to party preparations go.
    Tonight we'll make your son again a man.

(Enter CARLO. *As he draws close by,* EDDIE *exits.*
CARLO *is so lost in thought that he almost passes his father by.*
He pauses when he hears his father speak.)

VIN. It's sad, my son, your father you pass by,
    As if some loathsome stranger on the street.
    You act as if this morning you did die
    And post-death shambling zombiehood did meet.

CAR. O, father, dearest one, I could not bear
    For you to think my love for you had fled.
    Despondency does not mean I don't care
    Or that this form before you's joined the dead.
    It's just that life seems empty now, and sad,
    And there seems little prospect yet of joy.

VIN. At your age (listen now, and trust your dad),
    The world should seem to you a brilliant toy.

CAR. Speak not to me of "shoulds" in this mad globe,
    Which cast off "shoulds" long years before my birth.
    What shoulds? The dead should not shrug off death's robe!
    Young men should always feel life's full of mirth!
    A man should hand his son a better place
    In which to build a life that should know peace!
    There should be for each man a beauteous face
    Which makes pain go away and madness cease.
    No, "shoulds" you'll find won't sway me in the least.
    I've learned should's just a senseless bitter word.

VIN. Calm down, son, you're a man, not mindless beast.
　　　And now that I've your tortured anguish heard,
　　　It's time you cast it off, became like old,
　　　Became the son who caused a thousand sighs,
　　　Who danced around our enemies so bold,
　　　Dispatching those who dared again to rise.
　　　Your mental pallor's gone on long enough.
　　　You are my son. Someday you'll be the mayor.
　　　So show the world you're made of sterner stuff,
194　　　And start once more to act as if you care.

CAR. "Care" is one more word with little weight,
　　　For life's not black and white, but only grey,
　　　and I care not for what might be my fate
　　　and will do naught to grab one extra day.
　　　No wine can get me drunk enough to care.
　　　No woman make it worth the errant time
　　　To run my fingers through her golden hair.
　　　No staircase worth the effort of the climb.
　　　I've seen it all, I've tasted every sin.
　　　No longer do I care much if I lose,
　　　No longer seems it worth my while to win.
　　　It seems as if I wear another's shoes.

(CARLO *pauses, worn out by his own tirade.* VINCENT *places a hand on his son's shoulder.* CARLO *turns into an embrace.*)

CAR. For you, my father, I will try again
　　　To find some satisfaction on this orb,
　　　And join once more enthusiastic men
　　　In seizing all life's gifts I can absorb.

VIN. I welcome back my first and only heir.
　　　Let all your frozen fatal feelings fade.

Alive again you'll be and all things dare
Tonight once we commence the masquerade.

(*Exit* VINCENT.)

CAR. A masquerade? I know the man means well
And hopes to snare the stupor set in me,
But nothing's left to save me from this Hell
Nor magic spell my weary soul to free.
This night, I fear, may ruthlessly reveal
The very things he struggles to conceal.

ACT II.

City Hall. Night.

(VINCENT *addresses the assembled masked partygoers.*)

VIN. Welcome, friends, and friends-to-be! This ball
Does bring together all those not yet dead
Within the confines of a City Hall
Which centuries has stood while men have bled.
Let's take a moment, starting, to remember
How we are all that's left of what was life
And of our stand against those that dismember,
Destroy us, disembowel us, damn with strife
Our every human notion in this city—
The zombies, whose soiled name I spit as a curse.
Recall, as you peruse our world with pity
That only we can stop it getting worse.
Remember that humanity is ours,
That "let the dead stay dead" is our sole motto.
The zombies are as alien as Mars,

While we're mankind's last hope, a shining grotto.
So celebrate this gathering tonight
And raise a glass to what we represent.

CAR. If with those words my spirit he'd ignite,
He did instead aid in its dark descent.

(VINCENT waves happily to his son. CARLO raises one hand in response, a weak smile on his lips. A dance begins, and CARLO stands stage left and solemnly watches the roiling crowd.)

CAR. Life! Damned life! Is this all life is for?
Stumbling clowns in masks who can't forget
They're born of ordure and must die in gore?
Whose days are made of fear and woe and fret?
Is that a life? I'll make no life of this.
Had I been born before my time—perhaps!
But now—no thrill, no battle, no secret, tender kiss
Would take the place of death's own milky paps.
If I could make my flesh just cease to be,
I'd do it! Question not what I would choose.
I'd cut the cord, and set my soul asea
And worry not that I'd a thing to lose.
I'd leave now, but my father watches near
To make sure that my lips have formed a smile.
I wonder if he knows he's seeing mere
Falsehood on a face etched full of guile?

(EDDIE, slightly drunk, stumbles over. His arm is around a masked WOMAN.)

ED. Your father is a man of many graces,
Grand party-giving is his strongest point.
No better way exists to shed the traces

Of cruel despair in a life out of joint.

(EDDIE *holds the woman's chin, displaying it for* CARLO.)

ED. Look at this fair one. Beauty, is she not?
  More goddess true than any woman seen,
  A form the womb of heaven has begot
  To tempt me with the grandeur of a queen.

CAR. I've seen you drunk before, my good friend Eddie,
  But never past beyond the point of truth.
  Your words alone tell me that you are ready
  To pick up coffee and set down vermouth.

ED. It's not the wine that speaks, it's just your friend
  Who hopes your constant carping side to vex,
  And bring this cruel charade to wise, just end
  with help of sweet and tender female flesh.

(CARLO *shakes head sadly, denying the possibility.*)

CAR. No use, I fear. This thing has gone too far.
  Your tools have not the power to appease.
  Eddie, our clear friendship I'd not mar,
  But send her far away—she does not please.

WOM. I never dreamt that you'd heap cruel abuse
  On one whose sin was loving you too much.

(*The* WOMAN *leaves.*)

ED. I've never seen you wear a shorter fuse
  Can not tonight you lighten up a touch?

CAR. Give up, my friend! No secrets here tonight.
   My father planned this gloomy masquerade
   In hopes to set my somber soul alight.
   I'll have no part of this bereft charade.

(Enter DOLORES, *masked, attempting to pass for human. She pauses on the outskirts of the crowd.)*

CAR. And now, my last farewells to you I'll make.
   Goodbye, my friend, for it is growing late.
   Remember me when I was a young rake,
   And hate me not for leaving. Farewell. Wait!

*(*CARLO *notices* DOLORES.*)*

CAR. Who is that one who stands at party's edge
   Warily watching all those who pass by?
   As if she's made herself a solemn pledge,
   As if my own intransigence she'd try?
   Do you know her? Can you speak her name?

ED. Like all of us she hides beneath a mask.

CAR. Then find her out. You, hunter. She, the game.
   Be quick!

ED.   Your every wish becomes my task.

*(*EDDIE *hurls himself into the crowd.* DOLORES *evades him while* CARLO *watches.* EDDIE *returns, crestfallen.)*

ED. I've failed you, Carlo. Find her I cannot.
   It's just as if she's vanished like the dawn,
   Just when you had changed from cold to hot.

I'd hoped to celebrate, and now must mourn.

CAR. You've done your best, as friends are meant to do.
In losing her you've earned yourself no blame.
Know that you've always been forever true.
Our friendship long has never witnessed shame.
Do one more thing for our long friendship's sake,
And leave me here to think on this a while.

ED. I trust you still, and so your leave I'll take
And leave you with your thoughts as is your style.

(EDDIE *bows to his friend, and vanishes into the crowd.*)

CAR. Where is she? Where's the one I thought I saw
Who changed without a word my night to day?

(DOLORES *appears stage left, and watches him as he studies the crowd fruitlessly for her.*)

DOL. There stands the one my spirit wants to gnaw.
But heart says to my hungry spirit *stay*.

(CARLO *pauses in his search.*)

CAR. 'Twould torture be if one brief, blinding glimpse,
Was all of her I'd be allowed to taste.
She's vanished as if stolen off by imps,
This all too perfect vision, cool and chaste.
Until I saw her, I could not remember
What living my own life was really for,
But she's ignited some sad, sleepy ember
Inside of me, and breached my shuttered door.
I could have any woman who is here,

Or, for what it's worth, have any man.
My father's power sways all in this sphere
Who'd latch upon me for what gain they can.
But this fair one, who makes instead to hide,
Has something different in her form and soul
Than all those who would claim to take my side—
Only she can make me once more whole!

(DOLORES *moves forward and addresses the audience.*)

DOL. Beneath this mask is cold and lifeless flesh,
    Beneath this breast a heart that's dry and still.
    Yet seeing him my soul still wants to mesh
    And disobey God's law as lovers will.
    I am a zombie, and that one is man,
    And there should be between us naught but pain.
    Of intercourse between us there's a ban,
    Each other's visage should bring dark disdain.
    Enough of "shoulds"! It's shoulds that forged today,
    A world dissolved to bloodshed and to war,
    Escape from which no one can find a way.
    Is this what our creator made us for?
    So here I snuck, my father knowing not.
    His daughter dear desires something new,
    Unfettered by the world the plague begot,
    Expecting not to see this princely view.

(DOLORES *sighs as she stares at* CARLO *through the crowd.*)

DOL. But I was fool to come, myself to tease.
    Nothing but tragedy can come of this.

(DOLORES *starts to go, but at this moment* CARLO *catches up with her.*)

CAR. Lady! Tell me! How may I you please?
    What must I do to from you earn a kiss?

DOL. Tempt me not, for I was fool to come.
    'Tis better that we simply parted thus.

CAR. Say not those words which set me out of plumb.
    I beg you of our meeting do not fuss,
    Unless it is to say that by my side
    You'll stay, ignoring what the world might do.
    There's something in you close to what a bride
    Should have. A shining spirit clean and new.

(DOLORES *speaks an aside to the audience.*)

DOL. He speaks of brides. Remembers he the rhyme?
    How borrowed, blue, and old, and new should be
    Embodied in the bride at that rich time
    She walks the aisle? How true those words for me.
    Borrowed is my undead zombie soul.
    Blue my skin, except where it is grey.
    Old my bones which crack each time I stroll.
    New my fleshly hunger every day.
    How could a man in whom the blood still flows
    See anything but monster in my form?
    Leave him I must before the truth he knows,
    To let him keep his fantasy of norm.

(DOLORES *tries once more to leave.*)

CAR. Wait, my lady, why will you not speak
    Sweet words to me? Instead you make to go.
    I swear, my lady, my heart's blood will leak
    Until your name I'm privileged to know.

DOL. If truth you knew, you would not make that wish.
　　If I leave now we've nothing to regret.

CAR. You make yourself as slipp'ry as a fish
　　That tries to skip between a sailor's net,
　　But you will find in this case that the reel
　　Which seeks to pull you in won't let you go
　　As easily as that. So do not feel
　　I'll let you vanish 'fore your name I know.
　　I love you though I yet know not your name.
　　I love you though I've never seen your face.
　　In finding you I end the lover's game
　　I've played for years. For others I've no space.

DOL. If only love could keep such sure a course
　　And future promise anything but tears.

CAR. My vow I give that there'll be no remorse.
　　Just say you'll stay beside me through the years.

DOL. But no, it cannot be, this thing called love
　　Though I would wish some other fate were so.

CAR. Too late for flight, my pure, white, captured dove.
　　I'll take our future, whether joy or woe.

(VINCENT spins upstage and claps hands. He moves downstage to speak.)

VIN. Friends old and new, I've watched you party well
　　And set yourself to celebration's task
　　Now time bids us to break the magic spell—
　　We're reached the hour where we all unmask.

DOL. Alas, kind sir, with that I really must
    Say my farewell and from the party part.

(CARLO *seizes her hand.*)

CAR. Your fingers cool should never leave my own
    Till I have warmed them in the hearth of love.

DOL. No warming of this flesh can e'er be known
    By wooer's hand, by heart, nor thickest glove.

CAR. Did not my words romantic buy your trust?
    You have my mind, my soul, my life, my heart.

DOL. You have my hand.

CAR.   I'll keep it till you tell
    The holy syllables that make your name.
    I'll keep it till I know your face as well
    And both our hearts have merged into the same.

(CARLO *reaches for her mask.* DOLORES *touches his wrist with his free hand.*)

DOL. Not here, surrounded by this drunken mass.

CAR. Name time and place and I will swiftly fly,
    Will dare each mountain, cross each treacherous pass,
    To see your face. Then gladly I will die.

DOL. It will not come to that, let us both pray.

CAR. Since we'll together stay till our last breath
    Has left our lips, I do not fear the day.

In finding you I've lost my fear of death.

DOL. I fear not death, I fear what death may bring.

CAR. I fear the loss of you, and that is all.
　　Tell me where we'll meet, and make me king.
　　My life's begun the evening of this ball.

DOL. You know the graveyard at this island's tip?
　　Meet me at rosy dawn beside the gate.

CAR. To be with you to charnel house I'd skip.
　　For glimpse of you, I'd embrace any fate.

DOL. Now drop my hand.

CAR.　　　　　You'll be there? Do you swear?

DOL. If swearing makes you drop my hand, I do.
CAR. Then here's your hand. Not easily I'll bear
　　The time till it is grasped again.

DOL.　　　　　Ado!

(DOLORES *races through the crowd.* CARLO *follows her with his eyes.*
DOLORES *pauses* once *and looks back over her shoulder before exiting.*)

CAR. Life! Grand life! My outlook she's reversed!
　　I feel as if a new life now begins,
　　Her blessings rescuing what was Carlo cursed.
　　True love absolves a man of many sins.
　　My gloom has gone, and now the future's bright
　　Bathing me in true love's cleansing light.

ACT III.

The graveyard's main gate. Dawn.

(Enter CARLO and EDDIE, *stumbling on stage, obviously drunk. They are having a conversation which it is apparent they have been in the midst of for some time.*)

CAR. I tell you that she stepped from out of dreams
    to drag me from this nighttime of my life.

ED. I must admit that your demeanor seems
    Improved. But to already call her wife?
    Who is this one on whom you pin so much?
    Her face, her name, are secrets still to you,
    And though I'm glad she's changed you with her touch,
    How can you swear to be forever true?

CAR. Do not ask me to sense make of love's magic.
    Why two hearts yearn can never be explained.
    Cheer up, dear friend, true love is never tragic.
    Start looking happy. Lose that look so pained.
    I'm much too high to harbor any doubts,
    So think you not to sway me with your fears.
    I'll suffer all her frowns, moues, snits and pouts,
    And gladly help her through all future tears.

ED. I've never seen your confidence so sure
    At least not when it came to woman's sex.
    Mayhap you'll marshal something to endure
    And 'scape the often hidden marriage hex.

CAR. Love and marriage, laughter, children, age,

Welcome's the chance to put those garments on.
Now that this stranger's turned another page,
My book of life's less dreary. I'm less wan.

ED. But why her? What has she done to break down
The wall you've built around your secret self?

CAR. Seeing her, I saw myself a clown
Who'd put the best of me upon a shelf.
And though my friends did everything they could,
I heeded nothing of the things they said.
In seeing her I saw that I was good
And stirred myself back from the walking dead.
Tonight I'll see her while you stand your guard
Ensuring none disturbs us as we meet.

ED. I am myself disturbed that this foul yard
Should be the spot for lover's tryst discreet.
There is not love nor life nor safety here.
I wish that you had chosen other ground.

CAR. My love, not I, did choose the setting where
Together both our futures may be found.
I too admit that if I'd had the choice,
I would have picked less danger-fraught a spot,
But when she named the place I gave no voice
To my concern, just blessed my lucky lot.
I will protect her here, I make my vow,
Here or anywhere our fortunes trend.
An odd place to start off, I will allow,
But I care not what omens do portend.
Go now, and see that we are left alone
To worship here with Cupid's progeny.

ED. If any pass, with sword I will atone.
　　You'll have your time to woo her decently.

(The friends clasp hands. EDDIE exits.)

CAR. And now to wait, beside death's lit'ral door,
　　Praying that she comes to keep her word.
　　But wait! She is a lady at the core,
　　That she should fail a promise is absurd.

(While CARLO paces the gate, DOLORES appears on stage on the gate's other side. Her manner is subdued.)

DOL. I'm here, my noble prince, as you have said,
　　To finish out this dance we've both begun.

CAR. More than my words. I hope our wills are wed,
　　And that your heart by my own has been won.
　　We stand on either side of this great fence
　　Which bars the dead from living. Come to me
　　And we will all our hopes and dreams commence.
　　Our fates are now entwined, you will agree.

DOL. This gate you see may be too hard to breach
　　And means more than you yet could even guess.
　　I think I may be ever past your reach,
　　And love is doomed, with no chance of success.

CAR. Your voice, so sad, it tears my very being.
　　Let me come close, the sadness I will steal.

DOL. Can it be true love that I am seeing?
　　Do you swear this love of yours is real?
　　This world has things that are not what they seem,

And beauty may be purely in your mind.
Will your true love vanish in a dream?
Once the truth is out, can you stay kind?

car. You talk as if you hide a wicked heart
Inside what seems to me an angel's form.
There's naught you could have done, for my own part,
Could make me lose sight of perfection's corm.
There's nothing you could say or see or plan
Could reach the roots of what today has found.
You are my woman, and I am your man.
Let our love in its rightful place be crowned.

DOL. He speaks so ardently, his words ring true,
And truth to tell, my ardor's also strong.

(DOLORES *slides between the bars of the gate.*)

CAR. The human angel entertains my view,
And now all will be right, and nothing wrong.
And now, your name! Dispel this empty void.
Speak quick the word to fill my hungry soul,
A name that means for me joy unalloyed.
End my ears' most unbecoming greed.

DOL. Call me Dolores.

CAR.   Dolores are you called.
You're angel, and you bear an angel's name.
Your singing name does leave me more enthralled.
All other words than that will leave me tame.
Dolores! Three syllables which ignite
Within my spirit an infectious bliss.
And now, Dolores, set the world aright,

And grace this vagrant's lips with angel's kiss.

DOL. Alas, I fear my lips would leave you cold.
　　Other lips will have what you require.

CAR. You joke with me because I have been bold.
　　I'm sure your lips will set my soul afire.
　　Do you think I seek to toy with you?
　　I might have once, but now that's not my style.
　　Step closer now, I long for better view.
　　An inch away from you is like a mile.

(CARLO *extends a hand.* DOLORES *does not move closer to grasp it.*)

CAR. You hesitate, Dolores, could it be
　　Your feelings fail to truly mirror mine?

DOL. No, Carlo, your heart and my own agree.

CAR. Why hesitate from making your lips mine?

DOL. I fear that our first kiss will be our last,
　　That but one kiss is all the fates allow.

CAR. Don't doubt my love. All other girls are past,
　　And this one seeks no more the earth to plow.

DOL. It's more than that. There's much you cannot guess
　　About what lies beneath this gaudy mask.
　　If I submit, our lives will be a mess.

CAR. Let us dare it, then, that's all I ask.

(*After a momentary pause,* DOLORES *takes* CARLO'*s hand.*)

DOL. You swear that you will stay forever true.

CAR. I swear that you have bound my heart in chains.
  I swear—

DOL. Enough. I pray we do not rue
  This madness. Love conquers, and no sanity remains.

(DOLORES *leans forward to offer her lips. They chastely kiss.*)

CAR. Your lips, so cool. Your fine, fair cheeks like ice.
  The touch of you relieves the lustful thirst
  That's been in me since God did roll the dice,
  And let me see you, and my notions burst.
  My fever makes your own hot lips seem cold.

DOL. You would go on?

CAR. I would go on to Hell
  To follow through this kiss with one more bold
  Causing heaven itself to randy swell.

DOL. Curse God who has abandoned this poor world,
  For letting pass the things that happen next.

CAR. Do you see me fight destiny unfurled?
  Together, all despair will be perplexed.

(DOLORES *and* CARLO *kiss, more passionately this time, eyes closed.* DOLORES' *mask slips, but she does not realize it.* CARLO *opens his eyes first, and sees the pallor of her shredded face.* DOLORES *senses that something is wrong and opens her eyes slowly.* CARLO *backs away, puts a finger to his lips.* DOLORES *does not move, expecting the worst.*)

CAR. You're dead.

DOL.   Yes, dead. And now what will you do?

CAR. I cannot do, I cannot even think.
    I kissed your lips, and now your lips are blue.

DOL. My lips are blue. What's grey you'll find will stink.

CAR. You kiss me, but I always thought your race
    Would eat me up without a second thought.

DOL. I'll eat you up, but first I would embrace
    And eat you not the way that zombies ought.
    I'd gobble you up as lovers often do
    And press myself against your fresh, pink skin.
    Love makes me chose romance instead of grue
    An act my people think a zombie sin.
    I've said my peace. But you've not answered me.
    You owe me that much, even if you're made sick.

CAR. Forgive my silent lips for what I see.

(CARLO comes closer. DOLORES has not yet moved as she waits for his response.)

CAR. Your kind has warred on mine since undead were.
    No congress 'tween us save the rending blow.
    But to me you are frankincense and myrrh.
    To me you're poetry, all else is prose.
    Your skin is different, eyes of color mottled.
    Your smell is not my own, your flesh, it rots.
    But with one look from you all doubt is throttled.

I love you, though no blood within you clots.
I love you still, it matters not your state.
Living or zombie, to me is meaningless.
As soon would I care about an ounce of weight,
As seek from Cupid's bow for some redress.

DOL. O, Carlo, I had dared not even hope
That our meeting could cause a valid bliss.

CAR. If you're my hangman, I accept the rope
Enough of words. Speak further in a kiss.

(The lovers embrace. After a moment, a growing clatter can be heard from offstage. Enter EDDIE, *backing in, fencing with* LEOPOLD, *King of Zombies, father to* DOLORES.*)*

ED. Begone, dead thing! You have no business here!
My friend and master's private in a tryst.

LEO. A grave your master's privacy will bear
Should here I find my daughter has been kissed.

CAR. Who speaks of daughter with a sword in hand?

DOL. My noble father Leopold comes near
King of all the zombies in this land.
If we don't fly, your future I do fear.

CAR. I cannot leave a true and trusting friend
To deal for my sake 'gainst the living dead.
I'll intervene and bring this to an end.
No man will ever battle in my stead.

*(*CARLO *draws his sword.)*

CAR. Eddie, you no longer fight alone.

(EDDIE turns and for the first time notices Dolores unmasked.)

ED. A welcome sword you bear, but what is this?
    You meet with that? Have your senses flown?

(While EDDIE is distracted, LEOPOLD makes a mortal wound.)

ED. To think I die so you a corpse could kiss.

(CARLO catches EDDIE as he falls.)

CAR. Speak not of death. Of death I'll not allow
    A word from out your lips. Just lie and rest.

LEO. The devil a second death I will endow.
    Beneath my heel I'll crush another pest.

(As LEOPOLD lunges for CARLO, DOLORES interposes herself between father and lover.)

DOL. Father, no, you cannot hurt this boy.
    I love him, and he loves me back as well.

LEO. If love you have, it's something I'll destroy.
    Before you two will love, you'll go to Hell.

(LEOPOLD tries to reach CARLO with his sword as CARLO comforts EDDIE, but DOLORES is able to hold him back.)

DOL. If me you love, you'll then do this at least,
    One here's been killed tonight, so let the other live.

LEO. For you, my daughter, he'll not need a priest.
    No last confessions will he have to give.

(LEOPOLD storms off, dragging his daughter behind him.)

ED. I thought I'd last far longer than this age.
    Grow old, have kids, all life's treasure's hoard.
    But now I'm being ushered from the stage,
    One undead having slashed me with a sword.

CAR. Rest up, dear friend, it's far too soon to die.
    We've many long, carousing years ahead.

ED. I know you far too well. Don't try to lie.
    Before mere minutes pass I shall be dead.

CAR. Eddie, listen, let us hurry home,
    Before from you more precious blood can ooze.

ED. Too late! Oh, God, I had so far to roam.
    To think my life I could so early lose.
    Goodbye, Carlo, I tried my very best
    To be your friend through times best and times worst
    And now it seems that I have failed the test.
    My life is over and my spirit cursed.

(EDDIE dies.)

CAR. Wake up, dear friend, you go away too soon.
    There still was much that we had both to do.
    I thought my wedding day you'll play a tune,
    When Dolores and I forged life of something new.
    Who thought that true love could birth such distress?

Not death but rather, new life it should bring.
And now my neat world's been made such a mess,
Best friend slain by sullen zombie king.

(CARLO *hefts* EDDIE *in his arms, and prepares to carry him home.*)

CAR. Forgive me, friend, your death and also this—
Regardless of the guilt brought by your fall
I love Dolores' cold, firm, undead kiss.
I love her still, submit to siren's call.
Dolores, I will have you or know why.
If your love can't be mine, I'd rather die.

215

ACT IV.

Dolores' bedroom. That afternoon.

(DOLORES *tosses in bed while* MARY, *her maid, wrings her hands.*)

MA. I've kept your father's house for many years,
Since zombie plague made me be born again
And in that time I've witnessed many tears
Fall from your eyes due to the acts of men.
Love's not an easy game to have to play.
The rules are senseless if you're live or dead.
I'd hoped to be in heaven by today;
Instead we're still by Cupid's fever led.

DOL. It's not a fever; fevers are what pass,
And what I feel will never dare to fade.

MA. I know inside it feels that way, my lass,
But I am older. Listen to your maid.

I've loved many, obsessed on each in turn.
But now I swear I could not list their names.
Though once my body and my brain did burn,
My memories cast them off like childish games.

DOL. My heart sings true! Don't say that I'm a child,
Who's playing with a toy that she'll forget.
The feelings coursing through me aren't mild,
And father's turned my happiness to fret.

MA. Then tell me, child, what's brought you to this state,
And this old fool will help you if she can.

DOL. If you could aid my struggle with this fate
You'll stand beside me when they read the bann.

MA. A father's wishes must not be denied,
But I will lend a sympathetic ear,
For there's no pain as great as love denied.
So speak. Let me the situation hear.

DOL. I met him only yesterday, this man,
And though by now mere hours have been spent,
It seems that years are gone and that we can
Be sure that we are for each other meant.

MA. Who is this one who in you's made the change?
Where met you he who made your heart to fall?

DOL. This one whom my whole life did rearrange
I met last night at living Mayor's ball.

MA. You dared the ball against your father's will?
Torment swore he to any who dared go.

DOL. What will he do to me? He cannot kill
    My form or heart. Inside me love does grow.
    And I would risk my father's violent rage,
    Or any punishments the Gods would bear,
    For without my love, the world is but a cage.
    Any pain's worth glimpse of Carlo fair.

MA. Carlo, no, you must not speak that name!
    Is he the one who makes your heart to pulse?
    Our enemy's fair son? Have you no shame?
    He's living, and the mere thought does revulse.

DOL. I care not what you or my father feel,
    What foolish rules my carefree heart does break.
    The love that runs inside of me is real.

MA. My lass, I fear you do a grand mistake.

DOL. It cannot be. Who wrote these foul commandments?
    Who said that those alive by us be eaten?
    I say that love's a thing that perchance rents
    The rules. Those foolish things can be beaten.

(Enter LEOPOLD.*)*

LEO. No! The thing that should be beaten wears your form.
    You shall not mate with foul still-breathing thing.
    I'll beat you till your limbs again are warm,
    And remember once again that I am king.
    Begone, Mary, this you should not see.
    You are aware, I know, how discipline goes,
    But as you are not fully family,
    I'll not have you stand by to count the blows.

MA. Let me stay, I sad consequences fear
  And severance of your love which should not pass.

LEO. Begone, my maid, what happens you'll not hear.

DOL. It's all right, Mary. Alone I'll drink his glass.

(Exit MARY.*)*

LEO. Now I will speak as fathers do, and warn
  With stern pronouncements of what will transpire.
  'Twill make you wish you'd not been once more born.
  Unfailing service is what I require.
  Need love and gratitude be requested
  Of one whom I have brought through these mad times?
  When I think of all I have invested
  To raise you, and now this, it seems a crime.
  Forget him. This first time I'll ask polite,
  But then all niceties from my demeanor fade,
  And if I do not see you are contrite,
  As daughter you will know a failing grade,
  And suffer all indignities within my power,
  As I am suffering yours due to your tryst.
  I'll let you think upon this for an hour.

DOL. No minute, hour, lifetime, I insist,
  Holds time enough to from me love erase,
  Or end this thing which you saw born last night.

LEO. I warn you, daughter, you must learn your place.
  A world where your will conquers mine's not right.

DOL. Most noble father, I seek no fight with you.

My love for you has long known no extreme,
But now I've found a man as daughters do,
And I must go to him, as love's rules deem.

LEO. Ah, that's the problem. "Man" is what you said.
You've set your eyes on men when men are past.
Keep your love on a leash. Stay with the dead.
Of arguments let this one be the last.

DOL. If that be so, my father, it's your choice,
Of whether you will fight this happy thing,
Or join with me and Carlo to rejoice
That love, dear love, has made our hearts to sing.

219
·

*(*LEOPOLD, *enraged, slaps his daughter.)*

LEO. Don't speak of choices to one who's had none,
Who was pushed back to life to bond the dead.
I have no "choice" in whether war is done,
And in my presence I'll not hear this madness said.
The world exists, we cannot make our own.
The rules are written, which we cannot edit.
No feelings in a woman's tender zone
Can tip scales the direction that you credit.

DO. But, father—

LEO.   No. "But father" I'll hear not.
The case is closed, with no room for appeals.
Carlo is alive, while you do rot,
And with that fact your love can make no deals.
No love can be between our races two.
Learn this well, your father does implore.
To change that fact there's nothing you can do;

Dolores shall see Carlo nevermore.

(Exit LEOPOLD. *Enter* MARY.*)*

MA. There, there, girl, that's it, give yourself to tears.
　　I've cried them oft myself in years gone by.
　　Lovers are such flighty fickle dears,
　　That he'd have left you anyway to cry.

DOL. Not this time. Our true love is strong.
　　'Twill overcome whatever fathers say.
　　Our future bright together will be long.
　　Love's vibrant "yes" wins over parent's "nay."

MA. If only I'd your naïve confidence
　　When I was younger, it would have been strange
　　To see if I'd in my life's skein made rents,
　　Or my own father's will made any change.

DOL. You know then how it feels within my place.
　　Your heart was once a mirror to mine made.
　　Help this time the lovers win the race.
　　Help me to my man become a maid.

MA. Ah, lass, I wish there was a way to do
　　The acts of Cupid, but I have no bow.
　　Perhaps your only answer's to eschew
　　The very thing you wish. 'Twas ever so.

DOL. It will not be this time, that I do swear,
　　If it means end of me, of everything!
　　There's nothing that I would not gladly dare.
　　I'd fight the world to make the angels sing.

MA. You'd really for this Carlo risk it all?

DOL. If you've an answer, any price I'd pay.

MA. I think that I can help you vault this wall.
 If you are unafraid there is a way.

DOL. What is it? Name it and it will be done.

MA. I'd hate to raise your hopes with crazy lie.

DO. I'll take lies if with them this be done.

MA. Then know what I have learned of those who die.
 I've heard that we come back—

DOL.   We all know that.
 Those words bring nothing new to end my pain.

MA. Hear me out, girl, it is not that pat.
 What I mean is that they come back again.
 The living first come back to become us,
 And that's accomplished through the worldwide plague
 Involving not the slightest bit of fuss.
 The manner that this happens is still vague.
 But time to time I hear a silly rumor
 Of dead instead of coming, going back,
 And death is cut from their souls like a tumor.

DOL. Of how to do this thing you have the knack?

MA. I know the details not of how this works,
 For there are some things it's best not to know,
 And there are times I feel that madness lurks

221
.

In going places we're not meant to go.
But I know one for whom the things arcane
Are simple as to us our ABC's.
But he's an unforgiving one and I would fain
Become involved with him though he's the keys.

DOL. You must take me to him, give your word!
And having done so tell my father naught.

MA. That this should work is patently absurd.
And think if you are by your father caught.

DOL. I'm caught by Carlo. I so little care
For what another thinks that I am free
To fly to heaven like a bird in air.
In finding love, fear has no hold on me.
Say that you'll do it. Let us make to leave
And find this one who'll set all things aright.

MA. I'll do it for you though I fear I'll grieve
And with this thing unnatural turn day to night.
I'll send a message to him so we'll meet
And make you to the image of your love.

DOL. Tell him he should make himself be fleet
As eagles soaring through the skies above.

MA. Go now to your father with the news
That you your virgin senses have regained,
And hope that he your imprisonment eschews
So we can leave here to meet the mystic bard.

DOL. At this point if you feel that it is just
I'd tell falsehoods to King of Kings himself.

(Exit DOLORES, *leaving* MARY *momentarily alone.)*

MA. The girl is mad with love and that's a shame,
    For love is surely the worst kind of madness.
    I pray that once we're done there'll be no blame
    For true love must too often end in sadness.

(A handful of pebbles rattle off the wall. MARY *moves to the window.)*

MA. What's out there? Leave me shadow, with my fear
    That anything I do will end with guilt.

*(*CARLO *answers from offstage.)*

CAR. Dolores, it is Carlo, my dead dear,
    Ready to bury my sword down to the hilt
    In anyone who stands between our lips.

MA. He thinks I am my lady. I will talk
    As if I'm her and see if falsehood slips.
    What brings you here? Visit you to balk?

CAR. I came, sweet love, because I have a plan
    To end objections families may feel.
    There's but one way together that we can
    Disarm their hate so wedding bells can peal.
    If we were both the same, we'd need not run
    From hate, but rather towards our bliss.

MA. It seems that here two minds have thought as one,
    And with true love there's nothing that's amiss.

CA. If both the same we could somehow arrange,

There'd be no need for war between our kin.
By making to one race another change
We'll rise above the earth's tumultuous din.

MA. You're right that you have nailed the only way
  For happiness to be two lover's fates.

(*Enter* LEOPOLD, *with* DOLORES *trailing.*)

LEO. Whom do you speak with? Hold there, villain! Stay!

(LEOPOLD *rushes to the window.*)

LEO. Look, he leaps like magic o'er the gates!
  Who was that, maid, what did here just transpire?
  Was that a brigand sent to bear my daughter hence?
  Do you with living fiends tonight conspire
  To undertake a brutal crime immense?

(MARY *falls to her knees.*)

MA. My lord, your every wish becomes my deed.
  I've spent my second life here serving you.
  Look not upon me as a weaker reed,
  You've only but to say and I will do.

(DOLORES *studies* MARY *nervously.*)

DOL. I'm sure it was some creature of the night
  Scrounging for one last meal to stay alive.
  And hearing us draw near it did take flight
  Before we could its animal life deprive.

LEO. I guess you're right. Discord had made me jumpy.

I make each harmless creak into a threat.
Our path these past few hours has been quite bumpy.
We will have peace in this fine household yet.

(Exit LEOPOLD. DOLORES *pauses by the door to make sure he has not remained to listen.)*

DOL. Bless your soul! To save me you did grovel.
  My gratitude could not be more profound.

MA. A true love such as yours is something novel.
  In my long life no other has been found.

DOL. So tell me, was that Carlo in the street?
  It was, I know! What was it brought him here?

MA. He brought with him a brilliant plan that matches
  The one that you and I have just contrived.
  Like minds a like way out of sadness hatches.
  Two start points have one destination arrived.

DOL. Then he will love me when I am as he?

MA. Your story cannot have another end.
  A celebration out of this must be.
  Love's reputation we hereby defend.

DOL. True joy awaits me, and my solid flesh,
  Once rigor mortis leaves and I wax fresh.

ACT V.

The interior of the graveyard. Night.

(Enter CARLO. *He wanders the graveyard, a shovel over his shoulders.)*

CAR. Where are your bones, friend? Sleeping time has passed.
    This act alone cannot be carried through.
    Though I'm the one who made you breathe your last,
    I need your help to weave this strange skein through.
    There's no one living I find I can trust,
    So now's the time for me to you uncover,
    And you to like a dog shake off death's rust,
    So I can pleasure prove with lady love.

*(*CARLO *finds* EDDIE'S *grave, center stage.)*

CAR. Ah, here you are, dear Eddie, noble friend.

*(*CARLO *digs.)*

CAR. Ashes to ashes, dust to dust, 'twas said,
    But life's no longer guaranteed that end,
    And dead rise up as if but out of bed.

*(*EDDIE *suddenly reaches up out of the grave to grab* CARLO'S *ankle.)*

CAR. Impatient friend, I work fast as I can.
    Forever waits, so try to patient be.
    Awake again you'll be a diff'rent man,
    And then I hope your new form will help me.

*(*CARLO *lends his friend a hand, and* EDDIE *climbs out of the grave.)*

ED. So this is what death feels like. I once feared
    The fetid breath of death upon my cheek.
    I trembled as my last few moments neared.

All courage fled. I was left soft and meek.
But now that I have sliced the ebon veil,
I see how foolish were my moments tense.
By dying so, I've grasped the holy grail,
And suddenly the stuff of life makes sense.

CAR. I'm glad, friend, all makes sense from where you sit,
　　For you are where I do soon hope to be.

ED. You are not ready, Carlo. You're too fit.
　　No reason for you turning like as me.

CAR. My lady love's a zombie, such as you.
　　Fate has living flesh by zombies eaten,
　　But you'll help me escape the undead stew.
　　Tonight this madness by me will be beaten.

ED. I do admit in you I see a meal,
　　Though friendship bids me bypass this first bite.

CA. For myself you're thanked, and commonweal
　　Will surely thank you once they see the light,
　　For once they see the things that love can do,
　　No longer will we one another kill.
　　With sacrifice I'll my fair maiden woo,
　　And make the waters of this world stand still.

ED. What is it that you ask in friendship's name?

(CARLO *passes the shovel to* EDDIE.)

CAR. Tonight, I'll die, and come back as another.
　　I'll kill myself, but to life's ember tame,
　　You'll to plant me in the ground, my brother.

ED. When I first living saw you with that girl,
    I thought that you had given up your mind.
    But now to me she seems a perfect pearl,
    And you're the one who seems of the wrong kind.
    I pledge my strength to with you disjoint mend.
    You only speak the word. I'll meet your need.

CAR. My heart knew that on you it could depend.
    Stand back, the time has come to do the deed.

(CARLO plunges a knife deeply into his own stomach.)

CAR. Such pain! It burns! But I will bear it well,
    If agony will fair Dolores bring.
    And now, I sleep, though just for but a spell.
    O Death, hear I my dear beloved sing?

(CARLO staggers back, and tumbles into the grave.)

ED. Rest well, I know the comfort of that bed.
    It carried me hither from one life to next.
    Now it's your turn to lie here in my stead,
    To prove that death can be forever vexed.

(EDDIE scatters a handful of earth over CARLO.)

ED. And now I leave my friend to where I'll wait
    For his grand transformation to occur.
    And once he's gained his love-struck chosen state,
    I'll see him wed, for True Love nothing can deter.

(Exit EDDIE, stage right. Enter DOLORES, stage left.)

DOL. Here I return to where Carlo declared
    Eternal love for me, so it is right,
    That here the gap between us is repaired.
    I'll drink magician's potion here tonight.
    My maid waits yon so I may all alone
    Contemplate incipient reunion
    of two who now our race's hate atone,
    and shatter any doubts. Love's no illusion.

(DOLORES *pulls a vial from her cloak and raises it overhead.*)

DOL. This drink will soon my barren flesh infuse
    With stuff of life. I can no more postpone
    The strictures of my plague-like death to lose.
    Soon this cold heart will ne'er more be alone.

(DOLORES *drinks the potion. She grasps her throat and falls into the grave,
vanishing from view.* EDDIE *returns once more to center stage.*)

ED. I thought I heard my lord and master stir.
    Yet I sense nothing here that is amiss.
    'Twas probably just the whining of a cur.
    I'll go, and not return till lovers kiss.

(EDDIE *exits. Within the grave, the lovers stir.*)

CAR. Is that my darling's hip close next to mine?

DO. It is! Together we will be at last!
    Has my skin at last a pallor that's like thine?

CAR. It must! Let's rise and take each other's cast.

(Both DOLORES *and* CARLO *stand. Their heads and shoulders now pro-
trude from the grave. It can clearly be seen that* CARLO *has a grayish pallor,
while* DOLORES' *skin is fair. They look upon their own hands first, and
not each other.)*

DO. The bard's wild potion worked. My skin is fair.
    Memory hides from me when last was so.

CAR. I've joined the dead, but little do I care,
    As long as down the aisle we soon must go.

*(They look at each other now. Shocked by what they see, they scramble from
the pit. The grave yawns between them.)*

CAR. As zombie suitor I was to arrive.
    Why have you gone and changed the other way?

DO. But I thought we'd agreed I would contrive
    To like a snake shed skin of blue and grey,
    And join you in your world of living folk.
    Why did you rather two steps backwards choose?

CAR. We tried to fix this thing, instead we broke
    The sad machine of love. Must we then lose?

(The lovers consider each other intently.)

DOL. Love cannot lose. Do you so soon forget?
    If you've a pulse or not to you I'm bound.

CAR. You're right, for looking, I still long to pet
    The liquefaction of your curves so round.
    Come to me, love, though places we did switch,
    And let's forget our difference of race.

Beside the grand abyss of this death ditch
I swear your heart I love, not nature of your face.

(The lovers embrace.)

DOL. Let's to our fathers' hence and spread the news.

(Enter LEOPOLD, *stage right.)*

LEO. To me this treachery comes as no surprise.
　　How dare your father's kindness you abuse?

(Enter VINCENT, *stage left.)*

VIN. My son, it's time you shed this grim disguise.

LEO. Disguises both they wear, enemy foul.
　　It's time to wash them off and end this play.
　　To see my daughter like this makes me howl
　　My anger to the Gods. End this I say!

VIN. On this one point I'm with you, zombie king.
　　This travesty of love must not go on.
　　This tableau pains me with ungrateful sting.
　　If you can't stop this I'll make war upon
　　Your zombie kin as you have never seen,
　　And find a way the earth of you to rid.

LEO. It's not my side that's birthed this madness mean.
　　It's you, you old buffoon, and your damned kid.

(In their anger, LEOPOLD *and* VINCENT *forget their children. The two men draw their swords and begin to fight.)*

VIN. Don't dare you in my sight defame my son.
　　　Look homeward, blame your own deceitful bitch!

LEO. I'll kill you, man, and after you are done,
　　　Cement you down! You'll never leave your ditch!

(Enter EDDIE.*)*

LEO. Prepare to die!

VIN. 　　　　　　Prepare to—

ED. 　　　　　　　　Stop this now!

*(*EDDIE *comes between King* LEOPOLD *and Mayor* VINCENT.*)*

ED. I've seen enough of violence this past day.
　　　The races must become fast friends enow,
　　　And end this mad desire to rend and slay.

VIN. It cannot end as long as they embrace.
　　　Call off their love, and end this cruel charade.

LEO. Once they say goodbyes, we'll leave this place,
　　　Once they have cleaned themselves and shut this masquerade.

DOL. They still don't understand what love has wrought
　　　Nor comprehend our metamorphosis.

CAR. Their anger I fear will be ever taught.
　　　I think that we will never vanquish this.

ED. I love you both. I'll end this impasse chill.

(EDDIE *reaches into the grave and removes the vial from which Dolores had sipped. He offers the vial to King* LEOPOLD.)

ED. King, surely your exertion raised a thirst.

(LEOPOLD *drinks.*)

ED. And you, Lord Mayor, I guess I'll have to kill.

(EDDIE *runs* VINCENT *through with his sword.*)

ED. All will be clear once you two are reversed.

(*As soon as* EDDIE *removes his sword,* VINCENT *tumbles into the grave.* LEOPOLD *grabs his throat, and follows.*)

ED. Let's leave this ground, and vanish till they wake.
    Tonight we've more than made a match for you.
    We're done that, but with our whole lives at stake,
    Remodeled all our world to something new.

(*Exit* EDDIE.)

CAR. Come now, my love, our joyful future meet,
    And from each other nevermore do part.

DOL. I need no more to make my life complete.
    Between us two we do share but one heart.

(*The lovers kiss and exit. Enter* JONATHAN, *the gravedigger from the prologue, followed by* SAM, *the zombie.*)

JON. And so we reach the climax of this play,
    Which in its five acts sought to fill you in

On how zombie and living reached this day,
Moving from enemies to accepting kin.
We've made our peace with how the plague has shaped
Our sordid world. We've ended all our wars.
Yet if you think that this world has been raped,
It's not a very different one from yours.
Our curtain falls. Go back now to your lives.
Take what you wish as you tonight return
To lovers, parents, children, husbands, wives.
Remember to be kind to those who yearn.

SAM. Living or dead, love lies in wait for you.
    Begrudge it not. Or who knows what we'll do?

(Exeunt omnes.)

THE FINAL CHARGE OF MR. ELECTRICO

*When he came to me, he touched me on the brow, and on the nose, and on the chin,
and he said to me, in a whisper, "Live forever." And I decided to.*
-Ray Bradbury, *Paris Review* interview

*M*r. Electrico had once believed he was going to live forever.

And as he sat on one corner of a spare bed at his grandson's house—a bed which his pained lower back signaled was somehow far harder than the string of cots which to his far younger self had seemed so soft—he looked down at the sword in his trembling hands, and still, all these many years later, thought...why *shouldn't* he have fooled himself into thinking that? He'd told so many kids so many times they'd never die that after a while it had seemed only fair he should join them in the immortality he'd been extravagantly granting.

Considering his decades on the carnival circuit, such wishful thinking was surely inevitable.

Count how often those inviting tent flaps unfolded at the beginnings of his shows, multiply that by the thousands filing in tugging eager children who were then instructed to squat in the front rows, add the host of times he surrendered to the embrace of the electric chair and felt its power pass through him, letting his skin tingle and his hair stand on end, boost it all by the number of slashes he made with his sword while reaching forward to knight the closest kids with shouts of "Live forever!"...

...and a sensation had begun to expand within him which insisted—the words he'd uttered were no con game.

And he'd deserved to taste their power, too.

No one could go through those motions for so many performances, mouth those same two words that many times, without beginning to believe. He dared anyone else to try it. Not that anyone else ever would. They couldn't. The days of carnivals were long over. Besides, it wouldn't be fair for the charge to merely pass through him, and have none of it remain. Something had to stick, right? Some small part?

Yet...why should he be so lucky? Those who'd toured with him, the only ones to whom he could have talked about this and have them understand, had already taken their leave.

The Fat Lady had been the first to go, back when they were both still on the road. Her heart gave out in her sleep, the sad price demanded by her trade. At least she went peaceful. (He liked to think she did. Does anyone ever truly go peaceful?) The Skeleton Man, though, hadn't been that lucky. He was carried away by cigarettes. Last time Mr. Electrico had seen him, when he visited to reminisce about the old days, the man could barely speak above a whisper. Not much reminiscing got done, except in their own heads. Those wheezy lungs had kept them both too focused on the future, short though it was, to enjoy wandering through the past.

As for the Illustrated Man, Mr. Electrico was never quite sure exactly what had happened to him. No one would say. When he showed up for the memorial service, the relatives wouldn't even look him in the eye. And those tattoos, they didn't seem quite so pretty when viewed in the open coffin on which the Illustrated Man had insisted. Mr. Electrico remembered how once they'd been marvelous.

How once they'd *all* been marvelous.

The jugglers, the ticket takers, the drivers, all gone, gone, gone. There had been too many funerals over too many decades, and he'd gone to as many as he could, for his friends deserved to be shown a little respect, but then, after a time, there were no more funerals to attend. Now only he remained.

So...maybe the electricity had done something after all. He was still around, wasn't he? The last man standing. Okay, so the hand which had once held the sword shook, and during the night, he often had to get up half a dozen times to piss, and when he woke in the morning, sometimes—not always, but sometimes—he wasn't sure where he was. But all that was better than the alternative, right?

Sure would have been nice if one of the others—any one of the others, he wasn't picky—had still been around, so they could have shared a place. Would have been nice, too, if his son was still speaking with him, so *they* could have shared a place. No fixing that, though. Mr. Electrico doubted forgiveness was even possible. It was sweet of his grandson to step up like this, even if the kid didn't understand the carny life his grandpa used to lead. But maybe that was the only reason he *was* willing to step up.

Josh.

It was Josh, wasn't it?

That's right.

Josh.

Mr. Electrico wished he could show the kid who he really was, and why, wished he could explain it all in the way he'd never been able to do for his son, whose empathy had been crushed by having to live through it. And once he could have. The photos would have helped. And the newspaper clippings, filled with awe and wonder. And if only he still owned the costume he'd once worn, red silk with yellow piping zigzagging down the sleeves to make it look as if lightning was about to come out of his fingertips. But those were all gone, all of it, every scrap of memorabilia, each battered souvenir, lost to rundown apartments he'd abandoned with rent unpaid, and evictions which had left his possessions dissolving in the rain, and small-town pawnshops he'd see the once but never again.

And drink, oh, the drink. To that above all those physical manifestations of his memories had been sacrificed, sometimes willingly, sometimes not, as his path narrowed to whatever this life of his had turned out to be.

Only the sword, remarkably, remained. Even he wasn't entirely sure how.

He held it out before him as he used to do at each show—more an extension of his arm than a piece of metal—and closed his eyes.

He could almost see them then—the faces in the front row filled with amazement, kid after kid shocked to see what coursed through him as he sat in that chair showered with sparks, faces which would soon themselves be literally shocked as he tapped their brows and shouted in the tent then what he whispered in the small borrowed bedroom now—

"Live forever!"

And when he had, he truly thought they could.

All these years later, he raised the sword high above his head, and there he was, in front of thousands of people blurred together by memory, forgettable faces with no names to go with them. But there was one face which stood out from all the rest. One face which had gained a name.

Mr. Electrico saw it then, the face of the kid who'd come back, the face of the kid who'd brought him a magic trick, the face of a kid he'd welcomed into the tent and introduced to his friends, the face of a kid which was also in a former life the face of a friend, a friend who'd died in his arms in the Ardennes Forest in 1918, during the Great War.

Or was that last but a lie he'd told, the kind of thing you cough up to a rube to keep them happy and empty their pockets? It had been so long since their last encounter one Labor Day weekend that he couldn't be sure, couldn't remember whether he'd been sincere, or was only planting the seeds for a long con which never had the chance to play out.

No, that he couldn't remember.

But he remembered the day when the carnival stopped by Lake Michigan, near Waukegan, Illinois, and the kid to whom Mr. Electrico had seemed to matter so much.

He remembered that kid, and wondered whether he was the one who'd prove his words more than just words. The one who truly would live forever.

That kid named...Ray, wasn't it?

Yes. Ray.

• • •

Ray hadn't been the first to come back—kids were always ditching their parents and returning to say the things they wouldn't dare unless they were alone with him—but he was the first to come back who didn't also ask to join him. They were always asking to take off, believing that hitting the road with a carnival was the solution to whatever their problems happened to be. Splitting from an abusive household could be a good thing, sure, Mr. Electrico had done the same himself when he was a kid, but having done so, he'd learned the hard way—why bring the carny life into it? That was no answer. But then, it never was.

He kept waiting for the kid to ask him, too, ask for help in running away, the way he himself had once asked for help from another who'd earlier carried his name. First when Ray pulled out that beginner's magic trick he'd bought at the Five and Dime and begged him to explain how it worked, and then when he was brought into the tent and introduced to the others, where Mr. Electrico could see the kid's eyes grow large as he took in the Bearded Lady and the Alligator Boy and all the rest of them, saw how they treated each other when they were by themselves without the rubes around, as if the fantastic were common, and the common fantastic, and finally out along the sand dunes, where they sat and talked of their lives, and Mr. Electrico was moved to say something he'd never said before, about how the two of them had known each other in past lifetimes.

But Ray never asked that question Mr. Electrico had come to know too well. And it was only later that Mr. Electrico realized the thought had never even occurred to Ray at all.

They talked for hours, about Ferris wheels and movie stars, rocket ships and life on Mars, about comic strips which promised more than real life ever could, about things that might have been and things that never were...but then it was time for Mr. Electrico to head back for his evening shows—the final performances before he'd have to move on. There were tears in Ray's eyes as they parted, which Mr. Electrico thought meant the kid would then ask the question, before the opportunity to do so was gone forever...but he did not.

He often wondered what those tears had meant. He wished he could have tracked the kid down and asked him. He suspected if found that the kid would have understood what his grandson couldn't and his son never even wanted to try. But he'd never learned anything more than his given name, and so a reunion was impossible.

Mr. Electrico wished they *had* known each other before in the trenches, the way he'd told him, because that would have meant there was a chance they'd see each other again in the future. But he knew now, as he knew he'd known then, that there was no coming back in this life, that once a person was gone he was gone, one reason he fought so hard against his body's signals that it was time to leave.

He didn't want to leave.

Mr. Electrico snapped out of his reverie, suddenly aware of the streets down which he walked, realizing—he had no idea where he was. What made it worse was that at the same time—he was also uncertain whether this confusion was because he'd wandered, while lost in thoughts of the past, to a neighborhood he'd never encountered before, or if, cruelly, he no longer recognized a place with which he should he familiar. He hoped it was the former, because the latter... well, that was happening more often now.

Closing his eyes and concentrating hard, he remembered.

He'd left his grandson's home for a walk in the sun—Josh had insisted he go out, said it wasn't good for him to sit alone in that spare room all day. So Mr. Electrico had headed to the park, starting his rambling there as he always did, because he knew its openness would bring back his carnival days, and thoughts of that moment the caravan would arrive at a new location, and study an open field before beginning to set up. If he could position himself properly, and keep the benches and path lights and playground equipment at his back, he could almost pretend it was still the past. He'd stay there forever if he could.

But eventually, his joints had told him he'd better get moving again, so he grabbed a hot dog that hadn't tasted as good as one he might have gotten on the midway, then headed on to look in store windows filled with things he no longer wanted nor needed, if he ever did, then studied the posters outside a theater advertising movies he would never bother seeing, his afternoon reminding him too much of things he would never do.

But once he'd spent enough time wasting time, enough to keep Josh happy at least, and was ready to turn back...he no longer recalled how to get home. He stood on a street corner trying to remember, but not trying too hard, because the failure that was more often starting to accompany such trying would be too painful.

So he meandered until he made his way back to the park—he could remember how to get there, at least—and once there, as he stared out across the grass on which one wasn't supposed to walk, he again briefly tried to decide which way he should turn next to find his way back to his grandson. But he couldn't choose, so instead, he sat on a bench and wished, as the darkness settled around him, that he could still spread wide his hands and light up the night.

• • •

Which is where his grandson found him still sitting the following morning.

Josh wasn't alone as he walked up the path toward Mr. Electrico. There was a policeman by his side, which told Mr. Electrico that no, Josh truly didn't understand.

He did not like police officers. It was nothing personal. No one who'd worked a carnival ever did.

"What are you doing here, Grandpa?" asked Josh, as he slid onto wooden slats still covered with dew.

"Just resting," said Mr. Electrico, unwilling to reveal the truth, especially not with a cop there to bear witness. "Thinking. Remembering."

"All night? Here?"

"And why not? I can do those things on a park bench as easily as anywhere else."

Josh leaned in more closely to his grandfather, so only the two of them could hear what he was to say next.

"You forgot again," he whispered. "Didn't you?"

"I did not," Mr. Electrico insisted, hoping he'd been able to imbue his words with confidence. He'd made so many believe so much, surely he could make one man believe that.

"That's not true, Grandpa," said Josh. "We both know that. If we didn't find you, who knows how long you'd have been out here alone."

"I was just taking my time, that's all," he said, his words less certain. The power to pretend, a power about which he'd once been so proud, had long ago diminished. But he still had to try. "I'd have gotten home eventually. I always do."

"Not always," said Josh, his voice still a whisper. "This wasn't the first time. Remember?"

Mr. Electrico felt his grandson's hand on his shoulder, and though the touch was gentle and though it was meant with love, it brought back memories of other park benches, and other touches, ones not so gentle, which had been meant to make him move along. He stayed silent, and tried not to let those feeling show.

"So you're saying the officer and I should just leave you here then? You'll have no problem getting back on your own?"

At first, Mr. Electrico said nothing. He looked off again toward the unbroken stretch of cool, green grass, and imagined a tent rising there. But tents would rise no more. He sighed.

"I guess I've sat here long enough," Mr. Electrico said finally. "We can go."

As he stood, he could hear his knees crack. He guessed he probably wasn't the only one who'd heard them.

"The officer said he'd drive us home," said Josh, gesturing at the police car which had been left idling on the outskirts of the park.

"I can walk," said Mr. Electrico, even as he felt a pounding in his chest. "I'm not dead yet."

Besides, he thought...he'd been in the back of too many police cars. Sure, it had been decades since the last time. But still. He remembered that claustrophobic feeling, all those doors with no handles. No, sir. Not today. Not yet. He stretched, partially because he needed it after having been curled up on a park bench all night, and partially because he needed Josh to point him in the right direction so they could get started, and was delaying because he didn't want to have to admit it.

"Shall we?" he said, and tilted his head in a vague circle he hoped might accidentally approximate the correct direction.

Josh hesitated for a moment, looking as if he was about to speak... then shrugged instead and began walking.

Mr. Electrico followed, trying his best to memorize the streets—some of which seemed familiar to him, and some not, as if buildings had been shuffled overnight—between the park and his grandson's house. They were silent all the way there, though Mr. Electrico could tell, from the grim expression on his grandson's face, that a speech was building which he would not want to hear. Once they arrived, Josh waved at the couch in the living room.

"We can't go on this way," he said. "I know you know that, Grandpa."

"We?" said Mr. Electrico. "I'm tired. Can we do this later?"

Josh nodded, and Mr. Electrico went up to his room—slowly, as all stairs were taken slowly these days—where he fell asleep immediately, a thing which he hadn't allowed himself in the park. Oh, he'd been tired, and he'd desperately wanted to nod off, but a life spent on the road had taught him that was never to be done. He hadn't even been able to bring himself to nap while there, only listen to the crickets and look at the stars, both those present that night and those which existed only in memory. So sleep came quick now, as did dreams of his old life, and an afternoon by Lake Michigan, and a boy named Ray.

When he woke, he could remember little of the dreams, only that he *had* dreamt, which he did not like. It seemed forgetfulness, which was now so much a part of his life, was spreading to his dreams as well.

How long before he forgot it all?

243
.

• • •

Mr. Electrico managed to avoid "the talk" Josh kept insisting they have, making him think he still had some of the gift of gab which had served him so well during his carny days, but then, one morning, he woke and looked under his bed for the sword which would allow him to perform the ritual meant to remind him of who he'd once been, and he found nothing but dust bunnies, a sock he'd thought he'd lost, and a depression created in the carpeting by a long, rectangular box which had lain there since his grandson had taken him in.

His sword, the only memento that remained, was gone.

He shouted his grandson's name, so upset he didn't have to search for it even for a split second. No answer came, but Mr. Electrico suspected that could have been because his voice was no longer loud enough to carry downstairs. His knees were unfortunately not the only things giving out. He tried again, more forcefully, to use the voice he'd once owned when he'd captivated crowds, but though his mind remembered, his lungs would not.

"Josh!"

There was still no answer, so he headed slowly to the top of the stairs and called out again. His grandson was not normally gone so early in the day, so it was strange he shouldn't be there now. As Mr. Electrico was about to take his first step down, a figure came into view from the living room.

Mr. Electrico froze. It wasn't Josh.

It was the kid.

Ray.

He seemed exactly as he'd been all those years before, unchanged by time. And in one hand, the sword. Ray laughed as he made a few passes through the air with the metal, marking the air between them.

"You were looking for this," he said, his voice as frozen in time as was his face.

"What are you doing here?" asked Mr. Electrico.

"What do you think?" he said, leaping up one step, then back down again, repeating the move several times with glee. Mr. Electrico remembered what it was like to leap, but not when he'd last been able to do it. "What I've been doing ever since the day we met—living forever."

"That's...not possible," Mr. Electrico said. *Or was it?* he thought. "Where have you been? Why are you here now?"

"It seemed as if you needed me," said Ray, pausing in his prancing to look up. "Needed me to find this. I doubted you'd have been able to on your own."

Ray flipped the sword in his hand so that its hilt was now pointed up toward the top of the stairs. It was an offering. An invitation. One Mr. Electrico desperately wanted to accept. But in that moment, he didn't have the strength to walk down to receive it. His knees buckled, and he dropped to sit on the top step, suddenly unable to stand any longer.

Mr. Electrico was glad Josh wasn't present to see the weakness which had stolen over him. And so, of course, in that moment, from behind Ray came the sound of the front door being unlocked. Ray smiled, a buoyant smile Mr. Electrico recognized, and then looked briefly over one shoulder, unalarmed. He knelt, laying the sword down sideways across the bottom step, the blade so long it stuck out through the bannister.

"There," said Ray. "It's yours again. No one should take it from you."

And then Ray backed out of sight, vanishing into the living room, just before Josh came into view from the front foyer. Mr. Electrico found himself without the breath to speak, so Josh was startled on seeing him there, at first not even noticing the sword.

"Grandpa, why are you sitting up there like that?"

Mr. Electrico heard the love in his voice, but he also heard the exasperation, and knew he should answer immediately. Josh had lately been accusing him of getting slow, and a snappy answer would help contradict that, but he had none. All he could think was—how is it that Josh missed seeing Ray? Before Mr. Electrico could think of anything to say, Josh noticed the sword on the bottom step, and his expression darkened.

"So you found it," he said. "I'm surprised. How did you manage to do that?"

"You?" said Mr. Electrico. "You're the one who took my sword? Not..."

Mr. Electrico fell to silence. How could he dare reveal what he'd seen before Josh arrived home? His grandson was already having trouble accepting what he'd become, and that he'd mistakenly believed a boy he hadn't seen in half a century had taken his sword would be...too much.

"Not what?" said Josh.

"Nothing. It's just that...for a moment, I thought...never mind. But why? Why did you do it?"

"I had to, Grandpa. You're not safe with it anymore. Maybe you can be trusted with it when I'm here to supervise, but when you're alone? No."

"That's not true, Josh."

Mr. Electrico found himself trembling, whether from fear or anger he couldn't tell. But maybe it was neither, and only the trembling that came with the years.

"Sadly, it is true. You're not who you once were, Grandpa. And after we got back from the park, after you fell asleep, I started realizing... you could get hurt, without even meaning to."

As Josh spoke, he was hesitant in a way Mr. Electrico had never seen before, at times rocking from one foot to the other, at times seeming about to step over the sword and join him on the top step. Instead, he stayed in place, continuing to squeeze words out, words obviously as difficult to speak as they were to hear.

"It's not your fault," Josh said, louder than he'd left off. "So I had to, you see? And look at you here with the sword again. You could have been hurt retrieving it. What if you'd fallen off the ladder and broken your neck? You shouldn't be doing things like that, doing the things you once did. I wouldn't want to find you that way. I love you, Grandpa. You know that don't you? This is for your own good."

"What's this about a ladder, Josh? I didn't climb any ladder."

"Oh, Grandpa, have you forgotten that already? You had to have used a ladder, or else how would you have gotten it down from where I stored it in the garage? If you can't even remember that, it's just one more reason you shouldn't have it."

Josh stooped to pick up the sword, then turned toward the garage.

"You can't do this, Josh," said Mr. Electrico, rising swiftly to his feet. The sudden movement left him dizzy, forcing him to press one hand against the wall to remain steady. "That's mine! That's all I have left."

"Then what's it doing down here with you up there? You must have dropped it. Don't you see? You might have cut yourself. Or fallen and run yourself through. No. No more. If you want to keep living here, please. Don't try to find this again."

"Josh," he said, as his grandson vanished, seeming no more or less real than the boy who had vanished on his arrival. Mr. Electrico would have shouted if he could, but he had no more energy with which to shout.

"Later, Grandpa," said Josh upon his return from the garage. "We'll talk more later. We have some decisions to make."

Mr. Electrico said nothing as Josh walked up the stairs and squeezed past to his own bedroom. He did not *want* to talk more later. At least, not with Josh. He knew what was coming for him, he knew what those decisions would mean, and talking would only bring that fate toward him more quickly.

• • •

Mr. Electrico waited until he could no longer hear Josh's television vibrating through the thin walls and was sure his grandson was asleep, then snuck out of the house and stood on the front lawn. He'd head toward the park, he decided, where he'd spent most of the previous night.

He loved the park, the way his scanning of the unpopulated vista brought back memories of the beginnings of things—the tents still unrolled, the Ferris wheel unconstructed, the rubes asleep in their homes, and he needed that feeling now more than ever. That was almost the best part, those moments of before when anything could happen. It felt as if anything could happen tonight. But which way should he turn?

He could still remember where the park was, couldn't he?

No. He couldn't.

As he stood in indecision, fearful of choosing the wrong way, even more fearful of choosing no way at all, his breath turned to mist in the cool night air, and as that cloud pulsed, appearing and disappearing with each exhalation, through it, off on the nearest corner, under a streetlight, he could see Ray, waving the sword over his head, doing mock battle with a moth which hovered above him.

Mr. Electrico's sword.

And then the kid danced out of the spotlight and into the darkness.

Mr. Electrico took off after him, perhaps, based on what his knees were telling him, more quickly than he should have, but he didn't dare lose him. He could make out his outline in the distance, always on the verge of disappearing, and as Mr. Electrico ran, so ran Ray. They moved through the night this way, twisting and turning along the maze of the subdivisions, the kid continually pausing off in the distance just long enough to be sure he was seen, but no longer, and then taking off again as soon as Mr. Electrico started after him again.

By the time Mr. Electrico arrived at the park, he was gasping, and sure he could not have gone a single step further. For a moment, as he looked around, he thought he'd lost the kid, but there he was, sitting not on a bench, sitting not on the grass, but off in the empty playground, plopped on a mound of sand in front of the rut beneath the swings, a mound kicked high by the feet of a thousand thousand children.

The kid smiled, patting the sand beside him, and as Mr. Electrico settled down slowly, his legs protesting as they bent, he remembered the two of them having been side by side like that before, so many decades ago, when he had been so much younger, and the kid had been...

...exactly the same.

"Why are you here?" asked Mr. Electrico, having to catch his breath to get even that single short sentence out.

"Why are you *here*?" asked the kid, waving the sword to encompass the park.

And then Mr. Electrico *did* know, know what he hadn't known before, but merely suspected.

"Because I can almost see Lake Michigan," he said. The past and the present rubbed up against each other in this place. It was what called him here time and again. Because if he squinted, and imagined, and remembered, he could see from one to the other.

They sat in silence for awhile, looking off into the distance. Eventually, Mr. Electrico closed his eyes. Sometimes, in this place, he could see much better with them closed. But he could not see far enough. Not yet.

"Did you bring me another trick?" he asked. "Another puzzle to solve?"

"I did."

The kid rose, pointed the sword to his head, then allowed it to drop to his toes with a flourish, as if by lowering a sword, he was raising a curtain on himself. He bowed theatrically.

"You? You're the trick?"

Ray nodded and smiled.

"That's not a trick," said Mr. Electrico. "You staying the same, me growing older...that's a joke."

"So how come neither of us is laughing?" said the kid, settling back down beside him in the sand. "No, it's not a joke. I wouldn't do that to you. It is, indeed, a trick. Last time we were together, you showed me the secret to how one worked. This time, it's my turn to show you."

Mr. Electrico wanted to learn that trick, that secret. But there was something else which in that moment he wanted more.

"I'd like my sword back," he said.

"In a moment."

The kid used the sword to make circles in the air in front of them, then figure eights, then x's, then finally circles again.

"You said we'd met before in a former life. Was that a lie you were telling me? A part of your act?"

"I don't think so," he said. And then, more forcefully, certain for the first time: "No."

"You said I was your friend. Was *that* a lie?"

"No."

There had been no hesitation that time.

"So we were friends in the last life," said Ray. "We are friends in this one. And we will be friends in the next one as well."

"I'm glad of that," said Mr. Electrico. "But you still haven't answered my question, not fully. Why are you here?"

"Because I wanted to thank you," said Ray. "I've been wanting to do that for a long time, but I never had the chance. I could never reach you, not until now, when you were so close, because though I couldn't come nearer to you, you could come nearer to me. The day I met you, the day you made sparks come out my ears and told me to live forever, that was the day everything changed. That was the day you gave me the future, the day I learned how strange and wonderful the world really was. That was the day...the day I decided to become a writer. I could never thank you, because I could never track you down. I tried to, I really did, but only now...only now..."

Ray shrugged.

"Anyway...thank you."

"You remembered," said Mr. Electrico quietly.

"Yes," whispered Ray.

"You remembered me telling you to live forever."

Ray nodded.

"And did you live forever?"

"I did," said Ray. "Thanks to you, I will."

"So why haven't you changed? And why have I?"

"That's the magic, you see," said Ray. "Because no one has yet to do *this*."

The kid stood, and with a gesture Mr. Electrico recognized as if he were gazing upon it in a mirror, because he had done it thousands of times himself, leaned down, extended the sword, and tapped him on the center of his forehead.

"Live forever!" Ray shouted, with a voice that boomed far too loud for one so small. For a moment, the world seemed on fire. Mr. Electrico's skin prickled, and his hair stood on end, as he sensed the charge coruscating through him and connecting with a dormant engine within. Then, as the kid pressed the sword back into Mr. Electrico's hand, the sky—whether it had been truly ablaze, or whether it had been just the old electricity running through his eyes anew—faded.

"It's yours now," said Ray. "It always was yours."

Mr. Electrico leapt up, made a giddy hop, and struck his own slashes through the air. He laughed, feeling complete once more.

"Ready to join me?" asked the kid. He gestured behind them, away from the shadow of Lake Michigan.

Mr. Electrico turned, and in the distance, where suddenly it was daylight, could see the tents flapping in a gentle breeze. He could make out the banners, looking as fresh as the day they were first painted, covered with the images of his friends, images larger than life, but no larger than they lived on in his memory—the Sword Swallower and the Bearded Lady and the Illustrated Man and—

—and look—on the largest stretch of canvas in the carnival—there he was, Mr. Electrico, bigger than life himself, too, but no bigger than life should be, his hair ablaze, his eyes sparking, his fingertips flashing lightning, fully again who he used to be.

Who he was again.

"Live forever," Mr. Electrico whispered. "Yes...let's."

He took Ray's hand, and together, they headed toward the carnival.

A MOST EXTRAORDINARY MAN

*M*rs. Sappleton hadn't thought of that odd Mr. Nuttel since the day he'd fled gibbering from her parlor, due to—or so her niece Vera had said—"a horror of dogs." But as she held a letter addressed from the man's sister in the States, the one who had taken such pleasant meals with her and Vera four years before, it all came flooding back.

"A most extraordinary man," she whispered while studying the envelope, a muttering which caused her niece to ask of whom she spoke. Nothing much escaped the girl's attention, Mrs. Sappleton long ago noticed, often in such a way as to be disturbing.

"Mr. Framton Nuttel," said Mrs. Sappleton. "You remember, that young man who—"

"Oh, I remember *him*, Auntie," said Vera, smiling in a way which Mrs. Sappleton thought, if looked at from the right angle, could almost have been taken for a smirk.

"If you remember him so, then he managed to make a far greater impression on you than he did on me," said Mrs. Sappleton.

"Oh, we shared many things before you came downstairs to join us. Many things."

"And from what you told me, they were not at all things an impressionable girl your age should have heard. Mad dogs on the banks of the Ganges. Sleeping in graves. The young man should have known better."

"But he was sick, Auntie. We should endeavor to forgive him."

"It is good of you to think so, to be able to find in yourself that mercy," said Mrs. Sappleton, and as she held the envelope up to the sunlight which streamed in through the large, open French window, her curiosity changed the subject. "It seems his sister has written me for the first time since that letter of introduction her brother had carried. I wonder why. What could it possibly be about?"

"Oh, read it, Auntie, do!" said Vera, clapping her hands. Mrs. Sappleton was pleased to see the girl, who had only just turned sixteen, show some enthusiasm again. She hadn't seemed quite herself in recent months, had not, in fact, been the girl Mrs. Sappleton helped raise since Mr. Nuttel's brief, eccentric visit, a passing strange coincidence.

Mrs. Sappleton retrieved a letter opener from a low bureau in one corner of the room, slit the envelope lengthwise, cleared her throat, and began to read.

"My dear Mrs. Sappleton," she began. "I wish I were writing you this morning under better circumstances."

Something about the young woman's phrasing made Mrs. Sappleton pause. As she scanned ahead down the page, a sudden shock coursed through her and weakened her knees. She sat down suddenly, her hand went limp, and the letter fluttered to the rug. Sensing her mistress' distress, Bertie, her husband's little brown spaniel, padded over and licked with concern at the tips of her fingers.

"What wrong?" asked Vera, in a tone suffused with equal parts excitement and worry, though it would have required extensive study to discern which was which.

Mrs. Sappleton waved the hand not being snuffled by the spaniel in vague circles before her, as if searching there for the words she could possibly say that would make the subject matter suitable for Vera's ears. Finding none, she dropped that hand in her lap and spoke in a whisper.

"I don't know that I can..." she began weakly, then fell to silence.

"Then let me, Auntie!"

Before Mrs. Sappleton could object, Vera had scooped up the letter, and holding it tightly, stood bolt upright before her. Her eyes were bright, as if she were bursting with pride while preparing to recite a poem in school. She cleared her throat, and began to read the unexpected correspondence with an impeccable pronunciation.

"I wish I were writing under better circumstances," she said, strangely channeling the intonations of Miss Nuttel's speech, even though Vera had been but eleven when the two had last spoken. "I have the unfortunate duty of informing you that my beloved brother, whose time on this Earth was so tortured, and whose path through this world was so rocky, has died. I had hoped that the time he spent with you, which as I have so often expressed had been so refreshing for me, might prove equally so for him, might calm his fretful soul, but it was not to be so. He found no cure there. Framton returned from his stay with you as agitated as when he'd departed from my side. He was jittery as ever, starting at the slightest sound, his eyes always darting, his head constantly swiveling atop his shoulders as if he was fearful of something none of the rest of us could see. Eventually, the exhaustion of dealing with his jangled nerves became too much for him, and he...I will be blunt with you, Mrs. Sappleton. He chose to depart this life.

"I do not blame you, because I remember you and your niece with kindness, and am sure that you each did your best, with your hospitality and your charm, to part the dark clouds which hovered unceasingly over him. Alas, his ailment proved too great to be lifted by any human power. I hope he is now abiding with the One Who in His Grace and Mercy may bring all peace to those who would but ask it of Him.

"I hope that if Fate allows I may return to see you and your niece once more someday. Vera was a very interesting young girl, and I am sure that by now she has blossomed into a very interesting young woman. You are both often in my thoughts. Please keep Framton in yours.

"Yours most sincerely, Miss Edith Nuttel"

Vera stopped speaking, but her eyes did not lift from the page. Keeping her head down, her lips moved as she reread a section of the letter.

"Auntie, what did Miss Edith mean when she wrote that, 'he chose to depart this life'? What exactly happened to Mr. Nuttel?"

Mrs. Sappleton looked wearily at her niece, whose eyes glistened as if she knew more of the answer than her question would have you believe.

TELL ME LIKE YOU DONE BEFORE

"I'm tired, Vera," she said, letting her head drop back against the Morris chair. "Let us talk about this together later."

"Yes, Auntie," said Vera. She folded the letter carefully and slipped it into a pocket. Smiling, she left the drawing room and headed to her bedroom, where she read the letter over and over until it grew far too dark to continue reading, at which point she sat motionless in that darkness and recited it from memory.

. . .

The following morning, Mr. Sappleton stepped from the lawn in through the parlor's large open French window and called out to his wife, "Dearie, have you seen Bertie? I can't find him anywhere." He held his shotgun in the crook of one elbow, and his white mackintosh, as yet unmuddied by the day's hunt, was draped over the other.

"That's not like him," said Mrs. Sappleton. "He's usually nipping at your heels by now, begging to be taken along."

"He's not the only one who hasn't been behaving like himself lately," Mr. Sappleton said grumpily.

"Hush, John, she'll hear you."

"And what if she does? A bit of frank talk would do the girl some good. She's been behaving strangely lately. You know that as well as I."

"Oh, I'm sure she'll grow out of it, John. All girls eventually do."

"All girls eventually do what, Auntie?" asked Vera, coming silently into the room.

"How about you?" said Mr. Sappleton roughly to his niece. "Have you seen Bertie?"

Vera placed a forefinger to one pale cheek and tapped it there until her eyes lit up.

"Not since this morning," she said. "I heard him scratching at the door to be let out. He'd spotted a bird he hoped would make him a good breakfast, and I let him have his way. Now what was this about girls?"

Mr. Sappleton harrumphed and stepped over to the open window, where he stared off toward the moor, and the snipe which he hoped waited for him beyond.

"I'm heading off to hunt with those brothers of yours," he said to his wife, "though it doesn't seem right somehow without Bertie. I'll see you later, dearie."

He then dipped his chin toward his niece.

"You, too, Vera."

And then he was gone.

"Will you tell me about girls now, Auntie?" Vera asked as soon as they were alone.

"In a moment," said Mrs. Sappleton, sighing. "But before I do, would you please put this out at the postbox?"

She reached into the folds of her skirt and pulled out an envelope.

"I didn't sleep well last night, and so I wrote a letter of condolence to poor Miss Nuttel. I can't imagine what it would be like to have one's brother..."

Mrs. Sappleton's voice trailed off, not wishing to expose her niece to such kinds of thoughts.

"Have one's brother what?" asked Vera.

"Never you mind right now," said Mrs. Sappleton firmly. "Just put the letter out front, and then we'll have some tea and talk. Now that you're sixteen, and you're not a girl anymore, we can talk woman to woman. It's long past time for that."

"Yes, Auntie," said Vera, curtsying. She then turned and skipped away toward the front door, like the innocent girl her aunt had first taken in.

Mrs. Sappleton moved to the open window through which she hoped to see one final glimpse of her husband's back, but he had already vanished into the distance. She hoped he would be returning soon. It was early, but something already did not seem right about this day.

Her reverie was interrupted by a high-pitched scream.

Mrs. Sappleton hurried toward the sound, and found her niece at the open front door, staring down at the welcome mat on which was curled the bleeding body of Bertie, quite dead. The letter opener which she had so recently used was plunged into his poor chest, and his eyes stared at them accusingly, as if there'd been something they could have done, but had chosen not to. Mrs. Sappleton grabbed Vera and pulled her to her bosom.

"Stop looking, Vera," she said sternly. "Woman now or not, you shouldn't have to see this."

But even as Mrs. Sappleton pressed her niece against her bosom, Vera twisted her head ever so slightly so that she could peek at the remains of the little brown spaniel, his body twisted, his fur matted with blood. Her expression, unseen by her aunt, was one of both horror and glee.

• • •

Mrs. Sappleton sat by the open window, praying for her husband and two younger brothers to arrive home from the marshes soon. But she knew, even as she was engaged in the practice of supplication, that they of course had no idea they had any need to hurry. As far as they believed, it was a day like any other, save for the fact that Bertie was off hunting on his own just as they were, another male, though a four-legged one, doing a male's business, and therefore there was no need for alarm. For the trio of hunters, the day was no different, except for the absence of a dog. While for Mrs. Sappleton, the day was no different, save for the horrid presence of one.

"This is all the fault of a ghost," said Vera, startling her aunt. She'd entered the room so quietly that Mrs. Sappleton had thought herself still alone with her reverie.

"Whose ghost?" Mrs. Sappleton asked reflexively, but realizing the nature of what they were speaking, she quickly changed direction. "There is no such thing as ghosts."

"But, oh, Auntie, there is!" said Vera, wringing her hands before her. "And now that Mr. Nuttel is deceased, his ghost must be mad, just as he was—"

"Vera! There is no need to be insulting! Especially not to the dead."

"—and his spirit has traveled here, and has taken revenge on poor Bertie. Remember, he—"

Vera hesitated a moment before continuing, as if struggling to keep straight the facts of a tale told long ago.

"—he had a horror of dogs."

"I remember no such thing," said Mrs. Sappleton. "I only remember that you told me so."

"Maybe now that Bertie has passed," said Vera, "poor Mr. Nuttel's soul can rest in peace."

"And maybe you can stop telling such fanciful tales," Mrs. Sappleton said sternly. "Whatever has come over you these recent months? I hardly know when you are telling the truth and when you are..."

Here Mrs. Sappleton stammered, because she had been raised properly by her own aunt, and did not like to make such an accusation as she was about to utter.

"...when you are not."

"Oh, Auntie, I have always tried to tell you the truth. It's just that I can't help myself sometimes. I am a believer in romance at short notice."

"Well, I believe we've had enough of such storytelling and speculation. Let us stick to rational, concrete facts, shall we? No more fabulations."

"If you insist," said Vera, her hand moving to the cloth of her blouse and feeling Mr. Nuttel's letter through the fabric there.

"What's that you have, Vera?"

"Nothing, Auntie," she said, turning quickly away.

"Whatever you've hidden, you must give it to me at once. As I've told you, there will be no secrets in this home."

Mrs. Sappleton stood and approached Vera with one hand outstretched, but before she could compel her niece to produce what had been hidden, her brothers bounded through the open window and into the room.

"Hullo, sister," said Edward, the older of her brothers. He surveyed the room with a smile which turned into a puzzled frown when he did not behold that which he sought.

"Has Bertie returned?" asked Ronnie, her younger. "If not, your husband must be disconsolate without him. You should have seen how he was moping without him on our hunt. I can only imagine how lonely he must be now if his spaniel has not yet turned up."

"Imagine?" asked Mrs. Sappleton anxiously. "Why must we imagine? Where is my husband?"

"You mean he has not yet returned?" asked Edward. "He should have beaten us here by quite a large margin. He left us more than an hour ago."

"Yes," said Ronnie. "Hunting just wasn't the same without Bertie, he said, and so he abandoned us to return for a look. We expected to find them here, frolicking together. Where could they both be?"

Before anyone could answer, Vera leapt up, pointing with a shaking hand toward the open window.

"Lock it!" she shouted. "This is all Mr. Nuttel's fault! He's coming for me just as he came for Bertie!"

"Bertie?" said Ronnie. "What happened to Bertie?"

"Who's Mr. Nuttel?" said Edward. "And why would he be coming for you?"

"I certainly won't be locking any doors," said Mrs. Sappleton. "How else will your uncle be able to get in upon his return? Whatever has come over you?"

"I don't care," said Vera, beginning to cry. "I don't care about any of that. Lock it, lock it you must. I've done something, Auntie. I've done something horrible, and now a haunting has befallen us all."

Her aunt and uncles tried to get her to tell what she had done, but they could pry nothing from her save tears. As she was inconsolable, Mrs. Sappleton slipped her a jigger of rum and led her up to her bedroom. Edward called out from behind the two women as they fled the parlor.

"I still don't understand," he said. "Who's Mr. Nuttel?"

• • •

Somewhere, a dog barked, and it woke Vera to the darkness of her room. She felt somewhat dizzy—whether it was from the alcohol or the excitement of recent events she could not say—and for a moment she wondered if all that she recalled having passed during the preceding day had been but a dream. Hearing that bark of Bertie's surely meant it was so, because how could he bark if he was...

But then the dog barked yet again, and she shrugged off all symptoms of sleep as easily as she tossed aside her covers. She sat up, heart beating wildly. It surely sounded like Bertie, but...Bertie could not be alive. She remembered it all now, and there was no doubt as to what had occurred. She had seen him dead. Murdered.

After what Mr. Nuttel had done to Bertie, was she now being haunted by Bertie's ghost as well? Was the spirit of the poor creature bringing this upon their heads as the consequence of all her fabrications?

She tiptoed to the window, hoping that in the slowly increasing moonlight she could spot whatever beast it was that had made the sound. Perhaps (she told herself, even though she doubted it could be so) she had only mistaken an owl for a spaniel. But as she stared out her window and down across the lawn, no further barking came, and so she had no idea in which direction to look in hopes of locating it.

Then she saw something—a white glow that grew more prominent as the moon rose in the sky. Her heart jumped in her chest. Was this Mr. Nuttel's ghost, come to punish her? She stared, willing herself not to blink, waiting for the shimmering blotch to move, as surely it must...but it did not. Then she realized—it was nothing more than her uncle's white mackintosh, reflecting the moonlight. Had he left it hanging on a tree in the yard upon his return? But if so, why had none of them noticed it before?

She slid open the window and scuttled down the trellis, ignoring the occasional scratch of a thorn. She would retrieve the mackintosh and bring it back to Auntie and Uncle, who had to be home by now, home and asleep the next room over, and things would again be as they had been. But once she dropped to the ground and began walking toward the glow, she saw by the shifting of its outline that—it wasn't just the coat, it was her uncle himself, leaning motionless against the tree, head tilted back against the bark, studying the night sky as she approached.

"Uncle, what are you doing out here?" asked Vera. "You have worried poor Auntie so much!"

He did not answer her. She drew nearer and touched his hand so he would look down and notice her. Could he have fallen asleep out here in the cool air? But...no. Now that she was before him, she could see...his hair was matted with blood, mirroring Bertie's fur. But no knife had made his wounds.

He had been struck by a rock.

She tugged at his hand, and his head fell forward, his chin against his chest. His eyes, though wide, saw her not.

She shrieked, pulling back her hand, and as she did so, her Uncle toppled forward, knocking her off her feet, pinning her beneath him to the lawn. She could not move, could barely breathe from the sheer weight of him, and soon lost consciousness beneath the stars.

• • •

When Vera woke, Auntie was peering down at her, a stern expression on her face.

"What are you doing out here in the cold and damp, Vera?" she asked. "This is no place for a young girl to sleep."

"But Uncle—"

"What about Uncle? He still has yet to return."

Vera groggily propped herself up on her elbows. There was no white mackintosh. No Uncle. And she looked down the length of her nightshirt, as far as she could tell, there was no blood either.

"I saw him," insisted Vera. "He was here. He had been hurt, and he was—"

"I thought we agreed there would be no more fanciful tales. And especially none so hurtful to me as that."

"But I'm not lying, I—"

"Enough!" barked Mrs. Sappleton, louder than Vera had ever remembered her.

Mrs. Sappleton yanked her niece to her feet and pulled her roughly toward the house.

"Let's get you back to your room," she said.

"But I don't want to go there," said Vera as she was pulled in through the open window and up the stairs. She looked back at it in horror and grew hysterical. It had all begun with an open window, a window which her aunt now refused to lock.

"I don't want to be alone," she howled. "Please, Auntie, don't leave me alone tonight. You mustn't. You can't!"

Mrs. Sappleton pushed Vera into her bed, but as she arranged the covers and looked down at her trembling niece, her heart softened.

"Move over slightly, child," she said. "Allow me to get in bed beside you, and we'll sleep as we first did when you came to live with Uncle and me. All will be better in the morning. You'll see. Things are always better in the morning."

Were they? Vera had no way of knowing, but as she snuggled closer against her Auntie, she found comfort there, and fell quickly asleep. She did not dream, and if there was further barking in the night, she either did not hear it or slept so deeply that it did not wake her.

• • •

When Vera woke to the bright sunshine streaming into her room through the window she had opened and climbed through the night before, she felt a clammy dampness about her, and her first thought was, "Not again."

To wet yourself at her age, especially after being told you were a woman, was embarrassing enough, but to do so while your Auntie was sleeping beside you was positively unbearable. Vera disentangled herself from her Auntie and as she pulled away she realized...the wetness was not her own.

She tilted her head back toward Auntie's face ever so slowly, somehow knowing what she would find there, and saw her wrinkled cheeks covered in blood. The blanket which had been pulled to her neck was soaked as well. Vera leapt back, rolling off the bed and onto the Oriental rug, unintentionally pulling the soiled blanket with her, which made her shriek even more, and she slapped at it, coiling herself in it more and more the harder she fought to free herself, until she finally broke away and could toss the sodden blanket aside.

And there, now that she could see again, was Framton Nuttel, sitting on the sill of the open window, wearing her uncle's white mackintosh, the front of which was drenched with blood.

"Hello, Vera," he said. It was only when he spoke that she noticed his hands were scarlet, too.

"You're...alive? But I thought—"

"You thought so many things. Too many things. Like your story about the tragedy that befell your dead uncles and the eccentricity of your pining aunt. My nervous condition had me on the edge, Vera. And your fancies pushed me over that edge."

"But your sister's letter? She said—"

"My sister said nothing. My sister—thanks to you, thanks to what you forced me to become—is no longer capable of anything. *I* wrote that letter. And then I returned. Returned to tell you that you are a bad little girl. And to make you pay. And to make all who loved you and all whom you loved pay."

He made a move to rise, but Vera held a hand toward him and he paused.

"Stay where you are," she said. "I have but to make a sound, and my uncles will be in here immediately. Then they will thrash you for what you have done."

Mr. Nuttel smiled, but now there was a flicker there that remained from the nervous uncertainty of old.

"Your uncles are not with us, Vera. They returned to their own homes and spent the night with their own families. You and I are the only living things within earshot."

"They are too here," said Vera, setting her jaw. "They could not bear to leave their sister alone without her husband, and so they remained in the guest room. You know nothing of a brother's love, Mr. Nuttel. All I need to do is scream. And believe me. I will."

He knew there was no one else there, he *knew* it, but yet when the words fell from her lips, she told the lie with such flair, that for a fleeting moment, he believed her, just as he had believed her when she had told him that ridiculous story so many months ago. So when she inhaled as if to scream, he hesitated when he should have leapt upon her, and she instead leapt upon him, pushing him out the open window.

As he tumbled back, she slammed the window shut, locking it quickly, regretting the falsity of her lie, and wishing that her uncles had been there to rescue her. But they of course were not.

She could see Mr. Nuttel rise to his feet and hobble around the house, and suddenly remembered—the open window downstairs through which Auntie had hoped her husband would return, but through which he would never step again—Auntie had left it open, she had *insisted* on leaving it open, why had she not believed her?

She raced downstairs, and into the parlor, and did not find Mr. Nuttel there. She was in time! The fall had made him lame, and had given her the moments she needed. She leapt at the door, began slamming it on its hinges, but before she could seal herself inside, Mr. Nuttel blocked it with a bloody hand. She could hear the bones of his fingers crack as the door hit them, but his face showed no pain. His madness had transported him beyond its reach.

He bruited the door open violently, the force of which knocked her back onto the rug. He stepped through the open window looking so, so tall.

"Mr. Nuttel," she said, voice quivering, seeking in her mind for some tale that would divert him, and finding none. "What is it you are planning to do to me? Am I to suffer the same fate as Bertie and Uncle and Auntie?"

"Oh, no," he said, letting the white mackintosh, now stained with red, fall from his shoulders and revealing that what lay beneath was equally as horrifying and bloodied. "I have something very special planned for you, Vera. Because, you see, romance at short notice is also *my* specialty..."

THIS IS WHERE THE TITLE GOES

*T*his opening sentence is supposed to make you stop breathing. This next sentence is supposed to allow you to start again, even as you forget you are holding a book or magazine. This third sentence you read is supposed to make you forget the act of reading, as if the words were your life instead of your dream. This fourth sentence, closing the first paragraph, should have you captured, and cause you to realize that there is nothing more important you could possibly be doing right now than reading this.

As you read on, you realize you were right to do so. The words, tumbling along like trained acrobats, make the ringing of the phone disappear. The rumble in your stomach lessens. The thoughts of that errand you had long put off and planned to finally accomplish today turn to vapor and are absorbed by the porous prose before you.

Here, three paragraphs along, is where you meet someone about whom within you rise uncertain feelings. You're unsure of his motives, and even less sure of the motives of the author. The next few sentences will introduce you to him further, the character, not the author, telling you how he feels as he moves through the dense air of the scene, but you can't make up your mind quickly as to whether you're to take him as a hero or a villain. It unnerves you to be made to feel so gray, when up until now your emotions have been stirred in black and white. During the course of this next sentence you will be given a few fragments of physical description, far too vague for you to assemble the mental equivalent of a police sketch; just enough for you to put a picture together of him in your head, but not so much detail that you will be unable to contribute in his creation. You should feel, if the words do their job properly, that there is as much of you in him as there is of the words themselves.

You realize that he seems unsure of whether he can accomplish the deeds that are set out before him, but he will try anyway. You realize that you like stories about people who strive in the face of failure, perhaps because you need the encouragement yourself. You also realize, far more importantly, that unlike the protagonist, the author does not seem unsure of accomplishing *his* task, and neither do you feel unsure about accomplishing your own, which at the moment is to make your way slowly down this page.

The author makes this man seem a nice enough person, and it begins to dawn that you should be rooting for him. And just when you've made the decision to hand him your heart, as your veins begin to pulse in concert with the page, along comes a treacherous paragraph, an ice floe built of consonants and vowels. He is handed his first setback here, and you want to freeze the words upon the page. These next are the sentences that tell you about those who want to stop him. You do not like them, even though they are given a few random appealing characteristics, perhaps to throw you off guard. One keeps delicate pets; another is kind to his aged mother. You're not sure why the author tells you these details. It makes you dislike these threatening men all the more.

They lay the first trap for him here, and to you it seems foolproof. There seems no escape. Even as your conscious mind can think of nothing but the story, you worry, and with one thumb you feel for how many pages remain, wondering for how long a time you can continue to live in this world. Can the story be over so soon? You hope not, but surely, no way out remains. During this next sentence you do not breath, and in fact, you do not begin to do so again until the seemingly distant beginning of the next paragraph.

Time moves more slowly now. You need to know what happens next, and yet the faster you rush toward the answer, the further it seems to recede from you. You look up, and the light in the room seems denser somehow, as if it is spilling through the windows in liquid form. It comes between you and the page, and you must wipe it away from the page, as if a party had gone on too long, and someone had spilled a drink across an heirloom tablecloth.

Here is where, startlingly, the protagonist whom you have come to feel a friend tricks them both and gets away in a manner that surprises you. The writer, however, makes sure that even as you are surprised, you do not feel tricked. The words before you are thus living paradoxes, preserved on the page, pinned by metaphor. The next sentence you make yourself read twice. This is the sentence where you learn exactly how he did that, how he pulled it off, the character, not the writer, and you realize that you could have done it yourself if you had been as smart, or if your god had been this writer. Here, as you pause to let it all sink in, is where you're supposed to laugh at the audacity of it all.

You suddenly notice that your eyes no longer ache, as they had been doing up until the time you settled in with this story. Or rather, you remember that you have forgotten to notice the pain that existed up until you first read the words, "This is Where the Title Goes." The words have clogged the pores of your mind, allowing nothing else to enter. Pain can no longer find a home here.

This paragraph will tell you more about the city where the action takes place. You feel its pathways beneath your feet as if the city was your own. The man whom you have come to feel is your doppelgänger moves through it, not only for reasons of plot, but also for reasons of verisimilitude. He interacts, in a guarded fashion, both with those who seem quite like him and also those peculiarly unlike him, in an attempt, or so you sense, to enact a grand plan. But the skeins of that plan are too loose for your fingers to do anything but slip through as you try to grab it. You like this city and wish you could live there. Perhaps, walking down a dark street, you might come across this man, who would wrap you in that complex fabric.

But instead of your face, it is another's he sees as he walks through the shadow. He turns his head at the softness of a sigh, and so, when you least expected it, this is the sentence where you learn what it is like to be in love. As he gazes at her, you know that her hair is the hair of the girl you sat behind in homeroom in the eighth grade, and her skin a texture that you have only before seen in dreams. You know, looking at her in the portrait you have painted in your mind, that he would do anything for her, perhaps even give up the grand plan on which by now you have chosen to depend so greatly. Only she can divert him from his path. And you know that she could do the same to you.

He tries to go, and she does not let him, and by the way the words lean together you know that she was sent here, that she is a last resort, and now choices must be made which cannot then be retrieved. The next sentence rips something inside of you. Here, a further sentence on, is where you're supposed to cry.

A space comes next, a skipped line, just the height and width of a single narrow band across the page, and in that space is the death of all of his hopes and dreams. She was the reason for doing the things he has chosen to do, and now, he has no reason. In that small break between this paragraph and the next, everything changes. You cannot bear to truly know it. The author knows that of you, and so he chooses not to show you his face as he turns from her body, her face blank against the pavement, her gun on the floor between them, with one shot fired as they struggled.

· · ·

He goes ahead with his plan anyway, even though there is no longer anyone whom to him is worth doing things *for*. He has in a moment decided to instead do things for the person she used to be. For the person who wanted a world in which this story could end as it does.

If you, reading these words, were a different sort of person, you might have been able to arrive at this second paragraph after the ominous break still thinking that all was as it was before, and that the reason he goes on is the same. But it is not, and it can never be again. Whatever will be done will no longer be done for victories that he can truly savor. Any triumph that occurs will not arrive as a success for him, no matter how charmed his life from here on. Any triumph that comes he will have risked for you alone, and for those like you.

This is the sentence that lets you know that the prize is almost within his grasp. This is the sentence that tells you exactly how those who would stop him have conspired for one final attempt to put him down. These conflicting sentences wrestle with each other before you, and until one can erase the other from the page, their twin exertions leave you with only one thought.

You are worried that the one in whom you have invested so much will fail.

By now it is as important to you that he achieve his goal as it is that you achieve your own. You have not had cause to hope for so very long. The walls about you no longer seem quite so in need of paint. The paths worn in your thin carpeting no longer seem so obvious. Your aggravated lower-back pain appears to have been replaced by the spine of a twenty year old.

This is the sentence that misleads you one last time. This paragraph is full of words like "gutted," "bloody," and "explosion," and unfortunately, momentarily, it allows you to think that the evil might triumph over the good. That the goal, once done for love, now done for the need of only itself, is forever over the horizon, and will not be reached in either your lifetime, or the lifetime of the story itself.

But then...it is all over. The plans of the one you have come to see as your second self have all come together. There is triumph in the air. In your room, as you read these words that come so close upon the end of the story, you feel its breeze upon your face. The tapestry, once so loosely woven that it seemed as if all sense would at the last moment slip through, has been tugged tight, and the image of truth and beauty painstakingly created on its surface is at last visible. The image there burns into your heart. It could be no other way. You touch your cheek and find a tear there, but you are smiling.

The story's final sentence is coming along now. There. There it is. It just went by. It's going now, almost gone entirely, a perfume that you were privileged to inhale briefly and once, but is now no longer yours alone.

You let those last words ring in your mind, repeating the final sentence again. You let the pages slip from your fingers onto an end table, but before you rise to go to bed, you will pick them up again. You will copy those final words over onto a small slip of paper that you will carry in your wallet, and when you grow depressed you will retrieve it to place your lips once more around those words and dream of being the person you were meant to be.

You have at last, after all of your searching, after all of your ceaseless reading, after a lifetime of needless regret and failed promises, finally read the perfect story.

LIVE PEOPLE DON'T UNDERSTAND

Everybody knows in their bones that something is eternal,
and that something has to do with humans.
–Our Town, Act III

Emily remembered what it was like to be alive.

In fact, at first, she had forgotten that she was dead. She lay in a coffin, the confines of which she could not yet bring herself to see, and thought herself newly risen from a nap. Gazing upward, she wondered why the familiar ceiling above, the one under which she had shared a marriage bed with her husband George, had been replaced by stars.

Adding to her puzzle, she sensed other sleepers stretched out nearby. Their presence made her uncomfortable. It had been difficult enough for her to grow accustomed to being a wife, to sleeping with another beside her—she remembered her nervousness on her wedding night and smiled—but to have strangers nearby her as well was more than should be asked of her. Their closeness here did not make sense, but then, dreams on waking often lost their sense, and so she did not let herself worry much about her confusion. She trusted that she would understand soon enough. But then she remembered those who should have been nearby, and all those feelings faded, to be replaced by a greater loneliness than she had ever felt in her life.

If she asked, perhaps these strangers would tell her why George was not at her side—the two of them had yet to spend a night apart, which was exactly as it was supposed to be—and where her newborn baby had gone. She had just had the baby, hadn't she? George, Jr. was four by now, and could cope without her there every moment, but the little one...it must be hungry without Emily there to share her milk.

She couldn't even remember whether she'd had a boy or a girl—how could that be?—but she knew that she had to find her baby.

She had to find her George.

"Wake up," she shouted. It rattled her to do so, because she was not a person accustomed to shouting. "Oh, you must wake up and talk to me. Where am I? What is this place? Help me, won't you? Help me understand. One moment I was at home in my bed in Grover's Corners, and the next I'm waking from a nap...where? Hello? You can't fool me. You're out there, you can hear me, I know it. Stop trying to pretend that you're still asleep. It just won't work, not when I need you so badly."

"Hush," came an old woman's voice to her left. Or at least Emily thought her to be old. The voice sounded vaguely familiar, but Emily could not place it, because the woman's throat was drier and raspier than she remembered it.

"I can't," said Emily. "I won't. Really now, I don't see how you can ask me to be still, not when there are so many unanswered questions."

"Nonetheless, just hush," insisted the woman, and as she continued to speak, Emily realized who she was. "You'll get used to unanswered questions. Soon enough, they'll no longer bother you so much."

"Really now, you shouldn't be talking that way, Mrs. Soames," said Emily, ill at ease at talking so sternly to an elder. "It is Mrs. Soames, isn't it? Forgive me for saying so, but there's no need for you to be so rude."

"There's no need to be anything any longer," said Mrs. Soames. "Which is precisely my point. Just settle down and let me be."

"How can you sleep away the day that way?" said Emily. She did not pause to consider what forces could have possibly brought them together at this time. "It's Emily, Mrs. Soames. Remember how much you enjoyed my wedding? You always loved a good party. I remember that about you. How can you just lie there when there is so much out there to live for?"

A rich burst of laughter came from somewhere off to Emily's right. The sound startled her, but gave her no offense. She did not feel that her emotions were being mocked, and remembering back to another who would chuckle with a wisdom Emily had not yet earned, she realized who it was who lay so close beside her, and felt loved and embraced.

"Mrs. Gibbs?" she whispered, stunned to see her mother-in-law there, and yet pleased by her presence.

"Can't you get her to keep quiet?" said Mrs. Soames.

"Don't be so hard on Emily," said Mrs. Gibbs, as the woman's laughter died down. "She's only a child. The two of us had plenty of time to make our peace with what would come here. But she was at the beginning of things. Besides, don't you remember how you felt when you first got here, even with all that preparation? Don't you remember what it was like when you first took your place?"

Emily listened, and listened hard, for the answer meant everything, but there was only a long silence, as if Mrs. Soames was having difficulty remembering how to speak, let alone the moments of her arrival in this place, whatever this place was.

"Vaguely," Mrs. Soames finally said. "Yes. Yes, I *do* remember. Only...I don't think I want to remember."

"Well, there you go," said Mrs. Gibbs. "But you weren't always like that, let me tell you. She's young yet, in more ways than one. She can't help but remember."

Emily waited for Mrs. Soames and Mrs. Gibbs to address her again, instead of just bantering amongst themselves, but instead, their conversation petered out, and they fell to silence. Emily called out to them again.

"I think I know where I am," said Emily, astonished. "I'm still dreaming, aren't I?"

"No, dear," said Mrs. Gibbs, her voice sleepy. "All that happened before, up until the time you found yourself here, that was the dream, dear. Let it go."

"I can't." Anguished, she began to cry, but no tears came. She thought to touch her face to find out how it could possibly be that the weeping failed to dampen her cheeks, but her arms would not move, no matter how hard she tried. Struggling like that, the truth of her situation came upon her with a suddenness that was sickening. "I'm dead, aren't I?"

"No need to say it that way," said Mrs. Gibbs. "It's really not so bad. The experience can become quite pleasant after a while, actually. Now you rest, girl."

"Please," said Mrs. Soames.

"I can't!" she said, feeling herself grow hysterical. How ridiculous was that, to be dead and hysterical? She refused to be either. George wouldn't want her to be either. "Don't you see? I'll never be able to let go!"

"Enough," said Mrs. Soames. "Someone's coming! Behave!"

"What if it's a thief?" said Emily, made fearful by the sound of unsteady footsteps trudging up the hill. George was supposed to protect her from such things, but now her only comfort was in two old women, and what could they do? "What if he's here to rob us?"

"Don't be silly, girl," said Mrs. Gibbs. "You have nothing more which anyone would wish to steal."

There was so much more that Emily needed to say right then, but before she could respond further, she sensed her poor dear husband above. George was there, right at the edges of the newly turned dirt of her grave. She was shocked by how much death had distracted her, for until that moment, she had not been aware of his approach. He seemed different to her, though, than when she had seen him last.

"Mrs. Gibbs," she said. "What's happened to your son? He's so...old."

"Tempus fugit, dear," she said. "You'll learn that soon enough."

"Could I really have been asleep so long?" said Emily. "It must have been years. But he's here! He still remembers us, Mrs. Gibbs."

"That isn't always a good thing, dear. No, not at all. And he's here to see you, not me. Listen."

"Emily," George moaned. He dropped to his knees directly above Emily's head. As he sobbed, she wished she could touch his lined cheek to comfort him, but she could do nothing. "I'm sorry, I'm so sorry."

"You needn't apologize, George. Not you."

She could feel a wrenching in his heart, could feel his essence seeking her out but not being able to find her. Their two hearts had once beat as one, destined for each other from the very start, but now, his lone heart was barely a heart at all. She pleaded for a way to break the barrier that kept them apart, but it was useless. Though he was alive to her, she was dead in all ways to him. His fingers bunched in the wet dirt, pawing it like a soggy blanket that he hoped to pull from across her face.

"No one should have to die in such a horrible way," he said, gasping. "I cannot change that, so I will myself to forget it. But I can't do that either, Emily, no matter how hard I try. Do you forgive me after all these years, Emily? Could you?"

He wanted an answer from her, one that she, in turn, wanted to give, and he listened for words she could not make him hear. But she would forgive him anything, could not recall having ever wavered from such a thought, in part because she knew that he could not possibly do anything that it would actually be necessary for her to forgive, not in a thousand lifetimes. Not George.

The urgency of his yearning was overpowering, though, and it came back to her then, not all of it, not the details, just enough to know what had delivered her to her final resting place. Her mother had told her during those few times when she'd tried to impart the lesson of womanhood to her, that some women were not built for childbirth. How unfortunate for Emily to have to learn that first hand. But at least...at least their baby lived. She had that much to be thankful for. At least she had seen that much before she vanished from her first world and was forced to take her place in the next one.

"Don't blame yourself, George," said Emily. "You need to be strong for our child."

Emily wondered how old their littlest one would be, considering the sprinkling of gray in George's hair, and wanted to ask him, but he would not have heard, had heard none of it up until then. Feeling his pleas unanswered, he fell forward, and sobbed into the dirt, his cheek pressed so close to her that she could almost feel his breath.

"I shouldn't have done it," he said. "I know that. I even knew it then. But I was a coward. And I'll keep paying for that until the day I die."

George stood suddenly, and shook off his raw emotions as easily as he slapped the dirt off his knees. She felt her window on him closing down to be replaced by the face that he let the world see.

"I'll try to forget you," he said, a coldness to his voice. "With enough time, perhaps I could do that. But I doubt I'll ever be able to forget what I did. Goodbye, Emily."

He ran off too quickly, stumbling as he had when he'd arrived. Emily could not hold on to him, so she held onto his words.

"What did he mean?" asked Emily. "He was your son, Mrs. Gibbs. Is your son. Help me understand."

"Better not to know," said Mrs. Gibbs. "Let him just go. Let it all go."

"Should I?" said Emily. "Really? But you know. I can tell. You've figured it out. Why won't you tell me?"

"Because I care about you, dear. You'll be much happier that way."

"Then I'll have to ask Mrs. Soames to help. Mrs. Soames!"

No matter how Emily whined, she could not rouse the woman. She had slipped off to her final sleep. Only Mrs. Gibbs was left, perhaps invigorated by the visit from her son. Emily had no choice but to badger her mother-in-law further.

"But you must tell me what he was talking about," said Emily. "You must! Why was he asking for my forgiveness? He's your son, you know him best. I don't remember him ever doing anything I'd need to forgive! Do you?"

There was a sudden silence, and in that space, months seemed to pass.

"Mrs. Gibbs!"

"Dear?"

"George, Mrs. Gibbs. Tell me about George."

Mrs. Gibbs sighed.

"It's much better that way," said Mrs. Gibbs, "to not remember. I'd rather not think about my son, if you don't mind. And you should do the same."

"No! I could never do that. This is my life—"

"*Was* your life, dear."

"—and I can't let it go as if none of it happened. I need to remember. How sad he was up there! What could have happened to make him so sad? Don't you care? You're his mother!"

With no seeming provocation, Mrs. Soames spoke up.

"If you really must know—" she began.

"Hush!" said Mrs. Gibbs. "Now I'll say it. Hush! Don't tell her any more! It will only bring more pain. She's here to learn to put the pain away, not to pick it up again."

"Tell me what?" said Emily. "I have to know."

"You *can* go back, you know," said Mrs. Soames. "You can go back and see how it was. How it used to be. Others have done it before."

"It isn't a good idea, though," said Mrs. Gibbs softly.

"I'm going to do it anyway!" shouted Emily. "I have to do it! I have to know again, to feel."

"Feelings are overrated, dear," said Mrs. Gibbs. "You'll learn that soon enough, whatever you do. So you might as well take the easy way. Walk around the pain, don't walk through it. That's always the better way."

"I don't care!"

"Oh, give up," said Mrs. Soames. "You're not going to talk her out of it. She's a tough one, all right. The sooner she gets it out of her system, the sooner we'll all manage to get some rest."

"I can see that you're right, Mrs. Soames," said Mrs. Gibbs. "I guess you knew better all along. So go, dear. You won't be able to change anything, you know. That much will always be true. But you'll be able to see. And it will hurt, dear, it will hurt a great deal. Knowing what you know now, how you'll end up, how there's no permanent way back, well, it won't be pretty. Are you sure you want to do this?"

"As long as I can see my Georgie again, see what it's like to be alive, that's all that matters."

"You're braver than I ever was," said Mrs. Gibbs. "And a great deal more foolish. But I knew that when you became a Gibbs, Emily. No matter. I suspect that you'll feel quite differently when you come back."

"If I can see my George, I'm not coming back. I'm never—"

Before another syllable could pass through her stiff lips, the stars above Emily were replaced by her husband's eyes. There was no strength in them as he looked down at her. She saw only fear.

"What's wrong?" she asked. He was young again, his hair dark, his face smooth. And she was young again herself. She could feel her baby struggling within her to be born. All seemed well with the child—her experience with George, Jr., had taught her so—and there should have been no reason for her husband to be afraid.

"I don't know," he said.

She remembered having done this all before, remembered herself asking, and him answering, just that way the last time, but now, there was a difference. This time, the surface of things revealed the truth beneath. When in response to her questions about his demeanor, he'd said, "I don't know," she could tell that he was lying. She *knew*.

Emily was stunned by this revelation. George had never lied to her before. But then, shifting her head on the sweat-soaked pillow, she corrected herself. Her worldview was not the same as it had been mere moments before. She now knew that she had only *believed* that George had never lied to her before. Mrs. Gibbs had been right in telling her that she would see things she did not wish to see. And what was worse, though she could watch events unfold, she found that she could not change her words, could not respond using the new information she had earned.

"But everything will be all right, won't it, George?" she said. "The baby—our baby will be all right, won't it? Tell me that the baby will be all right, George."

She already knew what he would say, but still, Emily was distressed when George could find no other words than the words he had spoken before.

"I don't know," he repeated.

Emily lay in the bedroom in which she'd expected to be when she instead woke to find herself in her grave. She could see all the possessions that once were hers, and the happiness at seeing them brought tears welling up, but because she could change nothing about this scene, they were tears from the pain of childbirth that her new self only interpreted as joyous. She was happy to feel them wet her cheeks as they could not do before, to know life again, but that joy did not stay long, for she could also see the bedroom as if from above, as if she'd lifted the top off a doll's house to peer down. And so when George turned his back on her in her pain, Emily could see that his action was not entirely motivated because he was overcome with grief, though that is what her earthly self would have thought, *had* thought years before. With the eyes in her body, she could see George reaching to the end table for a glass of water, but with God's eyes, with the sight she had been given, she could see through him and around him and beyond him to the other side, watch helplessly as he slipped a small vial from his shirt pocket and tilted its clear contents into her drink.

"Here," he said, his voice leaden, and this time she knew that it was not so in a tone of concern. "This should make you feel better."

He held the glass to her lips, and as the liquid touched her tongue, the emotions that barreled through her grew even more grotesquely twin. Her living self, the one that knew of nothing but the living, and thought the dead were impossibly far away, was relieved to feel George's left hand at the back of her head, comforting her, urging her to drink deeply. She was loved. She was protected. Her new self, the one with the blinders of life burned away, saw things with sudden clarity as they really were, saw into George, and could see the panic there in him. She knew him then as wife should never know her husband. He did not want this child, had not even wanted their first child, was not entirely sure that he had ever really wanted her at all. He had always felt himself trapped by his snap decision to stay in Grover's Corners. It had all become too much for him.

And so with trembling fingers he held the poison to her lips. He planned to tell his family and friends that she had died in childbirth. They would be surprised, but would not disbelieve. After all, such things were not so unusual. It was known to happen from time to time, just as her mother had warned her.

But she'd never figured it would happen to her.

And truth to tell, it hadn't happened. But only he would ever know. George, and now, most unexpectedly, Emily as well.

She drank deeply, and soon felt the movements of her baby slow, and realized that she had been wrong, that it, too, had died, and as she began to sleep for what was meant to be the final time, she looked into her husband's eyes and thought, with knowledge of the grave and with complete sincerity, "Poor, poor George."

And then her husband was gone, her baby was gone, and she was back on the hill under an open sky, where she was meant to be boiled down to her essence in preparation for the world to come.

"I'm going back," she said, to no one in particular. The stars had no answer, but at least one of her neighbors did.

"Is that you, Emily? Still worrying away at the world, I see. Don't you remember? You've already been back."

"Not the way I plan to go back now. You don't know about George, what he's done. I've got to go back for real."

"You can't do that, dear."

"Don't patronize me, Mrs. Gibbs."

"I'm not, dear. It's only that no one has ever gone back that way before."

"I'll do it. Just watch me."

"You know it will only mean more pain. You've learned that much already, haven't you?"

"It doesn't matter," said Emily. "I've got to see my George, see him now, see him and say more to him than the shallow things I said before. After what he's done, I've got to tell him something. Live people don't understand."

"They never will, dear," said Mrs. Gibbs.

"I can't let myself believe that. George will be different. George will understand. I'll make him understand."

"You can't *make* the living do anything."

"It doesn't matter. George will listen to me. I know he will."

"Oh, my boy will listen all right. But you're not the pretty girl you once were. If you go before him as you are now, and he sees you again, like this, he'll have to listen. You'll certainly get his attention. The true question is, will he *hear?*"

"I'll make him hear," said Emily, with the confidence possessed only by the newly dead. "You watch."

"I don't believe I will, dear. It's terribly tiring staying awake like this for you. I believe I'll rest for a while. And don't worry about the likes of us, dear. We'll still be here when you get back."

Emily listened for the sound of her mother-in-law sleeping, and the sounds of all the others around her who made up the history of Grover's Corners, but there was nothing—no breathing, no snoring, no hint that there was any life there. And in truth, there was not. But Emily refused to sleep the sleep of the dead, not when George was out there, his double crime still a fresh wound in her mind.

All of the strength that had been missing before, when George had wailed above her, coursed through her explosively now. Her hands, which had been tied by invisible bonds, now pushed against and through the flimsy wooden roof of her coffin. Carrying her will before her like a torch, she pierced the dirt above like a swimmer surfacing after a dive, and found herself on the hillside, looking down at the few distant lights of the town she so loved. She wished she could feel the wind against her face, but could not. Her torn and leathery skin was beyond that now. She looked down at her headstone, at the dates beneath her name that insulted her with their brevity.

"I was so young," she said.

"We all were," said Mrs. Gibbs with a final yawn, before turning back to sleep. "Now go do whatever it is you think you have to do."

Emily walked down the gravel roadway up which she had been carried. She remembered that now, remembered it all, though when it had occurred she had still been taking her first brief nap. Along the way she passed so many sleepers, and as she saw them, she felt their presence in a way she never had when as a child she played hide-and-seek among the tombstones. How could she have missed them?

She wanted to call out to them all to join her, to return to their loved ones as she was doing, but she knew they would not listen. Unlike Mrs. Gibbs and Mrs. Soames, they were long gone, and would not have responded no matter how loudly Emily called. The part that belonged to the living had been completely burned away, so that all that remained was the eternal.

What she and George had was eternal, too. She would never forget that. And once she reminded George of that fact, he would be unable to forget it either.

She thudded noisily through the home that she and George had once lived in together. Her heart sank to see the clutter that he had allowed to overgrow the place she used to keep so clean. The piles were high and the dust was thick. It was late, and he was surely to bed, and that is where she found him. She sensed no others in the house. Her baby was dead, but where was George, Jr.? Perhaps he was spending the night with a cousin, which was just as well. She wouldn't have wanted him to hear what was to come.

Their half-full marriage bed looked bleak, and even though George was in the bed alone, he was curled as far away as possible from the side Emily had once occupied. He teetered at the edge of the mattress. Emily could not help but pause before the site where she had died. George, as if in his sleep sensing her there, turned fitfully. She spoke his name, but words were not enough to wake him. Her lungs did not seem to house the strength of her limbs, and so her words were but a whisper.

She leaned over to touch a shoulder, and his eyes snapped open.

"Emily," he said. His eyes were still full of fear, but it was not solely of Emily. It was of everything, as if there was no longer a part of the world that did not torment him. And he looked so old! Even older than when she had last seen him. Now his hair was completely white, and his skin was so wrinkled as to match the face she remembered on his grandfather. No wonder George, Jr. was not here; he was long gone to a life of his own.

How much time had passed in slumber? How much life had been lost?

"I'm so sorry, Emily," he said.

"I know that, George," she said, leaving her fingers pressed against him. He did not move, just lay there and studied her with eyes near tears.

"I cannot stop dreaming of you," he said. "Even when I'm awake, I dream of you. How can I ever make you understand, Emily? I can barely understand myself. I was so afraid. I thought I knew how to make my fear go away. But after what I did to you, after what I did to the baby, it only became worse."

"I know that all already, George. I've been given that gift. And that's why I'm here. That's why I've come back. To tell you that there's no reason to be afraid. No reason at all."

He smiled then, and sighed. From the strength of that sigh, it seemed to have been the first one he had allowed himself in a long while.

"Do you really mean that?" he said.

"Yes. Yes, I do, George. Life is wonderful, you see. I want to make sure you understand that."

"I do. I know that now, Emily."

"I'm glad," she said. "I love you, George."

"And I love you, too, Emily," he said, lapsing into sobs. "I'm sorry I never realized that until it was too late."

"It's never too late," said Emily.

And then she killed him.

• • •

George remembered what it was like to be alive, but the stars above did not surprise him. He was not for a moment fooled that he still remained in such a state. There was no more life in him, and he knew how, and he knew why. He shuddered there in the grave beside his wife.

"It was all so terrible, wasn't it?" he said. "And silly. And pointless. How did we ever bear it, Emily? Emily?"

She was sleeping more deeply now, having done what she needed to do. There was no George out there whose presence in the world of the living kept calling her back.

His cry beside her woke her from her slumber.

"But it was wonderful, too, at times," she said, her voice still soft with the dreams of what would come. "Only we hardly ever knew it."

"If only we could have."

"I don't think that's possible, George, not for live people. That peace and that beauty was beyond us. I love you, George. Now you go back to sleep. Go back to sleep until we are made ready to meet again."

"I can't, Emily. There's something...I sense that there's still something out there."

"Don't be silly, George. It's time to wean yourself of all that."

"Wait! Listen!"

There was a shuffling on the rough road coming up the hill towards them, the hill beyond which the town of Grover's Corners had grown nearer to the graveyard. A middle-aged man stood over them, stooped with sorrow, his face achingly familiar to George.

"Why, it's like looking in a mirror," said George. "It's George, Jr., come to visit us. And look at him. How long have I been here?"

"He's far too old to be called junior any more, George. And he's not here to visit us, darling. He's here to visit himself."

"He seems so sad."

"That's because he still thinks of us from time to time. He thinks he lost us both too soon. How sweet."

George looked up at his son and felt the guilt that only the newly dead know.

"I don't want anyone to feel such sadness because of me, Emily. It reminds me of the way I couldn't help but feel about you. Couldn't we—shouldn't we—do something?"

"No, George. It's not the same with children. At least not with our child. His pain is different. It's not our place."

"Are you sure?" said George. "I feel it. I feel it right now. I have that choice. I could come back and free him from that burden. I know I could."

George's fingers twitched as his son shed tears by the tombstone above them. But before he could lift his arm towards the surface, Emily roused herself from her great slumber and snaked her hand through the mud to lace her fingers through his.

"No, George," she whispered with a yawn. "Let him be. He may be blind, but soon enough, he'll see. Soon enough, one by one, all of them will."

While George was focused on his wife's eternal touch, he realized that his son had stolen away. He did not know how much time had passed. He realized that he had been sleeping. By now, George might even have joined them through the natural coursing of time, though he did not sense his son in the ground nearby.

He called once more to Emily, but this time she did not answer. She had already been weaned of this world for once and always, as he would soon be, too. He looked forward to that moment.

As he felt himself drift back to sleep, maybe for the last time, he studied the swimming stars above. Someone had once told him about stars, how it took the light from them millions of years to get to Earth. It didn't seem possible, even with the promise of what was to come, that time could stretch on that long.

He could no longer feel Emily's fingers wrapped in his own, but he knew in his heart that they were still there. Millions of years. They were hurtling towards him. As the light raced above and the living raced below, George was ready to spend that time exactly where he was.

THE MAN WHO WOULDN'T WORK MIRACLES

"But he perceived that his miracle had miscarried, and with that
a great disgust of miracles came upon him."
-H. G. Wells, "The Man Who Could Work Miracles"

"*W*ell, at least I don't have a brain tumor," George told himself with less joy than he'd imagined such news would bring as, exhausted from broken sleep, he staggered out to his car after having listened to his doctor's diagnosis. But he'd been hoping for more than just a reprieve. Learning from a lengthy and annoying series of tests what *wasn't* going on in his head didn't help him much when he so desperately wanted to know what *was*.

His MRI had come back clean, as had all the other tests. Lying on his back being rocked this way and that while goggles kept him in the dark and monitored his eye movements yielded nothing. He had no infections. His blood pressure was neither elevated nor depressed. No particles had become loose in his inner ear. There were no signs that after all these years (and how many there had been was a number about which he was sometimes uncertain), he'd spontaneously developed Ménière's. After weeks of being poked and prodded and tossed and spun and never feeling nausea those times technicians were sure he would, no clues could be found to explain why the world often (but only under very specific, very limited conditions) refused to stop spinning.

"Unfortunately"—or so the doctor had said—"we sometimes don't get to find out the nature of these things. Sometimes we have to be content that the cause isn't a life-threatening one, the occurrences are rare, and they aren't getting worse."

But George's vertigo *was* getting worse, wasn't it? After all, for most of his life, such a thing had never happened, and then, several months before (or so it seemed), he'd suddenly started waking in the middle of the night to the sensation of the world spinning while he remained still in the eye of a storm.

So far, that unsettling feeling had kept itself to the night, but how could he trust, even with the medicine his doctor had prescribed, that it wouldn't escape into his days? How could he dare to drive home?

But he did. It wasn't as if he could wish himself there.

He smiled at the thought of that, and wasn't entirely sure why.

• • •

George had never been much of a dreamer. He couldn't remember his parents ever having to wake him from a childhood nightmare, had never, as his friends growing up had, been plagued by dreams of showing up to school unprepared for surprise tests, and when coworkers told him of their own dreams and looked expectantly at him, waiting for him to reciprocate, he had nothing to share. In fact, he'd long suspected he was the rare individual who didn't dream at all. But whenever he'd make that claim, he was told that was an impossibility—everybody dreams—and those who think they don't simply aren't aware of doing it. He'd shrug, willing to accept that those who told him this were right, even though he never had proof of it.

Until two months back, when proof came in the form of horrific dreams invading his nights.

They were always the same.

The world had exploded, with every building torn from its foundations and every tree ripped from the earth and flung into the sky. The air was filled with shrapnel which orbited about him, leaving him dizzy but oddly untouched. He couldn't understand what had happened, why everything he knew had been destroyed, how he could remain firmly on the ground while the contents of the world rattled around him, and he waved his arms wildly, begging the maelstrom which surrounded him to stop, commanding it to stop, pleading with it to stop stop stop—

And then he'd wake, covered in a sweat which had been absent in dream, thanks to the force of the winds which had rocked him, the real, waking world back with him once more, spinning uncontrollably, his hands clutching for his mattress through the sheets to prevent his spasming body from tumbling to the floor. After a few moments, and many gasping breaths, the sensation of a planet unmoored would fade, then the dizziness would follow, and finally the nausea.

And then George would sit up on the edge of the bed, regretting he'd ever found out that yes, he, too, could dream.

• • •

He realized he was spending more time at the bar than he used to, and he wasn't entirely sure why. Had he started drinking only after the dreams began, or was that before? The memory of which of the two had come first escaped him. All he knew was that something drew him there for as many beers as he could handle and still make it home. And for the late-night conversations with friends, of course, because he embraced both in his efforts to forget.

Or was that remember?

When he asked his friends what they thought the repetitive dreams might mean, whether the dreams were the cause of the vertigo or the vertigo the cause of the dreams, he didn't get the answer he expected. He thought there'd be some debate over which the catalyst and which the result, but no.

"Who cares what the dreams mean?" Todd said, cutting through the chatter of the others. "Whether the chicken or the egg came first doesn't matter, as long as you get to eat."

"I don't know which one of us has had too much to drink," said George, "but what you just said doesn't make much sense."

"What I mean is that you're remembering dreams, that's all that's important," said his friend. "After all these years, that's a miracle."

"There's no such things as miracles," said George. And after saying it, he paused, for as he said it, before he even finished saying it, he remembered having heard those words before, and with that memory came another uncertainty to add to that of the dream mystery of cause and effect, for he was unsure whether the syllables had previously been spoken—on many nights, in many bars—by himself or by another.

"So you say," said Todd, who then laughed. Which made George even more unsure of what was truly his past and what only half-forgotten dream. He frowned, and looked down into his drink.

"You know what would be a miracle?" said George. He paused then, leaving a space as he contemplated uttering words so familiar they almost felt scripted rather than something he thought up on the spot.

"What?" said his friend. "What would be a miracle?"

George almost said them then, those words on his tongue which had come to him too quickly, frightening him with their sudden and overly confident appearance...but then he swallowed them, and the last contents of his mug as well.

"It would be a miracle if you'd get off my case," said George instead, who then ordered another round of beer for them all, after which Todd and the others *did* get off his case, leaving him to his thoughts, until, aided by another round, and still another, and yet one more, he could think no more of miracles, or doctor visits, or the disturbing nature of déjà vu, or the furious and insistent spinning of the Earth.

· · ·

But though George had made sure he could not consciously think of any of those things, he could still dream, for drink only silenced so much, and that night he did. This time, he could barely see the ruin of the planet as a swirl of haze clouded his vision. Rough winds tugged at him while twisted girders, as if flung from the hand of God, came close to smashing against his head. He ducked, and dodged, and almost lost his footing as all the contents of the world spun about him—he tried to turn look away from what he thought were tumbling bodies, but in dream, he couldn't control his own body as much as he would have liked—and when he woke, the world was still spinning...

Though this time, it was not from any disorder which his doctors could not diagnose. This spinning was something he knew.

His head was being squeezed in the vise of a hangover, one which he knew had been well-earned, even though in the bright light of morning, it was little-remembered. The fact he alone was the cause of this particular spinning, though, masking what he'd come to expect, did not make the pain any less.

He stumbled to the bathroom, finding it difficult to remain upright, ready to heave, and as he dropped to his knees and stared at the bowl, knowing what would inevitably come next, he muttered, "Oh, God, I wish I hadn't had so much to drink last night."

And upon speaking those words, he was suddenly sober, his head no longer dizzy, the world no longer spinning, his stomach no longer roiling.

"That's odd," he thought, reaching out to flush the toilet, even though, surprisingly, there was no need of it.

George could hear the ringing of a phone over the swirling of the water, and rushed back to his bedroom more quickly than he'd been able to exit it. He snatched up his cell to hear the worried voice of his closest friend from the night before.

"So what happened?" Todd said.

"What do you mean?" asked George.

"Well, where'd you go?"

"Go? I didn't...wait, what? What are you talking about?"

"Come on, you know what I mean. You weren't yourself last night. Why'd you really have to take off so early? The bar still had beer left. Who was it? There had to be someone. Spill!"

As Todd laughed, George could feel his knees weaken, and he allowed himself to drop onto the bed. He hadn't gone anywhere the previous night...had he? He was sure he'd closed the place down. That's what he and his friends always did, and that's what he'd been certain they'd just done again.

"Leave early? Is that what I did? Are you sure?"

"Wow, talking like that, you must be even drunker than when you left us. Did you head somewhere else to get it on after you ditched us? You must have. Or did you bring a bottle home?"

"I'll call you back later," said George, abruptly ending the call. He tossed his phone on a night table and then flopped back onto the bed.

"What the Hell could have happened last night?" he whispered.

He mulled over the events of the night before, and would have sworn he'd never abandoned his friends, but matched them drink for drink all the way to last call, after which they'd grabbed a six pack because they still didn't want the night to end and drank in the park the way they had as teenagers, not giving up until they could barely walk. But according to Todd, none of that had happened.

Could he really have left early?

Based on what his head and stomach were telling him, he guessed his friend was right. There was no other explanation for his lack of a hangover. He stared at the ceiling, and wondered.

"I wish..." he said. "I wish...I wish I could remember what's really going on."

And then he did.

. . .

He remembered it all.

He remembered his time in a bar with friends more than a century before, and that they'd been discussing miracles, and how, in the midst of his scoffing, he'd—to the great surprise of all, including himself—suddenly performed one. He remembered how, in the hours after, he'd caused the dead wood of his walking stick to bloom with roses, dredged a swamp, and even sent a constable to Hell—literally. He remembered how in his desire to prolong the night, a night during which, under the cover of darkness, he would perform even more miracles in order to better humanity, he stopped the Earth from spinning on its axis, and how everything upon the planet's surface broke free from the force of that frozen rotation, and in an instant, the world was destroyed, all it contents filling the sky as they would later come to fill his dreams.

Until he wished his wishes away, wished that first miracle and even his knowledge of it away, and put the world back as it had been before.

And he remembered what came next.

He remembered the first time he was afflicted by vertigo-inducing dreams, also more than a century prior, how they'd asserted them-selves long ago in a time before everyone else on the planet but him had been born, knocking at his subconscious again and again until dreams unlocked memory. And how, once the power to work miracles returned, and he realized what he had foolishly (or so he thought at the time) cast off, he swore that this time, he would get it right.

And for a while, he did…

But then once more his wishes grew too big and too vague, with the results too disastrous. He started small, helping the helpless one at a time, but then his wish to end poverty, instead of bringing riches to the downtrodden, resulted in the death of millions of the poor, an ending to poverty he'd failed to predict. And he again put the world back, put himself back, the way it and he were before they both were changed.

But his blessing, his curse, his gift of godhood, would not lie dormant, and repeatedly knocked at the door of his mind until it had come alive once more. And repeatedly his hubris led to disaster, with the world undone more times than you would wish to know.

That initial destruction was followed by a world in turn made ash by fire, flooded, starved, frozen, split asunder, and any number of deadly fates, and George continued to swear, with each renewed bout of wishing, that this time he would get it right. He became acquainted with unintended consequences before the term had even been invented, and when it finally was, the two words reverberated within him, though that recognition could not prevent him from continuing the unfortunate pattern.

Sometimes he would become a king, sometimes a president, but no matter his promise that he would always remain benevolent, he always ended up accidentally wishing his way to dictatorship instead.

He became a superhero, too, with abilities rich and varied, but any superhero becomes a supervillain eventually if he has enough power and lives long enough, and George had and George did.

Always, after days, after months, and sometimes after years (actually, sometimes even after seconds), his eyes would open to what he had done, what he had become, and he would reset the world. Over and over, caught in a loop which had lasted more than one hundred years, mourning for having caused your death, and the deaths of your parents, and their parents, and so on, bringing you and them back to life countless times, then living briefly in wish-enforced ignorance before it began all over again.

Which brings us to now, when that loop, he decided, must end. Remembering it all, torn by it all, he swore he would no longer undo this world.

For he would no longer *do* anything.

He wanted a life, not a string of unconnected days lived over and over, with time passing, the world dying and being born again and again, but nothing progressing.

He now knew what was wrong—that his vertigo was a sign he had been sick of a disease his doctors could not see. For who could? He was sick of miracles, which meant...

There must be no more of them.

· · ·

As George moved through his day, there was many a call for a miracle. There always was, in this, the most flawed of all possible worlds, which his restored memory proved to him it was, but he left those calls unanswered, regardless of the itch they caused. Still, he could feel the tug of each.

So he noticed when a limping man struggled to finish crossing the street before the light could turn red on him, but left the man to that struggle. He neither cured the man's limp (which he'd learned by now might cause him to take unnecessary risks in the future with his newfound mobility, shortening his life more than any limp would have), nor silenced the car horns (which might have meant a driver would step from his car and look under the hood for a cause, at which point he could have been run over by an inattentive bicyclist), nor frozen the traffic in place (George did not even want to consider what *that* might have done).

And as he passed a newsstand, his eyes were drawn briefly to headlines which told of troubles far greater than one man attempting to cross a busy street—they trumpeted wars ongoing and wars yet to be, famine and brutality and disasters created both by man and by chance (each competing to see which could damage humanity more), and with difficulty, he forced himself to turn away. He could make it stop, any of it, all of it, had already made it stop, many times over, with the wave of a hand, the blink of an eye, a few syllables said sometimes sincerely, sometimes thoughtlessly...only what would that get him?

He knew what that would get him.

When he realized he would be late for work from too much studying of and failing to interfere with the obvious errors in the world around him, George did not, as he had so often done in years and decades past, close his eyes and reopen them only after he'd reappeared where he wished to be. He let nature—random, chaotic, unmediated nature—have its way with him, even though it meant arriving to a boss angry due to his lateness. And though the itch was strong within him, George did not send him to Hell, as he had once done to someone else so long ago, when this all began (and many other someone elses after that), but instead went to his desk and did his job, a coding job which, until he remembered, he did not know he did not really need.

Whatever he wanted, he could have had for the wishing of it, with no need to stare at a computer screen until headaches came, but what he wanted now most of all was not to destroy the world again. Well, *nearly* destroy the world, anyway. He'd come close before, too close, but luckily at the last minute had always been able to wish things back the way they were. What if next time, he were not so lucky? A stray wish could spell the end of everything.

So he moved through his day the way a normal person would, rooting out viruses with his brain, rather than a wish, and resisted all urges to make miracles. He let the microwave reheat his bland office coffee, rather than materializing a new one ground from exotic beans, ordered a sandwich with the others from the local coffee shop instead of substantiating the lobster he really wanted, and listened to Francine's boring stories when he could have silenced her. Tempting all, but the risks were much too great. And once his day was done, and he took stock of his actions, he was pleased. He fell asleep tired, but happy, knowing he could do this. He could do this.

298

Until the world began spinning even more wildly than it had before. But as he slept, and watched everything he'd ever known tumble madly, he could tell the change was more than just in the intensity of the destruction. This time the dream was different, more than just memory reasserting itself, since after all, there was no need of that, as the memories were already his once more. No, this message was even more demanding, and from its insistence, he knew what he was being told. He knew, as he suppressed his feeling of nausea from what roiled around him, what he was being commanded to do. He knew the one thing that would take away the dreams, take away the waking dizziness which followed, and at the same time, he knew he must not give in to the solution.

"No," he thought, denying the wishes the existence they craved. "You can't come back. I will wish no more. Better I alone am destroyed than the world entire."

He woke, dragged himself upright even though his brain sent signals for him to topple, and sat on the edge of the bed, swallowing his bile and breathing rhythmically until those feelings faded, readying himself for another day during which he knew he'd have to once more fight against the resurgence of miracles.

The miracles themselves had a different idea.

He headed for the office, leaving plenty of time to arrive early and not rile his boss—but more importantly, to not stir up temptation over what he could do to his boss if he unleashed his wishes. Before he got very far, though, he heard the screech of brakes, and turned to see a car had leapt the curb and was just about to hit him.

He ducked to one side, falling against a brick wall. As a woman helped him to his feet, he heard a cracking above, and looked up to see an air conditioner had broken free from a window. He rolled to one side as it fell toward him, and the machine smacked against the pavement where he'd just been.

"No," he insisted. "I will not work any more miracles. I won't!"

As he stood there, wondering how the universe would answer, a crushed car to his right and the remnants of an air conditioner to his left, the whine of an engine turned his attention to the sky, where a smoking helicopter jerked this way and that, challenging him to hold out a hand and stay its swift descent.

"I can't," he said. "Don't you see? I can't. I won't do this to the world—to myself—any longer."

But the miracles would not listen, and a rotor snapped free, nearly decapitating him. While he sensed it would not kill him, needing him alive to make those wishes real, he didn't want to endanger others, and so raced back to his bedroom—dodging an escaped hippopotamus from the zoo, leaping a crevasse which opened before his feet, and nearly drowning in a flooded subway car, all of which he survived without need of wishes—where he dove beneath his covers, comforted by the darkness.

"This world is not for me," he muttered. "Not anymore. I reject it! What am I to do with you? You don't want me to be a maker of miracles, that's clear from the way you twist them, yet you don't want me *not* to make miracles either. What do you want? Show me what you want. Show me!"

No answer came. George wasn't quite sure he was really expecting one, nor if it was coming, what shape it would take. So he continued to cower beneath those covers, enjoying the warmth blossoming from his breath, and wondered if that was where he should stay. Outside only destruction and amnesia waited, and he'd had enough of both.

Maybe he *would* stay there.

But then he heard a creaking, which he recognized, from his own strides across the bedroom, to be footsteps. Stay there? No. Whatever was behind the miracles would not allow that. George slowly pulled down the covers and peered over them, but only slightly, ready to quickly pull them up again if need be, not that a blanket would be much protection from what the weight of all miracles might throw at him. But it was no miracle, only a man, standing there looking like a walrus, dressed in the sort of clothing he hadn't since since, well, since all this began. His expression was not a happy one, and George lifted the edge of his blanket slightly under the force of his gaze.

"Just what do you think you're doing, young man?" the man said. "What's going on here? Your story is over. It ended more than one hundred years ago! So stop it. Stop it, do you hear?"

The man clapped his hands then, as if expecting George to hop to it, and though he sensed he should—hop to what? He had no idea. But George flung the covers aside and leapt from the bed anyway.

"Who are you and how did you get in here?" he asked. "This is no story, this is my life. What are you even talking about?"

The intruder's eyes softened sightly then, but George took no comfort in that. For the look was one usually given to a small child, or a pet.

"Don't you know me?" he said. "Don't you recognize me? Don't you… remember me?"

George stared, lost for a moment, but then…he remembered that, too. Yet how was what he now remembered even possible?

"That's right," said H. G. Wells, seeing George's recognition take hold. "I'm the one who made you."

"Did you now?"

"Don't be so impertinent! Of course I made you. Without me, you wouldn't have existed. I thought you up and set you on this path."

"But if it was you, if it was truly you, why would I still be *on* that path? No, something else must have made us both. It was the miracles that must have made us. The miracles want me to exist, and use them."

"But I made the miracles, too. Without me, they don't exist. Without me, *you* don't exist."

Wells waved his hands around the room, which suddenly seemed shabby to George, compared to all the other rooms he'd lived in over the century. Then Wells snapped his vest and grumbled.

"What am I saying?" he continued. "What miracles? There are no real miracles. This is just a story. This is just something fantastic I dreamed up. An entertainment, nothing more."

"You're sure of this how?" said George, frowning. "Because it all seemed so...real."

"Of course, I'm sure I—"

George held a hand up then, silencing Wells, who froze in place, his mouth half open, the fingers of one hand half-formed into a fist. George stepped nose to nose with the man who claimed to have created him. Ridiculous.

Then his eyes went wide and he nervously rushed to the window, where he only relaxed after he saw that outside, life went on. People walked, cars rolled, contrails crisscrossed the sky. Good. He'd only frozen one person, and not the world. He was worried there for a moment. He'd learned the hard way what would have been wrong with that. He spun away from that world and stepped back to the man turned statue.

Or was it just a man? He claimed to be his maker, and certainly acted more like one than a man. Did that mean he was...God? George supposed not, or else his minor miracle wouldn't have worked, for surely God's miracles could not be turned against him. There was only one way to find out the truth of this, so George waggled his fingers again, and the man continued speaking right where he had left off, apparently unaware of his temporary pause.

"—dreamed you up."

"Why do you think so? Why are you so sure?"

"Because—I did." said the man, pulling a newspaper from an inner pocket of his vest. "If you won't believe me, believe this. It's all there. You'll see."

He thrust the newspaper out toward George, who was hesitant to reach for it. It was folded to a page revealing a title—"The Man Who Could Work Miracles."

Miracles.

George ripped the pages from his visitor's hands, and began to read it, curious at first, then puzzled, then stunned. As he read the description of who he once was, but was no longer, his past captured in print, every word accurate, his knees buckled, and he sat down hard on the bed. He wanted to crumple the pages, toss them away, and pull the covers over his head again, but he knew it would do him no good. So he continued reading on, through his fledgling attempts to save the world, all the way to his first destruction of it, and then his first erasure and restoration, knowing that though the story as written ended there, it did not end there. The escape he'd sought, the escape detailed in the pages before him, wasn't an escape for long.

"How did you know all this happened?

"All that didn't *happen*, you see, not the way you think it. There was nothing to know. It came out of here."

The man tapped the center of his forehead.

"And what was supposed to happen next?" said George, pointing at the last paragraph of the story. "After."

"After? There wasn't supposed to be an after. I'm a writer, young man. I create openings and devise endings, and once I do that, I let them go. So after yours, I moved on to my next story and never thought any more about it. Well, until the movie, of course, but that's neither here nor there."

"A movie? About me?

"Why, yes," said Wells. "But let's not speak of it. For you'll find no answers there either."

"But how was I supposed to end?"

"I never gave it much thought. I assumed once the last page was turned, you'd have gone on to live the life you'd have lived without me. Perhaps it was a happy one, perhaps not, but once the final word was written, that was no longer up to me."

"If that had happened, I'd have been dead by now. That was more than a century ago."

"That isn't my problem. I'm a writer, not a god."

"And yet, you somehow gave me the power of one. And I can't get rid of it. Take it away from me, please! You can do that, at least."

"I'm sorry, but as I said, I don't know how to help you. This is all… very confusing. And I'm not easily confused. I don't even know why I'm here. Or *how* I am here. I'm no god—"

"Yes, yes, you're only a writer, you said that."

And as George looked back and forth from the man who said he'd written him into existence and whose story he had then run away with, to the printed story itself, and then the man again, frowning under a bushy mustache, he realized the one miracle worth making—a miracle which could put this all behind him at last.

. . .

George McWhirter—he'd long ago dropped the Fotheringay, feeling that surname would put off many readers—scrolled down the screen, giving his story one final read before sending it off to an editor. The only thing causing him trouble about this latest story, one concerning a man burdened with a gift which turned out to be more of a curse, and his efforts to escape it, was the title. He'd been vacillating all day.

"A Great Disgust of Miracles"?

No, not quite there. While it was indeed true, that didn't seem right.

"A Most Extraordinary Occurrence"?

Oh, it was, it truly was. But that still didn't really nail the tale.

"The Man Who Wouldn't Work Miracles"?

Ah, that was it.

And as George pressed send, shooting off his newest story to an editor, he knew that no, he *wouldn't* work them, no, not ever again.

Except with his words.

STORY NOTES

"TELL ME LIKE YOU DONE BEFORE"

If during my younger days I had chosen a different path, you wouldn't have been able to read this story, because it would never have existed.

Starting when I was a teenager, and into my mid-twenties, I not only wrote, but I acted. Which meant that as I was gathering rejection slips from *Analog, Amazing, The Magazine of Fantasy & Science Fiction,* and every other genre magazine that existed at the time, I was also inhabiting Bill Sikes in *Oliver,* Boris Kolenkhov in *You Can't Take It With You,* the Creature (the one who philosophized, and didn't just grunt) in *Frankenstein,* and...Lennie in *Of Mice and Men.*

I was passionate about both of these arts, but after much internal debate, came to the conclusion there was no way I could pursue them both and manage to hone my craft or maintain any level of professionalism. In the end, I chose writing.

And so here we are, you and I. And the reason *why* we are here is—

I was unwilling to put my future into the hands of others. Relying on editors, agents, and publishers is one thing, but to my mind, casting agents and directors were an entirely different sort of gatekeeper. Because of their differing roles, I felt that in writing, the art could come before the business, whereas in acting, the business had to come before the art.

What I mean by this is that in order to act, a creator needs a venue, a director, lights, and dozens of other components in place, and so would not be allowed to act until all those things came together *and* they then nailed an audition. Doing a monologue alone in a room wasn't acting. In order to perform my art, I'd need to wait to be given permission.

But to write, no permission was necessary. The art could come first. All I needed was a ream of paper and (back then) a typewriter. Regardless of whether I'd be successful in the business side of publishing that followed, I could still create a finished product. The art would exist whether the story sold in months, years, decades, after my death, or not at all. Following where my writing muse rather than my acting muse led meant I would not be putting my fate so much in the hands of others.

If I failed to sell any of my writing for a decade, I would still have many completed stories of which I could be proud. But if I failed to be cast in a role for those same ten years, I'd have...nothing.

I wasn't prepared to wait for others to allow me to create.

Which meant my final role on the stage was as Lennie in the Greenpoint Repertory Company's production of "Of Mice and Men." Inhabiting that character taught me a valuable lesson about Steinbeck's story which proved helpful to this one, even though the creation of "Tell Me Like You Done Before" was still more than twenty-five years away.

When I was cast as Lennie, I worried whether I'd be able to pull off each performance. Not because I doubted my acting abilities, but rather because I'd never been able to read the book or watch either the play or one of the filmed adaptations without bawling at the tragic ending. How would I be able to hold it together while living through those events?

It turned out I didn't need to worry. Because though the ending to "Of Mice and Men" was sad and depressing for the reader, the audience, and those characters who survived the events of the story, when one is inhabiting Lennie himself, that end turned out to be transcendent. Because in his final moments, Lennie achieves his goal. He can see what he's been working toward all along. And only in that moment does the story end for him.

So no, I did not cry during my final scene at each performance. And each night, post-play, I was happy. Giddy, even. While the rest of the cast, those who had to go on without me, were glum.

And then, years later, we come to "Tell Me Like You Done Before," in which I imagined a post-canon life for characters I'd known and (in some cases) loved since childhood.

I had the idea for this story at least a decade before I wrote the first sentence or figured out any details of the plot. I carried the seed around in the folds of my brain, waiting for the right catalyst to begin. Then came the 2009 Stoker Awards weekend in Burbank and an encounter with Stephen Jones, who was pulling together a zombie anthology titled *The Dead That Walk* and hoped I'd contribute. I returned home, energized as I so often am from such gatherings, and wrote the first draft of this story so quickly over the course of a weekend it was almost as if I was transcribing it rather than writing it for the first time.

That was a gift from my subconscious, which unbeknownst to me, had been working on the story all along, and had been awaiting my call.

The speed of this story's creation reminds me of the chestnut about an auto mechanic who stops to help a man whose car had broken down on a country road. It takes the mechanic five minutes to fix the problem, after which he charges the stranded driver $50 for the service. The man is outraged.

"Fifty dollars for five minutes work!" he protests.

"No," says the mechanic. "The $50 was for thirty years of experience. I tossed in the five minutes for free."

So think of this as a story which took ten years and a weekend to complete. This kind of thing doesn't happen often, perhaps only two or three times in my career—my stories usually grow quite slowly, like coral—but when it does, this writer knows enough to be grateful.

Originally published in The Dead That Walk, *edited by Stephen Jones, Ulysses Press, 2009*

[Publisher's Note—The reason this book found a home with Lethe Press is because my introduction to Scott's work came through reading *The Dead That Walk* for possible reprint tales to include in **my** zombie project for Prime Books, *Shambling Through History*. Scott's tale remains one of my favorites in the interstitial undead field; some time afterward, I met Scott at Readercon and expressed my enthusiasm for his Steinbeck homage…and he mentioned other pieces he had written in a similar vein. I casually mentioned my interest that I would love to publish a collection of homages and pastiches. And thus the strange world of publishing turns…—Steve Berman]

"WHAT WE STILL TALK ABOUT"

How much do I love Raymond Carver?

So much that I cried the day I opened the *New York Times* and discovered he'd died.

So much that I once read the entirety of my favorite story of his, "What We Talk About When We Talk About Love," to friend and writer Resa Nelson during a long drive to Readercon. (She wasn't the only friend to be subjected to such a performance.)

So much that even though I would appear to have been the target audience, and to the surprise of my friends, I boycotted Robert Altman's film *Short Cuts*, based on Carver's stories, after I read an interview with the director which made it clear he completely misunderstood what the writer was all about.

So much that I mourned the lost science fiction stories his wife said he was creating when he started out to be a published writer. "He had written some science-fiction stories but when he got into John Gardner's class at Chico State, he was no longer interested in writing about little green monsters," said Mary Ann Carver in *The Paris Review*. But *I* was interested. Oh, how I was interested!

So much that I'd asked Barry Malzberg to recreate what one of those lost stories might have been, and published his homage in the first issue of *Science Fiction Age* magazine.

This story that you just read (or are about to read, depending on how you deal with these sorts of explanatory notes) is not one of those, however.

For though inspired by Carver, it's not attempting to pass *as* Carver, but rather my attempt to explore the same territory he did, only set in the far, far future. Most of my stories seem to be love stories, too, my characters trying—sometimes succeeding, sometimes failing—to pierce the barriers that separate them. Often that aspect of a particular story is subtle, but other times it's far more obvious, as in this piece in which four far-future posthumans take a trip back to the place where the human race was born...and discover that Earth isn't quite what they expected.

Editor Peter Crowther picked it up for his anthology *Forbidden Planets*, published to celebrate the fiftieth anniversary of the classic film of the same name. His mandate for the book was quite broad, and so was able to accommodate my story of our own planet, and how it might eventually turn out to be quite forbidden itself.

Though the title of this tale (and the story as well) tips a hat to Carver, I think it still works even for those who don't catch the allusion. I hope the same can be said about all the stories in this collection, and that the stories stand on their own even for those unfamiliar with the giants on whose shoulders I've stood.

One final comment—

In 2003, I shared a draft of this story with the students of the Clarion Science Fiction & Fantasy Writers Workshop in East Lansing, Michigan when I was the Editor in Residence, because I believed that if they were making themselves vulnerable by allowing their unfinished work to be critiqued, I should make myself vulnerable as well. So I'd like to thank the other three teachers who were present during my time there—Kelly Link, Maureen McHugh, and James Patrick Kelly—as well the entire class that year for their comments which helped improve this story.

Originally published in Forbidden Planets, *edited by Peter Crowther, DAW Books, 2006*

"THE WORLD BREAKS"

This story sprang into my head—though exploded might be a better word—as I was flying home from a science-fiction convention. Some are exhausted by cons, needing to collapse and recover, but not me. I always head home energized. Plus cons, by acting as catalysts for me, stirring up both my intellect and emotions, tend to spark multiple story ideas.

But strange, this con...nothing.

At least not until I was in midair and reached for a copy of *Newsweek* which had been left behind in the seatback by a previous passenger on that plane. The cover story was on the Iraq War, and Maureen Dowd's column included the quote from which the title of the story is taken.

As soon as I read that quote, the post-apocalyptic story was there in its entirety—the manner in which the tale is told, the narrative arc, the ending. Thank you, nameless passenger who left your magazine on the plane rather than tossing it. Without you, this story would have never happened.

Pete Crowther bought it for the late, lamented *Postscripts*, the third time he published a story of mine in that bookazine. Thank you, Pete, for being so supportive of me, and thank you, Ernest Hemingway, for coming up with such a moving quote.

Originally published in Postscripts #19, edited by Peter Crowther and Nick Gevers, September 2009

"AND THE TREES WERE HAPPY"

When I was a child, as my parents would drive us home late at night from weekend visits to friends and relatives, my mother would tell my brother and me a tale of horror which grows more horrific upon reflection than it ever was at the time.

She'd often share a wonderfully spooky rendition of "The Monkey's Paw," but the story which has come to bother me in retrospect during the years since wasn't quite as scary. I don't know its title, or its origin, but it's about a young man who becomes involved with a woman who asks he prove his love for her by cutting out his mother's heart. Which, since that's the way obsessive love works in these stories, he does.

As he returns with the evidence of his deed, he stumbles, dropping the heart, and out from the bloody organ comes the mother's voice speaking with tender concern for her fallen child: "Are you hurt, my son?"

This telling did not come to disturb me until years later, because when you are a kid, you're too young to pay much attention to subtext. (At least, that's the kind of kid *I* was.) But for a mother to tell her son: no one will ever love you as much as I do, and those other women, the ones you think you love, well, loving them will hurt me... that seems like a perverse message to pass on to a child who's yet to even think of finding a mate.

I wonder if the repeated telling of this tale explains why I have such a love/hate relationship with Shel Silverstein's *The Giving Tree*. Even though it gets me to tear up every time, it's at the same time a fable wrapped around pro-parent propaganda designed to let kids know that no matter how you mistreat them, Mom and Dad will love you more than your friends ever will, more than your lovers ever will, more than anyone other than they ever will. (At least, that's the hidden message *I* find in it.)

My continuation of that story sets aside all such things, letting the original be nothing more than its bittersweet surface, rather than a naked attempt to indoctrinate.

And so, though I don't usually cry when reading my stories aloud, "And the Trees Were Happy" has conquered me every time. Sometimes, as I near the ending, my voice will crack, and I'll have to pause and collect myself.

I hope you sniffle a bit at the ending, too.

Originally published in Genius Loci, *edited by Jaym Gates, Ragnarok Publications, 2015*

"MY LIFE IS GOOD"

It's been more than forty years since Randy Newman first came into my life—a fact which my Marvel Comics Bullpen comrade Don McGregor, tormented in 1977 by our constant a cappella singings of "Short People," surely did not appreciate—and so that singer/song-writer has been part of my subconscious for two-thirds of my life. He's in me still today: I've probably strummed his "Political Science" on the ukulele as much if not more than any other song.

Which meant that when F. Brett Cox and Andy Duncan asked me to contribute to their anthology *Crossroads: Tales of the Southern Literary Fantastic,* Randy Newman was the first thing that came to mind.

Well, actually, the second thing. Because the first thing that came to mind when they cornered me during a loud Readercon party was, "Are you sure?"

Since I'd spent my first thirty years in Brooklyn, I didn't feel myself to be an eligible contributor for such a project. But they assured me that since I then lived in Maryland, and had been on the southern side of the Mason-Dixon Line for more than a decade, I was an honorary Southerner. And who was I to argue with not one, but two editors?

The opening line of my story will be familiar to anyone who's ever heard the song "Rednecks," which appears on the Randy Newman album *Good Old Boys.* But that's far from the only Randy Newman Easter Egg to be found there. And Newman is far from the only giant upon whose shoulders this story was written. The story also contains an homage to Kurt Vonnegut, Jr. (whose work influenced me greatly when I was young) via a nod to his character Eliot Rosewater, famous for a speech similar to the one I chose to have Newman utter during his incarnation as a science fiction writer. I'll leave it to you to locate the other Easter Eggs present for both of them, some more easily sussed out than others.

Once the anthology was released, I sent Newman a copy, hoping he wouldn't mind the metafictional use I had made of his life. In response, I received a letter suggesting I write more adventures about him, perhaps even a multi-volume series longer than *Remembrance of Things Past* in which he saves the universe over and over again.

(Who knows? Perhaps I'll take him up on that suggestion someday.)

He also invited me to attend a concert he was giving in D.C. at the offices of SiriusXM, which I happily did, sitting just a few feet away from him as he played the piano. It was one of the happiest days of my life.

Now you'll have to excuse me...I need to go strum "Political Science" on the ukulele once more.

Originally published in Crossroads: Tales of the Southern Literary Fantastic, *edited by F. Brett Cox and Andy Duncan, Tor Books, 2004*

"PITY THIS BUSY MONSTER NOT"

Long before I wrote my first short story at age sixteen—and submitted it *The Magazine of Fantasy & Science Fiction*, whence it was returned to me after a mere three days—I'd already written dozen of poems. Hundreds maybe. If you'd encountered me at Canarsie's Isaac Bildersee Junior High School—Junior High School 68—you'd have found me with a notebook under my arm which contained them all, and on the cover, a decal of the Silver Surfer...a hint at the flowery language you would unfortunately find were I to allow you to peek within.

And shy loner that I was, I probably wouldn't have allowed you.

It was in that school where I initially encountered the poetry of E. E. Cummings through a poem which was the first of his for many of us—"in Just-," with its balloon man who "whistles far and wee." Later, at South Shore High School, I was also taught "Buffalo Bill's," "next to of course god america I," and "Since Feeling is First."

But the poem from which the title of this story was taken I had to find later, as I explored the world of poetry on my own. And how could a line like that *not* end up as the title of a short story? It nestled in my mind for decades, a sleeper agent waiting to reveal itself once a story occurred to me which best embodied the emotions found in its final lines. When the poem and its suggested title finally found the story it deserved, it was a surprise, and yet...not. If I'm patient, all story problems eventually resolve in their own time.

But before I let you go on to the next story note, a few words about the "shy loner" I said I was back when I was first set on the path of this story. And that's who I was long before then...

When I was in kindergarten, my teacher wanted the class to dance around the room pretending to be flowers. We were to sing while twirling colorful scarves. Extremely shy, very serious, and somewhat repressed, I refused. It seemed silly, and I didn't intend to make a spectacle of myself, not even when the teacher threatened me by saying that if I wouldn't dance with the others (I was the only refusenik), I wouldn't be allowed to take part in the visit to the pet snake kept by the kids in the next classroom. I was adamant, and so I ended up sitting stubbornly alone while everybody else got to play with that snake.

Flash forward a decade or two, and my personality was quite different. I spontaneously hurled myself at Steve Gerber's feet in Times Square in a kind of improvised guerilla theater, begging him, while tourists watched wide-eyed, to return to the family he'd supposedly abandoned. I've acted in plays, done hundreds of panels and readings, was toastmaster at a Nebula Awards banquet, and will pretty much do anything in public, as long as it is good and kind, that seems as if it would be entertaining to me or to others.

How did the kid who wouldn't dance become the adult who doesn't worry much about what other people think?

A happy accident. And a very special teacher.

One day, when I was in the eighth grade, as I was eating lunch in the crowded cafeteria, a signup sheet came around for anyone who wanted to be part of the school's drama class the following year. My friend Scott Friedman and I made a big joke of it...and then both signed our names, thinking we were being funny.

And promptly forgot about it.

Until the following year, when I showed up to begin the ninth grade and was distressed to discover I was now enrolled in that class. But not my friend, however, because strangely, in order for the school to make the scheduling work, only students who'd been enrolled in Spanish class made it through, and my friend was taking French.

I was horrified. Here I was, the kind of person who did not want to be noticed, who would never do anything to deliberately bring attention to himself, and I was suddenly trapped in a class where the whole point seemed to be "Hey, look at me!" But the very weakness that made it seem so horrible to me is the same one which kept me there. I wasn't the sort to make waves. I did what was expected of me.

The earliest memory I have from the first of two terms is of being on stage alone while the entire drama class looked at me and I had to pretend to be a chicken hatching from an egg. I hated every moment of it. And yet, without it, I would have grown up to be invisible. I was the kind of person who would probably have ended up like John C. Reilly's character in *Chicago*, who sang "Mister Cellophane"—"You can look right through me, walk right by me, and never know I'm there."

How shy and withdrawn was I? So much so that when the class got ready to put on the play "Oliver" at the end of the year, I was never considered for the role of Bill Sikes, the evil villain of that play, even though I was the tallest kid in the class and by far the most physically suited for the role. I ended up as one of the many chorus people milling around in crowd scenes. I didn't even have a line, which was just as well, because if I'd had one, you probably wouldn't have even been able to hear my voice anyway.

And then a miracle happened—the actor who was playing that role had to drop out for some reason, and a new Bill Sikes needed to be found. The two teachers went around the room and asked all the other boys to audition—except me. One by one, they had everyone try out singing Sikes' menacing solo number in which he is an imposing, threatening figure, and when they were done, without me having been called upon to sing, I sheepishly raised my hand, not quite sure what made me do it, and said, "Excuse me, could I please give that song a try?" And when I sang, the teachers saw something in me that I didn't really see in myself, and gave me the part.

They spent months encouraging me to climb out of my shell and into the persona of this character who would walk around filled with confidence and not mind at all that he was being looked at, that he was being noticed. In teaching me how to walk, how to sing, how to project, how to move fearlessly through a world, they transformed me.

The two teachers who did this were Frank Cama and Freda Slavin. I've long lost track of Ms. Slavin, but when I was a freshman decades ago at SUNY Buffalo, I was able to write Mr. Cama a letter thanking him for my transformation. And the year the HWA's Stoker Awards banquet was going to be held on Long Island, I decided to track him down, since I knew he then practiced law there. I took him out to lunch to thank him once more...and was touched that he brought along that old letter of mine, which I reread, almost brought to tears by that token of my earlier gratitude. Gratitude which remains unchanged.

I've always believed that the most important things that happen in our lives happen by accident, without our planning for them. That's what led to my working at Marvel Comics, that's what led to meeting my wife, and that's what led to me being the person who some of you out there have come to know, someone who can live a joyous, unbounded life.

And the person I most have to thank for that is Frank Cama. Without him, these stories, this book, would likely not have existed for you to read.

Originally published in Adam's Ladder, *edited by Michael Bailey and Darren Speegle, Written Backwards, 2017*

"Opossums and Angels"

Certain stories move me so, I reread them as often as once a year.

There's Frederik Pohl's "Day Million," which though it hasn't inspired a specific story of my own, can certainly be seen in the effortless scientific posthuman miracles of "What We Still Talk About," found elsewhere in this volume, though that one was more directly inspired by Raymond Carver.

There's Harlan Ellison's "One Life, Furnished in Early Poverty," which again hasn't been the direct catalyst for one of my own stories, but whose longing and nostalgia can be felt, I think, in stories of mine such as "I Wish I Knew Where I Was Going," which can also be found in this book.

And then there's James Tiptree, Jr.'s—that is, Alice Sheldon's, for hers was the name behind the pseudonym—"The Women Men Don't See," which I first read in the 1975 collection *Warm Worlds and Otherwise*. It was, to my mind, the standout story even in a volume with included such powerful pieces as "Love is the Plan the Plan Is Death" (which won the Nebula Award for short story in 1974) and "The Girl Who Was Plugged In" (which won the Hugo Award for novella the same year). It addresses gender with a narrator who is magnificently drawn and extremely obtuse, a lesson on how to tell a story via the words *not* on the page.

Sheldon's collection also included an introduction by Robert Silverberg which because of the following two sentences became infamous in 1977 once the person behind the pen name was revealed:

"It has been suggested that Tiptree is female, a theory that I find absurd, for there is to me something ineluctably masculine about Tiptree's writing. I don't think the novels of Jane Austen could have been written by a man nor the stories of Ernest Hemingway by a woman, and in the same way I believe the author of the James Tiptree stories is male."

So Sheldon herself was—even in her own collection—a women men didn't see. Silverberg was willing to own up to his blindness, though, for as he later wrote to her once she was outed:

"*You* didn't fool me; *I* fooled *myself*, and so be it."

How did I feel about all this?

I began reading these stories when I was in my late teens, learned of the revelation when I was twenty-two, and at this distance can no longer recall how I reacted to the unmasking. All I remember, all I know, is that she was and is one of my favorite writers, and her stories *matter*.

It occurred to me one day that it would be intriguing to see what would happen were a character from "The Women Men Don't See" to meet a character from "The Screwfly Solution," another of the author's powerful stories on gender. And so, *this* story.

I believe this extrapolation on my two favorite Tiptree stories will work for readers with no prior knowledge of her or of either story.

And I do hope I've done her justice.

Original to this collection

"Fifth Dimension"

I don't think I'd be who I am today if it were not for Rod Serling. And not even being forbidden by my parents to watch *The Twilight Zone* after an episode caused me nightmares was able to stand in the way of that.

The episode which caused me to wake up screaming, resulting in a month-long ban on the series, was not the one you probably think, not the one with a frantic William Shatner gesticulating wildly at a gremlin on the wing of his plane in "Nightmare at 20,000 Feet." Instead, it was "Stopover in a Quiet Town," in which a couple wakes in a deserted suburb that's eventually revealed to be (spoiler alert for 1959!) a habitat created by aliens where they are now the pets of a small child.

I have no idea why that one got to me so then, but it didn't stop me from rushing back for more as soon as the punishment was over. I eventually had each *Twilight Zone* episode so well-memorized that when I was in college, I used to astound my friends by being able to spout the closing dialogue of an episode simply from them mentioning the title.

With that series so much a part of me, it would make sense that I wished there to be more. And thus, this story, which imagines the tales Rod Serling is off somewhere still telling.

At the time Ted Klein, editor of *The Twilight Zone* magazine, purchased this story, he'd previous rejected at least half a dozen of my tales. He worked just a few blocks away from my own office in midtown Manhattan, and once I made that sale, I reached out to see whether he'd like to have lunch, a thing I could have done before, but hadn't.

Why?

Because I was very deliberately trying, even as I attended conventions, to *not* come face to face with editors.

I was foolishly noble back then, and wanted editors to judge my stories entirely by the words on the page. I didn't want them to be biased in my favor by a pleasant encounter after a panel, or warm feelings from having a drink together at the bar. I didn't want acquaintanceship or friendship to blur their judgement. I only wanted to sell them a story if it was worthy.

So I didn't reach out to Klein in those early days before the sale and offer to buy him lunch and let me pick his brain.

And I can recall being at the 1979 World Fantasy Convention and turning down a friend's offer to be introduced to Jim Baen, because I didn't want his meeting of me to color his decisions on a manuscript.

But what I've learned after all these years is: None of that matters. Editors reject stories from their friends all the time, and purchase them from strangers, enemies even, and whatever I thought I was accomplishing when I was in my early years of submitting was pointless.

319
.

So please—if you're just starting out—don't do as I did. Don't hide yourself away. Let yourself be human, and the stories and sales will take care of themselves.

Originally published in The Twilight Zone, *April 1983, edited by T. E. D. Klein*

"I WISH I KNEW WHERE I WAS GOING"

Charles L. Grant was a master of atmospheric horror—not the kind that runs at you with a meat ax, but instead the sort that sneaks up on you. He always focussed on the existential terrors that make the hair rise at the back of your neck, not the ones which only turn your stomach.

In other words, he was my kind of writer.

And he was more than that. He was also one of the good guys. Plus he was a consummate editor as well.

I can remember him demonstrating that from the audience of a World Horror Convention panel when he explained, to the consternation of a few of the editors present, why the anthologies he edited would never be invitational only, and always be open calls, because that was the only way you truly find the best of the best. It meant more work for him, but he was willing to do it, because he cared about the field.

I liked him. I liked him a lot.

And so when editor Kealan Patrick Burke decided to honor him with the tribute anthology *Quietly Now*, I knew I wanted in.

My short story "I Wish I Knew Where I Was Going," a tale of missed opportunities and second chances, was my humble attempt to walk in Grant's footsteps. I hope it turned out to be more than just a pale echo, that it will chill readers as much as it did me.

I can never look back on the finished product without a touch of sadness, though, and not just due to the loss of Charles L. Grant. One of the contributors to the book, William Relling, Jr., committed suicide between selling the story and the book's publication, and there's a blank space in the book where his signature should be. So I never consider that book without also considering all the stories which will never be written by two talented writers.

Originally published in Quietly Now: A Tribute to Charles L. Grant, *edited by Kealan Patrick Burke, Borderlands Press, 2004*

"THE TREMBLING LIVING WIRE"

Though Stephen Jones is an editor who has been very good to me over the years, and was the one who purchased and published this Poe-inspired tale, he was not the editor who acted as the catalyst for its creation. Such is often the way.

I began writing "The Trembling Living Wire" because a different respected editor, Ellen Datlow, announced *Poe: New Tales Inspired by Edgar Allan Poe*, an entire anthology centered around honoring that author.

My tale was inspired by one of my favorite poems of his, knowledge of which is not at all necessary to appreciate the story. (Though those who already know of the one "who despisest an unimpassioned song" may pick up on certain background elements earlier than those who've never read the poem.) Poe's "Israfel" got me to thinking of the places we go in the service to our arts. Some of those places are darker than others, yielding darker results. I hope never to go as far as in this story.

Ellen didn't end up taking the tale, but the Jones anthology *Psycho-Mania!*, focussing on killers of the Robert Bloch *Psycho* sort, turned out to be the perfect place for it. And when the title was unveiled at the 2013 World Fantasy Convention in Brighton, twenty-three contributors were in attendance signing copies, resulting in my favorite book launch ever. I wish you could have been there with us!

Originally published in Psycho-Mania!, *edited by Stephen Jones, Constable & Robinson, 2013*

"A PLAGUE ON BOTH YOUR HOUSES"

As I mentioned in an earlier story note, I find conventions to be energizing, and I often head home with story ideas exploding out of me like the sparks off a Roman candle. Such was the case during my drive home from the 1992 World Horror Convention held in Nashville.

I left the con after a late dinner, planning to drive through the night to beat the traffic. In the dark somewhere between Tennessee and Maryland, the opening lines of this story came to me, and I scribbled them on the notepad I always keep in the car, confident ideas will come. Once I arrived home, the rest of the piece quickly spilled out of me.

So the words were easy. But then began the far more difficult task of trying to sell the thing.

After four years of being unable to place this story (one editor of a zombie-themed anthology even rejected the piece not because he didn't like it, but because he said he didn't care for Shakespeare!), and wanting it out in the world, I printed it up as a Halloween pamphlet that I circulated to friends and colleagues. Stephen Jones liked it so much it ended up being published in *The Mammoth Book of Best New Horror*, his 1997 collection of the best horror of 1996, and the piece was also nominated for a Stoker Award.

This is the only story of mine which ever started out as a self-published piece. Since it paid off so well for me, perhaps I should do it more often.

"A Plague on Both Your Houses" has never been mounted as a play, and has had only one public performance—a staged reading in New York prior to the Bram Stoker Awards banquet the year it was nominated. (It was the first of my eight Stoker nominations to date.) In order to pull it off, I drafted friends who were present that weekend to join me onstage. Readers who are familiar with the science fiction, fantasy, and horror fields will perhaps be the only ones to recognize them, so I list their names here for them, and so history might remember.

The cast included Michael Marano (Sam/Carlo), Ed Bryant (Vincent), David Honigsberg (Eddie), Gordon Van Gelder (Leopold), Vicki Rollins (Dolores), and Nina Kirki Hoffman (Mary/Woman Reveler).

Oh, how I wish we'd recorded that!

Originally published by the author as a Halloween chapbook, reprinted in The Mammoth Book of Best New Horror*: Volume 8, edited by Stephen Jones, Carroll & Graf, 1997*

"THE FINAL CHARGE OF MR. ELECTRICO"

The earliest science fiction or fantasy I can remember reading—once I'd absorbed all of Dr. Seuss, A. A. Milne, Hugh Lofting, and P. L. Travers (and yes, I consider these writers to fit in those categories)— was in short story collections I picked up at the same candy store on Avenue P in Brooklyn where I bought my earliest comics. Collections by Isaac Asimov, A. E. van Vogt...and of course, Ray Bradbury.

His stories were magical to me. What I wouldn't learn until years later, as I began my path to becoming a writer and the stories of the people behind the stories took on a nearly equal importance to the stories themselves, was that his life was magical as well.

He roller-skated around Hollywood as a kid, meeting movie stars such as Cary Grant, Mae West, and Laurel and Hardy. When he was ten, and decided to become a magician, the great Blackstone the Magician gave him a live rabbit. When he was fourteen, he met George Burns and Gracie Allen and wrote for their radio show.

But it was the encounter he had when he was twelve, and met a carnival entertainer who tapped him with an electrified sword which made his hair stand on end, and commanded him to "Live forever," which has captivated me the most.

We know what happened to Ray Bradbury after that. But I always wondered what happened to Mr. Electrico. Bradbury said he lost track of the man, and so had no idea. But I had an idea, one I'd been carrying around for years. And that idea became this story.

I was lucky enough to have had a chance to meet Bradbury several times, the last being during the 2009 San Diego Comic-Con. He never tapped me with an electrified sword, but those meetings were magical in their own way, and I'll do my best to live forever, too.

Originally published in GigaNotoSaurus, *January 2018, edited by Rashida J. Smith*

"A MOST EXTRAORDINARY MAN"

When editor Luis Ortiz asked writers for sequels, prequels, homages, and re-imaginings which would pay tribute to seminal horror stories for his new anthology, I knew I wanted in, but worried the classics I most wanted to honor would be snapped up by other authors before I had a chance to claim them. I turned out to be lucky.

Though E. T. A. Hoffmann's "The Sandman," Robert Louis Stevenson's "Strange Case of Dr. Jekyll and Mr. Hyde," Edgar Allan Poe's "The Lighthouse" and others all had been taken, no one had reserved either of the two tales which had long before captured my imagination—Lord Dunsany's "The Two Bottles of Relish" or Saki's "The Open Window."

I'd first encountered the Saki in Junior High School, where we were taught it in English class, but the Lord Dunsany tale I was left to find on my own, as it was, perhaps, seen as too gruesome to teach children, even though the horror was implied rather than shown.

When it came time to write, I ultimately went with the Saki, so if you've ever wondered what happened after the end of "The Open Window," this short story will tell you what I think went down. But who knows...I might someday do a riff on the Dunsany tale as well. Those bottles of relish are too tasty not to be revisited!

Originally published in The Monkey's Other Paw: Revived Classic Stories of Dread and the Dead, *edited by Luis Ortiz, NonStop Press, 2014*

"THIS IS WHERE THE TITLE GOES"

I have always loved stories about the telling of stories, as well as the metafictional titles that go with them. Italo Calvino's *If On a Winter's Night a Traveler* is one of my favorite books, and Manuel Puig's *Eternal Curse on the Reader of These Pages* is perhaps the title of which I am the most envious. Combine that love with my fascination by the skeleton that lies beneath the skin of story, and you get *this* story. In "This Is Where the Title Goes," I tried to peel that skin away, and rather than try to tell just a single story, try to tell *all* stories.

Of course, it will be up to you to determine whether I have told even one story. The positive reactions to my readings of it aloud at various conventions over the past years, however, have me believing I'm on to something, though. And that several academics have told me they teach this tale in their creative writing classes is extremely gratifying.

The story was originally published in *The Journal of Pulse-Pounding Narratives*, a magazine I miss deeply, edited by Alex Irvine and Thom Davidsohn. Alas, it only lasted two issues, and this statement in their final joint editorial indicates strongly there will be no more:

"It is our fondest wish that if there are young people out there who dream of running a zine, they will see the path of misery and despair that we have so foolishly trodden, and turn another way."

At the time I'd first read those words, I had already also turned another way. The two print magazines I'd previously edited, *Last Wave* and *Science Fiction Age*, were behind me, and now, as then, another such gig seems as unlikely as ever. Not due to the "misery and despair" Irvine and Davidsohn mentioned, for mine were both fun projects, but because I hear the call of unwritten stories far more loudly than I do that of unedited magazines, and until I run out of tales I think need telling, I'll be focusing my energies on those.

Originally published in The Journal of Pulse-Pounding Narratives *#2, 2004, edited by Alex Irvine and Thom Davidson*

"LIVE PEOPLE DON'T UNDERSTAND"

The third act of the Pulitzer Prize-winning play "Our Town" has always made me cry. (And here you thought it was only the ending to "Of Mice and Men" which has had that effect on me.) I guess I should have realized my blubbering meant it was only a matter of time before I'd create a short story out of Thornton Wilder's life-affirming concept. And, of course, what life-affirming short story is complete without zombies?

Although eventually published in the anthology *The Book of All Flesh*, edited by James Lowder, it was publisher, anthologist, and author Peter Crowther who should get credit for planting the seed for "Live People Don't Understand." Crowther invited me to write a story for an anthology he was working on devoted to Will Eisner's noir comic book character The Spirit. I immediately plotted out a tale in which Wildwood Cemetery, where The Spirit has his secret headquarters, and the Grover's Corners cemetery, where the newly dead congregate in "Our Town," were one and the same. Denny Colt was going to bring a murderer to justice only to discover at story's end that the client who'd hired him to do so...was actually the deceased.

The title of that incarnation was going to be "Spirits, Saints, and Poets," taking off on the Stage Manager's response after Emily asks him whether human beings ever fully realize life while they live it:

"The saints and poets, maybe—they do some."

When The Spirit anthology ended in limbo, I was too much in love with the concept to let the story die with it. It sat fallow for a while until I heard that James Lowder was putting together the zombie anthology *The Book of All Flesh*. I realized then how the plot could be restructured to build a story that could stand alone.

As much as I regret not getting a chance to play with The Spirit, the story as published turned out to be a much cleaner realization of what I wanted to say than it would have been originally.

With these notes causing me to think about "Our Town," and about my acting career such as it was which went on hold so many decades ago, I realize yet again that if I were ever to find time in my life to return to the stage, I sure would love to have a go at the Stage Manager role. Let's hang in there together, shall we? It just might happen someday.

Originally published in The Book of All Flesh, *edited by James Lowder, Eden Studios, 2004*

"THE MAN WHO WOULDN'T WORK MIRACLES"

My first exposure to the H.G. Wells tale "The Man Who Could Work Miracles" wasn't from the original 1898 short story, but rather from the 1936 film of the same name, directed by Lothar Mendes and starring Roland Young. It was in heavy rotation when I was a kid in Brooklyn, probably on WPIX, along with endless screenings of *King Kong*, *Mighty Joe Young*, *Godzilla*, *Invaders from Mars*, and *Invasion of the Body Snatchers*. I watched all of them whenever they were on, which I guess explains quite a bit about who I am and why this book exists.

And though no comic book ever influenced me to tie a towel around my neck, pretend it was a cape, and try to fly, this story *did* cause me to many times concentrate real hard and attempt to commit miracles. (Hey, I was a kid!) I never succeeded, no more than I was able to levitate objects by wriggling my fingers like Ray Walston on the TV show *My Favorite Martian*.

Oh, yes. I tried that, too.

Eventually, I stopped trying. But the H.G. Wells story has remained in the deep well of my subconscious for most of my life now, so it was inevitable I'd eventually ask…what happens next? I believe I started actively thinking about writing this story more than a decade before I finally did, a long gestation period for me.

But here it is, closing out a book that's something of a miracle all by itself. Which means, I guess, all that concentrating I did when I was a kid in an attempt to replicate the power granted to George

McWhirter Fotheringay worked...just not in the way I thought it would. Because the fact this book exists, and you exist to read it...that's the real miracle, and a much better one than any I could have imagined back in Brooklyn, where I was just beginning the make the acquaintance of those giants on whose shoulders I would someday perch.

Original to this collection

ACKNOWLEDGMENTS

*T*he stories in this collection would not exist without the direct influence of John Steinbeck, Raymond Carver, Ernest Hemingway, Shel Silverstein, Randy Newman, E. E. Cummings, Alice Sheldon, Rod Serling, Charles L. Grant, Edgar Allan Poe, William Shakespeare, Ray Bradbury, Saki, Italo Calvino, Manuel Puig, Thorton Wilder, and H.G. Wells. They are the giants on whose shoulders I stood while writing them.

But also...be aware these homage stories were not written to a deliberate plan. They are the merely the stories that happened as I bumbled along from idea to idea, writing whatever matched my mood at the time. Had I approached with intentionality the project of tipping my hat to all the writers who influenced me along the way and whose fingerprints can be found if closely inspecting my lifetime oeuvre, I might have also created stories more directly showing the effects of having read Joanna Russ, Roger Zelazny, Kate Wilhelm, Kurt Vonnegut, Jr., Thomas M. Disch, Robert McCloskey, Samuel R. Delany, Zenna Henderson, Theodore Sturgeon, Harlan Ellison, Madeleine L'Engle, Barry N. Malzberg, Jayne Anne Phillips, Angela Carter, Frederik Pohl, and countless others. And, of course, Stan Lee, Jack Kirby, and Steve Ditko. Who knows? Someday I might actually write those stories.

Many thanks to perspicacious editors Stephen Jones, Peter Crowther, Nick Gevers, Jaym Gates, F. Brett Cox, Andy Duncan, Michael Bailey, Darren Speegle, T. E. D. Klein, Kealan Patrick Burke, Rashida J. Smith, Luis Ortiz, Alex Irvine, Thom Davidsohn, and James Lowder, who were insightful and generous enough to have originally published the stories in this volume in their magazines and anthologies.

And a final thank you to publisher Steve Berman, who leapt on my passing comment during a Readercon one afternoon about the number of homages I'd made and offered to gather them together under the Lethe Books imprint; Andy Duncan, who was kinder to me in the introduction to this volume than I deserve; Matthew John Soffee, whose portraits of some of the writers who inspired the stories in this book came together into a perfect cover image; and Inkspiral Design for turning transforming that image into the beautiful final cover of this book.

ABOUT THE AUTHOR

Scott Edelman has published nearly 100 short stories in magazines such as *Analog, PostScripts, The Twilight Zone, and Dark Discoveries*, and in anthologies such as *Why New Yorkers Smoke, The Solaris Book of New Science Fiction: Volume Three, Crossroads: Southern Tales of the Fantastic, Once Upon a Galaxy, Moon Shots, Mars Probes, and Forbidden Planets.*

His collection of zombie fiction *What Will Come After* was a finalist for both the Stoker Award and the Shirley Jackson Memorial Award. His science fiction short fiction has been collected in *What We Still Talk About.* He is also the author of the Lambda Award-nominated novel *The Gift.* He has been a Bram Stoker Award finalist eight times, in the categories of Short Story and Long Fiction.

He worked as an assistant editor for Marvel Comics in the '70s, writing everything from display copy for superhero Slurpee cups to the famous Bullpen Bulletins pages. While there, he edited the Marvel-produced fan magazine *F.O.O.M.* (Friend of Ol' Marvel). He also wrote trade paperbacks such as *The Captain Midnight Action Book of Sports, Health and Nutrition* and *The Mighty Marvel Fun Book.*

In 1976, he left his staff position to go freelance, and worked for both Marvel and DC. His scripts appeared in *Captain Marvel, Master of Kung Fu, Omega the Unknown, Time Warp, House of Mystery, Weird War Tales, Welcome Back, Kotter* and other titles.

Additionally, Edelman worked for the Syfy Channel for more than thirteen years as editor of Science Fiction Weekly, SCI FI Wire, and Blastr. He was the founding editor of *Science Fiction Age*, which he edited during its entire eight-year run. He also edited *SCI FI* magazine, previously known as *Sci-Fi Entertainment*, for more a decade, as well as two other SF media magazines, *Sci-Fi Universe* and *Sci-Fi Flix.* He has been a four-time Hugo Award finalist for Best Editor.

Lightning Source UK Ltd.
Milton Keynes UK
UKHW041230140119
335543UK00002B/274/P